Other books by Larry W. Miller Jr.

Trials of an Archmage series:
Book I – Discovery
> Paperback ISBN: 9-595-25758-5
> Hard Cover ISBN: 0-595-65313-8

Book II - Pern and the Giant Forest
> Paperback ISBN: 0-595-30229-7

Book III - The Mystic Library **
> Paperback ISBN: 1-905166-40-0

Book IV - Ascension/Circle of Darkness
> Paperback ISBN: 0-595-41898-8

Other Fantasy Books:
Long Live the Queen
> Paperback ISBN: 0-595-27449-8

Balance Lost / A Strange Friendship
> Paperback ISBN: 978-1-4401-0693-4

Science Fiction Books:
The Conquest of New Eden/Sins of the Father
> Paperback ISBN: 0-595-37561-8

Droptroopers: Gauntlet of Fear
> Paperback ISBN: 978-0-595-47591-9

A Watery Crash
> Paperback ISBN: 978-1-44018-180-1

Adventure Books:
The Last Wizard of Earth
> Paperback ISBN: 978-1-45026-975-9

These titles are all available from www.iuniverse.com or www. bn.com except for "The Mystic Library" which is available from www. amazon.com. Now many of these titles are also available as e-books through www.iuniverse.com or http://ebooks.ebookmall.com .

a Kingdom of Unity

Long live the Queen III

By

LARRY W. MILLER JR.

iUniverse, Inc.
Bloomington

A Kingdom of Unity
Long live the Queen III

iUniverse books may be ordered through booksellers or by contacting:

iUniverse
1663 Liberty Drive
Bloomington, IN 47403
www.iuniverse.com
1-800-Authors (1-800-288-4677)

ISBN: 978-1-4620-5972-0 (sc)
ISBN: 978-1-4620-5973-7 (e)

Printed in the United States of America

iUniverse rev. date: 10/26/2011

Dedication:

I wrote this book while working at Tekserve POS. It took six months to accomplish during lunches and breaks. There were several people around me that were supportive during this time. First of all, Jesse, you listened as I ranted on as various parts of the book were written and I thank you for it. Hopefully, you will finish reading "Long Live the Queen", and then "Balance Lost", so you can read this one. But enough with the how this book was written, let's get to the why this book was written. It really all goes back to one person: my aunt Joann. She was the one that asked me: "What ever happened to Josh and Erica?" At the time, I answered that by writing "Balance lost". As it turns out, there were more stories to be told. After all, the two children are coming-of-age. The problems they faced as children only get larger when combined with the struggles of growing up. Another staunch supporter of this book has been my sister Julie. I hope you like it. Miguel, who sits beside me at work and puts up with me as I type away during break, thank you for "dealing with it". I would like to thank my extended family both in and out of TekServe for putting up with this crazy man that can watch movies in his head and writes them down. And finally, I would like to thank my mother. Without her none of this could have happened in the first place. I think back to when I first told her that I write books. I hadn't published any books at the time and the response was skeptical but hopeful. Now, 11 books later, I think it's finally starting to sink in that I meant what I said. I love you Mom and I always will. Enjoy the book.

CONTENTS

Queen Erica

This is the concept art for Queen Erica. You cannot see that her hair is red in this picture.

CHAPTER 1

S weat began to make Erica's ear itch as her workout stepped up to the next level. Erica had wanted this beating, and now she was getting it. The Captain of the guard had personally agreed to train her in the arts of war. She was a good student, but life in the palace had not prepared her for this. In fact, her previous life back in school had not prepared her for this either. She was not out of shape, exactly, she had just never been called to this extreme level of physical exertion. Even when the ancients helped her with her moves, she was physically drained afterwards. But she was the queen. She needed to be able to protect herself in this dangerous world. What was worse was that Josh had taken to his studies well and had become a truly gifted sorcerer. So it was the least she could do to become the best fighter she could be. After all, they had the people of their kingdom to consider. They could not appear weak or another duke or bandit would come in and try to take over again. She had to keep her guard up on multiple levels now. This reflection caused her to pause just a bit and the flat of a sword smacked her arm hard. She flinched back and rage began to take her. The ancients answered her call and soon this was a pitch battle for their lives. This had happened before and the quartermaster knew what to do. He splashed both combatants with the water bucket and they immediately broke out of the spell. The two lowered their swords and drooped as the rage left them.

Erica took off her helmet and her hair looked dreadful. Of course through the panting she didn't really much care. It was just as well that nobody important was around to notice anyway. She was a warrior, and warriors didn't have to look like porcelain dolls. She would head up and bathe soon. She just needed some time to catch her breath.

"You know that you have already improved your highness." The big armored figure told her. "It was not so long ago that you would have been laying on the ground trying to find the strength to breath in armor." He added and she nodded. She was just starting to feel a bit better and her breathing was slowing.

"I feel stronger." She replied. "Not as strong as you of course, but I am not as weak as I was." She elaborated. She handed her helmet and the sword to the quartermaster who accepted them with a small bow. She knew that he would have them cleaned and polished and sharpened where appropriate before she needed them again. She smiled at him and he withdrew.

Both of them made their way back into the castle. The courtyard was nice, but they were both tired and hunger would hit soon enough. Erica accepted the help warmly when the servants offered to remove her armor and get her cleaned up. This was a luxury she had felt uncomfortable with for her first years of rule here in the other world. Now that she was becoming a fine young woman, she allowed herself to be at ease with herself and her body and she no longer worried over what these people thought. She was still conscious of them and she never took them for granted. She just didn't fret so much over their administrations. She had just finished soaking in the tub when her valet brought fresh clothes for her to put on. She grudgingly left the warmth and soothing of the tub water and began to dry off with the huge towel that had been left within reach of the tub. The hearth was not lit now as the days were still quite warm this time of year. The castle was decorated with hanging plants and it all seemed so much more like home that way. It was in stark contrast to the cold stone gray walls that were there the rest of the year. She could just feel the pangs of hunger and her light step proved that the bath had been rejuvenating. She was in her court gown, the everyday one, not the special gold inlaid one. Her crown was the everyday circle. It had a single gem at its front to help her get it oriented correctly. Other than that, it looked very plain. It wasn't as though anyone would mistake her for a normal person. After all, she was a True Blood of the old heritage and she and her brother had done wonders since their unlikely ascension to the throne.

Erica strolled through the passageways of the castle with a light step and a tune humming in her mind. One of the toughest things for her since leaving the modern world was the loss of all of that culture. Music was played by hand here. There were no electric guitars, or boom boxes, or even a portable player. There was no power at all. She had sadly given it all up and lived with the songs in her memory. She was moving towards the receiving chamber. This was where she did her queenly duty each day. She heard the song in her head more loudly. Something was amiss here. She could here *Tainted Love* in the chamber beyond. It did not sound like the original; after all it was being played by a string quartet. Her steps became quicker as she approached the large double doors. The guards at the door nodded to her and opened the massive doors and the music flowed out into the hall. She could tell that she was smiling as she strolled into the room. Josh was there draped over the working throne and admiring his handiwork. The string quartet played on almost feverishly when they noticed the queen enter the chamber. Erica made her way across the large chamber and her walk became dancing by the time she reached the thrones and her brother. Her smile was infectious and he was beaming as she approached. She whirled and plopped down on her throne and continued her dance sitting down. When the music finished, she looked at her brother with true affection.

"What is the meaning of this? How did you do it?" She asked in a rush.

Josh held up his hands and straightened on his throne. "Hold on, they're not done yet." He cautioned and true to his words, the musicians started playing another highly recognizable tune.

Erica's eye lit up. "Happy Birthday; you remembered!" She said and she flung her arms around her younger brother. His discomfort was ignored for a few long moments and then she regained her composure and let go of him.

"It's not every day that you turn eighteen." He said. There is a

3

festival planned for this evening. I'm pretty sure you know about it already. Nobody around here can keep secrets from the queen." He said in a sardonic tone. "However, this musical interlude we planned in total secrecy. In fact, I have jotted down about a dozen songs for them to learn and they will present them to you as soon as they are confident that they have learned them." He said seriously. "After all, we wouldn't want to cause your royal majesty displeasure." He said with tongue planted in cheek.

She thumped him on the arm but her smile did not even dim. "Well, I don't know about this festival of yours, but the music is the best gift that I have ever gotten." She said and a slight tear began to well up in her eye. "I do so miss home." She said again.

Josh saw the cue and was ready to head it off. "Oh no, you know we can't go back there again. You remember what happened last time." The memories began to flood back about the imbalance of the dimensions and the nasty things that had resulted. "We have to stay put and make the best of this place as long as we rule." He said. She knew these things already, but it didn't hurt to hear him say it. It reminded her that she was not alone in her isolation.

Erica looked at her brother again. He had grown up quite a bit since they had come here. He took his responsibilities very seriously. Josh was going to be seventeen in a couple months and he already had the air of a man about him. He was confident and he was powerful. It was not just in the physical sense though, he was a powerful magician. The young man had really taken his studies seriously as well. He was well versed in local politics. He knew the trade routes and who controlled them. He knew the current population of their kingdom and who needed what. He handled requests from the people on a daily basis. He kept everything running smoothly. Yes, she had worried about him in the beginning, but he was a true hero. It was a wonder for her to realize that fact even now. The things he could do with just a thought were amazing. It sort made her jealous of his abilities. She had sworn to protect him, even if only to herself. She always felt that he was the weaker and thus the one who needed protection. He was her younger brother after all. Still, now that he had come into his own, he was impressive. His memory was flawless. He was gifted in many things like learning. He was not, however, very people-positive. Still, the people that he dealt with were able to look beyond that for they truly needed his other skills. Josh had been handling disputes in their newly formed court. They had a legal system now. There was now a system to control expenses on a governmental level. They had advisers and committees for less demanding tasks and somehow, Josh had handled it all. She shook her head to bring her thoughts back to the present. The string quartet was putting away their instruments and Erica thanked them with a nod when they departed and they all smiled and bowed respectfully back.

The caller stepped forth from the shadows. "Your majesties, it is time to commence the daily visitation." He said in a voice that was not shouting yet filled the great hall with sound. It was pretty impressive.

Erica felt the elation of moments before begin to ebb away. She hated the day to day grind. The notes of the song were still echoing through her mind and she chose to focus on that for a bit longer before grasping what was happening before her. Josh picked up on the hint and began to handle the business for her today. Hopefully the day would go off without incident.

The world was a troubled place away from the *civilized* lands. The elder races were having a conference about a new threat that seemed to come from nowhere and everywhere at once. In fact, it was not clear what the threat was. That was why this meeting had been called. The chairs had been grown for the occasion and the circle of elders represented almost every elder race in the nine kingdoms. By anyone's accounting this was an important affair.

"If I may, my distinguished colleagues, I suggest that we gather what we do know instead of whimpering and whining about what we don't know." The Grand Elf was older than anyone could remember but his hands did not shake and his mind was still as sharp as steel. His steely gray eyes swept the convocation and there were nods of ascent to his visual query. He finally rested his eyes upon the representatives of the Stone Lords. Made of living rock, they were the eldest of the elder races. Their slow and sedentary lifestyle usually left them unnoticed by the more fleeting peoples of the world. "If you don't mind, I'd like to hear from you first." The grand elf said with a smile that was practically painted on for he was not a happy man.

The delegate shifted in his seat of rock and the grating sound of stone on stone was unmistakable. "My fellow representatives..." He began very slowly. "It has come to the attention of our collective that rumblings deep in the ground have become a cause for concern." The words were delivered so slowly that the listener almost forgot the last word when the next one was delivered. "You must understand that this is only tentative information. No sightings have been linked to these tremors. The crystals do point to evil however, they all turned black." He said with finality that was not felt throughout the chamber. The group was relieved when the grand elf spoke again, he was much easier to listen to.

"So what you are telling is that your sensor crystals tell you that tremors are evil?" He asked, his tone was light, but his gaze was dangerous. "Perhaps you could be a bit more specific." He prompted.

The uncomfortable fidgeting ratcheted up and the sound of stone on stone was almost deafening. This was clearly a stall for time, as if this being needed any more of that. "We have no further information at this time." He admitted finally.

The grand high elf sighed as he understood the implications of what was said. The very ground did not know what was going on beneath it. The thought was not very reassuring. "Then I think we need to focus on anyone who has made a sighting. Are there any among us who have a report?" He asked. He pretty much knew the answer already, but was forced by protocol to ask the question. To his surprise, the king of the sprites raised his royal hand. With a nod the sprite king was allowed to take the floor.

"My good fellows, we of the sprite kingdom run as much of the forest as anybody. You all know what territory we cover. My people have spread out since the first discovery of trouble. No sightings have been reported thus far. Whatever this problem is, it does not exist above ground as yet. We have seen trees begin to wither though. Roots were tainted below ground near the ashen falls. I would suggest that any further investigation begin there." He said and his smug look showed that he was quite pleased with the group's overall shock.

The Grand high elf looked angry at first and then thoughtful. He was still not pleased when he finally reigned in his emotions and spoke. "So you have a location where the trouble exists? And when were you going to tell everyone about it?" He asked, his anger bubbling up to the surface again.

The Sprite King held up a finger. "It was obvious to me that someone needed to speak up, and so I did. Earlier, no one was going to do anything positive with the information, so I did not. I was not going to choose sides while my esteemed colleagues argued over what they would do. Now that there is a direction to go and a cohesive group to follow it, it is time for action." There were rumblings around the circle, but not really of disagreement. The complaints were for how the information was relayed as opposed to what was actually said. The Sprite King felt the dissension and he came to the conclusion that discretion was called for here. "My friends, I apologize for any affront you may have felt at my revelation. Do not be alarmed from my sense of timing. Instead, let us focus on this dilemma and see if we cannot determine what the root cause is. Once we determine that, we can take steps to rectify the problem." He offered and the grumbling settled down somewhat. He had ruffled a few feathers here and he was not sure how badly he had damaged relations among this elite group. He hoped that it was not too bad. He knew that the common enemy they would reveal would erase any misgivings they had about him now. He was anxious to get that investigation under way. "So if you will, my friends let us decide who is to investigate this mystery."

A beast of a man cleared his throat for attention. If he had been seen in the woods, he would have resembled a bear. Here, sitting in a chair grown from a tree stump, he defied casual description. He had a large double-bladed axe strapped across his massive shoulders and his leather outfit appeared to be cut from rough hides. His corded arms were crossed in front of his barrel of a chest. His voice was low and guttural.

"We will begin the investigation. The pack can cross the terrain required in no time at all and our fine senses will allow us to check places that cannot be seen." He said and the predator look in his fiery eyes was unmistakable. Suddenly everyone felt sorry for whatever was causing the problem.

It was the High Elf who recovered first. "Your suggestion holds merit. Is there a second on the floor?" He asked and several hands went up around the circle. He nodded to them in acceptance. "Then your motion has passed. You shall begin the investigation and be sure to keep this council informed of your progress." He said trying to keep the reins on his hunter friend at least a little bit. The old man stood up and held his arms wide. "I speak for the entire council when I say to you; good hunting!" Light applause followed the meeting-ending gesture and the council swiftly dissolved. Each of them was eager to get back to their peoples and tell them what was decided. It was so seldom that the council even convened that when it does, it was news.

The entire kingdom of the True Bloods was in attendance for the massive celebration. There were banners hung across the main thoroughfares of the city and everyone seemed happy and excited. This was a time for rejoicing. Queen Erica was to make an appearance. She was so beloved by the people that her birthday became a grand occasion. The guards of the palace proper were dressed in their finest parade uniforms. Their weapons were cleaned and polished and shone brightly in the afternoon sun. The food vendors were set up almost everywhere and the tabs were being paid by the crown today. Spirits would be supplied after the food was gone. The festival planning had gone off without a hitch. As far as anyone knew, the queen was still unaware of the proceedings outside her own home. Of course that would not last. No surprise party of this size could be air-tight security wise. A massive effort had been given though and the general feeling was that she would be totally surprised when her brother brought her out to the viewing area. A steady breeze kept the colorful banners and flags in constant motion. The temperature was about seventy-four degrees. It was perfect. The trumpeters were posted on the highest wall of the palace entrance and as the moment drew near, the tension in the crowd ratcheted up with the excitement. Finally, the horns blew out a fanfare. All eyes were glued to the balcony where the queen would appear shortly. It was as if everyone held their breath at the same time.

Josh had been ushering Erica through the palace and she did already know at least part of what was in store for her. She still had her regular court clothes on and Josh would not let her stop to change. She resented his bossing her around, but she also knew that he was up to something. Until she could figure out what, she would simply go along with whatever he was up to. They made their way to the reviewing stand and Josh stopped in front of her before she could part the curtains that were the only thing keeping her out of the public view at this point.

"Now, wait just a second." He said and she looked at him with a puzzled glance. Then she looked down. She had a ball gown on now. It was beautiful. It was teal with gold stitching making floral patterns around her hemline and waist. There were precious gems set into the fabric as well and it would make her glisten in the sunlight. Her head felt the weight of the royal crown. He had managed to summon that to her head as part of the total image. His magic was powerful. She felt the weight of her office upon her in that moment and then he stepped aside and let her step out onto the balcony. The crowd erupted in cheers and applause. Her radiance was only enhanced by the dazzling dress. She was no longer a child. She had come of age and the expectation was that she would soon marry and produce an heir. After all, that's what royalty did. The trumpeters played and the crowd stood as the anthem of the kingdom echoed out across the sea of humanity before her. Erica could not believe her eyes. It looked like everyone was there! The crowd was almost as big as the one for her coronation. This was amazing. She looked back and Josh was there smiling. He had worked his way onto the balcony behind her.

"How did you do this?" She asked; the shock was evident in her words. "I should have heard something about this." She gasped. She maintained her smile for the throng before her as their adulation poured over her and made her feel all warm and fuzzy inside. Josh just let her take it in for a few minutes more before he made his hand signal to the trumpeters. The string quartet had only been the beginning. Now the trumpeters sent their notes out over the crowd.

The theme from "Rocky" swept across the crowd and everyone turned to see the triumphant looks on the musician's faces. Erica's mouth fell open, despite herself. She recovered quickly enough, but her hands were shaking. She wanted to slap her brother, or give him a big hug. Neither felt just right though. The song ended and the crowd cheered again. It would soon be time to move back inside for the more formal part of the celebration. The grand dining hall would be full today and long into the night; but first she had a duty to tend to. It took a while, but eventually the crowd calmed down and awaited Erica's announcement.

Erica swept the crowd with her gaze. With the bright sunshine highlighting everything, it was a bit overwhelming. She could feel the good feelings emanating from the massive throng before her. It was bone-deep, the feeling of well-being they were putting upon her. She lifted her hand and held it out to them. "I thank you for this mighty greeting. It means a lot to me that you all have come to celebrate my birthday." She said and the crowd erupted into applause again. "If you will consider what we have done here in the past year, it is not difficult to understand why you are proud of me and I of you. Together we have accomplished a lot. Our sick have gotten better. Our hungry are being fed. Our trade with other kingdoms is on the rise. Our artisans are exporting their fine goods to wealthy nobles across the land and our reputation for fairness and hard work is spreading. Be proud of yourselves. I could not have accomplished this alone. It took all of us to make this change. You are here to celebrate me and I am here to celebrate each of you." She lowered her hand and then bowed to the crowd. "Thank you." She said with finality. The crowd whipped itself up into a frenzy and the music began again. It was no longer a formal engagement, it was now a party. Erica watched a few long moments more before retreating from all of that attention back into the safety of the palace.

Josh stood there beaming. He had pulled off several stunts for his sister today. Erica looked at him and saw the playful little boy he had been not so many years ago. He still had scars from his ordeals, but now they were faded and his new childish grin made her feel almost giggly. Of course that was no way for a queen to act. She wanted to scold him for putting her into this predicament, but she didn't have the heart. Instead, she swept past him and headed out into the hallway. The festivities outside could still be heard, but they were muffled by distance. It would be some time before that ended out there. The festivities inside were only just beginning as well. Erica made her way back to the reviewing room. There were lines of people to see her and her staff had done wonders to keep all of those people in line. She was thankful for that. A mad rush or a mob scene were things she desperately wanted to avoid. The page announced her at the door and all of those faces turned to her and began to bow. She felt embarrassed as she did every time this happened. Erica drew herself up to her full height and strolled across to the throne and sat down. She was still in her finest court regalia and the onlookers were properly impressed. She set down the scepter in its holder on the side of her throne. It was the equivalent of a modern day remote caddy. Josh had whipped it up to handle some organization for her while she worked. It was just one more thing she leaned on him for. She motioned for the staff to begin today's business. The first group of visitors were ushered up and they bowed again as they were presented to the queen.

"Your majesty, we are pleased and honored to be allowed this audience on your birthday. Please accept this small gift from our family on this momentous occasion." He said regally and she nodded to him as he held forth a bolt of cloth. It was fine work, gold with red flowers intricately stitched into the sides. It must have taken a long time to make. This meant that Josh had been doing all of this planning for longer than she had imagined. She hadn't noticed him come in but there he was sitting beside her on his throne. He was doing his best to be totally plain and unnoticeable. He was good at it. Life in high school had prepared him well for that. Still, he was a True Blood too. He could not hide in the shadows forever.

Erica swept her eyes back to her guests. "I thank you kindly for your gracious gift. I am certain that you will wish to stay for the festivities here in the palace. I look forward to dining with you this evening." She said and the man's eyes went wide. He almost fell over.

"Your... your majesty, I am most thankful for your offer. It is not commonplace to be seated with the queen. I would not miss this dinner for the world." He said and his family looked on with even more pride than was displayed at the unveiling of the material.

Erica was feeling a bit playful. "Good, I am looking forward to a lot of things. I am hoping that my brother can put on an exhibition of his skills for our entertainment as well. I think that will make the festivities extra special." She said and the look on Josh's face was priceless. He had not even considered such a performance. He would have to work on his illusions for some time before the show. She had effectively taken him out of the rest of the day's normal activities. If he was angered or frustrated by this, none of it showed on his face though. He simply smiled at his big sister.

"If that is what her majesty would like, then I'm sure that can be arranged." He said regally. There was no way out of it now. He had to come up with something fast. He already knew that he would do it and do it right. He just wasn't sure yet what that meant. He needed some reference material. "If you would excuse me your majesty, I shall begin with my preparations immediately." He said and bowed as he retreated from the now excited visitors that were lined up filling the room. Erica wondered what her brother had in mind, but knew that whatever it was it would be spectacular. She continued through the day without him with the aid of her staff of professional support. She was more than glad that they were there by the time it was said and done. She had received tons of gifts and almost all of them were top notch items that were not easy to afford for the citizens of this society. The items had been meant for rich foreigners. They were expertly crafted high-end items that had propelled this kingdom to the top of the global market. The sun was just starting to set and the candles were busily being lit in the main dining hall and the other preparations were well under way. This would be the largest dinner they had ever seated and it showed in the high level of activity Erica witnessed here. It had been almost four hours now and she had seen neither hide nor hair of her brother. It made her a bit nervous. When she couldn't keep an eye on him, he might be up to anything. With his magic, anything really meant *anything*!

Erica did not have time to stop and think too long here though; her personal servants were beckoning her back to her quarters. They kept muttering about getting her freshened up and out of that fine gown. Apparently she had been supposed to change before resuming daily work. It had them all up in a tizzy. To be honest enough, she was tired and could use a bath and some small refreshment before dealing with the crowds again. This was going to be a long day. So it was with some hope that she allowed herself to be taken away from all of the preparations. Whatever would happen, she would have to wait to see what it was.

Josh had been working feverishly on the imagery that he wanted. His conscious mind could only focus so hard, and he wanted to use things from his dreams. So it was with considerable effort that he began sifting through the imagery of his own sub-conscious. In fact it was a feat that only the most advanced of magicians could attempt. No one would have believed that you could walk among your own dreams while awake. However, Josh, and his unique perspective, was able to not only accomplish this feat, but to elaborate on what he saw while he was there. It allowed him to try things out before he would attempt to conjure them in the real world. It was something that no True Blood had ever managed to do in all of the written history found in the palace's hidden library. Josh had spent many hours down there learning all that he could to help control his magic. He was also looking for a way to make it cost him less of his own personal energy when he cast his spells. Part of that work was the physical training he had undergone to make sure that he had more personal energy in the first place. He was strong and fit now and he could still bring all of his mental faculties on line in the blink of an eye. He was basically a spell casting machine. He was building his choices as the hours slipped by. He could tell how long it was taking and he worried that it might not be ready in time. He didn't think that Erica knew how long it would take him when she proposed this display. He also did not realize that she had done it to get him out of the way for the remainder of the day. She *did* know how long it would take. He sent several images to his own memory after he was satisfied with them in his mind's eye. Then he stopped and sat down. He felt spent already. It was a lot of work trying to manifest things only in your mind. With the mental activity done, he realized that he was hungry. Hunger was one of those things that got forgotten along the way while deep in thought. He should be more careful.

Josh left the study room and headed to the kitchens. He was sure that someone there would take pity on him and feed him. They always did. Somehow they understood that he was on a unique schedule that could not be explained rationally. Most likely they did not care when he came in, only that he did. He was royalty after all. It might even brighten their day to help him, the poor True Blood, with his nourishment needs. He entered the kitchen and it was busier than he'd ever seen it before. There were people moving to and fro and pots on the boil. The smells were amazing and his stomach clenched as it realized he had just found the Promised Land.

"You there..." A voice called out to him. "Take this tray over to the hall will you?" The woman said and a few faces turned. Then recognition hit her and she almost dropped the tray. "Begging your pardon milord; I didn't know it was you." The color began to drain from her face and Josh thought she would pass out. Instead he surprised both of them.

"Never mind that, I shall take the tray as requested." He said and his grin showed the mischievousness behind the act. He took the tray from her trembling hands and happily left the kitchen. He would return quickly and get some of that tremendously good smelling food. He carried the tray past several people that were busily preparing this or that. They all looked at him in shock and he put on his best *I'm innocent* face. He spoke not a word to any of them. Instead, he simply left the tray on the table as requested and then headed back to the kitchen.

Once there he got a much more proper welcome. There was a tray of hearty food set aside on a small table that had been shoved into the corner and out of the way. A fresh stein of fruit nectar was placed beside it and a fresh loaf of bread was still steaming on a separate plate nearby. Yes, this was heaven. He sat down out of the way as best he could and began to wolf down the meal. His hunger had reached that nasty stage where you almost weren't hungry anymore. The food sat like rocks in his stomach but his taste buds were quite pleased with themselves. Nobody bothered him as he finished the plate and sat back to rub his stomach appreciatively. The cooks really knew their stuff. He had never eaten this well in the other world. Of course he was never royalty there either. He stood up and brought the plates to the sink for washing and a young woman took them with a warm smile.

"Thank you, milord." She replied with a slight curtsy that should have been impossible in front of a stack of dishes. She had made it look natural, almost practiced. Her eyes seemed to catch his attention, they were almost golden brown and her hair, tied up as it was, was almost a perfect match. He tried to shake off his feelings, but they kept after him as he retreated.

"Thank you." He managed to reply as he backed away and then lost himself in the crowd. He needed to get focused again if he was going to perform here. He stole away to the foyer that linked to the main dining hall. He would visualize the room there and prepare the final settings for his display. He got a wicked smirk on his face as he pictured his own shenanigans in the massive room filled with honored guests. It still took some time, but he eventually got everything the way he wanted it in his head. That was the key to his power. It was tedious and even mundane, but the work had to be done to ensure that the final production was flawless. He was only partially aware that the main hall had been filling up. The diners were making small talk around the gargantuan table. The overall noise level was rising and Josh drew himself up to his full height, swept his arms down to change his own clothing to the most regal stuff he could think of. One last check and then he was off into the room. He strolled in as if he had no cares in the world. He was smiling and nodding at the various people who were wishing him well. His title was a bit foggy. His sister was the queen by birthright of age. Simply put, she was older and so was in charge. He pictured himself as a second in command. Maybe that was not completely accurate, but it was close enough that no one questioned his authority. His own lineage was the same as his sister's so there would not be a question about that part of his ascendency. No, the real problem was that his people skills were nowhere near his sister's. He was a thinker and a planner. He could organize and prioritize. He had trouble with the emotional side of things. On top of that, he was sixteen going on seventeen. The hormones that would have simply made him uncomfortable at home were now driving him into a tizzy here. He was shy around women to say the least. His geeky past had not prepared him to be the kingdom's most eligible bachelor. Still, with all of the work he had put in he was toned and well defined for the lucky lady that did eventually catch his eye. Josh continued his walk until he reached the chairs at the head of the table. He glided into his subordinate throne and waited for his sister to arrive along with all of the other guests.

As he sat there, he realized just how successful this party had been. He had missed most of it, but he could tell that the citizenry present would be well fed and happy. He felt a sense of accomplishment in that. He knew that he was the driving force behind this bash. He was the instigator. It was true that he only started the ball rolling. Once he got the right people on the task, things pretty much fell together. So many people were involved now that he couldn't have told you just how many it had been. The bill was probably going to be astronomical for this one as well. The funny thing about that is that the money would be going to his community for the services rendered here today. It was just another way he would boost the local economy.

The trumpets blared again and everyone turned for it was the signal that the queen was in attendance. Erica entered the dining hall and several young girls ahead of her tossed rose petals to the floor. It looked like the bride in a wedding coming down the runway. The guests all bowed courteously and Josh simply stood up and waited. The fanfare continued until she had reached her seat. She waved one last time to her guests and then she sat down. The waiters brought massive silver trays of food. The spread was amazing. The sight and smells were almost magical. Everyone began eating. The normal protocols were not observed here. This was a party, not a royal function. Even though the queen was in attendance, everyone seated were allowed to enjoy themselves. This was not a political function. There were no foreign dignitaries here. There were no representatives of far away guilds or lands. None of the elder races were represented either. This was just a cozy local affair with only citizens of Erica's kingdom in attendance. The others would have to wait for a more formal occasion to strut their stuff. This day was not for them, it was for Erica and the people directly under her supervision. Since the standard delay between courses was non-existent, the meal moved along at a quick pace. There were acrobats performing in the western foyer to the dining hall and jugglers filled in the gaps between tumbling routines. When the desserts came out, the mood in the hall was one of contentment. However, that contentment would not last. Erica would see to that.

The queen stood and all of the people in the room bowed to her as one. She turned to Josh. "Well little brother, what do you have for us today?" She asked in a no-nonsense tone that anyone other than Josh would have been frightened of. Josh just smiled.

"You would like an exhibition of skill and flash?" He asked and she nodded. "Well then, I guess I had better come up with something then, shall I?" He retorted and the crowd's focus shifted to the wizard. Josh stood up and moved easily over to the area the tumblers had been using. They vacated it just as he arrived. Josh held up a hand to silence the murmurs that had been slowly rising in volume in expectation of this event. "I do this for my beloved sister. I do this because she asked me to, and I do this because I can." He said with a wink that startled a few giggles from the assembly. Then he closed his eyes and began the transformation.

Josh seemed to grow and distort. His fine robes were now no longer long enough to cover him. He had become almost twice as tall and he was building up mass. He was turning into something huge, with hair and muscled arms that could crush a tree trunk. He completed his transformation and a hill giant stood in the foyer. He held out his arms to the side and his new arm-span almost touched both foyer walls. Then he clapped his hands loudly and thunder shook. Suddenly, a clown outfit adorned the mighty hill giant. There was a lot of laughter at the display. Then the entire hall began to rain. It was not water that fell from the sky. Or rather the ceiling of the great dining hall, it was small hard candies. The diners were busily placing plates over their heads for cover as the magical sweets rained down around them. Then the music started. A calliope had formed against the wall and the standard circus song echoed throughout the chamber. Then the rain stopped and the table with all of the food began to change. It bent and warped from the center outward. The long rectangle was becoming a giant circle. Josh continued to concentrate and held his arms up as the spell completed. The table rose off of the floor and became brightly colored. Under that table were horses. They were magnificent beasts and they stood gallantly in their locations. The diners began to mount the horses and the make-shift merry-go-round began to turn as the horses trotted forth at a pleasant speed. Erica stood in amazement as she watched a real live merry-go-round. The hill giant began to shrink again and soon Josh was back to his old self. He only had one minor change; he now had wings. With a small amount of effort, he leaped and sailed to the top of the merry-go-round and stood at the peak in the middle.

"And now for my last trick of the evening..." He shouted above the merriment he had caused. "We are going to have a race." He said. There were shocked faces on the people below. "We cannot have it here of course, we are inside after all." He said. "So I have decided that we shall have it here." He said aloud. At his last syllable, the entire world seemed to shimmer and distort. He had teleported the entire party to an open prairie and the horses stopped trotting in their predetermined circle. Now they were lining up for the race. Erica was on the back of a mighty white horse with golden trim and jingle bells in the tack. She looked excited almost to the point of being hysterical. Then Josh took to the skies. With the ceiling no longer in the way, his wings could fly him anywhere. Then he landed before them in the grass. "On your mark!" He said and the horses all tensed up. "Get set." He said and he floated up effortlessly. "Go!" He shouted and the horses bolted forward in sheer exhilaration. The shrill screams from the diners showed how much they enjoyed the event. The horses raced on thundering hooves and billowing breath as they pounded the ground. The finish line was a normal tape streamer and the white horse of the queen charged forth and broke the tape across its mighty chest. Then, as if nothing had happened, they were all seated at the fine dining table once again. There was a moment of silent shock, and then the applause began to fill the chamber. Josh stood in the foyer the same as he had started and he bowed deeply to the crowd. There were whistles and cheers as he made his way back to his seat and sat down. He held up a chalice of the fruit nectar. All the other cups rose in answer to await his toast.

"To my sister, the queen, happy birthday!" He said, and the

answering happy birthdays filled the room as they all drank the toast.

Erica stood up as well. "I thank you for your gracious gifts and for the spectacle that we have all experienced this day. There is still much to do around our kingdom and we will still be tasked with heavy burdens. But this celebration shows that we have a fun side too. Life is not all about work. It is also about living. Thank you again for enjoying this day with me." The applause and the party went on into the night. The morning would bring its own challenges, it always did. They would enjoy tonight.

CHAPTER 2

Thurik, chief warrior of the Dark Hollows clan, representative of the beast men, made his way skillfully through the woodland area. He was sent to investigate this threat to the world. He knew very little about what he was looking for, only that he was sent to find out what was going on. His powerful arms and legs propelled him through the woods at breakneck speed. His thick fur protected him from the branches and brambles along the way. He was a predator of almost epic proportions. He was also highly intelligent. His powerful corded muscles were only icing on the cake for him. He was a thinker as well. He caught the scent of something and altered course in time to miss the deer in his path. It would have been an easy kill and quite a good meal, but he was not hungry just now. He was on a mission. He completed a gradual correction to get back onto the path he wanted and his stride never even shifted. He was making good time and he should reach the area that the sprites had mentioned within the hour. He could feel the excitement building within him as he got closer. It was like stalking a prey that you couldn't see; the closer you got to it, the more the frenzy took you. For all of the distance he had traveled so far, he was now incredibly close. He was not even winded. He had paced himself well. It would not be long now. He set his jaw in a hard line and lowered his head for just a bit more speed.

The Sprite King was worried. Yes, there were things being done about this troubling something under the ground. Yes, he had done his duty and reported it to the council. Inside he felt that they would be powerless against whatever was under there. The fact that the rock people had not even sensed them was notably dangerous. Who had that kind of protection magic? It was troubling beyond his normal capacity think it through. He needed advice. He would seek out the humans. They had done well by him in the past. It was something he had grown accustomed to doing recently. They had saved his people by returning the spirit tree. They had brought peace to the kingdom. He knew that the True Bloods were just and fair. He would seek them out again. He wondered what his own people would think of that, but he knew that without some kind of intervention, the world would remain in peril. Something inside of him told him that the elder races were ill-equipped to handle this problem. So it was that he began his journey back into human occupied lands.

Under the massive mountains, there was even more activity than any of the surface dwellers believed. The massive machinations were doing their work tirelessly. Forges were working around the clock and metal was being melted and reformed into something useful. What was being made were the objects of war. There were weapons, armor and mechanized carriages. Gunpowder in its coarsest form was being deployed on a scale to boggle the mind. The army that carried these weapons would be fierce and practically unstoppable. The depth of the industrial base was huge. It fell below the landscape farther than the highest tower rose above it. It looked bottomless. The dark ones worked and worked under sadistic taskmasters to accomplish this goal. It would be an army of unprecedented size. The best part of all of this preparation was that none of the races from the surface even knew of its existence. The plan was well underway. The Dark Lord looked on with hatred in his eyes. He had witnessed many things over the millennia that he presided over the darklings, but even he had never before seen such a mobilization as this. His glory would sweep the land like a choking shadow and extinguish all life on this insignificant little world. The thought brought a smile to his wretched face and his fierce fangs stuck out just a bit. Then he turned and struck his Lieutenant for no apparent reason and stormed off. His army would be ready to arrive soon; the light would know fear before it was extinguished. He promised himself that. He would take great pleasure from watching those pathetic weaklings on the surface squirm and struggle before they realized their true hopelessness and collapsed. That moment would be the real victory. He waited to savor that moment for all eternity.

The beast warrior began to feel fear as he approached the area of investigation. He slowed down his pace and began to sniff the air. His keen senses told him that something was extremely wrong here. Evil was in the air. There was soot and tar and saltpeter and sulfur he could detect right off the bat. He shook his head to try and clear it. The fear seemed to grab a hold of him like a giant fist. He stepped forward and it intensified sharply. It was as if he were pressing against a wall of fear. He made himself move ever closer. The trees looked all twisted and wrong. There were dead sprites here as well. Their bodies were blackened as if burnt from the inside and rotten. The fear was now like a massive weight pulling him down to the ground. He lifted his foot with considerable effort and stepped forward again. His mind was screaming at him to flee. His animal instincts tried to make him do exactly that. His own will was all that kept him from doing so. He stepped forward again and the ground seemed spongy. He swept his foot back a bit and used a stick to check the surrounding terrain for a safe path. The ground seemed to recoil from his touch. The darkness began to seep up out of the ground around him as he backed away in fear. This was some trick of the blackest evil. The tree trunks were turning black as well. The leaves were falling and rotting before they hit the ground. The smell of rot added to the feeling of foreboding he was trying to hold in check. He had a mission to do here. He needed to find out what was causing this. He knew that even as he felt his knees begin to shake and buckle. Thurik felt himself fall to the ground. The vines and plants that would normally have supported him were now entangling him and they were sapping away his strength even as he fought to rise again. His arms were held fast and his legs could do no better. The spongy ground began to envelop him and he tried to scream as the darkness overtook him. He was gone in minutes and the land returned to its former state. There were no clues that Thurik had ever been here at all. For now, the evil was safe.

In the home of the Dark Hollows clan, a cry rose up from all of the pack as one of their own was lost. No one knew how Thurik had met his end, but they hoped it was with honor. The mission to investigate the disturbance had just escalated. The area was now confirmed to be actively evil. There had been no warning of Thurik's demise. He had just blinked out of existence. That kind of loss had to be on purpose. Not many outsiders knew of the pack-link, but those who did knew that the last moments of life for any of the pack were shared by all. This time the pack received nothing. It was as if Thurik had been removed from the planet, not simply killed. It was a time for brief mourning and then quick and decisive action. A new investigator must be sent. This time they will send more than one. Secondly, the members of the council must be informed of this setback. They were counting on the report that Thurik would now never make. The situation was as serious as it got. Blood would have to be spilled to avenge the fallen member of the pack.

Mouse lay in the open grass watching the clouds roll lazily by. He had been given lands and a place to call his own. He was still young to be a stead holder, but he did what he could. His land was fertile enough, he was just stretched too thin to work it properly. Honestly, his life as a common street rat had not prepared him for his elevation to citizen and land owner. He was thankful to Josh and Erica, but he still felt dizzily in over his head. It was moments such as this one that reminded him of his own childhood. The dark alleyways and sewer paths he had traversed stealthily were still there in his mind.

He also remembered his taskmasters. The thought brought him a moment of unease as he put that safely away in his mind. Mouse had truly come far. He had managed to attract the attention of a nice girl and his farm that kept him out of trouble. His old rags had been replaced by rugged and suitable clothing. His old friends had not visited him since he had moved out of the city proper. Thinking back, they were really fellow refugees as opposed to actual friends. It was one of the things that made Erica so different at the time. He could still remember her look of compassion as he told the True Bloods of his life. As travelers made their way by his farm, he had heard only good stories of the boy and girl that had seemed so lost those years ago. It was like a dream that they shared. Still, he had done his part in writing that history. A smile crossed his lips upon that reflection. There was a startled cry and he sat bolt upright, broken away from his meandering thoughts. Mouse looked around towards the sound and saw a local farm girl staring in horror as a large black and white wolf approached the homestead. He got up quickly and ran towards the confrontation. That is, if it was a confrontation. The wolf was not in an aggressive posture and seemed to be taking the girl's panic with some humor. He ran up and came to an abrupt halt before the two of them. Mouse must have looked puzzled because the wolf burst out laughing.

"I have not dealt with your kind for a little while. I had forgotten how funny you are." He said in a voice that rang only inside the two human's heads. "You were the one that helped the True Bloods back when they were alone and scared?" The wolf asked and this time the voice was only in Mouse's mind.

"Yes sir, I helped them. Although I must admit, I only gave them guidance. They did most of the work themselves." He said and the wolf nodded.

"That is as it should have been." The wolf replied. "Send this girl away so that we may have a more relaxing conversation." The wolf ordered.

Mouse turned to the frightened girl. "Vicky is it?" The girl nodded. "Run along home now. There is no need to worry yourself over this guest. He will not harm either of us. Think no further on it. I shall come by later if you like." He said, hoping to forestall any questions she might have. The edge of fear still remained, but she was looking at Mouse now instead of the wolf. It was at least a change of focus.

"Okay, I'll leave." She said, her voice sounded shaken. Then she turned and started back towards her home which was the neighboring farm. At least for now, she was out of the way.

"Well done young man." The wolf complimented. "I sometimes fail to understand how the human mind works. You handled that situation properly. It is one of the reasons that I have come seeking you out." He said and Mouse tilted his head slightly in question. It was a very canine thing to do and the wolf did not miss the subtle shift. "You surprise me further." The wolf added. "Let us discuss just what needs to be done before events unfold here in the kingdom." He said and the two of them retreated to Mouse's farmhouse to talk. There the wolf laid out his plans and once he was fully understood, he left Mouse to ponder just what all of this was about. It was dark by the time the wolf left the humble abode.

"Remember, do exactly as I have instructed or all may be lost." He warned and Mouse nodded gravely.

"I will do everything you said." He replied sincerely. "I only hope that it will be enough." He added and it was the wolf's turn to nod gravely.

"So do I." The wolf muttered as it turned to leave. Then in a softer voice, meant only for himself he repeated it. "So do I."

Once the wolf was out of sight, Mouse began to pack his things. He had some traveling to do and then he would make the contacts that were required. He had a small hand-written list of the people and places he needed to go and a rough outline of when they had to be done by. He knew that it would be close. The distances involved were not insignificant and the people on the list were going to be hard to reach. However, he also knew that he could do it. Josh and Erica needed him again. He would not let them down. Of course they didn't know that they needed him and that's what made it all scarier. He would be alone on his quest. The wolf had told him that there could be no more assistance. The chances of being discovered were just too great. He would need all of his skills to pull this off. He pulled up the loose floorboard in the floor of his house and found his old dagger and rags. He had wondered if he would have need of them again. Now he had his answer. And so it was that Mouse became his old self and left the comfortable farmhouse he had been given to rejoin his old life of adventure. Despite all that he was giving up, he had to smile. The one thing that stuck with him from the wolf's speech was that nobody knew what he was up to. As long as it stayed that way, he was certain that he could accomplish everything on the laundry list he had been given. Then at the end, the royal family would know who had helped them again. He actually felt happy about the prospect of seeing them again. It had been a couple years and he had taken a shine for Erica. Curiosity made him wonder just how she looked now. Of course those kinds of thoughts were a distraction. He shoved them aside and headed off down the road towards his first destination. His determination was not reflected in his mannerisms. To all viewers, he looked just like a distraught beggar, trying to find his way again. Ironically, that was not too far from the truth. This time he hid the smile to stay in role. His one hand clenched on the hilt of his dagger. He was ready for this adventure, oh yes he was.

The dark army was near to completion. At least the equipment stage of it was. There were still a few logistical problems to hammer out, but overall, the progress had been acceptable. Of course in this case acceptable was so far beyond what anyone else had ever accomplished that they would need a new numbering system to count it. The amount of equipment was staggering. It was not the Dark Lord's job to find the troops to use this equipment. The Master had given that task to another, one whom he trusted implicitly. There would be an army to use these magnificent weapons of war. The war that was coming would sweep everything before it like a tidal wave of destruction. His eyes glowed red with the vision of it. Fire would engulf the land and allow him to summon his master. The plan was proceeding quite well, but there was still such a long way to go.

The only hitch in his plan so far was that the beast-men had somehow figured out that their investigator had met with an untimely end. The nosey little creatures had actually mobilized a significant force of their own to combat whatever unseen thing had taken their brethren down. He had plans for all of that, but the timing of it all was inconvenient. He wished he had more time to thwart this enemy, but time was something that he was always arguing with. The fact that his actions had remained secretive for so long was a testament to his thoughtful planning and careful calculations. He had done everything, and he had done it under everyone else's nose. There was some small satisfaction to that. He had done what so many before him had failed to do. He had gotten a foothold under the human world. In fact, he had brought many of his denizens of the lower planes with him. He didn't bring an army. That much power was still beyond him. If he could win the war he was about to launch, though, he could claim even more power as the world was enslaved and shrouded in utter darkness. The pain and fear would be palpable. The cries of the fallen would be music to his ears. Now these beast men were the only obstacle to the full realization of his plans. They had to be removed. He would use force if necessary, but he would much prefer to keep his forces hidden. He needed something much more subtle than that. He began to craft a new spell. It would require much of his personal strength and it would require many twisting and interwoven threads to carve out the reality he wanted them to see. Every detail had to be precise or the illusion would fail. He began to work on the task with renewed determination. These upstarts would not foil the plan he had worked so long and hard on. There was no way he would allow that. He got a slight chuckle at the thought of simply destroying every one of those beasts. Then he focused back on the task at hand. If successful, they would not even know that they had been duped. If he pulled this off, he could claim mastery of the illusionist arts. That would simply be another feather in his already heavy cap when it happened. When his master managed to claw through to this dimension, he would be well rewarded for his efforts. Glory would be his.

The Stone Lords were troubled. The vibrations that their crystals were giving off were ominous. The surface dwellers could not have realized the depth of the evil that was working its way towards them. The crystals were not even the same color now. Their vibrations were tainted and twisted. If this continued, they would shatter and the world would be lost to the darkness. So much magic was there to be released. It was more than frightening. The keepers of the crystals meditated and chanted to try and calm the crystals down. They were under the power of some outside influence. Whatever was pulling them out of balance was powerful indeed. The sacred vast chamber was set into the side of a great mountain. The mountain cave would be the interface between the Stone Lords and the surface dwellers. This was always the way. Of course the surface dwellers no longer even remembered of this place. It had become the most sacred place in Stone Lord society and thus its location was now protected. If a message was needed outside their world of rock and stone, it was taken there by an envoy. It would appear that this was one of those times.

The Chaplain stood up from his chanting and made his way slowly towards the message center. The chamber was round, almost four hundred feet across. The crystals of varying color and shape were grown right into the very rock wall itself. The lattices they created were attuned to the very fabric of reality as the stone lords saw it. Now those lattices were starting to fracture. The crystals were being pulled out of alignment. The forces required to do this were beyond imagining. The watchers documented all that the crystals did. Now they were nervous. The hooded stone lord priest completed the journey and his look gave no question that he was deadly serious.

"We need an urgent dispatch to the elders." He said in that grating stone speech that took longer than any other race in all of history. "Have one of our couriers take this message to the nearest surface settlement to be passed along to the elders. We cannot wait for our own envoy to reach the council." He ordered and the envoy bowed slowly and deeply. The Chaplain returned the bow and when all of the protocols had been observed, he began to write the message. The message was actually short, but in the stone lord fashion, it took hours to scribe. The envoy waited patiently and bowed once again once the message was given to him. He left at a brisk pace that would have been considered an insult if the Chaplain had not ordered him to hurry. All in all, two days had passed by the time the stone lord envoy cleared the settlement heading out for the nearest surface dweller settlement. The trembling in the ground told him which direction to go and he was on his way.

The dark army was not a single force. It was being made in three major pieces. The first group was the grunt soldiers. For this the evil ones had decided to deploy clay automatons. These creatures would fight until destroyed. They followed simple orders blindly and they were physically strong. The second and much more dangerous part of the army were the demons. A dull-witted mass of bodies was not an effective fighting force. You needed specialists in various combat maneuvers. You needed officers to direct your grunts around. These weren't being grown; they were being summoned from the ether realm. The evil one had sent his three generals out into our world to sow the seeds of war. The Dark Lord was only the first of the three generals. These generals were working independently of each other as well. They did not even know each other. Nor if they had, would they have cared. Their responsibility was limited to their task and their task alone. The evil one would punish those that failed in their duty and reward those that excelled. It was as simple as that. It was fear that kept each level of worker in line. It was the promise of sheer unmitigated brutality that fed that fear. To that end, the evil one demanded and received utmost loyalty upon pain of something worse than death. For these creatures had already died once before. No, their torment would be eternal. The mind had trouble wrapping around the concept, but it was a motivator beyond all others. It was this driving factor that would ensure victory when his troops finally hit the field. The darkness will rule. The Dark Lord smiled at the thought. He had performed his duties with such precision and care that failure was almost impossible. The only danger he was in now was whether or not he was discovered before he could use this equipment for the army he would see later. It was his worst fear, beyond what the evil one would do to him forever if he truly did fail. He would spare no expense to make sure that this did not happen. Even now, the beast men were making their best time towards his facility and he was just completing his conjuration. If all went as planned, his true genius would be revealed soon. The Master will be most pleased and The Dark Lord's position of power would be assured.

The thicket opened up into a grove before the beast men who scarcely paid it any attention at all. They were intent on finding the trouble and they were focused on the emanations of evil that they could sense with their fine instinctual driven senses. The darkness was before them. It was not far now. The general feeling was of rage and revenge. Unfortunately those strong emotions were also rather blinding. It was not the way a true thinker would have proceeded. They came in as a pack. The beast men were more beast than man just now and it was at this point that they were most vulnerable to what happened next...

The grove before them dropped. It fell and fell. The lead pack members dropped with it and their sudden howls of terror froze the members behind them. It was as if the world had swallowed up their fellows. None of it made any sense. The fallen ones were still screaming even as their lives were snuffed out. The loss was instantly felt among the ones that were perhaps a little more fortunate. They began to back up from the unbelievable scene before them, but it was too late. They were well within the trap that had been set for them. Crazed gibbons left the security of the tree line and entered the grove surrounding the remaining beast men. They were undead and rabid as they hooted and called after the shaken people. Then, as if on cue they all lunged forward and overwhelmed the beast men. The fighting was brutal, but the undead were ceaseless. They would continue even when broken in half by mighty hands. This was a fight that the unbalanced beast men could not win. None of them made it out of the grove. As the last one of them fell, the grove reverted to its normal appearance. It was still wooded, but a huge pit had been dug and then covered over with clever magic. The fallen ones had died on wooden spikes thrusting up from the sandy bottom. The undead monkeys were clay constructs. They were animated to be sure, but they were nothing more than tools. This entire battle had been run by the Dark Lord himself. He had single-handedly defeated this threat. This was why he had planned this so painstakingly. He was good at what he did, but it had to be utterly believable or the illusion would have fallen. If that had happened, then the beast men might have escaped, or worse, understood what was happening and communicated it to their brethren. No, he had to take them all out at once with none of them suspecting that he was involved. In that, the execution had been flawless. The clay creatures were throwing the bodies into the pit so that it could be filled in. There would be no traces left behind for anyone to find upon further investigation. His primary plan was once again secure.

The loss of so many of their pack brought frenzy to the remaining beast men and they had no clues as to what had happened to their fallen ones. The images they received were of panic and desperation. Then the images of the undead gibbons had come and true terror was felt. If the enemy could raise the dead, then the upcoming problem would have to be dealt with differently. Clubs and arrows would not stop an undead foe. Sure, you could slow one down, but it would continue its pursuit. This was bad news for the council. They would dispatch a single beast warrior to relay this information. Then the blood pact required them to hunt down the slayer of their warriors and bathe their claws in its blood. The code, after all, was the code. It was the only way the souls of the fallen could rest. Preparations began in earnest and soon the entire village was in motion. This would be the biggest hunt that they had ever undertaken. It was the stuff of legend.

Josh danced and spun as the music played. The string quartet he had commissioned to play more familiar music had done remarkably well given what he could remember of the songs in question. Each one had been a hit back home before they had ever come here. Erica's eyes lit up as each new one was played. It would have been the music of her senior prom, or at least be oldies there if it had gone out of style. In any case, the thought of prom and having lost yet another piece of the life she had left behind brought a fresh stab of pain to the young queen. Of course she could have as many parties here as she wanted, but that really wasn't the same thing. She also knew that the imbalance of the two worlds was such that traveling back and forth was almost impossible. The previous problems had made the fabric between them extremely fragile. It would be quite some time before they could return home. In fact, they pretty much had one trip left in them. That would be the one to retire. Until then this kingdom and its inhabitants were their home. Both of them had decided to simply make the best of it. They had started off on that path by simply throwing themselves into their work. Now they had other help with those mundane tasks and more free time began to surface. It would not be long before boredom would once again rear its ugly head, but not tonight. The party was still in full swing. That is, the after party. It was the equivalent of thirteenth century bar hopping. Both of the True Bloods were currently engaged in the celebration. They had bodyguards keeping watch over them at all times. The celebration was still in full swing when the strangers entered the inn. The music continued and the dancing continued, but the patrons started to separate to allow the newcomers access to the middle of the main hall. When they reached the dance floor, the music ground to an abrupt halt. The bodyguards immediately cordoned off the two rulers and the crowd spread back from the inevitable confrontation that they were certain they would be able to watch. The tension in the room ratcheted up and Josh and Erica stopped and turned to see what was going on. Mouths dropped all over the inn as the newcomers spread out into an aggressive formation. They were all heavily armed. They wore leather armor and it looked pitted and worn. The most amazing fact about the whole situation was that they were not human.

In fact, the newcomers were not even of the elder races. They were a product of the elder races. They were mostly men with the head of a bull. It was amazing how easily recognizable they were. Erica was practically beaming. Neither of them had ever met a Minotaur before and it was certain that they did not expect this to happen now. The aggressive stance was normal for any militaristic culture and the Minotaur culture certainly fit that description. In fact, they were all born with first rank. They earned promotion through time in grade and through valorous actions. These three Minotaurs were highly ranked, as their multiple beaded earpieces showed. Josh was the first one to step forward. The young man slid the guards aside with a wave of his hand and he stepped forward practically into the face of the lead Minotaur. You can say whatever you like about beast men, but these towered over the True Blood. Much to Josh's credit, he didn't even flinch.

"Welcome to our celebration." He said genially. "Is there something we can get for you?" He asked, playing the part of the host.

The Minotaur snorted. "I am Rutgart, and I am on a mission to talk to the True Bloods." He said in a gravelly voice that spoke more of impatience than anything else. "Are you them?" He asked directly. The guards all tensed as they awaited Josh's reaction.

"Actually, I am one of the True Bloods." He replied in a happy-go-lucky sort of way. "My name is Josh. I am pleased to meet you Rutgart." He said keeping his best smile firmly in place. "If you like we can talk in the back room here, or if you prefer we can return to the palace to hold a formal greeting." He offered.

"Time is short, our message is urgent; we shall meet in your back room." Rutgart replied in a gruff voice. "What are your terms?"

"Terms?" Josh asked; he had the strange feeling that he was missing something. "What terms are you referring to?" He asked directly.

"Bah, you do not know how to negotiate. Just lead us to your back room." Rutgart said with distaste. The group made their way back behind a nervous barmaid that would have much preferred to be anywhere else. Nobody spoke along the way and the tension was thick in the air.

Josh took the lead and offered seats to his new guests. They did not take them. They remained in their aggressive formation in the now cramped back room. The palace bodyguards were stuck outside in the hall where they were a little more than unhappy with the security arrangements. Erica was still safely on the dance floor, although there would be no more dancing tonight. The mood of the party had been broken and the patrons were paying their tabs and making their exits. The innkeeper was just as pleased to have it all over with. He could begin the cleanup of his establishment. So the rest of the inn was quiet as Josh started the ball rolling.

"Why don't you just tell me your message then?" He prodded. His stance was one of utter neutrality. If there was a combative bone in his body the Minotaurs could not see it. It probably disgusted them further that they were dealing with one so weak.

"We have grave news. The council of elders has dispatched an investigator to check on a disturbance below ground that has been reported by the Sprite King. That investigator has subsequently been killed and a secondary expedition force has been sent. At this time we do not know the status of that group. You are to be informed that the Grand Elf requests an audience with you and that your help will be required if this threat is what they think it is." Rutgart stopped. He had memorized the entire message word for word and now he was double checking mentally that he had left nothing out. When he was satisfied, he bowed to Josh. "That is all." He proclaimed formally.

Josh thought for a few seconds. He already trusted the Sprite King but he had never met the Grand Elf. Still, it would be an adventure and that made him smile. "Please tell his highness that I will be glad to meet with him. I never met the Grand Elf and look forward to the opportunity to do so." He said and waited as Rutgart copied the words into his memory. Once he got the confirmation of that, he continued. "Do you know what the nature of the threat is?" Josh queried carefully.

Rutgart snorted. "If I knew that, I'd be taking care of it." Then he paused. "Sorry, I am not one to deliver messages, I am a warrior. My axe will cleave anything that troubles me. It is the way of things." He said as if that explained everything. Josh got the feeling that no more information would be forthcoming here. But still he had to try.

"You said that the investigator was slain. Do you know how this was done?" He asked.

Rutgart shrugged his massive shoulders. It looked odd on such a massive person. "I have given you all that I know. May I have leave to go?" He asked, following the protocols, if only loosely.

Josh felt a twinge of anger at the rejection. He had precious little information and he was fairly certain that this big lummox had more than he was telling. Maybe it was not a lot more, but definitely more. Perhaps it was a matter of respect. "You are certain that you know no more? Or do I need to prove to you that I am also a warrior?" He asked in a challenging tone.

Rutgart Laughed deep and heartily. "You are no warrior!" He managed to reply after a few deep breaths to recover from his laughter. "You are a little thing, and of no consequence to the battlefield." He said in the merriest of tones, trying not to sound too condescending.

Josh stepped up to the mighty Minotaur. He could have gotten no closer, even though they were different sizes, the move was somehow intimidating. "You underestimate my value. I understand your perception, but you are wrong." Josh challenged. "Do you know anything useful, or should I just send you away?" He said in an aggressive voice that seemed to surprise the axe-wielding veteran before him.

"You talk big talk for such a puny thing. You amuse me and that is saying something here in a human settlement." The word human came out like a curse. "Perhaps the little warrior would like to prove himself before I tell you anything at all." He replied; making sure that Josh knew his bluff had been called. Unfortunately for Rutgart, Josh didn't know how to bluff.

Josh held up his hand and pointed to the door. "Very well, we shall go outside and I shall have a small demonstration for you. Then you can tell me all that you know or I shall send my own dispatch to report that you will no longer be joining your forces." Josh threatened. His tone was of steel and the Minotaur finally took direct offense. It was exactly what Josh had been going for here. Once he was angry, he would make mistakes. The group headed outside and the bodyguards nervously rejoined the group as they made their way out of the building much to the innkeeper's relief.

Once outside, Josh drew a line on the ground. He made it solid with a word and then he looked directly at Rutgart. "I have placed a barrier here on the ground. Do you have the strength to cross it?" He asked and Rutgart snorted. It was not so full of amusement as he had done before.

The Minotaur stepped forward and hit his foot on the unseen barrier. From his perspective, it looked just like any other line in the dirt. There was something amiss here. Josh taunted him further,

"Come on now. Cross it if you can." He waved his hands at Rutgart and the warrior's rage began to take over. With a bellow he lunged forward and toppled the barrier down. The impact dazed the large beast man, but otherwise he was unharmed. It was exactly as Josh had hoped it would be. He stepped forward and grabbed the Minotaur by his collar. Incredibly, Josh lifted Rutgart off of the ground and held him high in the air. Then he turned and threw the hapless warrior across the open compound. Rutgart skidded to a stop and looked back the way he had come dazed and confused. How had this child become so strong? Then his rage returned and he stood up, drawing his axe. The fire in his eyes burned deep red and he locked onto his target. He bellowed again and ran forward with his powerful legs taking tremendous strides. Josh simply stood his ground. The charge continued for an endless time that was only a couple of seconds in reality. Then Josh made a small move. He dropped into a stance and brought up his hand once more. The surprised Minotaur flew up into the air as if punched by a mighty dragon. He arced high over the ground and then before the impact with the ground, he slowed to a stop and floated there, mere inches from the ground. Josh stepped over to view his helpless opponent. "Have you seen enough?" He asked and Rutgart nodded emphatically. He lowered the beast man to the ground gently and then backed up a step to allow the beast man to get up with some dignity.

Rutgart picked his axe back up and sheathed it back across his back. His stance was one of acceptance. He made his way slowly around to Josh. "I apologize. I did not know that such warriors existed among the humans." He looked left and right and then back at Josh intently. "How is it that you are so strong?" He asked.

Josh smiled at the warrior before him. "There are more kinds of strength than just what your muscles can do." He said cryptically. "On a test of sheer strength, you would surely beat me every time. However, with a bit of work and a clever mind, the differences can be made up." He paused for a moment. Then he had to ask. "You remember our deal right? You need to tell me all that you know now." He insisted. Rutgart knelt down next to Josh. It put their eyes on an even keel.

"It will be my honor to tell you everything that I know to help you." He said formally. The two of them talked for over an hour before Rutgart left with Josh's message for the Grand High Elf.

CHAPTER 3

Erica and Josh later discussed the grave news and started putting together their contingency plan. According to the data that Josh had collected, the underworld was somehow pushing up against the crust of reality. It seemed so far-fetched, but it was obviously scaring the elder races terribly. If it could do that, then there was definitely something to this threat. The problem was that they did not have a militia of their own. They had guardsmen, for sure. They had security details and even local constables to police the streets. They did not have an organized military defense force. Perhaps it had been short-sightedness, or maybe even just wishful thinking, but they had put all of their energies into creating a society that was not war-like. They had trade partners, not allies. They had neighbors, not enemies. This would take some serious change in order to protect those people that now depended upon them fully. It was a heavy burden and just another such for these young people. In the beginning it was amazing just how needy the average citizen was. They had taken great strides towards making their people happy and more self-sufficient. Now all of that was potentially in jeopardy. The only true saving grace here was that they knew about the threat before it was at their gates. The time for preparative action was now. The only real question was where to begin...

"I thought I was supposed to be the warrior among us." Erica said with just a hint of whining in her tone. She was looking at her brother with mixed emotions. He had come to her with a problem that both of them needed to work together to fix. He had also put himself in harm's way to get that information. This was the point she was concentrating on now. "You had a duel with a minotaur!" She yelled at him. The change in volume started Josh a bit.

"I knew that we weren't really going to fight. It was all a big show. He needed to understand that we were strong enough to help him. Before that, he would tell me nothing. In fact, he said that to me directly. Honestly, what was I supposed to do?" He asked plaintively. Erica rolled her eyes, stopped to think and then let out a sigh. Her anger left her with that long exhale. She looked somewhat deflated. Josh took that as a good sign.

"Fine, so you got the news. He told you what specifically?" She challenged. He opened his mouth and she cut him off. "He told you that something is coming up from the ground and that it is evil. He told you those other beast-men had died trying to investigate this, whatever it is." She stopped, having lost the steam to continue.

Josh picked up the thread. "He also told me that he suspected that the evil whatever it is wanted to remain hidden until it could complete whatever diabolical plan it was engaged in." He added. "He also figured that when that plan reaches its conclusion, everyone in the world will be in danger." He finished. Josh scratched his head. "I realize that it's not a lot to go on. One thing it does is tell us that we are not prepared to defend this palace with force. Sure we can keep the peace in our society, but little else. We have no mobilized force to keep an enemy from these walls either. If there is going to be some kind of large scale fight, I want it to happen as far away from any civilian casualties as I can get it." He said with conviction.

Erica was taking it all in. "I agree with that." She responded to his last statement. The palace guards are good fighters. They are veterans of minor skirmishes over the years. When the dukes tried to take power here at the palace, they fought valiantly to hold them at bay. It was that delay that allowed us to bring our own force to bear." She was thinking tactically now. This was really Josh's forte, but she was expected to the warrior as well as the queen. "But even if we have all of the duty shifts on at once, we have barely three hundred of the palace guard. We have another two hundred or so as police down below. The constables are not trained in this kind of combat though. They are peace keepers. We cannot ask them to do more than prison duty if the fighting breaks out here." She concluded. Then she stopped her pacing and looked at her brother. "We need more men." She said in her most direct tone.

Josh lay back in the overstuffed chair. "I had reached that same conclusion. However, we do not know the time table involved either. Can we get recruits from our own populace? Do we have time to train those recruits before it all hits the fan? Can we house and feed these soldiers-in-training? Can we get enough equipment to outfit our own personal fighting force?" He stopped her before she objected. "Yes I know that I can produce the equipment, but that still doesn't answer the other questions does it?" He retorted. Erica shook her head. "I don't see how we can put together a defensive army with what we have. If we started training individuals now using our staff as the trainers, then the wall guards will suffer. The sentry rotation would be thrown out the window." Josh looked thoughtful. "Of course we are not sure that there is a threat to us here for sure. We could be worrying over nothing here." He told her and the look on Erica's face and the fist on her hip told him that it didn't fly with her. In all reality he could not have taken the easy way out either. The potential was too high to risk everything that they had worked for on the off chance that they were not invaded by some force. Even if this evil turned out to be nothing, a rival duke or lord could just as easily march on them. They needed to beef up the kingdom's defenses. He would need some expert advice for this task. The thought had pulled him away from the room and his sister, like it had done so many times before. When his eyes returned to focus on the here and now Erica was staring at him expectantly.

"I'm sorry, what did you say?" He asked and she let out a sigh of exasperation.

"I said; who can train the staff here in the palace. If there is an attack, they will want to take the palace as quickly as possible. We have seen it fall before, twice. We need to protect our own people and prevent this from happening again." She said in a rush. Her emotions were being strained here. She knew that her brother's mind worked differently than hers did, but surely he wasn't going to leave their staff on their own.

Josh blinked twice and looked at his sister again. "Oh those, I already have a plan for them." He replied calmly. When the time comes, they won't even be here. The palace will be completely empty." He added and Erica's face could not hide her shock.

"So you just want to give up the palace altogether?" She asked incredibly.

Josh just smiled. "I didn't say that. All I said is that when the time comes, they won't be here. I didn't specify where here will be." He said and a glimmer of a plan began to gain recognition in Erica's mind.

"Wait a minute; you want to move the palace?" She asked; her shock still quite evident.

Josh looked thoughtful for a moment. "Not exactly, I don't want the whole palace to move, only pieces of it." He said and Erica looked confused. He stepped up to elaborate. "Have you ever been caught in a maze?" He asked. Her memory flashed back to the intricate sewer system beneath the city. It was exactly the image he had wanted her to recall. "Imagine if you were caught in a maze of moving walls. What if an invading force could not retrace their steps? What if they cannot find their way further in or out? That is what I am working on for the staff. The enemy will never find them."

"That sounds like a good plan." A new voice said and both children jumped at the interruption. It was Josh who recognized the small green winged figure behind them.

"Your majesty..." He blurted out. "It's good to see you." He said jovially.

The Sprite King smiled at the two young people before him. "You have done wonderful things since your arrival here. I am both pleased and blessed to be seeing you again. I only regret that tidings are so grave for this visit." He said and the seriousness of his tone rang ominous to both True Bloods.

Erica knelt before the Sprite King. Partially to offer her own form of respect, but mainly because he was so much smaller it allowed her to see him more clearly. Either way, it made the tiny winged man happy. "So the rumor we received from the Minotaur was not a rumor at all, trouble is definitely coming this way?" She asked, getting down to business as usual.

The king shook his head. "I wish I could tell you for sure. In fact, I am surprised that you already know that something is up. It is a credit to you that you have already discovered at least that much. It is also surprising that the beast-men chose to tell you what they know. They are usually very secretive and protective of their information." He said warmly.

Josh answered that one. "It was not easy to convince him that we needed to know what he knew, but that is a tale for another time." He said, showing his maturity beyond his years. The twinkle in the king's eye showed that he understood that as well.

"Right you are Joshua." The Sprite King agreed. "We have very little information as you already have guessed. The fact that we know anything at all has to be some sort of weakness on the side of darkness. Still, the plans, whatever they are, are still hidden by the veil of ignorance. We have only a limited ability to penetrate that formidable barrier." He said and he pulled out his pipe and began to tamp in the tobacco.

Erica looked around. "Are you comfortable here? We can move to a better, and maybe more secure place, than this if you prefer." She offered.

"You are a pleasant hostess your majesty." The king responded. "There is no place more secure than your private quarters here in the palace." He replied honestly.

Josh pointed a finger at the small man. "You got in here without being detected." He warned. The Sprite King just smiled. "How secure can we really be?" He asked aloud."

The king bowed before the two humans. "You already knew me; I did not set off any alarms because you wanted me to come. If not, then an alarm would have been raised for sure. This land is linked to you two. Nothing can transpire here that you would not know." He said matter-of-factly.

Josh shook his head. "We lost the palace before because that is not true. Things can happen here without our knowledge of it. Our attunement to the earth is less than yours. I am sorry that this is so, but it is a truth. We must plan accordingly." He said with finality.

The Sprite King thought about this for a moment. He seemed to reach a decision, and then he changed his mind. Then he smiled at Josh. "If you cannot sense the world as I thought you had to have, then it is good that you realize that. Knowing your own limitations is important to keeping them from stopping you from doing whatever needs to be done." He said back. Then he changed tracks. "Seriously, the plan you have laid out for your palace staff is quite impressive. Most enemies would never even know that they had been duped. It is the sort of thing that I have come to expect from you young man." He said to Josh with obvious pleasure.

Josh tried to shake his head, but the Sprite King would hear none of it. "You have saved my people more than once. Humans rarely even see us. You don't seem to realize just how different you are from your parents or their parents." The mention of parents brought both children to full attention. "Honestly, they were good enough people, but I got the impression that they were temporary. They acted as if they were serving a prison term. They were looking forward to the day of their release and not living the days they had been given." His eyes swept both of the young royals. "You have made a difference in this land. You have united peoples to a common cause. You have made the average person's life better. These are things that royalty rarely even considers." He looked around the room. "You spend many hours in your chambers working on solutions to problems. You have both done so well that all that know you want to help you do more. Have you not noticed the attitude from your own people?" He asked. Erica was the one in tune with people. She blushed.

"Well, yes, I have noticed the general feeling of well-being from the populace. I figured they were just happier." She said meekly.

"They are that, but it is more than that. They feel that you care. They feel that you are looking out for them. This is because you are. You have been helping them. You listened and you took action when no one else had. Your decisions are just and fair. If you could live among the common people you could see for yourself just how much they care about you. I have my people out among your people. I have been taking an interest in all of your progress. I admit that it makes the elder races nervous. They do not understand you as much as I do. Once they figure out what your motivations are, they will applaud your efforts. You will see." He said and he blew smoke from his pipe up into the air to roll around above him before dissipating. "In fact, I am here to help you save your progress as it were." The look of confusion on both faces before him made the Sprite King chuckle. The sound broke the tension in the room. "The spirit tree tells us bits and pieces of the future. It is linked to the world as deeply as any creature upon it. However, as you know, its connection had been recently severed and reattached." He paused for a moment. "In fact, thank you again for that Josh." He added pleasantly. "Anyway, because of this the spirit tree cannot tell us exactly what is going on here. However, the images we have received are disturbing enough." He set down his pipe and the wisp of smoke terminated almost immediately as if he had willed it out. Perhaps he had. "The future of your kingdom here is in grave peril. Hordes of some dark nature will be swarming over it at some future date. We cannot tell exactly when, but I fear that the time is near. The tree shows us that you will need help to fight off whatever it is. We see new alliances and old ones working side by side. It is a powerful image. We see the elder races all but extinct and your efforts will be all that save them. Another prophetic and powerful image concerning you that one is. Finally, we see the joining of two great houses." He paused again on that statement. All the others he had thrown at them quickly as if to forestall any objections. There had been none.

Josh fought through to get up the nerve to ask the question burning in both of their brains. "Two houses, what two houses?" He asked.

The Sprite King smiled wide. "Your illustrious queen will marry." He said and it was obvious that he liked just how uncomfortable he had just made Erica.

"What?!" She exclaimed. "You tell us that we are facing an imminent attack and you want me to worry about getting married?" She blurted out all at once.

The Sprite King had expected this reaction; in fact he was enjoying it immensely. "You have already decided not to marry your brother. I've known both of you well enough to understand that. Your parents were brother and sister and so were their parents. So it is obvious that you will be breaking that particular tradition. However, you must consider the kingdom. If you are slain without an heir, the whole place would tumble into chaos." He turned to face Josh. "Oh I'm sure you could keep things together for a little while. You are strong and determined and quite clever. In the end, however, you are only mortal as well. Upon your passing, if nothing else, the kingdom would still fall. An heir is the only way to secure your legacy for the future." He winked at Erica. "I expect this will be a busy time for you young lady." He said chidingly. Erica stood defiant, her fists on her hips. "Seriously, you have to give at least some thought to this; no matter how uncomfortable it makes you. You owe it to your people. They deserve to be protected. It is the highest calling that we can have." He stopped and slumped a bit, his steam had been exhausted. Then he turned to Josh again. "You and I will discuss tactics later. I need to eat and rest before that and I do need to get back to my people to try to set up defenses there as well. We have much to do." He said and Josh simply nodded.

Erica was still flustered but not so much as to not read the tides of emotion here. She rang the bell that requested servers and in a flash a steward was there. The man was not altogether tall, but his distinguished appearance showed his position in the household. He had a very brief start at the sight of the Sprite King, but his professionalism saved him from any further reaction.

"Your majesty, what do you require?" He asked in that stuffy butler voice that Erica found so grating. She let it go now because of their guest.

"We need a meal brought up as soon as it can be arranged. We'll take it in the small dining room. We also need accommodations for our guest. Please see to it that he has a place to rest and that we are informed when it is done." She directed and with a curt bow, the steward left.

The trio watched as the man left. It was the Sprite King who broke the silence that lingered on afterward. "What a stuffy fellow." He said and both Josh and Erica laughed.

Josh shook his head. "You don't know the half of it. Erica has been after him to loosen up for months. No matter what we direct him to do, or order him to act like, he stays just the way he is. In a way it is almost comforting to know that some things will last." He said; the joviality running away from him at the end.

"There are places where decorum should be recognized. However, it can't be everywhere or you become like him. Watch yourselves that you do not become slaves to protocol like that. It kills the soul inside." The little King said, mimicking Josh's tone, if not quite so seriously.

It was not long before the steward returned and they were led to the small dining room. It was almost laughable. The *small* dining room would seat about thirty guests. However, relatively speaking it was the smallest one they had. The group had bowls of fresh vegetables before them. They had been steamed to lock in the flavor. Without any protocol at all, they just began eating. The Sprite King kept making noises. There would be a grunt here or a moan there. He was sampling each type of vegetable in the bowl and making his own assessment of the value of steaming the wonderful fruit of the land. So far, it appeared to be dead even.

The meal went on until all three of them had put down their utensils. Serving girls took the dishes away and they were left with hot tea and a tray of cookies. The sounds from their guest changed from grunts to yummy sounds. It turns out that he was looking for something *human* to eat. He could have had vegetables any time at home. He wanted something strange and exotic. The sugar cookies were doing the trick for him now.

Erica noticed the change and realized what was happening. She leaned over and whispered to one of the serving women. The girl nodded and hastened away. She returned in almost record time and brought forth a small handful of confections. This had been Erica's addition to the culinary treats available from the kitchen.

The sprite king looked at them and his smile looked a bit confused. "What are they?" He asked finally.

Erica smiled back at him. "They are gumdrops." She replied. "Let me know if you like them." She added and he took one. To his little hands they were almost huge. The sugar on the outside caught his attention first and his tongue checked it right away. Then he bit into the drop itself. He started chewing and chewing. This was a new sensation for him and his eyes belayed his age. He had temporarily become a child again. He tried to swallow, but more chewing would be required first. Then he took another bite and was amazed again that it really was different than anything he had ever eaten before. There were four different color drops and he could not wait to try some of the others.

"I assume that you find the dessert to your liking?" Erica asked putting that stuffy tone into her voice for emphasis.

The Sprite King didn't even notice the jab. "Oh yes, they are quite good these, gumdrops of yours." He replied as he grabbed a piece off of another one, this one was cherry red. He shoved a piece into his mouth and closed his eyes to savor the moment. Both Josh and Erica laughed and he looked around startled. Then he realized what he was doing and he started to laugh too. Bits of cherry gumdrop were trying to escape and he did his best not to lose any of the strange confections. The eating was pretty much over and they all moved to their chambers for some rest. The conversation would pick up again afterward, that was a certainty. What they did know of the Sprite King, he never did anything without a purpose. Erica was not sure that she wanted to hear the rest of what he had to say. But a part of her understood his point and honestly, she was eager enough to find someone to connect with. Josh was a good companion as little brothers went, but she needed something more, something with a deeper connection. Her position as queen had pretty much singled her out so that meeting somebody to get to know them had pretty much all but vanished. In fact, she was lonely. The revelation hurt a bit and she put it aside for now. She would rest, and then maybe get in some weapons practice before having to deal with the *thinkers* again.

Mouse had made his way through two villages seeking the first of his targets. Of course target implied that he would do something violent which was not what he was up to. No, the wolf had been specific about what he was to do. He needed to convince certain people that they should prepare their area for recruitment to something called the First Royal Army. He had not heard the term before, but he understood well enough what an army was. He was making good time, but the wolf had told him that time was working against him. He stepped up his pace just a bit more. He would be a bit sore tonight, but if it was that vital that he complete his mission, he would suffer a bit for the doing of it. He needed to believe that he was doing something important. Yes, he had been told, but that was all. He had helped the True Bloods before. He had been told then how important his part had been. He remembered well the feeling that had brought on. He longed to feel it again. He wanted to mean something. He didn't want just to be Mouse. He folded his coat a bit tighter and lowered his head into his stride to bump up his pace just a little bit more. He *would* mean something. He would do this thing right and he would save the day! The sounds of a cheering crowd filled his mind's eye and he smiled as the ground fled by him below. He would not fail.

The pack had traveled long and hard and they were nearly spent. The effort to find an answer for their losses was all-consuming. Messengers had been sent out but none had returned so far. The wave of terror around the infected area had swept outward and even this far out it seemed like a physical force. There was little they could do to fight this unseen enemy. Strength and courage was one thing, but hidden fear placed directly inside your brain touched the animal instincts. Those were powerful motivators. The pack lay on the thickets beneath the trees. Exhaustion had overcome many and the pack stopped to let them rest. Truth-be-told they were all feeling the effects. Never before had the entire pack been humbled like this. That simply added to the artificial fear they were all experiencing. As they lay there, they were unaware that they were being watched.

The Dark Lord eyed the fallen beasts with a smile. His plan had succeeded even better than he had anticipated. By simply increasing the area of effect, he had kept all of them further away from his project. The work continued on unabated. His master will surely be pleased. All that remained was to eliminate these broken beasts and be done with them. The only question left to him was how to do it. He had considered sending a dark beast of his own to do the deed, but if it failed then he would become a laughing stock. It was also possible that with a visible foe, the enemy might rally themselves up into something cohesive. That he could not have at this delicate stage. No, he needed something fast and sure. He would slaughter them all before they could scream. He knew just what to do now. He began the incantation to summon the demon he had in mind. He did not envy the beasts and their impending doom. He would have to make sure that he had a seat with a good view; he didn't want to miss a thing.

The Grand High Elf sat in the uncomfortable carriage. He was not sure why he had been talked into this foolhardy venture, but he knew that once he had agreed, there was no way out of it. They were traveling west. The wooden wheels were bouncing along in bone-jarring fashion in the well-worn ruts that posed for a road in these parts. Compared to the way his people got around, it was downright uncivilized. He kept grumbling under his breath but his companion did not even seem to notice his discomfort. In fact the other figure in the carriage was still somewhat of a mystery to him. The man, and he was human, stood quite a bit taller than the Grand Elf, and he possessed much of the grace that only the elder races could lay claim to. However, the similarities ended there. This man was big and powerful. His outfit covered everything, but there were ripped muscles under that cloak. The bouncing carriage was nothing to this man. It wouldn't have been too surprising to see him running along with the carriage and keeping pace with it. He looked like a hunter. Of course he was more than that. He was an adviser to one of the most influential human leaders the world had ever produced. They were on their way to the Kingdom of Hallowed Springs. They had been traveling this way for a day and a half and it was tiring to the aging elf. He still resisted the urge to ask if they had arrived yet. The first two times he had asked drew an ugly glare from the human whose patience was nowhere near that of an elf. They weren't even carrying a conversation along the way. It was just the squeaks and rumbles of the carriage broken by the occasional snort from the two horses that were pulling it. The driver was on top of the conveyance and his post was just as miserable, except that he could see where they were going. It had been a maddening journey thus far. Then, just as he was beginning to lose hope, the wheels stopped and the sounds of the driver stepping down could be heard. The big man stayed put as the driver made his way down to the passenger compartment. The door opened and the Royal Adviser exited the carriage and looked around checking for possible threats. His time as a royal guard was reflected in his thoughts and mannerisms. The Grand Elf stepped gingerly from the carriage and looked around as well. But for him it was not something he did for security. He was more interested in where they were. The trees off in the distance were taller than those around his neck of the woods. The road continued on past where they had stopped. It wound around and disappeared in either direction within a few hundred yards. They were stopped in front of a small building that was little more than a cabin. The soft yellow light in the window seemed somehow inviting. The driver led the horses around back to the barn that was placed there just out of sight of the main building. The remaining travelers made their way to the front door. The hunter knocked on the door irregularly for some kind of code. The door opened almost immediately after he had stopped. The two were ushered in and sat at a table. The cabin was indeed as small as it appeared on the outside. The cramped space was cluttered with things. The soft warm light of a fire beckoned to them. The trip had been rough on his weary bones. He couldn't have said just how far they had come. The only consolation that he had now was that the surroundings did not look familiar at all. They had gone far enough for that to be true. He sat at the table and waited.

"You have done well to get this far." A voice said from behind them and both men whirled around to see who had spoken. The raggedy man looked like he had long ago given up trying to fit in. In fact, he looked like he never actually fit in even if he had tried. His torn and tattered clothing hardly hid his reptilian skin. The Grand High Elf looked shocked first, and then he smiled.

"Forraguth! I had no idea you'd be around here." He exclaimed happily. The demi-human held out a strong scaly hand and The

High Elf shook it with gusto. It was not an easy feat for one of his considerable age, but he managed it as he had done for centuries. "Why are you all the way out here in the human lands?" He asked, trying not to let the word human sound like a curse for the sake of his companion.

Forraguth looked at his aged friend. In truth they were almost the same age, but a half-man, half-dragon aged somewhat differently than either species aged alone. "I'm surprised that you don't know." He replied, trying not to be to condescending to his old friend. "Something is going on and all of the kingdoms will be affected by it. I am here to seek council with the king." He elaborated.

"Then we are on similar missions it would seem." The high Elf said, stroking his lengthy beard with an absent minded hand. "You are right about strange things being afoot. I cannot even find out who is behind this thing, or for that matter what it is." He added with more than a hint of frustration coloring his tone.

"Take it easy my friend." Forraguth said in a calming tone that had just a twinge of magic to underscore the emotion. The effect was almost instant on his aged friend. "There will be answers, and soon I fear. We will have to face the fact that we elder races are unable to battle this threat alone." He looked at the rogue/adviser to the human king. "We will need the humans to help defeat this mighty foe, whoever it is." He concluded. Neither of them seemed all too happy about that admittance, but neither could they ignore it for the sake of their own arrogance either. It simply was the way it was. "Nevertheless, I intend to do all that I can before the offal hits the rocks. If we can stop this war before it starts, then we will be so much stronger than trying after it has gotten some momentum behind it."

It was time for the human to speak up then. "My lord agrees with you. It is the main reason that we are having this little get-together in the first place." He sat down with the elder representatives. "It is not only in our interests to see this affliction stopped, but it also helps your peoples as well. We have the manpower to mount a proper defense, but we do not know where to deploy. We have to have tactical information on the threat that you are obviously at least aware of. We also do not have some of the special skills that you posses that would help this mission reach a successful conclusion." He paused for a moment. "This really isn't the time to go into all of this. You need to speak with my lord to hash out the fine details. We will be leaving for that rendezvous in about six hours. If you require rest, then a place will be provided for you. Consider me your host on this venture. I have already arranged a meal to be brought to you and if there is anything you need, just ask and I shall do my best to accommodate you." He stood back up, excusing himself from this conversation. "I bid you good day gentlemen, and success to us all." He said and he stepped back into the corner of the cabin and sat down. When he settled in fully, he vanished. It was some kind of magic the two others presumed, but it left no trace. It was a good trick.

True to the human's word, a meal arrived at the door and the three young servers laid it all out without a word. They finished their work and departed without a greeting or even a whisper among themselves. The discipline was almost staggering. The two eyed each other and then they took in the food table. It was a truly remarkable feast before them and they settled in to enjoy it. It wasn't long before both of them were leaning back in their chair holding their burdened stomachs. The coziness of the cabin seemed to envelop them and sleep took them both. Whatever discussion they would have had was lost for now. They would have to wait.

CHAPTER 4

Rest was something the Sprite King got precious little of lately. His people were so troubled that their emotions drained upon their leader. Here, away from the mass of his own people, he could finally get some sleep. He had never before known the peace he felt here. The palace was a fortress of relaxation for him that he hadn't ever even dreamt of. Still, he was not here for his own bodily requirements. He was on a mission. It was also a mission that would lead him back to his people soon enough. He got up and freshened up before meeting with Josh and Erica in their chambers.

The two leaders were already clean and ready. There were some baked goods that smelled of sugar on a silver tray beside the seat he was offered. They were some cinnamon confection and the pungent odor of them made him take two. He had not really felt all that hungry, but when it hit his mouth, he ate greedily. When all of it was consumed, and that was a major feat for one of his size, the tray was taken away and a fresh hot towel was handed over. In moments, all seemed right with the world. Of course it was an illusion, but it felt good while it lasted.

Josh opened the floor of discussion with his first question. "Do you know from which direction the trouble will come?" He asked plainly. It was a good starting point and the Sprite King nodded to the young prince.

"The..." He searched for the right word. "Infestation will come from the southwest." He finished and Josh mentally looked in that direction. His far sight was like an astral travel. His mind's eye swept through the palace wall and out southwest over the morning countryside. The shops were not open yet, but the vendors were getting ready. The colorful canvas sun blocks were being extended over precious spoilable goods. He flew over them while no one noticed. In truth he was not really there. He was only seeing what they were up to. He swept out farther, hoping to catch a glimpse of something, anything that was out of the ordinary. It all looked peaceful and productive. Normally he would have smiled at that recognition. Now, he frowned.

"Well, whatever it is, it isn't happening yet." He said finally.

The Sprite King laughed. "Do you think I would wait until the last minute to tell you of an impending attack?" He looked almost amazed. "I think you understand me less than I thought." He added, a bit put out.

Josh shook his head. "No, it's not that. I was pretty sure that I wouldn't find anything when I looked, but I had to do it. I had to feel that everything was still okay for now." He replied, his tone suggested a deeper meaning and the Sprite King rarely missed such a cue.

"Yes, I understand. As leader I have great responsibility to my people too. You fear for them, as is your station. You fear for them more than you fear for yourself. It is the sign of a good leader. Selflessness is one of the cornerstones of public service." The King concluded with a grin.

It was Erica's turn to shake her head. "I just wish the politicians at home could hear you say that. They are more concerned with lining their own pockets with cash than with the well-being of their constituents." She replied.

The Sprite King shook his head woefully. "Then it is time for your home to change its leadership. Any leader who has failed so miserably should be removed from his post. He should accept his failure and come to terms with his people for his short-comings." He said with conviction in his heart and steel in his tone. He truly believed what he was saying and it showed.

Josh held up his hands. "You'll get no argument from me on that one. I think the whole lot of those crooks back home should be taken out and shot." He said jokingly, but the tone was wrong and the Sprite King started to build a rage.

Erica sensed that and tried to handle the situation. "Josh didn't mean to actually execute the rulers; life is too precious to him for that. He was just trying to lighten the mood; unsuccessfully I might add." She said flashing him a warning look. Josh backed down suitably.

"Yes, I am sorry. I meant no offense. It was just hard to forget that our old leaders were no better than the rogue guild here." he said and the Sprite King nodded.

"Yes, I can see how that would be troubling." He paused for the briefest of instants. "But more troubling is how you both call this other place home. You cannot return there I am told. *This* is your home now. Until you can accept that, you will not be everything that your people need in this crisis." He warned and both of the young rulers let their heads drop. "You need to be totally committed to the preservation of *this* world. Can you do that?" He asked.

Josh and Erica reached out and clasped hands. This was an important moment for them. They saw the same commitment in each other's eyes. Then they let their hands drop. Josh looked down to allow his sister to have the floor. Erica made direct eye contact with the Sprite King. "Yes, we can do that." She announced.

The Sprite King nodded quickly but his face was not of joy. "Humph, it's about time too. You two have been gallivanting around like you're on some kind of vacation. This is serious work and it requires all of you to do it. You cannot think of this as a temporary position. You are here for life. I will help you all that I can, but ultimately the work to be done will be yours and yours alone." His admonishment was over. It was unmistakable how his demeanor changed. There was a lighter tone to his voice when he spoke again as well.

"So, how about we go over some real tactics then son?" He asked and Josh was relieved to have something he could sink his mental teeth into. He and the Sprite King talked quite some time and Erica made her royal exit to go and take care of the daily business of the court. By the time she was out of session, the Sprite King was gone and Josh was busily preparing things she did not understand. She sighed and left him to it. She felt tired, and just a bit apprehensive. There was some kind of trouble on the horizon, sure, but who was she supposed to marry? Her head hurt trying to figure that one out. She felt the beginnings of a panic attack coming on and put the thought away for now. Prince Charming could wait.

The Stone Lords had heard of the troubles the surface dwellers were having with the infected area, so they had dispatched their own representative to investigate the occurrence that was causing so much commotion amongst the elder races. However, Stone Lords were the very bedrock of society. Everything fluttered about compared to them. The representative made excellent time for his kind, but that was still slow progress by anyone else's measure. It would still be quite some time before he would reach the area in question. On the bright side, as he traveled, he sampled the rock and questioned everything along the way. If there was something up, he would find it. So it was, with the determination of a mountain, the Stone Lord associate made his best pace to the site where so many of the surface dwellers had been lost.

Forraguth stood tall and stretched. They were outside again and he was much more comfortable there than cramped up in any human building. No matter how grand they tried to make their structures, they simply paled next to the majesty that nature had provided. It was not arrogance, but simple fact that drove him to that conclusion. He had seen just about everything that the human race had to offer. He saw congested cities with their high populations and ripe smell; there were cozy farmhouses that could barely fit him through their door. None of it was for him. None of it felt right. There was something so … artificial about it all. He finished his mighty stretch and then got ready to depart. They were going to meet this human leader today; he was looking forward to getting business out of the way. He hated waiting; it was just something that made his skin crawl. He was restless by nature. He longed to be moving again. As he flashed a grin to his comrade, the Grand High Elf sighed. He preferred the open spaces as well, maybe not the same ones, but the tops of the trees the elves protected in the forest were more beautiful than anything he had seen anywhere else in the world. It was this common belief in the power of nature that linked all of the elder races. It was also something that separated them from the human populace. Humans tended to treat the land as a resource to be cultivated or demolished to make way for something they *built*. There was none of the harmony that nature displayed in even its smallest creations. The Grand elf wondered why the humans were so blind to this. Of course he had wondered this countless times over his long life. There were no answers. He also had to admit that some of the humans understood and embraced nature. There were specialties within the human equation that allowed communing with nature. However, they were the exceptions, not the norm. During his reflections, the preparations to leave were completed and all of them were happy enough to be back on the road, such as it was, once again. This trip was to be shorter and thus less taxing on the elf's weary bones. The compartment was cramped though with the addition of Forraguth. However, his stabilizing weight was more than enough compensation for the space he consumed inside the craft. This trip had just gotten better. All that remained was to find out what the king was up to and how they were supposed to help him. After that, the future was just an impenetrable cloud of confusion. It was another sign of a diabolical presence at work. It would take a lot of energy to block his vision. Nevertheless, blocked it was. He made a note to bring that up in the upcoming meeting as well.

Mouse had covered a lot more ground and he was now ready to confront his first target. The man in question was openly known as a merchant of one of the more respected guilds. His name was Travis. The thought of meeting with a man of wealth and power made Mouse nervous. He was still pretty young for an important mission such as this. However, his own lust for recognition would drive him on when his brain faltered. This Travis was supposed to be eating at the Inn. Of course it was general meal time for the midday meal so that was not overly surprising. However, Mouse didn't know what this Travis looked like yet. He could enter the Inn and look around, but he didn't want to tip off Travis or worse yet, set off any of the local inhabitants into a frame of mind of distrust. His mission was to get key people in the communities to gather their strength for the upcoming defensive stand. Anything he did that would jeopardize their trust would certainly make his mission that much more difficult. It was a sure bet that this Travis would not stay in the Inn forever. Mouse would simply get a good spot and observe the patrons as they exited. He would try to spot his man that way. He settled into a good spot. His ability to blend in served him well here. He had always been wise to the ways of the street. He had grown up trying to fend for himself in and around the smaller villages around the palace. He understood the hidden pecking order of the various guilds and he also understood how to avoid any complications with them. He made himself small and unnoticeable. At his new height, it had been a bit more difficult than it used to be, but he managed it without too much trouble. He would just have to wait now and hope that nobody passes by and notices him while he worked on his excuse for being here in the first place. His eyes showed none of the amount of thought his brain was processing. It was one of his safety features; he could always look dumb until someone gave up. He didn't have to dazzle anyone with his intellect here. In fact, if he had done so, it would have brought him the wrong attention. So he pretended to be a chameleon and remain unseen from any dangerous prying eyes. He would worry about fighting or running later. Hiding was his first and best choice... for now.

The day stretched out and the various patrons of the Inn began to depart. This was one of the bigger villages, it was almost a town. The population was large enough to have more than one Inn, but only just. He watched intently, while maintaining his obscure persona. Nobody came out that would fit the description he had been given. That was odd. The other Inn was much less costly and tended to have a rougher clientele. This one had been his best bet for a random encounter to emerge. But alas, it had not done so. He held his position for another hour before thinking about giving up. He had just started to move when the man he was looking for exited the Inn. He was dressed in suspenders and a puffy sleeved shirt that bespoke of wealth. His boots were just over the calf and had a large turn down area in the leather. It was yet another example of opulence. He had rings on his fingers and a diamond in his left ear. He walked like one who had eaten too much and for too long a time. That explained his tardiness at leaving. However, he was not alone. A serving wench was with him and his probably drunken stammer brought forth an irritating giggle from the young lady. So Mouse kept to the shadows and followed the pair around to the back of the Inn. The lady had a key to an external entrance to the upper floor of the establishment. Apparently, such a house of ill repute was meant to be separate from the main business of running the Inn. That was why a separate entrance had been required. It was obvious that this man would not be ready to talk once he emerged from this place so Mouse resigned himself once again to waiting. He would follow this man and find out where he lived, eventually. His mission could not falter. He had to do all of the steps that the wolf gave him. Josh and Erica needed him again. He munched on a piece of dried flatbread and waited patiently in the shadows for the drunken merchant to emerge. After the probable hangover, the man would be ready to approach tomorrow.

The Sprite King had departed and both children breathed a sigh of relief. As much as they liked the tiny old man, he was difficult to predict. The duties of the palace had been interrupted and a backlog of visitations needed to be seen to. Both of the young rulers steeled themselves for the mental load they were about to bear. This was going to be a long day.

On the bright side, they were comfortable enough. Instead of their more regal accoutrements, they were clothed in hunter's leathers. Once broken in, these were some of the most comfortable clothes anyone could wear. It was like a second skin. Erica had felt a twinge at one of her latest work-out sessions and Josh simply liked looking plain and uninteresting. In truth, the people were amazed at what he could do, but they were also intimidated by the young man. The love for him was almost equal to that of his sister, but the appearance of that love was scarce. He tried not to let it get to him, but it did hurt inside to feel the lack of affection from the very people he served. Of course he did not let that get in the way of doing his duties as he saw them. He was still dedicated to the people heart and soul. It could be no other way.

The petitioners filed in through the customary process and within no time they had actually caught up to current requests. The staff on hand at the palace knew their jobs and the flow were handled in a professionally personal manner. It was one of the secrets to this regime that they allowed good help to be just that, good help. When the last scheduled person filed out, both of the True Bloods breathed a sigh of relief. According to the time candle in the corner, six hours had ticked off. It was a good day, and not as long as they had feared. The two began their trek from the viewing room back up to their private quarters. They still shared a massive room, but there had been some changes. There was now a large divider that had been erected to allow some semblance of privacy between the brother and sister. It had been considered a good idea to maintain both of their sanity. The room was still quite large. In fact it was larger than both of their rooms would have been at home. There was no drywall here though. This was stone on stone construction and the seams had been packed with mud and gravel to create almost natural cement. The workmanship was really top notch, but then again, it was a royal palace. Only royalty could afford such meticulous attention to detail.

Josh had placed a large square table on his side of the large room. It had a miniature recreation of the surrounding landscape and tiny models of the buildings surrounding the palace. It was just like one he had seen in a role-playing shop. This was his tactical map. He had small flags that he could place to order around his units. The trouble was that so far, he had no units. However, he had a plan. The table would soon be populated and he would also have soldiers in the field. His mind was already gathering the details. His magic worked by simple thought but the exacting details had to be visualized or the magic would fail. His mind was well trained now and he could pull images from it with almost freakish speed. However, he still had to concentrate fully on the image to make it appear. This had been his weak spot before. It would be his strength now. If all went as he had planned, the fight would happen without him actually having to be present to witness it. He hoped that it was so; all he could do now was plan and do his best to make sure everything went off without a hitch.

The Dark Lord completed his work. The weapons and armor were ready. The siege vehicles were also prepared. He had but to report his success and his part of this massive plan would be complete. He set the glyphs in place in the darkest chamber. The fires lit around him in the sconces by his will alone and then he knelt before the shimmering disc that floated in the air before him. A wind blew through the chamber as the pressures equalized between dimensions. The Dark Lord could feel the presence he sought. It made his skin crawl to be in the presence of one so evil. He lowered his head even further to denote his subservience to his master. The fires all extinguished and the Dark Lord knew fear.

"You have disturbed me in a key moment in time. Your message had better be important." The Master warned. It was everything he could do not to shake as he steadied himself to report.

"The equipment you asked for is complete. Everything has been made ready for your troops Milord." He said, hoping against all hope that it would be enough to stem the tide of anger and hatred he felt from his superior. There was a pause that seemed like an eternity.

"Then you have done well." The demonic voice said. "I will be sending troops to that realm within a few hours. Prepare to receive my army and when all is complete, I shall personally take charge and drive the vermin before us. The moment of my victory is at hand." He said, and his rolling evil laugh shook the chamber. Then the connection was broken and the Dark Lord was alone again in the darkness. His eyes could see well enough even in this pitch black. He had a great sense of relief over the leader's reaction. He had done well and he would be rewarded. It was all that he had toiled for all these years. The secrets and the work were finally going to pay dividends. He would be somebody important in the new regime of this world. He stood and headed out of the chamber to make ready for the army he expected to arrive any time now.

The king of Hallowed Springs and its smaller villages sat in his throne. He was bored. It was a common enough occurrence. But he had plans that would alleviate the problem. Soon enough, he would be worried. Soon enough, he would have more to think on than he would wish on anyone. His only hope was that he would be up to the task when it fell into his lap. But for now, all he could do was wait. The chamber he was in was ornately carved and he knew each and every fresco well. He had grown up here and he had served as king now for nine years. His gray hair was an attest to the struggles that such responsibility put on a man. However, his set jaw and determined eyes bore the more likely resemblance to his character than did the crown and fine jewels that adorned his head and frame. The sword at his side was not for ornamentation either. He had fought to defend his people and his way of life. He had stopped usurpers and bandits before. He understood what it took to make a kingdom run. He had set up many of the rules and regulations regarding everything from trade, to limited birth rates for overpopulated areas. His own wealth had increased accordingly. The power of his small realm had increased by border skirmishes that he had planned and executed to precision. He didn't take enough to be considered dangerous by the more powerful neighboring duchies, but he slowly expanded his influence. His people were fed and clothed and they paid their taxes to him. All was well with the world from his point of view. That is, until the threat of invasion brought the whole thing into focus for him. He had planned to leave his entire domain for his son to rule. The prince was liked well enough to be able to assume the throne without too much trouble. The real problem now was whether or not it would be there for him to take. The rumor mill had been cranking out stories of massive evil armies and strange new weapons. Normally, this would not have caused him too much concern. After all, people tell their children all kinds of things to keep them in line. A leader had a lot of children, all of the people under his influence were like children to be directed and disciplined when necessary. No, he would not have given any of it true credence until he had been questioned by the elder races. They never jumped on any bandwagon. They watched and waited with the patience their longer life spans allowed. If they were worried, then something dire was on the horizon. He had dispatched a courier to bring in the representatives so that they could discuss just what was going on and what should be done about it. If all went well, his son would attend the meeting. The more experience he got dealing with the elder races, the more prepared he will be for it when he sat in this chair.

He had hoped to retire and let his son rule, but most kings died to relinquish their thrones. His health was not all that bad, but his age was definitely starting to catch up with him. There were aches and pains and creaky bones working their way into his everyday life. He resented those little reminders of mortality, but was powerless to do much about them. What he had in his favor was the best medicine available and magic that could prolong his life for quite some time. Not indefinitely to be sure, but much longer than naturally possible. Of course that would mean his son would have to wait longer for his inheritance, but was that such a high price to pay for the enlarging kingdom he would receive? The lookout had told him that the carriage was visible from the castle walls. The meeting he had been awaiting was not far away now. At least this day would provide something interesting for him to ponder. His own boredom had caused much of the grief that he dished out each day. He picked up a peach from a bowl next to his throne. He turned it over in his hand to inspect it for blemishes or bruises. It looked perfect as it always did. He knew that servants spent a lot of time picking out his royal produce. He was almost thankful that they had done such a good job. If his own arrogance had let him be thankful for what was rightfully his, then he might have. However, he was the king. He expected to be treated so well.

There was a commotion outside the chamber doors and the old man did his best not to look interested. His royal crown was starting to get heavy and he felt like slouching in the chair. He resisted the urge to do just that. He had guests. He was not sure who yet, but he knew that they had come to see him. The caller stepped to the side of the door as it opened. When Forraguth stepped through the open doors, the king's heart skipped a beat. The half dragon stood quite a bit taller than his staff did and the ancient looking elf with him seemed to radiate power. They crossed the vast chamber with the inlaid tile floor. They ignored the finery around them to focus on the lone human on the throne. This was who they came to see. The carriage driver was behind them a respectful distance and the doors were closed behind them. The room was silent except for the footfalls of the moving group. When they reached the correct distance, all of them stopped and bowed to the king. Movement off to the side proved that the prince was in attendance as well. This meeting could progress now.

"Please rise, oh dignitaries from the other realms." The king said bringing forth his pragmatic speaking voice. "You have traveled far to reach me, do you require refreshment?" He asked and they both shook their heads.

The Grand High Elf stepped forward one step. "Our message is urgent. There is no time to waste on pleasantries. We must discuss the impending threat to allow for the most equitable solution possible." The elf said trying to appeal to the human's baser instincts of financial expansion. The arrow hit the mark squarely.

"How equitable are we talking?" The king asked, his brow furrowing in suspicion.

"Oh, it is a bargain you must agree. We are here to save as many of your people as we can while also trying to save our own." The elf said and the king leaned back a bit.

"Ah, so this is a mission of mercy you are on?" He asked, trying to measure whether or not these beings were wasting his time.

"The enemy is on the move. We cannot tell from where exactly yet, but they are coming. The only question is how do you plan to keep them from ravaging your kingdom and populace?"

"My guards have been defending this castle for quite some time. My skirmishers are more than capable of defending my borders. I have been fighting with one group or another for my entire rule here. Do not fear whether or not I can defend my people." The king said in a dangerous tone. "The real question is what do *you* want?" He retorted. "If you have come to enlist our aid in defending you, then we can start talking price. If you are suggesting that we need your help, you are sadly mistaken. Either way, your next words will determine if we have further business to discuss or not." He warned. He could tell that the half-dragon was ready to burst; his temper was only barely held in check. The Elf seemed unfazed by the direct verbal assault.

It was a long moment and the silence between them strung it out even farther. It was the Grand High Elf who spoke next. "I can see that you are not interested in truly protecting your people, let alone assist in helping ours." He smiled as the king's look of shock registered. "It is therefore, you that is wasting our time. I bid you good day and good luck. I know that you are going to need it just to survive." He said and he and Forraguth turned and paraded out of the chamber. The guards allowed them to leave without hesitation. Truth-be-told the elder races made them nervous with such close proximity to their king. The carriage driver simply hung his head as he followed along, emotionally deflated.

"Please sirs, don't leave just yet." A younger voice called out to them from the corridor beyond. The group turned to see who was speaking. All of them were surprised to see who it was. The finery he wore made it clear that this was the prince. His young shoulders were just beginning to broaden and fill out, and his beard was only just beginning to come in, but his eyes were razor sharp and his brow was furrowed with concern.

"If I could have a few moments of your precious time, perhaps we could come to some sort of arrangement." He added, hoping to sway the foreign dignitaries from leaving empty-handed. "Let us talk in my private chambers. If you don't like what I have to say, then you can leave with no questions asked." He prompted with hope flavoring his tone.

"Very well young one, we shall listen to what you have to say." The elf held up a bony finger for caution. "This had better not be a further waste of our time. We have precious little to spare." He warned and the prince shook his head violently.

"I assure you that my intentions are honorable. Please follow me." He led the group down several corridors and finally ended up at an ornate door that looked just like any other door in the ancient castle. "This is my place here." He added needlessly. "Step inside quickly and we can get on with this." He said as he ushered them all into the chambers beyond.

Inside, it looked like a separate building. There were skins on the cold stone floor and curtains framed each wall. A large hearth in the center of the far wall had a raging fire within. It was warm and cozy in here. The furnishings were large cushions and the group did their best to take a seat and try to retain some dignity. It was not a simple feat. As free and easy as this room seemed, it did not reflect the look in the Prince's eyes.

"Look, I understand where my father is coming from." He began as a form of explanation. "He has been doing business as usual for as long as anyone can remember. He has never faced a threat like the one you are predicting. He has fought minor skirmishes for unwanted bits of land that his neighbors didn't feel the need to argue over. He is not prepared for what you say is coming." He said with no humor in his tone at all. In fact, his sincerity was almost a physical thing. "We need your advice." He concluded. He looked around as if to check for spies. "My father will never admit to anyone, let alone an outsider, that we could have a weakness. He comes from an era where weakness is rewarded by conquest. Strength is the only thing that he will respond to." Then the young man looked troubled. "He will never ask you for help. He can't. It is just not possible for him to do so." Then the young man smiled. "That's why I am here to do it." He said and eyebrows rose at the sudden change in tone. The last statement was downright jovial.

"So you are telling us that the king could not ask us for help, even though we were offering it." The elf said with a pause. "But he can ask us for help through you?" He added in question and the prince merely nodded. There was another moment of delay and the tension in the room was getting pretty thick.

"You must understand that he is old and tired. He's not ready to give up his comfortable chair and authority yet, but he is beyond the day when adventure would have called to him." There was a slight shift and no one in the room missed it. "The castle itself is defendable enough. The palace guard is efficient and they have trained side by side for most of their career. When the wave of enemy units comes, they will be able to hold the limited spaces. I am much more worried about the general populace. As you know, it takes a lot of people just to support the castle. The local villages give and give, but what are we giving back? If the horde comes and wipes them out, then they might just as well have breached the walls and sacked the castle. We will have nothing to maintain this fortress with. We could not withstand a blockade and they would eventually kill us all." The Prince looked almost eager. "We need to take the fight to them." He said at last. His own ideas had been much more radical than that of his father. Because of this, they had been rejected out of hand.

"There is merit in what you say." The high elf began. "I believe that I speak for my comrades here when I say that I am glad that someone around here still has a brain." He said in a biting tone that held only a small measure of the sting he wanted to put into it. "There are a few things you can do to, as you say, bring the fight to the enemy." We can help you with this, but we will need some assurances in return." He said and his wizened eyes were boring straight through the prince. "We will need protection."

The prince took it all in. He nodded at first and then he shook his head. "I understand what you are saying, but there is more information I need to make a proper decision. Not the least of which is; Protection from what?" He asked and the High Elf begrudgingly felt his estimate of the young man's abilities increase a little.

"Of course." He replied at first. "We do not know the nature of the threat at this time. All we have are glimpses from prophesies and some more attuned sources telling us what they think they saw." He said as a full disclaimer for what he was going to say next. "But, from what we understand, there is an army of evil creatures in preparation and it is believed that they are nearing completion and almost ready to march." He said and then he took a deep breath. "Of course we have not been able to verify that. That may be impossible until the enemy finally makes their first open move."

The Prince just sat there for a long moment. "An army." He repeated. "That definitely sounds serious." He seemed to be sizing up his chances with his current forces. "We have an army too, albeit a smaller one as such things go. But they are battle hardened and ready to go. Cannot we defeat this enemy on our own?" He asked.

The two emissaries looked at each other and then back at the prince. "We honestly don't know. Without knowing the strength and tactics of either side, we have no idea how well your defenses will hold against the unknown attackers." There was a long momentary pause for both sides to think on what was said. "It is still our belief that you have a good chance to survive. We are just not certain of it." He said and the bold truth of it shone through. "This is a gamble for us all." He added.

It was not what he had wanted to hear, he had hoped for something much more concrete from these important men. However, it was the most he was likely ever going to get. So the Prince considered his options carefully. "When it comes down to fighting, will some of your people fight with us, or simply hide while we redirect the enemy away from you?" He asked. His eyes were hard now.

Forraguth leaned forward, his eyes meeting the Prince's with that same granite hardness. "You will not be able to keep me out of this fight." He replied. "However, our old and sick cannot join the battle. Much as you're old and sick cannot fight. We need to protect these people for both of our sakes. If you can take care of that matter, then I can focus fully on the battle plan itself. I will work directly with your commanders to achieve the best defense that our combined force can muster." He leaned back again and crossed his massive scaled legs. "Is that sufficient?" He asked in a bemused tone.

Before the prince could respond, the Grand High Elf spoke up. "My people also have fighters among us. We are not many, but we are ferocious and proud. We also have magic that may be of service. If you can see to it that our non-combatants are taken care of, then we too shall join you on the battlefield." He stated without preamble.

The Prince felt goose bumps at the thought of seeing a half-dragon in action. If things weren't so dire, he would have been excited. Then he focused back on the questions at hand. "Yes, we can help your old and sick. We have an underground storage facility that houses supplies for the winter. It is fully supplied at this time and we even have healers available to house there. Our own people were going to hide away there and there will still be enough room. At least it is safer than being out in the open. There is a contingency exit should the cache be discovered. It may not be that easy to retreat from, but it is not hopeless." He stopped as he noticed the approving nods from his guests. "I want to focus more on keeping the enemy from the city in the first place. I don't want to fight street to street if we can stop the onrush outside of any civilian population." He stated flatly.

Forraguth smiled. "My sentiments exactly." He retorted. "I want to bloody my axe in a pool of enemy and not have to worry about picking specific targets. The rage will let me cleave them down rapidly. I need open space for this. We will need to set up a skirmish line outside of your stone walls." He said and it was the Elf's turn to nod in approval.

"The very grounds will have traps and illusions shall be spread across it. If we can cause confusion among the enemy, then your shock troops will have an easier time of it. For just as my large friend here says, the more of them we kill before they reach the walls, the better chance we have of preventing a breach."

The Prince shook himself. It was too much to be believed. A real enemy was coming and these men were able to help him do something about it. It was just the thing he needed to show his father that he could manage things. His sensitive and caring ways were not weakness. The King loathed his son for his weakness. It was an image that both of them hoped would change. This battle would be the catalyst for that change. The prince just hoped he was taking the correct path. It felt right. That was a very good sign.

"Very well gentlemen. I shall move forward with the preparations. We will work together to make things right." He said and he held out his hand and both visitors shook it in turn.

Forraguth smiled. "Good, I think we can be assured that the enemy will never know what hit it." The smile almost turned into a snarl and the Prince realized, not for the first time, how scary a half dragon could be.

CHAPTER 5

Erica was working out again. The thoughts that had been running through her mind had distracted her terribly. There was nothing like a good strenuous workout to put things back into perspective. Her sword was beginning to feel a bit light. Her muscles had been beefing up of late with all of the exercise. Her trainer looked on and he seemed to make a decision.

"Your majesty, if I may, I can see that your strength is increasing. I would suggest that you consider a change of weapon." He said. He could see the worried look on her face. "Oh, a sword is good, don't get me wrong." He added hastily. "But there are things out there that a sword is less effective against." He stepped over to the weapons rack. "It's time you met one of my personal favorites." He said as he held forth a hammer.

Erica set her sword into the rack and then took the offered hammer. It was heavier than her sword by at least a third. The handle was of some hard wood wrapped with a leather thong. The head was made of iron and it reminded her of a sledge hammer. The only difference was that the head was not flat. It had small pyramids shaped in it to distribute the blow to pressure points. The leather thong ended in a wrist strap that would allow her to maintain the weapon even if she had somehow let go of it. It felt warm and dangerous. She swung it a few times to get a feel for the weight. The feel of it was amazing.

The practice dummy was behind her and she turned to face it. She was about to strike when the Guard Captain, her trainer, cautioned her to take it slowly at first.

"Make sure you are ready for the kick back. A sword slices through a target. A hammer bounces off. If you are not ready, it will come back and smash you as well as your target." He warned.

She immediately saw the danger in that. Erica swung the hammer up in a wide arc and smashed the dummy. As predicted, it bounced off of the practice figure and swung back in her direction. She nimbly dodged it and pulled back. The sound it made was deafening. The metal plate that covered the straw dummy was visibly dented from the impact. This weapon could bash even an armored enemy. The initial shock sent a spasm through her arm and she felt just a bit sore. It would take a bit more strength before this weapon was comfortable. She dropped into stance and swung again. This time the hammer hit with a glancing blow and deflected toward the rear of the dummy and pulled her forward and off balance.

"Don't swing it like a sword." Her mentor cautioned. "If you lose your stance in battle you can be beaten easily. The hammer is used by only the stoutest of warriors. You must maintain a low center of gravity and strike with direct hits that are opposite angles from the bone inside the target." He said all in a rush.

"You mean you can break bones with this?" She asked feeling a bit shocked. "I thought it was for dulling your opponent. If you hit them in the head they will be unable to concentrate or attack." She offered.

"If you hit them in the head you will crush their skull. This is a true weapon, not some child's toy. The battle hammer can crush bone and sinew with almost equal ease. The cost of this power is in physical strength. You must apply the force to accomplish the goal. It is the epitome of melee combat. This is no hit and dodge tool. You must strike your opponent down with a single blow. The weapon swings slowly because of its weight. You must have a good opening to use it and be mindful of your own vulnerability while it is in motion." He said. She could still feel the weight of it as it hung in her hand.

Erica felt the stirring inside her brain. The ancients knew about this weapon as well. There were some of them that were overjoyed to have it in hand again. Still others were woeful that she had fallen down this path. She asked them for help. With a swinging motion that displayed full agility and amazing efficiency, Erica thrust forward, the hammer made its own path from her to the dummy. The loud clank sound was followed by yet another as the power of the deflection was used to speed the hammer to its next target. The arc was that of a figure eight and the dummy was hit four times in different places when Erica backed up and set the hammer head down on the ground while still holding the handle. Her shoulder was sore and her forearm ached. But she felt more powerful than the sword had ever made her feel. Erica found that she was breathing heavy again too. She would definitely have to work out more.

Her trainer simply looked on in awe. "That was quite a brilliant display of hammer work." He commented and Erica blushed. "I am certain that since you are only now discovering the weapon that the ancients had something to do with that?" He queried and she nodded. He returned her nod and chuckled. "I was hoping they would have something to tell you." He added thoughtfully.

"I can see that this is much heavier than I am used to. My arm is sore and my shoulder." She said in a tone that did not mean complaining. "I will need to get stronger before I can reliably use this weapon." She told him and he nodded yet again.

"It is wise that you are open to new experiences." He told her in a kindly way. "However, you must remember that you have limits. The ancients can guide your hand but they cannot lift the weapon for you. You must train every other day with weights in order to gain the muscle needed to be proficient with the hammer. You will need to add more meat to your food as well. The demands you will be putting on your body may require the services of a healer as well. Do not overwork yourself needlessly. I will be here to help you with that. Promise me that you will at least listen to me concerning your own safety." He stated flatly.

Erica looked into his eyes. She saw just what she knew she would see, a concerned man who wanted to protect a young lady from herself and others. She was actually touched by it. "I promise." She told him and he smiled and nodded his acceptance.

"Then we should be getting you cleaned up so that you can get on with whatever other duties call to you. Your body needs to rest from this exertion for now." He commanded and it was Erica's turn to nod. The two of them left the practice field and headed back towards the castle proper. Josh met them at the entrance.

"Looks like the two of you have been at it again." He said, just a bit chidingly.

Erica looked at him with a flash of anger, but it disappeared just as quickly. "I'm sore, if that's what you mean." She retorted. She tried to push past him into the castle, but he resisted.

"Okay, tell me where it hurts." He said like a doctor would have with just a hint of condescending mixed into his tone.

Erica seemed a bit taken aback. "I don't have time for this. I need to get cleaned up and then off to the reviewing chamber for daily business." She almost whined at him. If it had been a year ago, it would have been a whine. The years she spent as queen had actually grown her up somewhat.

Josh looked concerned now. "No really, where does it hurt?" He asked and both of the combatants looked at him blankly.

Erica realized that she wasn't getting away until Josh was satisfied so she sighed heavily. "Okay, my arm and shoulder hurt a bit now." She replied, rubbing the affected shoulder.

Josh snorted. "It's no wonder considering you were swinging a sledge hammer so fast." He replied but before she could pull away he had gone into his trance. His hand was resting on her injured shoulder and she could feel the magic as it started to do its job. The muscles and tendons stopped complaining and the bruising she had taken earlier in the day was fading rapidly. Josh was still focused on the healing and he pulled away when the spell ended. He looked like someone had punched him in the gut. "There was more damage there than you mentioned, but it is all better now." He said; his strength was obviously lower now. The deeper magic always took a heavy toll upon him. He backed away as Erica rotated her shoulder approvingly.

"Yes, that's much better." She said with a joyful lilt in her voice. She smiled at her brother and then pushed past him to go and clean up as was her plan before this interruption. In the back of her mind though, she had to admit that she was grateful for the work. He was really good at his job.

The Guard Captain just shook his head. "I don't know how you do that, but it is a skill I wish you could teach. Our troops could use someone with that skill on hand at all times." He said only partially joking. Then he, too left to clean up. Unlike the queen, he would have to do the job himself. He nodded to Josh and retired from view. Josh had felt the drain, but because of his own work-outs, he was much faster at recovering than he had once been. Already the bounce was back in his step. He decided to head down to the archives and do a little research. The quest for knowledge was never-ending.

The Dark Lord had awaited the new arrival. The evil one, his master, had promised to send him the personnel he needed to begin this war. He had the equipment ready to go and he was getting antsy to begin. The chamber was once again lined with candles and the stench of blood was evident in the recent sacrifice that he had offered. He knelt in the middle of the five pointed star and awaited the word that the transfer was to begin. A strong smell of sulfur swept the room and a dark smile crossed his lips. It was time. The shimmering vortex formed like a cloud in the air before him and a cloven hoof stepped through onto the stone floor. The creature that followed that first step was one he had not met before, but it was obvious that this was at least his equal among the rank and file of the master. He maintained his bow until the being completed the transference. Then, he permitted himself to gaze upon the new arrival. The demon before him was impressive. It had the lower half of a goat and the upper half of a really strong man. The twisted horns protruding from its head was the classic demon form. However, this one was even worse than normal. The limbs had been twisted as well and the joints seemed to move in crazy direction. This demon had undergone so much savagery that it was not to be believed.

"I am the Dark Lord." He announced to the newcomer. "The preparations are complete." He added and the recent arrival nodded, well sort of. It somehow made its intentions clear with those jerky movements of impossibly twisted body parts.

"Very good. I am General Forrack. My troops will be made and summoned from several sources. However, the first unit to arrive will be coming within the next hand of days." He said and the Dark Lord bowed.

"Of course, all is in readiness for the grand plan." The Dark Lord tried to be energetic and helpful. He somehow fell short of the mark.

"You know nothing of the plan. All you have to do is follow orders. I will take care of the rest. Now begone from my sight and I shall begin the preparations that will summon my troops from the ether realm." He ordered and the Dark Lord bowed and retreated. He made sure not to take his eyes off of the new general until he had fully departed to the next chamber.

Once outside, he began to vent his new anger. "I don't believe this! I personally set up all of the equipment for the new offensive and now I'm being tossed out like a common underling! I am the Dark Lord! I am the one who was entrusted to accomplish the impossible and remain undetected while doing it! I am the one that humanity will fear when it is all said and done! I will have my respect!" He began to lose his current rage and it started to burn into hate. "This General Forrack had better watch his back. I will have the last laugh, he can count on that." He stomped away to look after his own phase of the plan. There was not much left to do, but complacency at this late stage could cost them everything. He would not fall into that trap. His time was coming, he would soon find glory.

Inside General Forrack turned back to the portal he had just come from. The upstart calling himself the Dark Lord had been sent away in order for him to take care of the more sensitive part of this transference. He made the signs and spoke the words of power. The portal opened wider and changed color to a bright orange, like fire. He felt the pull from the other side and resisted it through the power of his own will.

"It is time brothers. I command you to take your rightful place in this realm and make it bleed. We are the masters and we shall bring forth utter darkness on all those who seek the light." He said and his words were answered with howls and cheers. Then, the first troops started pouring through the open link between worlds. The troops were filing in and lining up in the chamber. They would soon overrun it and need to go outside, but for now, their existence was still secretive. That would change in good time, but for now it was the best route to take in an unknown world with unknown loyalties.

The General stood as high as his misshapen body could reach. "You have come and our time is at hand." He paraded before the troops even as the portal fizzled and went out. "The time for our retribution on the living is now. We have stolen the power to travel between worlds and now we are here. The world shall tremble in fear when they see us." He lifted both twisted arms over his head. "Prepare yourselves for the hunt; we leave tonight to find out just how badly we outmatch these humans." He said and the yips and howls coming from his troops told him that they were ready to advance as well. The gear they would need was already here and it would not be long before they were joined by whatever the other leg of the forces consisted of. These were shock troops. They were mostly lesser demon or wisps, or even an occasional goblin. They were all considered to be undead. The magic fire that burned in their bellies drove them ever onward. It was a thirst or hunger that could not be quenched. They were the lieutenants of this coming war.

The new arrivals began to select their gear. The chamber adjacent of the summoning chamber contained a vast warehouse of goods. The Dark Lord had already moved on. The implements of war were an amazing sight for the warriors and they took no small pleasure from divvying up all that they found. It was not long before the General was ordering his troops around and placing them into ranks for inspection. This war was going to happen, that much the fool got right. He was a pawn in the grand scheme of things. Imagine calling himself a Dark Lord. The General laughed a low guttural laugh that made hairs stand up on the back of your neck. He mused to himself. "If he actually saw a Dark Lord, he would die on the spot to avoid becoming something so wretched and powerful." The statement brought laughter from the troops around him and soon the entire area was ignited in laughter as the army began to form. Of course this was just the first step of the process. There was still so much to do. General Forrath dismissed the troops for now and then made his way to a quieter spot where he could begin his conjurations. Oh yes, he still had so far to go, but the end was finally in sight. The glory that insignificant Dark Lord wanted would surely belong to Forrath for the taking when the master arrived.

Mouse had done his level best to convince his target that he was telling the truth. He had no signet ring to support his claim. He had no formal paper to back him up. All he had was the word of a wolf. Well, he had that and he had truth on his side. Rumors of an impending invasion had already begun to circulate so it was even more difficult to get his point across. He looked like just another panic stricken peasant with an overactive imagination. Unfortunately for everyone, this time it was not the case.

"Excuse me Mr. Strasser, but what I have to say is important." He began against the resistance he was already getting. "I have been sent to contact several individuals, leaders of their communities, to get them ready for an incoming invasion." He said in a rush.

"Invasion huh? I keep hearing about this invasion and that army. Honestly I'm sick of it. Just leave me in peace." The merchant replied. He tried to step away but Mouse had him cornered pretty well in this cramped inn's dining area.

"This is serious. I was sent by a wolf to contact specific individuals and you are on the top of the list. You must believe me or our cause may be lost." He pleaded to the unhappy merchant.

"Top of the list you say... Why is that young man?" He asked in challenge, perhaps spotting a way out of this trap.

Mouse looked down for a second. "I don't know. I wrote down the names as the wolf told them to me. You were the first one mentioned. You must be the most important." He paused for a moment, his own confidence starting to slip. "Or at least you were the closest one." He admitted.

"If I believe you, and I don't say that I do, what would this wolf have me do?" He asked, still not seeing a way out of this conversation.

"Oh that's easy, he wants you to speak with your people and get them prepared for the summons from the queen for aid. They will need an army to defend the kingdom and without at least some preparation ahead of time, they will not be ready before the attack comes." Mouse rattled off. It was the part that the wolf had made him memorize.

"Then you know when the attack will come?" He asked as a brief moment of shock hit his face before his control reigned it in again.

"No, I don't know when, but it takes quite a while to recruit and outfit an army. If the enemy has been working in secret all of this time, then they surely have the advantage in the preparation phase. It would be suicide for us not to consider the threat and plan accordingly." He said, his steam was almost spent now, but his passion for the mission remained. It was this unquestioning passion that was the final factor in Ludwig Strasser's final decision.

"So you need recruits for a royal army." He said, rolling the idea over in his mind and looking for cracks that might suggest a lie on this young man's part. The logic was sound though. Other than a lack of real gritty information, the message was intact. "Okay, I will talk to a few people. I know who is able-bodied and who isn't around here. It is another fact that may have singled me out for this mission of yours concerning this community. If you are leading me astray for some reason, I can't figure out what you'd gain by us being ready for a summons that doesn't come. All I can tell is that you believe in what you are saying. So whether it is truth or fiction, I must act accordingly and comply." The merchant paused again. "Who do I check in with?"

Mouse looked at him carefully. "Nobody, this is your only notice. We do not report to anybody, except the queen. When the time comes, all of the glory will be yours for your preparedness. I am just a messenger, but you are one of the doers. You are a key piece in the game that is to play out. It is a game that none of us can afford to lose." Mouse felt that this meeting was wrapping up and it suddenly got uncomfortable. "I had better be going, I have more people to talk to and you have business to attend to. Good luck to us all." He said and he started to back away.

Mr. Strasser stopped him with a firm handshake. "Good luck to us all." He repeated and released the iron grip.

Mouse left in a hurry and disappeared down the street in no time. He felt uplifted by the successful conclusion to at least one of his stops. He couldn't imagine what was coming to this village, but now he could picture the people standing tall to defend it behind the leadership of Mr. Strasser. As he left the village itself, he took one more look back to try to remember just what they were going to be fighting for. It was just the motivation he needed to get a move on and hot-foot it towards the next destination. It was not as far as the first one had taken him, a mere three days away, but he was now anxious to get on with it. The more time he gave the people to get ready, the more lives they could collectively save. He felt that it was worth anything he could do to help. Behind him the village went on and the stranger left unnoticed. Only one man knew what was going to happen and that one man began to make his plans. With an unknown amount of time left, there was no time to waste. He vowed that he would be ready.

Forraguth and the High Elf had stayed on for three days and discussed battle plans and tactics. The Prince had taken a whole set of notes which was impressive. Most people did not know how to read or write. After that, they each made their own way out of the kingdom leaving behind promises to return when the actual fighting started. The general feeling was that the King could impede any real progress if the Prince let him know what was going on. Still, the plans were good and solid and the fact that the king required so many servants to go anywhere helped the Prince keep his activities secret. He did not know what his destiny would bring him, but he did know that it was much better to be prepared than not.

And so it was that the Prince had people working all over the kingdom while the King was blissfully unaware. The impending doom would be met with at least some organized resistance. Hopefully it would be enough. There was always the feeling that they could be doing something more, but nobody could put a finger on just what that something more was. Defenses were being erected and weapons, albeit crude ones, were being fashioned by local artisans. The young men were being trained in the use of those weapons by employing wooden practice versions of them. The markets stayed open late and people were generally happier to be busy, so it was a winning solution all over the kingdom. The Prince was making points in the eyes of the public. He did not share the accolades that Josh and Erica had earned, but he was quickly becoming a household name locally.

The coffers of the castle were the worrying factor. If the King found out about the expenditures, the whole game would be up. However, with the commerce being up as it was, the taxes on goods were rolling in at an upgraded rate as well. They would not drain the finances; they would only skim a bit off of the top. The damage had been minimized, but was it minimized enough? Only time would tell now.

Josh had been working on another project. His magic was centered on his ability to visualize the target he wanted to create or change and then concentrating on it so fully that it became reality. He was getting quite good at it too. But boredom was a major factor in life in this world and Josh being fully obsessive and compulsive and just a bit attention deficit challenged found himself drawn to new and better things constantly. This new project was one he had been thinking on and off on for over a month. Now he felt that he was close to a solution. What was he trying to create? Street lights. The current system of lighting in his city was candle power, now candles offered a wide array of light and concealment possibilities, but the open flame made them a bit dangerous for say, a merchant that sells straw for instance. He continued his research and found that there were alternatives to using fire to light his city. They had glow worms. The worms themselves had very short life spans, but their excrement glowed for several hours. Josh was working on a pumping system that could recharge the lights with fresh droppings. It would be the first underground plumbing system. In addition, he needed to visualize a pump. Both of these things he had seen before, but he knew little of how they worked. This would make visualization of the item next to impossible. How simple it would be to just visualize the result and get what you wanted, but it wasn't how things worked. Complex machinery had to be envisioned throughout in order to function. If only he had gotten a hold of some exploded diagrams. Then things would be relatively simple. Those things did not exist here in this world though. It made him long to be home for just an afternoon. Of course he knew that was impossible. The barrier between worlds was so fragile now that travel back and forth had been forbidden.

Josh had heard in school that some systems of water pumping had used gravity for most of the power and he wondered if that could work here. He decided to try a few small scale models to see if he could make it work before working on the full size pieces. He sat in front of the large empty oaken table. His hands were palms down on the edge of the table and he closed his eyes and began to picture what he wanted. He could see the cobblestone streets, the shops and houses, and the light poles with the glass balls at the top for the light to escape from. He saw the shadows that the light would throw and he even saw the grass at the edges of the streets. He concentrated on each and every detail. He began to see the pipes under the ground and large tower in the background that held the reserve of the glowing worm juice. Then he pictured a valve system to move the juice from pipe to pipe. As he watched, in his mind, the bulbs filled and lit up. The streets were treated with a green glowing light. He opened his eyes and superimposed the image in his mind over that of the table and the town appeared fuzzy at first but it sharpened with his mental effort. In moments, the entire town was staged on the table. The small street lights were lit and he smiled as he looked at all of it. Then, the green light faded and it went dark again. His smile faded with the glow. What had gone wrong? He looked over the highly articulated model and then he realized the flaw in his logic. He could let gravity pump the fluid to the bulbs, but he needed a system to take it away once the glow faded so that it could be replenished. The model before him would have made a model railroader whistle in appreciation. It was flawless right down to the shingles on the roof. There was gravel beside the buildings and even the small tufts of grass waving in the breeze that would have been there if it had been real. Josh breathed a sigh and willed the image away. In seconds the table looked normal again. The drain on Josh had been small, so he was not ready to give up yet. He needed to think on it a bit more, then he would be ready to try again.

A voice from behind him made him turn. "How are you young man?" It said and he knew that voice.

Startled, but recovering quickly, Josh replied. "You promised not to interfere anymore." He said in an almost menacing tone. "I have kept my end of our bargain and not gone home for even a second." He said and the hurt in that statement caught him.

The man before him nodded. "Yes, you have been honorable, I admit that freely." He said with just the hint of a smile. "But what is coming worries me enough to see what you are going to do about it." The Guardian of Balance said.

Josh looked puzzled for a minute. "Do about what?" He asked and The Guardian shook his head.

"You know exactly what I am referring to. You were told by the Sprite King about the invasion. What have you done about that problem?" He asked; feeling just a bit exasperated with the very powerful young man before him.

"I plan to animate scarecrows to fight off the main horde outside of the city itself. I can support them with magic as I see it through my magnifier. Then we will have moved our people out and away from the illusionary city and they will be safe in the real one." Josh said like he was describing his breakfast this morning.

It was The Guardian's turn to look puzzled. "What illusionary city?" He queried.

Josh grinned at him. "This one" he replied and waved his hand over the table. The miniature city appeared again. Since he had called it up before, it was much easier this time to make it become real. The difference this time was that people were bustling about in a panic trying to get away from an unseen horror. There were fires placed here and there and it was obvious that the city were under siege.

The Guardian looked closely at the model on the table. There were no shimmering effects on it. The illusion was so perfect that it looked absolutely real. It looked too real. He reached out and touched one of the roofs and it dented in from his touch. He pulled his hand back quickly. "This is no illusion!" He exclaimed. "You have somehow constructed a replica of your city to the minutest detail. How did you do this?" He asked. Josh simply shrugged. "No, this is amazing workmanship, how did you do this?" The Guardian asked again.

Josh smiled at him. "C'mon, you know a magician never tells you his tricks. It would spoil the illusion for you." He said and chuckled at the expression on The Guardian's face. It was a really classic befuddlement. Then Josh turned serious again and faced the model. "As you can see when the enemy arrives, they will be in a reproduction of the city. The only difference is that it will be life size. Oh, and that I have some special plans laid out for how to keep them there for a long time. He added monsters to the display. They were attacking anyone and anything they could find. As they advanced, the walls behind them changed. It was something very subtle. They looked the same, but now there were barricades keeping them from retreating. The fighting kept them occupied so nobody noticed the changes. Then, when the attacking force neared the center of the city, more walls changed and they were completely trapped inside of it all. Then the ground dropped out below them and they were trapped in a large pit the size of a market square in the real city. The threat had been completely neutralized. Josh looked up at the Protector. "Is that what you wanted to know?"

The Guardian looked at the model long and hard. "It is most impressive, I admit." He said, scratching his head in thought. "How are you going to make sure that the enemy falls for your *illusion*?"He asked."

Josh smiled bigger this time. "You just did." He said and Josh vanished, the table vanished, the walls to the room vanished. The Guardian stood there alone in a room of white nothingness. Then a form showed itself and Josh stepped forward out of the filter of white. "As you can see, I have duplicated the sights, sounds and even the smells of our fair city. The duplicate will be undetectable from the original. The original will be in its same place, but shifted in time a couple of seconds. That required a lot less energy than actually moving the city would have." Josh sat down and a chair formed under him as he did so. The Guardian felt that he may have been showing off, but with power like that, he could afford to. "Is that all that you need? Are you satisfied?" He asked and the Guardian of Balance nodded.

"For now" he said and then he pointed at the talented magician. "Know this; the problem you face is not just your problem. This is a world-wide event that is coming. If it succeeds, then this world will fall from human habitation. If that happens, then you and your parents will never again meet. You cannot escape to that place when this one collapses into chaos. This new enemy *must* be stopped. Do you understand?" The Guardian asked and his tone was dangerous. He was one of the only people who could rival Josh's power after all.

Josh looked at him and nodded. "Yes, I understand."

In a flash, The Guardian was gone. His messages were always brief, but they were also important. Josh felt that he had better double check all of his images before the final moment came. It simply would not do to fail because he was ill-prepared.

Erica found herself working harder and harder to master the new weapon. The hammer suited her well. It was bold and dangerous, the same as she viewed herself. Of course she kept hearing about this posture here and that stance there from the Guard Captain, her personal mentor. That meant that she was on the right path though. The man had no tolerance for incompetency and if she hadn't made him throw his hands into the air, then she was competent. That felt good even as she took another swing at the now nearly dismantled dummy. There was a crew already setting up another one. She had gone through two of them in as many days. The general feeling was that they were all glad that she wasn't angry with *them*. If someone with that much power and force was mad at you, it was a serious problem. However hard she worked, Erica remained true to herself. She was calling upon the ancients less and less as her body learned the stages and steps on her own. The muscle memory would help her even if the ancients were not there. It was somewhat of a comforting thought. Erica finished another string of blows and when it was all done, the remnants of the practice dummy fell over and became just so much debris strewn all over the floor. She backed away and let the hammer set gently onto the stone floor. Her breathing was not the desperate panting it had been just a short while ago. She was adjusting to the new weight almost easily. She noticed that her shield hand was used quite a bit less than her attack hand. Even though she used both on the single weapon, it was out of balance. She stood up and turned to her teacher.

"I feel that this is wrong." She told him. He looked surprised at first and then his brows lowered and he looked at her suspicious.

"Oh, how so?" He asked in a low voice that meant 'This had better be good'.

Erica looked at him and then at her hands. "It's uneven." She replied. "I keep using my right hand more than my left and it throws off my balance and stance enough to become annoying." She said and the Guard Captain smiled.

"I was wondering how long it would take you to notice that." He said with a slight chuckle. The look on her face told him not to be condescending about it and he held up his hands in mock defense. "It's good that you noticed it, really." He said and her stance changed only slightly, but it was for the better.

The Captain stepped over to a fancy box about twenty inches long, eleven inches wide, and eight inches deep. It was ringed with fancy iron work and the lock that sealed it closed looked ornately enhanced as well. He pulled a key from around his neck and opened the lock. Then he opened the small box and brought out the new weapons. "I had these made for you earlier; I was just trying to get you ready to use them before I handed them over." He said and she saw the two golden hammers for the first time.

Erica laid down the one she had been swinging. The new ones were smaller and about one third the weight of the big two-hander she had been using. The leather wrapping on the handle was oiled up and wound tight. The hammers seemed to be made of one piece of metal. She was not certain how this was possible since the blacksmith probably didn't have the facilities to accomplish that. However, they were engraved with decorative marks that made it clear that they belonged to her. One was of her family crest. Another was of the crown. She held them up side by side and they were identically weighted and balanced. They gripped well and instantly became part of her arms, an extension of her own body. A feeling of exhilaration spread through her and she smiled hugely as she turned back to the practice dummy that had just been set up while she was distracted.

She started her attack and the Guard Captain gasped as she made it a dance of death. Like a ballerina, she was spinning and striking. High and low strikes were seamless and the arcs her hammers played were like a ribbon around her athletic body. She danced around the target and the repeated blows on the metal plating were ringing in her ears like sweet music. When she completed her run, the dummy that had just been put up could no longer be used, it had been crushed in some places, and literally destroyed in others. She felt so happy that she was not even winded. She turned back to the Captain and he was standing there staring at her dumbfounded.

"What is it?" She asked when he failed to speak.

"Did you call upon the ancients?" He asked, already guessing he knew the answer.

Erica thought back to the sequence she had just performed. "No, I don't think so. To be honest, I was simply letting the weapons and the moment take me away. It was beautiful was it not?" She asked hopefully.

He shook his head. "Yes, it was most impressive. What I don't understand is where you learned how to do that. I only just handed you the hammers and you attack as if you were born with them in your hands." He said, a bit of worry underlining his mood.

Erica blushed. "They just feel right. Where ever did you get them?" She asked, still a bit giddy from the new-found strength she possessed.

"I... I had them forged by the dwarves. Nobody knows hammers better than they do. It cost a lot of coin, but they are supposed to be the best." He said, turning just a shade redder with the embarrassment. "I knew that you were meant for two handed combat. It seemed the best way to fit you to your strengths." He said almost admittedly.

Erica stepped up quickly and hugged the gigantic man. "Well, they're perfect." She giggled. "Thank you." She released the big man and then went to put her new hammers away. The Captain handed her the key. Then they both headed off to do their duties. Erica sighed. It seemed that duty was all she had if it weren't for these work-outs. She carried her box as if it weighed nothing. Her mood was much brighter and the rest of the day would fly by while she dreamed of working out again.

The Guard Captain shook his head. He knew that the hammers were somehow enchanted, but he didn't know exactly how. He had no choice but to trust the dwarves who made them. If he told the queen about it, she would only have more questions that he couldn't answer. It was better that she didn't know. He made his way back to the barracks and let his mind wonder about the amazing ability of a first time hammer fighter. It was not the first time that she had surprised him, but it was the first time that it had happened without the aid of the ancients. That made him nervous, like a tickle deep in the back of his brain somewhere. He wasn't sure what, if anything, he could do about it, but he knew that it would bother him until he could figure it all out. He just hoped that it wasn't dangerous or anything while his feeble mind worked on the problem. He chuckled to himself at that. He had always been strong, his mind was not the reason he had climbed to the position he now held. Why did he think it would serve him well now to be smart? Oh well, there was a barracks to inspect and maybe some skull thumping would take his mind off of these troubling thoughts. He grinned at the prospect and pretty much forgot about that minor little itch.

CHAPTER 6

B ack in court, Josh was listening to two merchants squabble over who was allowed to work what street corner with their mobile peddler's carts. Erica stepped in casually and then slinked her way around behind the tapestry wall to emerge regally next to her throne. The two stopped bickering immediately and bowed to the queen. Their collective "Your majesty's" seemed a bit grating.

"What I am hearing is that you have a dispute over a piece of land barely larger than both of you cover if you lay down, is that right?" She asked and both men lowered their heads.

"Yes, your majesty." They answered in unison. It sounded odd for them to be in such synchronization and somehow not get along very well.

Erica looked at one and then the other. "You have three options that I can see." She held up three fingers. "One, you can ask for me to rule which of you gets the spot and the other one will be unhappy no matter how this all turns out." She said and they both nodded their understanding of her first point. "Secondly, you could arrange to share the area by determining whose cart is there during what hours of the day. The market is open all day along and some carts are open into the night." She said. Then her eyes turned grim. "Or you could go with number three. In number three I ban both of you from doing business in the city and then you can peddle your wares elsewhere." She looked at them both with hard eyes. "So gentlemen what have you decided?" She asked, and all eyes turned to the two merchants who had been so focused on each other that they were unprepared for this verbal assault. They looked at each other, both of them felt trapped, in fact they were trapped. They seemed to reach an agreement although neither of them spoke.

"Your majesty" one of them finally said meekly. "We can share the space." He said and Erica nodded to him.

"Of course you can. As long as you do not sell the same thing, you can both do a thriving business in that prime location." She said in a triumphant tone. "Then she looked over to the caller. "What other sort of business do we have here?" She asked directly.

The man looked at the other petitioners and they looked like deer caught in the headlights. They could not find a way out of this court. The queen was suddenly a hard-liner. They were accustomed to her being so lenient and giving. This was something none of them had anticipated and they wanted nothing of it. However, they were all still there and could not make a retreat without calling attention to themselves. The caller recognized this and found a way to let all of them off the hook at the same time.

"There is no extra business today your majesty." He announced and there was a collective sigh of relief.

Erica stood up and smiled. "Well then, my work here is done." She said and she traipsed out of the court while everyone watched her. It was one of the most unusual things any of them had seen in this court. Josh simply looked on in shock. He looked at the other petitioners who were filing out of the court, happy to be clear of the place. He shook his head and stood up.

The caller looked at Josh as if he were going to say something, then he too turned away and left the chamber. Josh stood there a few minutes more. The echoes of the footsteps faded away and he suddenly felt lost here. He made his way back towards their quarters. Once he got there, he found Erica lounging away and eating some sort of confections that had been hastily brought upon her request. There was a fancy box right next to her.

"What is that box?" Josh asked and Erica's eyes lit up.

"That is my new personal weapon set." She said gleefully. "They're really special. Let me show you them." She said almost in a rush. Her giddiness was setting off red flags in Josh's mind. Erica picked up the box and set it on the table. She used a small key to unlock the box and then she opened it and pulled out two hammers.

"Those look really cool." Josh said, understanding that something was wrong here, but now knowing what it was. "Where did you get them?" He asked.

Erica only glanced at him; she seemed to be infatuated with the weaponry in her hands. "The Guard Captain gave them to me. They are so much nicer than the practice hammer he had me use. These are much faster and more elegant." She said.

Josh rubbed his chin in thought. "I see." He said to stop the silence between them from stretching out any longer. Erica kept her eyes firmly glued to the hammers. She didn't even notice her brother any more. "Who made them, do you know?" He asked.

Absently, Erica replied. "They were made for me." Her gaze was still fixed upon the glowing hammers. Perhaps that was part of their enchantment. Josh knew that they were enchanted. The glow could have been faked, but that mystic aura could not have been.

"They are magical hammers." Josh stated bluntly. "Do you want me to check what kind of magic it is? He asked. Erica became immediately defensive and protective.

"No, you cannot take them from me." She protested. She hugged the hammers close to her and turned away part way.

Josh sighed. "I don't want to take them from you, I just wanted to see how balanced they were." He said and her eyes sparkled.

"Oh, they're perfect. They are an exact match and they fit my hands well. They are an extension of me. They complete me." She said, not truly realizing what she had said.

Now Josh was worried. "They complete you?" He asked. "How do they do that?" He added, trying to get her to see what she was doing.

Erica looked at him with a brief flash of anger. "Stay away from me." She said as she pulled back from him. "Leave me be." She reiterated.

Josh held up his hands defensively. "Don't worry; I'm not here to make you unhappy. It's me, you know, your brother. I just wanted to know what has changed recently. Do you realize that you are acting differently?" He asked trying to take her focus off of the hammers she was clutching so tightly. He strongly suspected that it was these hammers that had a hold on his sister. Somehow, they were either evil, or simply misunderstood. He needed to find out which in order to save his sister from herself.

"I am the queen." She said tartly. "I can act any way that I please." She told him boldly.

Josh nodded. "Yes, that is true. However, the question still stands. Do you know that you are acting differently than normal?" He pressed and she crawled even deeper into her shell.

"I am who I am, you cannot control me. I am the queen and what I say goes. So drop this and never mention it again." She ordered. "I have so decreed and it is now illegal to bring this up again." She paused as if trying to think of something to add weight to her statement. "If you don't want to spend time in the dungeons, then you had better listen." She warned.

Josh was appalled. She knew that he had been captured once before and tortured in a dungeon. He still had scars all over his body from that ordeal. He then knew that her mind was not her own. Something, probably the hammers, had affected Erica and she was now a danger to everything that they had worked for. Of all of the problems that he had contingency plans worked out for, this was the one he had never foreseen. Somehow, he had always imagined his sister being sympathetic to the cause and the people of their kingdom. Now he realized that it was not so. Whoever she had become under this new influence, she was no longer the sister that he had known and loved. She was now something else. She had become an enemy. This was not good news. She knew everything he had done and planned to do. She could personally bring down the entire kingdom through revolt. Everything had been so intricately balanced that it would not take that much damage to make her presence felt. As the leader of this land, it was her place to keep the kingdom going in the right direction. But something, something evil, has gotten a hold of her, and now everyone was in grave danger. Josh felt his mind whipping through possibilities. None of them sounded good from his perspective.

Josh finally decided to defuse the situation for now. "Never mind, I will go and see what is going on with the preparations. You just stay here and rest." He said.

Erica almost pouted. "I'm going for another work-out." She proclaimed. "I'll see you when I get back." She added in a tone that suggested that he should not push his luck.

"Fine, you go and do that. I can send for you if there is trouble that you need to be concerned with." He said and she waved a hand dismissively. Again, this was starkly out of character. Josh made his way out of their quarters and down the long staircase to the lower level. He needed help to determine what had happened and how to repair it. First of all, he needed to know where the hammers came from. To that end, he headed directly for the barracks. The Guard Captain had given her those accursed hammers; it was possible that he knew where they came from.

The General had been summoning his minions for hours. Even his twisted body could only take so much drain. He finished the latest casting and then he slumped down. His hands were raw from the conjuring. The sacrifice's blood had long been dried up and the candles were flickering out their last meager rays of light. The whole chamber would need resetting before he could continue anyway. He was feeling the weariness that was beyond death. Since he was not a member of the mortal plane, he was not subject to dehydration and disease as those fleshy enemy mages were. He was quite powerful and his undead body could maintain for much longer periods between rests. However, he had reached the end of that particular rope. The masses of summoned creatures had only added to his ever expanding army and that meant that his power base was improving. It was a good sign and one that he did everything he could to encourage. The original plan had been to recruit a certain number of demons and lesser beasts to stage the first wave of this fight. He had since abandoned those numbers for a considerable upgrade of personnel. His army, incomplete as it still was already numbered in the thousands. Soon they would be tens of thousands. Then he would add his constructs to the mix and the mightiest army ever assembled would march out into the human encampments and destroy everything in their path. With the weapons and siege vehicles, he already had everything he would need before the final assault began. The equipment was important, but not nearly so important as his troops would be. He had already decided to have the Dark Lord killed whenever he showed his face. It was just easier that way when describing things to the master. If his rival had been less cocky and more supportive, then maybe he would have let him ride his coat tails with the master. As it was, he could not afford to let this upstart upstage him should he get terribly lucky during the battles ahead. It just made sense to eliminate that possibility before it could materialize. The General snarled as he let himself lie down. The next wave would be coming soon and he needed to be ready for it. This will be the most amazing army that has ever marched. The glory he would receive would be beyond measure.

Josh made his way to the barracks. It was not a meal time so the troops should be inside doing whatever it was they did when they were not out killing or saving someone. He figured that it was a no-brainer to find all of them in one place. The Captain was sure to be there to oversee his charges. He needed only a few moments to at least begin to get to the bottom of this hammer problem.

"Ten Hut!" was shouted as soon as Josh entered the building. All of the troops stood at attention. Josh failed to realize that his own personal status would make him outrank everyone here. He tried not to blush, but he was definitely embarrassed.

"Carry on." He said and the tense shoulders all the way down the long building relaxed. He walked through the shifting bodies as each guard went through his personal gear. They were performing maintenance on all of the equipment that they had been issued. Based on the worn look of all of the cleaning equipment, it must happen all the time. Josh mused to himself. He stepped up to a man, he didn't know his name.

"Excuse me, where might I find the Guard Captain?" He asked.

"Sir, uh your majesty, the Captain is in his quarters at the end of the hall sir." The man responded in an almost shout. Josh blinked at the ferocity of it but thanked him and moved on. He was thankful to have a destination now so that he would not have to talk to any more of these men. They seemed too motivated to him. Dad had talked about ROTC when he got older and how he was glad that he hadn't stayed in that world. He was more powerful here. The hall was so long that he almost forgot why he was there. He reached the door at the end of it and knocked three times.

"Who is it?" A voice called out from inside the room. "It'd better be damned important!" He added and Josh felt a twinge of worry. Then the door swung open violently. The Guard Captain stood there flabbergasted. He had obviously just thrown on some pants and the rest of him looked equally disheveled. "Oh, your majesty, a thousand pardons." He said, trying to muster whatever was left of his dignity and bowed.

This Josh could react to. "I need a few moments of your time." He said and the Captain almost responded. "We can talk in your room if it is secure enough." He added.

The Captain stepped back into his room and waved Josh in. As ruffled and unready as the Captain looked, his room was exactly the opposite. It was neat and tidy beyond normal measure. In fact it was spotless. The corners on the bed were exactly folded and the boots underneath it were placed in exactly the right spot and were polished to a brilliant shine. Josh pulled himself away from his impromptu inspection and brought himself back to task.

"I am worried about Erica." He said flatly.

The Captain quickly came to full alertness. "The queen? Is she in danger? Where?" He rifled off his questions and Josh held up his hands.

"As far as I can tell, she is not in physical danger, but there is a problem and I think you may have had something to do with it." He said and the Captain felt automatic rejection at the notion, but he forced himself to listen further.

"If this is about the training, then I must tell you that she asked me to do it." He said, trying to make excuses for something he did not know of.

"It's not that. She needs to be trained and you were available. No, it's the hammers." Josh said and the Captain's chin dropped.

"Oh, those" He said almost sardonically. "I was afraid that something like this would happen." He said and his tone suggested deep sadness.

Josh looked surprised. "You did? Why did you give them to her if you suspected a problem?" He asked flatly. His anger was starting to surface and nobody in the kingdom ever wanted to see Josh angry.

"I, I didn't realize it until after I gave them to her." He said. He stopped and Josh had to prompt him to continue. "It was right after she got them that I knew something was amiss. She picked them up normally and then she smiled and used the hammers like a master. She had not even been taught how to dual wield weapons and she was dancing around the practice dummy as if she had been doing it all of her life." He explained. "I should have brought it up then, I know, but I was distracted by duties. I figured that if she already knew how to use them, then my job of training just became easier." He said honestly. "I didn't think that anything bad could happen from her being more skillful." He added to try and alleviate the guilt he was feeling.

"Where did you get those hammers?" Josh asked, ignoring the Captain's plea for acceptance from him.

"I ordered them from a merchant in town. They are dwarf made, the best makers of hammers anywhere. It took weeks to get them here and another couple of days readying her majesty to use them." He said.

Josh thought about the situation. "I need you to take me to this merchant. We have to do something before the general public finds out about her change of heart." Josh said dangerously.

"Of course your majesty, I'll do anything you ask." He replied. He seemed happier that the focus had shifted from him. He still felt guilty, but now he could actually take action to remedy the problem and thus retain his honor. "Just let me get ready and we'll go there now." He added, trying to be as helpful as possible.

Josh took the cue and retreated from the Guard Captain's room. The men in the barracks had disappeared. He didn't even know where they had gone. There was no sign that they had even been here. Everything was clean and straight. The barracks were ready for inspection. Josh had to wonder about how this had been accomplished. It was only a few minutes ago that he had entered the Captain's room after all. He headed to the door. The barracks was long so it took a couple of minutes to cross it. When he got to the door he opened it and froze. Fear danced on his spine as he looked out at the evening sky. So it had not been just a few minutes. Something was terribly wrong, again. There was a guard posted at the entrance to the barracks and Josh made his way over and smiled.

"What time is it now?" He asked and the guard looked at him a bit gruffly.

"It's two hours past when my relief should have been here." He answered, and then he realized who he was talking to and he stammered. "Sorry your majesty, it is about forty minutes past evening meal." He put in quickly before Josh could lose his temper.

Josh put his head on the numbers and calculated out just how long he had been gone. It was over six hours that he had been in that small room with the Captain. It didn't make sense at all. In fact, the man should be coming any moment now. He looked back into the barracks and the empty hall was really creepy. Then he realized that if the Captain were still under the effects of whatever had stalled time, then he would not be coming out for quite some time. Josh turned back to the guard.

"I'm sorry that you have been left on duty for too long, but I must ask you not to let anyone into the barracks. I will send a relief man to you as soon as I can, but in the meantime, you must continue to safeguard this place. Something is wrong. I need to sound an alarm and get to the bottom of this." Josh stopped to make sure that the sleepy guard was keeping up. Something in Josh's tone had awakened the man completely.

"You can count on me milord." He replied when Josh didn't walk away.

"Good." He said simply and then headed back towards the palace. Josh was thinking to himself just how much this stunk of conspiracy. First the queen receives hammers that make her not want to be queen, or worse, turn her into a bad one. Then the man who gave her the hammers falls under a mysterious time spell. This was high level magic; there could be no doubt about that. Someone was going to take the time to make the connections he was only beginning to make. The problem was who would be left to make those connections if the invasion came now. The timing was too costly to be coincidence. This had to be some sort of plot. He stepped up his pace and wondered just how bad the damage already was.

The Dark Lord had planned well. He knew that the new General would try and overshadow his own preparations and he was not prepared to just lie down and let the new-comer steal his fame when the master comes. No, he took steps to escalate his position and now that the army was here, he was ready to launch his attack. He had managed to convince a particularly weak-minded fool to give the queen his special hammers. Once she had them, it was no problem at all to convince her to keep them. The magic was working flawlessly. They would corrupt the young girl from the inside and she would lose her public support, or even her throne. The kingdom of the True Bloods would be defenseless when the army invaded. The only problem was that there were two True Bloods. He had plans concerning the upstart wizard, but he needed to be careful. It was said that this True Blood was more gifted than most of his predecessors. If that was true he might actually be a threat. If that is so, then the threat must be eliminated before the invasion truly begins. He had set up a time lock spell on the Guard Captain. The pawn had no idea how important a role he played in his own demise, but he might still be useful. If the conspiracy were discovered, then they would come to this weak-minded oaf for help and they would be ensnared in his elaborate trap. It was gloriously simple as evil plots went. The more time that the queen spent with the weapons, the more her will would be subjugated to his own. He would soon control one of the major kingdoms of this world. He just needed more time alone with the queen. He had already secreted himself away inside the palace. With one of his abilities, camouflage, he could hide almost anywhere. Right now, he was behind a portrait in the main gallery of the castle. He could see the queen even as she coveted the golden hammers. His plan was working so perfectly that he could scarcely believe it. He smiled evilly as he watched the young wizard find his way back to the palace. He had a rude awakening heading for him that young one. The anticipation was only heightening his abilities and he lusted for the vengeance he would bring down upon the General when he made this house fall by his own hand. Yes, he would savor that moment.

Josh continued up the steps to the entrance of the palace. The guards were there, and they looked to be staring straight ahead, but none of them challenged Josh as he approached. Something was wrong here. He continued on until he could see their eyes. All he could see was white. Their eyes were rolled up into the backs of their heads. They were not conscious. How they were still standing he could not fathom. His earlier fears now escalated as he raced into the palace at a full run. There were more guards; these were lying on the floor. There were also downed servants and workers. He knew that he was too late to initiate his copy of the palace. He had somehow been taken out of the equation. He wanted to get at the ones responsible for this. He had no clue yet who they were, or even what all they had done. He was moving from room to room looking for somebody, anybody that was able to tell him what was going on. He stopped short when he heard the laugh. He was just outside of the throne room. Josh steeled himself for the confrontation and stepped into the room. There were two figures there. Erica stood in front of the throne and some dark demonic looking thing sat upon it. Erica still had the hammers in her hands. It looked as if she had never let go of them. Her arms were shaking terribly from the effort to hold onto them. He wanted to help her, but whoever that was in the throne was by far the bigger threat.

Josh tried to put all of his authority into his voice. "Who are you and what do you think you are doing sitting on that throne?" He asked with determination and anger in his tone. It was not the authority he had been hoping for, but it was powerful. Although, based on the lack of reaction, it was not nearly powerful enough. "I say again? Who are you?" Josh said a bit louder this time. The temperature in the room began to rise with his emotions. The Dark Lord noticed the change and was instantly impressed.

"You amuse me little one." He said in a gnarly voice that would peel paint. "I shall answer your desperate question." He continued and Josh readied himself for anything. "I am called the Dark Lord." He said, the creepiness of him was accompanied by a terrible stench that wafted over towards Josh.

Josh balled his fists. "You need to get away from her throne and release my sister!" He said and his tone was loud, but also dangerous. The Dark Lord raised an eyebrow.

"It is true that you have thwarted my attempts in the past. However, you did not even know that I existed. Now that we are face to face, I realize that you cannot hinder my efforts any longer. Fear will keep you in line." He said with a chuckle.

Josh rose to the challenge. "I do not fear you." He said clearly in an even lower voice.

The Dark Lord laughed loudly. "Then you are a fool. I am the bringer of destruction. I will personally see to it that this kingdom falls into eternal darkness. Your people, and their souls, are lost now. It is inevitable." He said and Josh felt the rage welling up within him.

"I will stop you and the people will be saved." Josh muttered. His own confidence was beginning to waver. The thought of that brought him to a new realization. "You are manipulating me." He said and the Dark Lord looked surprised.

"You are stronger than your sister. She is still unaware of that fact." He said and in a self-amusing gesture, he waved his hand and Erica stepped to the side and started dancing.

"Stop it. Let her go!" Josh fumed. "I will fight you here and now." He promised and the Dark Lord laughed again.

"Is that what you think I want?" He stood up from the throne and looked around the palace. "This palace of yours disgusts me. I don't want it. I want to see it destroyed. Your sister is a part of that plan. You, however, are not." The Dark Lord swept both hands forward and a cloud of darkness formed before him. It buzzed and crackled with some sort of dark energy.

Josh felt the shift in powers. He had the image he wanted in his mind. He only hoped that it would work here and now. So many things were in question just now. He spit forth the image as a physical thing and a screen came into existence and surrounded the Dark Lord. It was basically a screened porch around the evil being. However, Josh had not stopped there. The screen was nearly indestructible and was also electrified. The dark cloud swept forth and Josh ducked down to let most of it pass him by. The cloud contained lightning and he went flying when it struck out at him and then it followed his sliding body on the floor. The Dark Lord reached far enough forward at the end of his spell that he touched the screen. Like a bug zapper, he was stuck to the screen and it was sending current through him. He could not let go.

Josh felt the wall as he slid to a stop. It was a violent impact, but he had suffered worse. His vision was being clouded by the darkness and he started focusing on the light at the fringes of his mind. He brought that light back to center and the dark cloud was replaced by the light. The lightning mercifully stopped as well. Josh propped himself up on one elbow to see what was happening with the Dark Lord. The evil being was smoking now as the electricity from Josh's mind continued to flow unabated by logical things like fuses or circuit breakers. The smell of rot and decay was now burning rot and decay. This room would have to be fumigated.

Movement out of the corner of Josh's eye made him turn just as the hammer swung. Erica swung with all her might to smash in her brother's head. His last second duck was all that had saved him from the unexpected blow. The miss took her off balance and that made the secondary swing miss by less than an inch. Josh was in a fight for his life and he couldn't hit back. He also could not concentrate on the Dark Lord. The dance they were stepping to was a lethal ballet of feints and swings. Josh knew that this was not his element. She could kill him with a well connected blow. He also knew that he couldn't strike her down. This was not her doing. This was not her fault. His morals had him tied up pretty well inside and concentration was failing him. He was physically fit as well from his studies, but he was not really combat trained. So it was still a defense that he was deploying. His mind tried to race ahead of each swing and make sure that he wasn't there. The whoosh of air as yet another close call buzzed by him seemed deafening.

"Erica, see what you are doing!" He shouted and she swung again. This time he dodged straight backward from an overhand chopping move and the hammer struck the stone floor hard enough to crack it. She was swinging for the bleachers now. Her arms were still shaking from sheer exhaustion, but she had the false determination of the possessed mind. Josh swept forward and pushed for all his might and Erica flew backwards from the impact. She caught herself and did a somersault to end up standing a few feet away and glaring at Josh. It was just the few seconds he needed. He quickly formed the image in his mind and in a flash; Erica was standing there in a straight jacket. Her golden hammers were next to her on the floor. She looked down at them and being unable to pick them up began to scream in terror and rage. She stooped down to try and touch them with her face and Josh grabbed her jacket by the straps and pulled her away from the evil influence. With a little distance from the hammers, she started to calm down a bit. Josh turned back to the Dark Lord.

"It is over, you are finished here." He told the creature and he let the electricity end. The Dark Lord looked like he had been in a deep fryer for too long. His rage was almost a physical thing.

"You cannot kill me, I am already dead!" He shouted triumphantly. "I shall still win the day." He said and he found that his limbs were not working so well. The cartilage and tendons had been fused. The muscle fibers had been cooked. He tried to move forward and fell over. The sound of him hitting the stone was something Josh would never like to hear again. Something broke inside the demon and his torment was something out of a nightmare. He gasped a few times and then he surprised Josh completely.

"I shall be back. This is not over." The fallen body of the demon vanished and all that was left were some charred remains and that awful smell. The hammers had disappeared with him as well. Josh shook his head and headed to his sister. He pulled her to him and looked into her eyes.

"Is it you?" He asked. She groaned, she seemed to be just waking up.

"Wha- what happened?" She asked and Josh dispelled the straight jacket.

"You've had a rough day." Josh replied. "Just take it easy now." He said trying to be gentle as he laid her down on the stone floor. With a casual thought, a pillow appeared in his hand and he placed it under her head. "We can talk about this later. I need to see just how much damage was done." He said. He got up to check on the rest of the palace, but he didn't get far.

"Josh, wait." Her plea sounded so desperate he froze in place. Josh knelt down next to his sister. "I remember everything." She said. A tear rolled down her cheek. "I tried to kill you." She sobbed.

Josh hugged her tightly. "Yes you did, but you weren't you. That monster had somehow controlled you through those hammers." He explained and she looked around frightened.

"The hammers! Are they still here?" She asked almost frantic.

Josh pressed her back down. "No, they disappeared with the demon. Just rest now. We can talk about everything later. There were people down all over the palace; I want to make sure that they get back up." He said and he left before she could call him back. In moments, aides and servants came in and tended to Erica until her brother could return. It had been a close call, but the palace was once again secure.

The Dark Lord appeared before the General. His broken and burnt body still smoldered in places and the General laughed. "I can see that you have tried to usurp power and failed." He said with no trace of the amusement he had just displayed. "Your failure may have cost us the True Blood kingdom. If that is so the master will have some special punishment set aside for you I am sure." He said and he stepped over to the broken Lord on the stone floor. He stomped down and broke another limb and the wail the Dark Lord let out echoed through the underground chamber. It was music to the General's ears.

"Take him away and make sure that he is properly tortured." He ordered and two cronies came and scooped up the broken and burnt body. As they turned to take him away the General added further instructions. "I want to hear his screams any time that I check in on him night or day. Is that understood?" He asked and his tone suggested that they had better be sure.

"Yes sir, General, it shall be done." They answered in unison. They hauled away the Dark Lord. His future was set and his fate was secured. It would not go well for him. He had failed. The only thing he had to cling to was his promise to that upstart human. Whatever it took, whatever he had to endure, he would fulfill his promise and kill that young man. All of this was his fault. He had thwarted the plan. He had caused this disgrace to come about. That wizard would pay with interest for all that the Dark Lord now faced. Even through the pain and nausea, he managed to smile. His revenge would be sweet.

Life in the palace had changed with that attack. Josh had managed to revive almost all of the staff. The only ones that he could not had been killed by those evil hammers. It was a hard thing to deal with. The queen had killed three of her own staff members in a rage that none of them could have foreseen. The very foundation of trust among the staff had been shaken. Josh did his best, but the pain and anguish would live on for quite a while. The full invasion had not even begun yet. It was only some advanced force that had come in and almost won a victory against them. In his heart, Josh knew that he had almost been defeated before he had even fought. Somehow, the people being brought back now did not make him feel all that much better. It was his failure that had caused them to be down in the first place. He should have seen this coming. He had been making plans for an army, not some infiltrator. He was angry with himself over that shortfall. Even with it being totally unfair, he was still the harshest taskmaster that he had ever had. He constantly pushed himself harder and farther. There was no excuse for weakness or stupidity. He had to be perfect. It was a deep source of stress for him and now that stress had become depression. Those around him could see it, but he paid scant notice to their attempts to cheer him up. He had, after all was said and done, saved them and the rest of the palace from takeover. The rumors were flying that he had even battled the queen herself. Even for a wizard, that could not have been an easy feat. Josh busied himself with the recovery effort and he addressed needs as he found them. Of course the ones that went unnoticed were his own.

Meanwhile, Erica had been moved to her quarters. She was recovering no better than Josh was. She was riddled with regret, she had tried to kill her own brother, and she had killed some staff members. The fresh thought brought a fresh tear and the servants just let her cry. They had tried to console her, but consolation was not going to come easy. The queen had done terrible things and even though she was not in control, she was aware of what had transpired. It was simply devastating to the normally outgoing and personable young woman who was supposed to be protecting these people. Then a horrifying thought occurred to her, what happened to the Guard Captain? Could he have been in on the incursion from the start? He had given her the hammers that had caused all of this mess. She was sure that he knew something was wrong. Maybe he was too afraid of Josh to tell him what he had done. She decided that she needed to know.

"Where is the Captain of the Guard? I must see him." She said and the servants tried to calm her down again. They brought her warm towels and soup. She was pampered and soothed. They would keep these idle thoughts away for now. It had been part of their instructions. In truth the instructions were to protect the staff, not Erica. The spell around the Guard Captain might still be in effect. Josh didn't want anyone else falling into that trap. He would go down and try to figure out how to spring the trapped man later. For now, he was blissfully unaware that he had been imprisoned. So Erica did not have access to the good Captain. Without that access, her mind began to weave tales of worry through her dreams. She slept more than she was awake thanks to the medicinal leaves that had been applied to her skin. She was attended around the clock. It was not for two days that Josh finally made it back around to his sister. When he did enter the room, he looked tired, very tired. It happened to be one of the moments that Erica was awake. She reached up for him.

"Josh, is it really you?" She asked, hoping that she was awake this time. Her grief mingled with her dreams had made her grip on reality just a bit shaky. Josh hated that it had been necessary, but he had put the fires out and the palace was returning slowly to normal.

Josh smiled at his sister, it was a weary smile. "I thought that was my line." He quipped and she smiled warmly at him.

"It is you. I couldn't have dreamed that." She said, glad to finally be back among the real and normal. That is, if you considered either of them normal.

Josh stroked her hair. Her pony tail had been undone for her extended stay in bed and then he backed away. "I know that you have had a tough time of this. In truth, it's going to get tougher before it gets better. But I think I can help at least a little bit with that. I have smoothed over the staff and I have offered condolences to the families of the fallen. Business is taking a four day hiatus and you should be up and around by morning. The evil presence is no longer within the palace. I've walked all of it to make sure. You can rest more if that's what you need." He offered.

Erica sat upright quickly. "No, I don't want to rest anymore. The dreams will come and they are bad." She said almost child-like.

Josh looked at the keepers he had placed on his sister. They stood there waiting patiently. "You have done well; I am in your debt." He told them and they bowed.

The lead servant, a midwife from the village, spoke up. "We did naught but our duty sire, we are pleased to have been of service." She said and the others nodded again.

Josh looked directly at the middle-aged lady in the apron and smiled. "I accept that. I wonder if I have your approval to allow my sister to get out of bed." He asked and there was a gasp from one of the lesser lady servants.

"Your majesty may do as he wishes," was the reply. Then, as if she could tell what he was going to say next. "She has rested enough; a little exercise would do her mind and body good." She added.

Josh bowed to her. "I thank you for your candor. If you would please withdraw with your agents, I shall get to the business of getting her exercised." He said and they all withdrew from the chamber.

Erica sighed. "What a relief. You know, they haven't left me for a second?" She asked exasperated. "I couldn't even think out loud for fear that one of them would race right on over and change my leaves to put me back under." She said and Josh knelt down next to her and unfastened the straps.

"I'm sorry for these." He said. "We had to make sure that you were yourself before we could release you physically." He said apologetically. "There was a lot to do and I couldn't afford to wonder where you were or what you were up to." He continued.

Erica hugged him. "Under the circumstances, I think you did an excellent job." She muttered into his ear before they separated again. "Still, I think I may owe you a beating sooner or later for some of this treatment." She added. "Did they really need to keep me sedated?" She asked.

Josh looked at the floor a second and then back at his sister. "Even though that was not my idea, I authorized it. I figured if you could not move, then all you would do is stew about what had happened. If you did that, then you would remember everything and not be able to do anything about it. I figured it was much easier on you this way." He explained.

Erica wanted to protest, but she thought about what he had said. She tried to imagine just lying there thinking about killing those poor people. The thought even now made her cringe. She shook it off and looked at her brother anew. He really had grown up. He understood things better than she had given him credit for. "Perhaps you're right." She admitted finally. "It doesn't get you off the hook, but I understand why you did it." She continued.

Josh turned all serious on her and the change was subtle, but unmistakable. "If the opening attack has been sent, and I believe it has now, then the full-on attack on our kingdom cannot be far behind. We need to move now to protect our people. This was just too close of a call." He said, the weight of an entire kingdom rested on his shoulders. He had been bearing that for her ever since she had picked up those blasted hammers. Maybe that beating could wait a little bit longer.

"Yes, you're right. We need to move on this now. I know that you have already made plans. What can I do to help?" She asked. Her look of concern seemed to take some of the weight off of Josh and his back straightened just a little.

Josh nodded. "I have already done most of the preparations for the spell. What I need now is for you to sell it to the people. Magic can only go so far and after that, we will need the help of the very people we are trying to save. They need to understand that what we are doing is to protect them." He paused. His thoughts were racing through his plans. Erica understood this and waited patiently. She had seen this before. "We have another problem as well." He said warily. "We will need volunteers for combat troops." He said and Erica looked at him skeptically. "I know, I know." He told her defensively. "But it is still true." He said feeling a bit lost.

"Where do we get volunteers from?" She asked practically. This was odd for it was usually Josh to be the practical one. She was uncomfortable in the role. Josh simply shrugged.

"I don't know. I have been thinking on it on and off and I find no answers. We could post a billboard in the square, but it would be like announcing that we are about to go to war, please grab a sword and come with us." He said and the bitterness in the statement was a good indicator of how he felt about war, and that plan of action.

Erica nodded, but thought a little more before responding. "Well, either way, we need to get the word to the people. An announcement of some kind is in order. I don't know how we can recruit for a military force, but I do know that the people would want to know that they are in danger. More importantly, they would want to know that we are doing something about it." She said. It was Josh's turn to nod. "Yes I think we need to make a proclamation." She said at last. "I mean, it's not like we can go on TV and tell everybody at once. We need to send messengers and get the town criers in action. We can do this relatively quickly. The real problem now is what do we say?" She said and Josh looked more thoughtful than he had a moment ago. It was a nice change from the defeatism he was beginning to feel.

"I'll get to work on that. You get the people ready for you proclamation." He said. The two headed for their various tasks. The trouble the elder races had been worrying about was practically at their doorstep now. They had to act fast.

CHAPTER 7

The Kingdom of the True Bloods was not the only one getting ready for the *secret invasion*. The forest was full of all kinds of races. The trees were even lending a limb so to speak when it came to detection and preparation. The invading force would have trouble navigating any protected lands. The Stone lords were making woodland routes impassable for all but a special few. The elves had prepared their repelling force. This menace was expected to reach every people. The truth seekers were in an uproar. The doom they were foretelling was too much for them to handle. Evil was coming and it was not like any other threat that they had ever faced. The Sprites were busily ferrying things to and fro in an effort to support their allies. The dwarves had sequestered themselves away inside of the great mountain of stone. They would remain there like a family in a bomb shelter. If this was truly the end of their world, they would sit it out and await whatever came next.

The beast-men were making body armor and heavier weapons. It was their destiny to meet whatever they faced head on. Their warrior's code demanded nothing less of them. Their grim faces told the true story behind all of that courage, but nobody was going to point that out to them. Everyone's nerves were stretched pretty tight as it was. With all of this hustle and bustle going on, it was an odd thing that a lone human had made his way into the encampment of the great elves unchallenged by the guards. It was an unprecedented bit of gall to come here in the first place. He looked unimposing enough, but his aura was what gave him safe passage. He was pure. He held no ill will towards any of the elder races. He strolled purposefully through the encampment and he stopped before the hollow tree stump that was the temporary home of the grand high elf himself.

Finally, after all of that traveling, he was challenged. "Just where do you think you are going?" Asked the elf in a dangerous voice that should have made this human cower away in fear. It did not.

Mouse looked at the guard directly. "I am here to see the Grand High Elf." He said plainly.

"The scouting reports told us that you were coming, and that nothing seemed to be deterring you, even our own defense structures." The guard continued, still not believing the audacity of this human when faced with such higher numbers that it was laughable. "What has given you such determination?" He asked.

Mouse held his chin high; this elf was not even making him nervous. His mission was way too important for that to happen. "I am trying to do my part to save the world." He said flatly. "Can I see the Grand High Elf now?" He asked directly. The wolf had told him that this would be a difficult stop on his tour, but that it was sublimely necessary. He held onto the knowledge that he was doing the right thing. Nothing could stand in his way for long. The elf guard seemed to be thinking for a long moment when the Grand High Elf stepped out of the stump.

Mouse immediately bowed to the wise and powerful leader. "Please, your grace, if I may have a few moments of your precious time..." Mouse said formally and the elf guards bowed to their leader, although not as quickly as Mouse had.

"You are an interesting young fellow." The Grand High Elf said and his tone held the humor he had intended. "So you are trying to save the world." He said with grandiose praise. "That is an admirable goal. Just how do you intend to do that young man?" He asked, his curiosity finally bringing him around to his point of interest.

"Actually king sir, I am trying to do my part in saving the world. I am not strong, or smart enough to do the deed by myself." Mouse replied, almost apologetically. "I have been sent by a wolf to meet with several members of society and you are next on my list." He said directly. Mouse knew not to waste the High Elf's time.

"I believe that you have my attention now young man. Is your message to be private or should we continue this conversation right here, just outside my quarters?" The old Elf said with almost a chuckle.

"Inside would be better milord." Mouse said. "One never knows how secure a particular area is." He cautioned. The High elf nodded and then waved a hand to escort Mouse into his inner sanctum. The stump had appeared to be rather small from the outside, but much of this space was actually below ground. Mouse found himself in a small hovel of creature comforts. The high elf sat across from him in the cramped space and the two of them sat before a small lit fire.

"Now then, perhaps you could tell me what is so important that you needed to come all this way to tell me." The Grand High Elf prompted as he lit his pipe with but a finger. Mouse realized that elves had magic, but he had never seen it used so mundanely. It was just so matter-of-fact that it startled the young man.

"Yes sir, right away." Mouse stammered.

"Relax. Just tell me what you need to. We can take it from there." The Elf prompted again.

"Yes sir." Mouse said. His head bowed down a bit in apology. "Well, I have been rallying important people among the human populace trying to convince them to make ready their defenses and to find volunteers to aid the True Bloods in assembling an army when the invasion comes." He said all in a rush.

The High Elf looked stern. "I hope you weren't looking for volunteers here." He said and Mouse shook his head.

"No sir. That is not my message for you. No. You are to stop helping the humans and to move your people north." Mouse said as if he understood all of the complex things involved with what he had just said.

"What?" The High elf said, sure he had heard the young man wrongly.

Mouse took in a deep breath. "Sir, you are to stop helping the human kingdom here and to move all of your people that you can north." He repeated.

"How far north?" The elf asked, being ever more patient than he felt he needed to here.

"The wolf did not say." Mouse said regretfully. "All he did say was that if you didn't go north, you will be slaughtered by the invading army when it comes." He said so absolutely that he could have been reading it out of a history book. "Please move your people to save their lives." Mouse implored. His belief in his message was so strong that his concern for the elder races was genuine.

"I have commitments, what am I supposed to tell the Prince when he doesn't see us at the time of battle?" He asked, his personal rage was beginning to bubble up. This young upstart was telling him, the leader of his people, what to do.

"I, I don't have all of the answers sir. I am only a messenger. I have been told that you will all die if you do not go north immediately. That is all that I am supposed to tell you." Mouse said and his own face was starting to look grim. "Please sir, do not tempt fate by staying put. Please move your people so that they may live to continue to enrich this world." He said. For a young human, this Mouse was well spoken.

"I will need some time to think on this. What consequences do we have to fear from you if we do not heed your warning?" The Elf asked. He braced himself for the response, but when it came he was still surprised.

"What, nothing from me. I am not a threat to you in any way. As I said, I am only a messenger and I will take my leave of you as soon as this conversation is over. I have other stops to make, other lives to save. My mission cannot be delayed." He said and he almost smiled. But the grim reality of it was he was worried that he wouldn't get to everybody before it was too late. The thought nagged at the young man constantly.

"Then I bid you safe journey." The High elf said. He bowed to Mouse and it was time for the young man to leave.

Mouse made his way out of the cozy spot and back past the guards. He turned back to see the the High Elf watching him. "Don't take too long to decide, we don't know how much time is left." He said and he turned and headed east. He still had more people to go see and as he just told the elf, he didn't know how much time the world had left. He needed to hurry.

The High Elf moved back inside his small home and sat down. He pulled a bowl from under the small table and filled it from a pitcher he kept nearby. Next he dropped several flower petals of differing colors into the bowl and began to chant. The flowers began to dissolve into the water and the colors began to bleed together. They made a swirling pattern of brilliant colors and once the chant was completed, they were pulled and twisted into forms. The High Elf was looking at the True Bloods. More specifically, he was looking at Josh. The young wizard was busily preparing some massive spell. From this angle, he could not tell what it was about, so he decided to speak up.

"Excuse me young one." The ancient Elf said with that old and crackly voice. Josh turned to the sound and recognition lit up his face.

"Sir, what brings your image around to my part of the world?" Josh asked with exactly the right amount of decorum for this impromptu meeting.

"I have just had a visitor. He was a young man and he told me that I need to move my people north in order to save them from the upcoming event." He said and Josh looked startled.

"You said a man, a human?" Josh asked. The elf nodded. "Curious, do you know who it was?" Josh asked.

"Yes, he said his name was Mouse." The High Elf said and Josh's eyes gave away his surprise.

"Mouse came all the way out to see you?" Josh shook his head. "He is an honest and trustworthy soul, but I don't know why he would tell you these things." Josh added when he noticed the Elf's concern.

"The message was clear, and he said it came from a wolf." The Elf told Josh and this new information startled him yet again.

"The wolf? Wow, you get messages from strange but very trustworthy people." Josh iterated at the firm brow raise of the Grand High Elf. "My guess is that Mouse was sent to you by the wolf. The wolf is wise. Very wise. I actually think it is another creature disguised as a wolf, but that's not important right now. The important thing is it warned you to move. I would start packing now. Don't wait for further confirmation. Move now and report to me when it is done and I will forward your status on to whomever you need to tell." Josh said, having picked up on some of the Elf's wavelength. It was the High Elf's turn to be surprised.

"But how?" He said in that startled voice.

Josh smiled at him. "Come on, it wasn't that hard to figure out. You are not in the deep forest right now. You are in a temporary location. For that to be true, then you must be helping someone outside of your normal influences. Therefore, whoever that is needs you for something and when you move unexpectedly, they will be surprised to say the least. So, I can help by contacting them and letting them know why you are moving and hopefully help them with whatever it was you were going to do." Josh said, following his own mental thread all the way through.

The Grand High Elf did not startle easily and he found that the experience was not entirely enjoyable, but his recovery was quick as well. "Young man, I get tired of underestimating you." He said gruffly, but there was no sting in it. "I will take care of contacting the Prince of..." He trailed off as if struck in mid-sentence. Sounds of screaming and orders being barked came from the distance and were audible through the link. The High Elf looked somber. "It may already be too late." He said and he waved his hand and broke the link

Josh looked at the wall where the disk had been. His neck hairs were standing on end. "The attack had come." He needed to move now. There was no time to waste. He turned to his aides who were busily looking disinterested in the conversation he had been just having. His startled cry demanded their attention.

"We need to mobilize the people now!" He shouted at them. "The enemy is upon us and we have no time to lose. Get the people to the shelters that I have already set up. The false city is even now being completed. Move everybody now." Josh ran away from the stammering aides as they scrambled to comply with his orders. He had to finish his construct before the enemy came. He hoped that the elves still had a chance but the gnawing in his stomach reminded him that he didn't think so. He hit the window of the palace and he looked out. Sure enough, the people were already scrambling. Off in the distance, the rumble of large siege weapons and the pounding of marching feet brought all of his fears to the fore. The enemy had mobilized and they were here now. He began to concentrate and his defenses, so painstaking planned, came into existence. At least he had that much going for him. He started working on his straw people. He began to visualize them in great numbers littering the fields. They would be totally unobtrusive to an advancing army. Then, when the moment of surprise would be best handled, they would rise up and attack. He continued to see them in his mind's eye. The field was becoming cluttered with the constructs. They had rudimentary weapons like farm implements. But they were going to be many. They would almost make an army themselves. Fortunately, he could lose them all and still save lives among his people. They were expendable. He could already feel the pull on his body as his magic continued to draw from his pool. He would be useless in the fight itself if he wasn't careful. He could hear footsteps behind him. He finished his current batch and sighed. Then he turned around to see who had come.

Erica looked at him expectantly. "Well, what do we do now?" She asked. Josh looked at her blankly. He was still a bit out of it from the power drain. Erica looked exasperated. "We don't have time to move all of the people, what should we do about it?" She asked again. Josh's eyes snapped into focus.

"We must take the fight to them then." Josh replied. His outer defenses were up, but they were weak compared to what he wanted to put up. A flash of regret made him doubt for a second until his rational mind shoved it away for another time. "Split the guard detail in half. Put half of them on perimeter defense here at the palace. Then, send the rest out to the front. Do not have them deploy directly against the enemy. Have them defend our citizens as they flee. There is no offensive at this time, we are in retreat. We must save as many lives as we can before we can afford to regroup and bring the true fight to the enemy." He said with solid confidence.

"You got it, I'm on my way." The queen said and she bolted away. Josh looked at the dark horde coming their way and he shivered.

These weren't troops, they were unholy creations. Demons and devils seemed to be driving some sort of clay constructs before them. Fear kept most of the people from fighting back. Hopefully, it would save their lives. Somehow, Josh felt that the enemy would slaughter even the helpless as they continued on into the city. Erica's words, "What do we do now?" Echoed in his mind. He shared her question truthfully. He was more in shock than anything else. This was not good.

He kept trying to see a way out, but nothing came to him. The false city would hold the enemy for a short time. That is, it would if the demons could not see through the magic itself. If that happened, all bets were off on any defense they might be able to muster here. He saw people being ushered out of harm's way and for the little relief that provided, the overall picture still had him tied up in knots. Josh stood at the window. "What do we do now?" He asked himself softly.

The General had finally gotten to the point where his confidence was equal to the task at hand. He ordered his troops out into the world. The plan had so many spires that it looked like a spiked ball. His army was so vast that he could afford to send a few thousand troops to this village and still have a sizable enough force to sack the city beyond. The human infestation would be wiped from this miserable ball of mud. His claws were aching for blood and he went with the main force to get this party started. The world was not ready for him, he knew that. He was ready to win it over for his master. The glory of the conquest and the raw violence called to his dark and twisted soul. His lust flamed the rest of his force and soon they were all in a frenzy of death and destruction. He watched as his front line made their way through one unsuspecting village after another. The dead and dying were spreading before him like a red carpet. The poor humans had been caught unawares. The feeble farming equipment they employed would not help them against the denizens of the dark planes. The armored savage troops dealt death without mercy or remorse. This was just the first of a long line of battles and there were very few casualties on the dark army's side. The buildings were ablaze and the fields were trampled. There would be nothing left when it was all done. The General smiled, it was not a pleasant look.

"Bring us around; I want another pass to make sure that none of the scum is left behind." He shouted and his troops obediently sent their wave back over what was left of the village they had just destroyed. They left no survivors. Satisfied, they began their trek north to the next village. The sun shone brightly upon them and even though it was warm, they did not like it. Once this war was over, he would see to it that it never shone again. The General spit and then headed his troops out into the fields north of the village. There was much more to do before the sun set this day and brought relief in the form of darkness.

The prince had sent out his people as scouts all around his father's kingdom. The fool on the throne would not believe that they were in any danger, so he did nothing. Still, the do nothing plans at least didn't get in the way of his own plans. He had worried over how long it would be before the enemy arrived. The first calls were ringing out in the city below him. Could this be the time? He looked out anxiously as the chain of callers relayed the message to his royal ears.

"Sire, the enemy has sacked Beaverton and Northswitch to the south. They are crossing the field and trampling or burning everything on the way. They will hit the outlying villages within the day. The scouts expect them to slow the army only a very small amount. They aren't taking any prisoners. They leave the dead in the streets and they make a special pass to make sure that they are all dead. This is a genocidal attack." The messenger said. His own face was grim as the Prince's.

The Prince looked down at his hands, they were not shaking. That said something. He felt the butterflies that had been plaguing his stomach vanish. It was now time to act. "Take a message back to the troops." He said boldly. "Pull in all the scouts and fortify the southern pass. I want all of our defenses ready to hold the pass as long as we can. Have the city guard begin evacuation of the city from the southern tip northward. Move everybody we can out of the way of the invaders." He stopped to wonder briefly where the elf was, but did not say anything aloud. "We appear to be on our own now. May god be with us as we try to hold out long enough for at least some of our people to survive." He said and the messenger repeated back his message. Then he left at a good pace and the Prince watched him go for only the briefest of moments. His mind was on the battlefield. He could not see it, but his imagination was up to the task of providing him with sufficient ugliness to make him cringe. He looked out the window once again. "They're taking no prisoners." He muttered to himself. He only hoped that it could be stopped before there was nobody left.

The dark army advanced from the villages with their appetite for destruction well engaged. They were still destroying everything in their path. While this was ultimately a crushing blow to the human settlements they did find, it did make their progress across the filthy green lands take painstakingly longer than they had hoped. The blood lust would fade and they would have to be whipped up again. The clay constructs did not face such difficulties though. They continued to trample and smash anything their masters called out. In fact, it had cost them more than one of these golems because they would continue until either the object was destroyed, or they were. It was a difficulty that was only partially foreseen. Even with these minor setbacks, they were still advancing on the humans. This land would support no more life and the winter would finish off anyone they missed. The plan was still intact and in the distance the first major city could be seen. There was a small mountain pass in the way, but it would not prove to be any more difficult than crossing to this plain had been. It was just another obstacle to be overcome. The master had to be watching this first push. This was the General's chance to shine. He licked his lips in anticipation of the death blows he would deliver to the puny human scum. He was suddenly thankful that there were so many humans to be found. It meant that his battle would last long enough to really enjoy.

Mouse had made his way through to yet another of his stops when the attack came. Unfortunately, he did not have time to complete the rest of his mission. The citizens he had helped would be pressed enough. The ones he couldn't reach had even less chance. It struck him in the heart. Had he failed? Now only time would tell. He needed to finish this stop at least. He continued through the streets, keeping to the shadows as he had done so many times before in his youth. Here, his background as a common street rat served him well. He knew how to blend in and become unnoticeable. He knew how to survive here. It was true that the sewers here would be unfamiliar, but how much did you really need to know about them to affect an escape? He was still making progress when the advancing wave of clay monstrosities rounded the corner, smashing and crushing anything they found. The demons with them were throwing fire from their hands. If it was magic, it was one of the worst kinds. The buildings were ablaze. Even the buildings made from stone were somehow burning. The plumes of smoke rose into the air in billows and the sounds of screaming and dying people could be heard. Mouse had his dagger out and his stance suggested that he should not be messed with. Not that such posturing would deter these attackers, but he had to try something. He stayed ahead of the wave but not by far. He could still see them and he felt this opportunity slipping away from him. The wolf had not told him what to do if the enemy actually arrived. There would be no time now for these people to recruit for the royal army. There were so many evil things here. The creatures seemed to pour out of every crack and crevice. They were swarming like locusts over the poor townspeople. There was little hope that this town would survive. There was no organized resistance. There were only small pockets of armed men here and there. They were easily dispatched by the overwhelming horde that befell them.

Mouse switched tactics. He no longer looked to go further into the town. It would only keep him in the eyes of the enemy for more time than he felt comfortable with. In fact, it already had accomplished that. No, he would make for a cautious retreat. He followed a wall until he hit the alley and he turned quickly and silently down it. He could still hear the sounds of the battle behind him as he found the sewer grate and with more effort than he remembered needing, he lifted the grate and slipped down into the sewer. This was not a major city; but it was more than a village, but not much more. There were sewers here and for that he was grateful, but it did not cover the entire town. In this particular area, the sewers were only servicing the industrial base in the center above. That meant that he did not have access to the whole town down here, but neither did the enemy have full access to him. The thought of steaming hot water, or some form of melted slag dropping down from above was more than a little frightening. However, it was much safer down here than up on the streets. So he followed the flow of the sewers. Nobody ever built a sewage system to keep the sewage in the habitation; it always flowed away to some water source. He was banking on that. Mouse didn't feel that it would be too far to get out of the town, but he was almost at a trot. The quicker he was out of here the better. The sounds of combat reached him every once in a while as he made his way past other sewer grates. He hoped that those sounds would mask whatever sound he made while traversing this underground duct work. He didn't even pause at these junctions. As far as he was concerned, the less time spent by an opening meant the less chance of being discovered. He was a bit surprised that more people had not found their way down here. It seemed too obvious to him. The sounds of commotion faded away as he finally cleared the town walls. He had traveled a remarkable distance and he found himself at an outlet into a local lake. He was safely away from the immediate threat. The big problem was what should he do now? He made his way west, trying to steer clear of the confrontation. He needed time to think. The end of the world had started. He had been given an important task, and he had come up short. The thought was so heavy that he felt like lying down and crying. Of course that was exactly the wrong thing to do. His logical mind told him that he was being foolish. He had no control over when the enemy would attack. He had pushed himself harder and faster at each stop and he had gone farther than he thought possible before the hammer fell. He had done his duty. The problem was who was going to be around to tell him that. From what he did see, this dark army was not interested in taking prisoners. They were killing everyone. They were destroying everything. He needed to find something tangible to do. His hands were shaking now. His rage was beginning to build inside. It was like a small fire now, smoldering ever so slightly. However, it would not take much fanning for the flames to erupt and destroy him. The logical side of him understood that, but his emotional self would not listen. He stopped abruptly. "They must pay." He muttered to himself. He looked around. He was safe now. He did not know how long that would last, but for now he was certain of it. He sheathed his dagger and pulled out a small bag that a friend had given him. There was orange powder inside of the small leather bag. He would need a campfire to make this work. Mouse started gathering dry bits of leaves and wood to get one started. He would not sit by the sidelines anymore. His friend could, and would help him become more pivotal in the events that were playing out around him. Mouse would finally be important. As grim as the moment was, the young man smiled, despite himself.

Erica had raced around the palace and her staff was almost completely evacuated by the time she met up with her brother again. The town criers had done their job and the people of the True Blood's kingdom were all inside their homes or businesses. No one was outside on the streets. The market was empty. It looked like a ghost town. Josh saw Erica and she nodded to him. He lowered his head and closed his eyes. The image he had so painstakingly worked on now came up to the fore as he mentally beckoned. Then he gave his conjuration that spark of life. In moments, all of the people had been transported to the new locations. For them it was as if a flash of light blinded them for a fraction of an instant. Then it was business as usual. The town criers headed out to bring the people back out of their places of hiding. Life continued unabated in this hidden realm. Josh looked on with a smug satisfaction at the work he had done. Then he sobered and looked back at his sister. She had that same no-nonsense look and they both nodded at once. Josh pulled them back from the construct and put them back in the palace. Now they could see the real world. It was not nearly as tranquil as the one they had just left, but it was something they had known to expect. The invading army was nearing the city. They had not yet arrived and

Josh began to populate the real world city with artificial citizens to be slaughtered by the ruthless enemy. It was a risk, to be sure, but it was the best plan that he had come up with. Erica watched with interest as her brother gazed out of the window and the townspeople began appearing below. They were moving along in their daily lives just as Josh had seen from this window on countless days before. The fight would start soon and they would cower appropriately before they were splattered across the walls and stone floors by the hopefully clueless enemy horde.

However, his first line of defense troops was now engaging. The scarecrows stood up and attacked from the rear of the main horde. The element of surprise was actually more powerful than even Josh had imagined. The straw men slashed at demonic troops. Some of them were going down and it was suddenly obvious what the weakness of the enemy army was. When one of the demon troops went down, four or five of the clay constructs simply stopped moving. They were mindless automatons and without some form of direction, they were useless. Josh smiled and Erica drew her sword. She had adopted a larger sword since having used the hammer. She readied for Josh's word to enter the fray herself. Josh kept throwing scarecrows at the back of the dark forces line and more and more of them fell bringing down their clay counterparts. Even as they killed some non-existent citizens, they were going dead from lack of control. The battle was starting to blunt and the evil horde started to get confused. Josh felt a glimmer of hope and then the new sound came.

The siege engines were some sort of vehicle in the rear of the formation. They were even farther back than the scarecrow attack and they looked like iron cars. They were muscle powered, but they were also very long ranged. In fact, they seemed impossibly long-ranged for the era. Josh looked on in horror from the initial blast. He counted the seconds, waiting for the round to hit. When it did a full seven seconds later he was unprepared. A parapet simply disintegrated, sending debris scattering along the palisades. The imaginary people did not react to the blast because Josh had never programmed them to respond to such a devastating attack. They cringed like they were being attacked by ground troops. It looked out of place to Josh but apparently it was what the enemy was looking for. They rushed the

121

walls with a renewed battle cry. The scarecrows were trying to keep up with the charging beasts, but they were never meant for running. They were falling apart in the effort. Fires began to ignite all over the city. Josh knew that only a few warriors were here, and most of those were meant for scouting use only. Erica would attack when the time came, but he hoped that it would not come to that. If they lost her, it would just as disastrous to the kingdom as any enemy attack ever could be. He needed something to combat these new units. The problem was that he didn't know how gunpowder worked. He could not imagine it in his mind to make it become a reality. He could picture a bullet and a gun, but without the necessary chemicals inside to make them work, they would be only solid props. Canons were out of the question for basically the same reason. He needed more mundane weapons. He began to see links of barbed wire and he quickly began duplicating them all over the city. They sprang up like metal vines. He saw spikes in the street from every cobble. They would be impassable for any but the most desperate. He made his imaginary people flee to the north and they would encourage the enemy to follow them into his newly formed traps. It would take some real doing, but he was prepared to make a stand.

The General stood among his best troops. The city before him was only blocked by a small pass through the mountains. His advanced scouts had already determined that there was some small measure of defenses stationed there. "Good!" He shouted and the troops around him looked to see what he was talking about. "Let us go and crush this enemy!" He shouted and they all picked up his battle cry. They surged forth and filed into lesser and lesser columns as the terrain dictated. When they reached the pass they were six troops wide. With spiked clubs and massive shields, the leading edge moved into the pass. Rocks hurled down at them from the peak above as the humans started their defense. The second row lifted its shields to cover the head of the troops in front and many of the rocks bounced harmlessly off of them. Then, as their advance seemed to be unopposed, all bedlam broke loose. A large ball of fire dropped down on them from above and they had nowhere to scatter to. The troops were on fire and the first three lines of them went down, smoldering. Then, a loud thud hit the ground in front of them and it told them that a new combatant had entered the fray. Forraguth stood before the entire army of the evil horde and he smiled at them. It was most unnerving. His just over seven feet of height was impressive. His double bladed axe was gripped in his right hand. It would have been a two handed weapon for anyone else. He took a three quarter stance and glared at the fourth line of the enemy.

"Well, I'm waiting." He prompted them and they charged. Forraguth's blade sang through the air as he played it around with all of his mighty strength. He cleaved several bodies in half with his first swipe. However, his attacks did not stop there. He leaned forward and breathed another blast of fire. The ball of flame swept forward down the narrow channel and lit many more troops this time. The humans behind him gave a cheer and their arrows began to pick off individual targets that somehow escaped the blaze. The formation of dark troops had been broken. Shields were discarded and the few that still wanted to advance were trampled by those behind them. Forraguth continued his merciless onslaught. He stepped forward into the carnage and swept wave after wave of clay trooper out of the channel. Bodies were flying a respectable distance as he basically plowed through them. The human foot soldiers fell in behind him and brought their own formation forward. The emotional ride was a most dangerous high. Forraguth reached the other end of the pass and knew that he had made a mistake. The army was bottle-necked here, that is true, but they are also many. He could see out into the open just how terribly outnumbered they were. Now he was being targeted by their archers. A bit of the mountainside erupted from a siege engine blast. Forraguth turned and ran back into the pass. The human soldiers were startled and they bolted as well, their formation dissolving as fast as random chance would have it. The dark army paused a moment and the siege engines poured multiple hits into the pass. Fragments of rock and fire were suddenly filling the passageway and many of the soldiers went down. Forraguth himself had taken two arrows in the back. Those wounds were not serious thanks to the scaly skin of his heritage. No, his worse problem was that he was pinned beneath a particularly nasty sized boulder. The side of the pass had fallen into the center and it no longer could be called a pass. He cursed and spat, and heaved, but the mountainous boulder would not move. He was helpless here. He knew that it would not take long for the enemy to advance again. His defense of this pass was now in jeopardy. He cursed himself again for being a fool. He pulled in his personal strength and then he let out a wail such as no human had ever heard before. The sound seemed to reverberate through the air and the very rock itself. With that last effort, Forraguth had expended himself. He simply collapsed under the weight of the rock.

Impossibly, the sound he had made came echoing back, just softer. Then there were more sounds. The wail repeated more than an echo would explain. Then it got louder as they continued. The prince had been watching the pass from the safety of his tower using a scrying glass. Now he saw something he couldn't believe. Dragons were coming. Their massive bodies were dotting the skies like birds. But these were dangerous birds. They swept in three and four dragon wings that swept the enemy army with fire and acid. The troops simply dissolved. The clay constructs could not withstand that much damage. The demons, they were a different story. The siege engines were trying to fire upon the dragons, but the beasts were quite fast for their size and the shots missed and hit harmlessly off in the distance.

The General stood up and pulled his own bow from off of his back. The massive bow was at least ten feet long when strung. He held it up and a thick arrow was nocked. He pulled the string back and lifted the tip of the arrow. The General aimed carefully, being sure to lead his target. A reddish brown dragon swept in front of him, trying to burn away more of his command. He let the arrow fly and it struck the great beast in the neck. The startled cry and wing over plummet to the ground signaled a new level to the fighting. The remaining troops swarmed over the dragon and dispatched it quickly. This army was not going to go away easily. They had come for total conquest and they would settle for nothing less.

The elves had covered more distance than was commonly felt necessary. However, it had been to their benefit that they had. The sprites were telling them of the massive battles that had erupted all over the lands. The dark armies had marched and villages were being completely leveled. There were no survivors to report from all of the preliminary scouting runs. Then, as if they had asked the question out loud, the sprites told them of how the area that they had been bivouacked in had been destroyed as the army made its way towards the human city. If the elves had not moved, then they would have been among the first casualties of this war. The High Elf felt a sense of relief that they had been spared, at least so far, but he also felt a sense of shame that they had run before the city was attacked. Now the humans would have to fight this battle without the promised aid from the elves. He sent a simple prayer in hopes it would protect them. They continued north, as the wolf had instructed. None of them knew how far the enemy would advance. They did not know how far they needed to go to be safe. So all they could do was to continue and hope for the best. No matter how lucky the Grand High Elf felt, this running instead of fighting really stuck in his craw. It would take him quite a while to get over this day. He also made it a personal promise to thank the young human if he ever saw him again.

Josh moved forward with his troops, such as they were. A good portion of his beloved city had already been destroyed by the heavy pounding the siege engines were throwing at them. He hadn't yet lost any of his people though, so he felt a small stab of relief about that. His straw troops were limited, but he could see them as if he were above the battlefield on high. He had live, up to the second updates on what was going on and he was directing his constructs with pinpoint and deadly accuracy. The enemy army had hit the city gates and toppled them in. Josh reflected on how that was supposed to be impossible, but there it was for him to clearly see. Then they had gone after the illusionary people and they had slaughtered them as if they were the real thing. The image seemed to be holding up well. The fires started all over the place then. The city was bleeding smoke into the air in its agony. Stones were being smashed and the army was advancing with nothing but total destruction on their minds.

The constructs were keeping some of the vast invasion bottle-necked outside the city. Those that were already inside pretty much had free reign of the environment. Of course, they were moving around the city and they could find only a few scattered victims upon which to vent their rage. Josh kept moving walls even as he directed his scarecrow troops. He would even replenish his troops in an area that the enemy could not see so that they would not become wise to what he was doing. The smoke was beginning to obscure his vision though. The fires were a major problem, and one that he had not foreseen. He still needed a way to destroy those rolling wagons of destruction.

Josh had to admit that those siege engines were a marvel of design. Using only the things that were available in this time, they had managed to produce tanks. They were armored metal hulks with strong wheels and they were powered by the dirt equivalent of rowers. They were actually pedaling these cars into the battle. Whatever they had used to fire them was also potent enough. The range on these things was more than impressive, it was frightening. The shot that struck the stone walls had to weigh at least seventy-five founds. It would have taken large cannon to accomplish the same feat. He wanted to actually get hold of one of them to see how they worked. However, he would destroy them all if he could. They were causing so much damage that he was finding it difficult to concentrate. There was also the possibility that they could hit the building he was in. That thought did not fill him with confidence either. He needed to silence those guns, and quickly. He began thinking about various ways to do just that when Erica called out.

"Get out of the window!" She screamed and he started to turn towards her. She was already running and she tackled him at a full run. They collided and skidded along the floor just as the window disappeared. The window, a piece of the wall, and a portion of floor where Josh had just been standing were gone. The shot had ripped all of that away in an instant. Erica got up first and brushed herself off. Josh got up second and he looked stunned.

"That's it, your time of playing war is over, and we've got to get out of here." Erica stated and it was not a question.

Josh still looked dazed, but the wheels were still spinning behind those eyes. "You're right of course." Josh said at last. "I just have one more little thing to do before we go." He said and he bolted from the room. Erica gave chase. As far as she was concerned, he was her only ticket out of the city without being seen by the invaders, she was not going to let him out of her sight.

Josh ran down the passageway. He was heading somewhere specific and Erica simply followed. The exertion was enough that she didn't care where he was going; only that she could still see him. He darted into a doorway and she pulled up to a stop to see just where they were. She was confused by his choice; it was just a simple storeroom. How could this help them? She was ready to ask that very question when he looked at her and grinned mischievously. She suddenly got very worried. He was up to something.

Josh held up his hands and began to concentrate. Magical power was being pulled from all around them. His image was forming in his mind and he checked and double-checked each detail before moving on. Once he was satisfied, he pulled all of that magical energy to the image to give it form and substance. He heard Erica gasp as the spell completed. The storeroom was now filled with something that shouldn't be here. It was explosives.

Erica looked at her brother, confused. "I thought you couldn't materialize things you don't understand?" She prodded and he smiled at her with a big goofy grin.

"Oh, I'd say that our video rental cards have paid off dividends here. I may not be able to make guns, but I have seen truckloads of explosives in movies. I just can't make the truck work. I needed only this." He said and he held up a detonator. It was green with a red light on top and an arming toggle switch. It also had an antenna, presumably to remote detonate the ordinance that now seemed to fill the storage area of the palace. "We need to get out of here, but only far enough to set this off and watch the show." He said. He stepped forward and placed his hand on Erica's shoulder. He looked down with his eyes closed. He was picturing the target location for his spell. There was a blinding flash and then they were out in the countryside. They were on a hill, and they could see the army for what it truly was. It was a genocidal killing machine. The hill they were on had been stripped of all bushes and trees and there were dead animals littered about. The enemy was killing everything that lived.

The city lay sprawled before them and it was burning and partially demolished. The siege machines had finally reached the gates and they were lowering their booms to enter the city itself. Josh counted to fifty, allowing time for the rest of their support troops to get within the walls. When at last they all appeared to be inside, he pulled out the detonator.

Erica looked at him expectantly. "What I do now, I do for the good of all of our people." He said, a tear welling up in his eye. He gripped the detonator firmly and with his other hand flipped the toggle switch to arm the bomb. The red light started flashing to indicate that it had an active circuit. Josh took several deep breaths, perhaps steeling himself to actually commit the deed. Then he closed his eyes and pulled the trigger. There was a momentary pause. To the two of them on the hill, it seemed like forever. But then the sky was filled with debris and explosions of incredible magnitude began to rip across the city. Clay and demonic bodies began to fly as the building began to go up. Then, as if the rest had been some sort of signal, the main cache of explosives blew. Both of the True Bloods turned away and knelt down from the blast. A terrible wind blew at them and they took shelter from the backside of the hill. The shock wave swept out and after several seconds, rushed back into the void it had left behind. When both waves had passed, only then, did they work their way back up the hill to see what had truly happened. The sight was frightening; a mushroom cloud now hung over the city that was their home. There was no army, there were no siege engines. There were no demons or their troops. There was only small debris and melted stones. A crater rested where the palace once stood. The crater was massive. It had to be at least two hundred feet across. The city itself was completely decimated. There was nothing but ruins left. It was as if the eroding influence of a thousand years had suddenly been applied to the structures. This battle was over.

Josh felt the weight of all of that destruction upon his shoulders. He dropped to one knee and sobbed. Erica tried to console him, but what could she say? He knew what he was doing. He knew what would happen. He also knew that it was the only way to stop that evil army. The only catch was had he become evil himself? Only time and close observation would tell.

Erica wanted to bring Josh out of his funk. She wanted to help him to focus on something else, anything else. Nothing different came to mind though. She decided that duty was to be his focus. She knelt close to his ear. "We need to see if our people are all right." She said softly.

It was the one highlight to this whole mess. He *had* saved the people. Suddenly, his mind clung onto that thought and he needed desperately to verify that it was true. "Let's go then." He said and his voice had that strong will back in it. Erica breathed a sigh of relief. If they lost him, the kingdom would fall. In a flash they were standing on the cobble streets of their beloved city. Of course this was the fabricated duplicate, but it still looked like their city. The people were going about their business. Everything looked normal except the surrounding countryside. It was obviously a fake. It had no third dimension to it. It was just a mental image from Josh's mind. The city mad been modeled, surely, but the outside area beyond the walls had not. It was like a large photograph hanging just outside to give the illusion of reality. Still, the task itself had been remarkable and it had indeed worked. His people were safe, for now at least. They could not survive forever in here. The food supplies were limited and eventually, they needed to leave the city in order to maintain their livelihoods. This was just a temporary solution. In fact, the one it seemed to be helping most was Josh, himself. The weight of all of that responsibility was a bit easier to bear. He was actually smiling, if only a little. The lines in his face were not explainable by age; he was aging due to the stress.

As the two of them stood there, some of the townsfolk gathered around to see them. They had questions. After all, their temporary shelter was not a perfect copy. They knew they were somewhere else, but did not know where.

"Your majesties" A particularly bold peasant said, drawing their attention to him. "Might I inquire just where we are; and when can we return home?" He asked. The questions were bold, and straightforward. It was a thing of beauty.

Josh held up his hand as others began to echo the questions and add more of their own. "Please good people." He said and Erica was surprised that he was the one handling this crisis. "You have all been moved to this temporary duplicate of our fair city that I made. It was necessary in order to protect you from the invasion that has taken place." Josh said and worried faces met him as he scanned the crowd for their reaction. Josh turned a little depressed. "I am sorry to report that the city has been destroyed in my attempt to defeat the invading army. It will take a serious amount of rebuilding to restore our city to its former glory. I can help a lot with that, but I cannot do it all. There is simply too much there to be done for one man, even me to handle." He said and there were nods of acceptance around him.

The mood was bad, but Erica decided to rally the people. "We have all survived, and the enemy is dead!" She said and a cheer erupted among the assembly. "As hard is it will be to rebuild, we still have the people and the will to do it. We are going to be in much better shape than other kingdoms. We shall be the ones who will prosper in the wake of this tragedy. We will become a greater force for good in this world." She said and the crowd cheered again. She looked around and was satisfied with the response. "If you will forgive us, we must see to other business. There is still so much to do." She said, giving herself and her brother a way out of the spotlight. "In the meantime, go about your business as usual. We will be contacting you to let you know how we are going to go back to our old home and begin the rebuilding." She told them and they began to disperse.

Erica turned to Josh. "You see, that is why we do what we do. It is for their benefit that we go through all that we do." She said and his look was dubious. She shook her head. "Either way, we need to get back and see just what we can do for our home. The palace didn't even survive the blast."

Josh had been thinking on what she had said. Not now, but earlier. "No, we don't have time for that now. We need to help those other kingdoms repel the enemy horde." He said bluntly. Erica's look of surprise made him jump into an explanation. "You said it yourself. We are going to be a lot better off than other kingdoms. That means that we can strengthen our relations with these other kingdoms by helping them in their time of need." He said. As usual, he had already thought it out too much for Erica to find fault in his logic.

"Fine, at least we'll be doing something." She said. So far she had not been able to take an active part in any of her home's defenses.

It was starting to unnerve her that she relied so heavily upon her brother. "But we had better hurry though." She added and he nodded. Then Josh closed his eyes and began to concentrate. In moments, the calm and tranquil cobblestone street they had been standing on was now a besieged front gate. The enemy constructs were trying to break down the main gates to a fortress type city. Erica did not know which kingdom they were in, but Josh had managed to find it so they must have been here before at some time. Her steel was drawn and she braced herself along with a few other startled warriors. Josh drew himself up and held both hands up in a gesture of warding. The doors before them that had been creaking started to ice over. The ice was thickening and thickening. Then spider webs were lacing across it and the strength was still being poured on. The creaking stopped and it looked as solid as stone. In fact, that is what Josh put on it next. A wall of stone began to form and the troops backed away from the bizarre magician. They were grateful for the assistance, but they feared his powers. Erica, having been thwarted of yet another chance to bloody her sword leaped forward and actually scaled the wall that had just formed. She reached the top and peered out at the masses beyond. An arrow whizzed past her and she ducked her head. She looked back at the startled men.

"Bring out burning oil and tar!" She bellowed. The men did not even know who she was, but the voice of authority was universal and Erica had laid it on heavily. They rushed to comply with her orders. The noise outside the doors was somewhat muffled by the new reinforcement, but it was still there. The large vats of oil and tar were brought and dumped over the edge. The clay constructs up in the front melted from the heat. Others were splattered and a torch flew from the wall to ignite the mass of bodies at the foot of the gate. The demon troops backed away but the clay constructs were mindless. They simply kept battering away at the fortified defenses until they could no longer move. The fallen bodies of clay became yet another barrier to the front gate. For now, the front doors were secure.

Josh helped Erica down amid the cheering defenders. "Nice thinking sis." He said and she smiled briefly at him. She held her sword in the air. "Prepare yourselves for the next wave. This is only a minor setback for them." She ordered and the jovial faces turned serious once again.

A gruff looking man with veteran armor pushed and shoved his way to the newcomers. "The Captain would like a word with you two." He said and somehow he was heard over the tumult. The two young leaders followed obediently. They were escorted back away from the walls to a tent that was set up in what had to be the market square. It was the temporary military headquarters for this kingdom.

"All right, I'd like to know just what you thought you were doing." The Captain said. He was a burly man, at least six foot four and built like a muscled behemoth. Josh and Erica stopped in their tracks. It was Josh who found his voice first.

"We were just trying to help." He replied a bit meekly.

The Captain must have been speaking rhetorically because the reply was unexpected. He looked at the two intruders sharply. His gaze was like razor blades cutting through you on their way to something more important. "You are not part of my defense forces, that much is certain." He said finally. "Just who are you?" He asked.

This time it was Erica who spoke up. "I am Queen Erica, and this is Josh." She said with at least some refinement in her voice. Her warrior's outfit kind of spoiled the attempt though.

The Captain looked at both of them in turn and then he let out a tremendous laugh. "You two? You are supposed to be some sort of royalty? That's a good one!" He said and his laughter seemed to infuriate Josh. Erica realized just how unbelievable the claim was on the surface of it all. Nevertheless, it was totally true.

Josh stepped forward, his height was good, but he was still far shorter than this towering mountain of a man. "What she told you is true. We have come to help you defend your kingdom against this common threat. You can either take the help or tell us to go." He said and his voice became iron.

The Captain thought about this ridiculous situation again. "Okay, if you are royalty of some kind, then why aren't you defending your own kingdom just now. Surely it is under attack as well?" He asked.

Josh looked the giant of a man straight in the eyes. "It was." He said quietly. The Captain's eyebrows rose. "My people will have to rebuild the buildings, but the invaders were slaughtered." Josh said and the Captain stepped forward.

"You mean to tell me that you defeated the invaders?" He asked incredulity flavoring his tone thickly. It was obvious that he believed less and less of this story as the minutes ticked by. He decided to challenge it with details. "Was the army you faced as big as the one outside our gates right now?" He asked.

Josh scratched his head. "I haven't fully seen the enemy you face here yet, so I don't know the answer. However, I do have the numbers of what we faced. The army had about eight thousand of the clay constructs. There were about three hundred of the demon troops and ten captains, or whatever they call them. In addition, there were a dozen siege vehicles and that's what destroyed our city walls." Josh said as if he were ticking items off a grocery list. There was no emotion behind it, it was merely relayed facts. His delivery was almost as frightening as the facts he portrayed.

The Captain scratched his chin in thought. "The numbers you tell me are at least close to what my scouts have reported. Although I have not seen these 'siege vehicles' you speak of. Perhaps that's something they are holding for the right moment to unleash." He said thoughtfully.

"That was what I was thinking. It also tells me that you need to get your men back from the walls before they are buried alive behind them. The bombardment should start as soon as they realize that ground troops alone will not get them into your city." Josh said logically. The Captain actually seemed to be taking him more seriously now.

The question Josh most feared was the next one voiced. "How did you defeat this army?" The Captain asked reservedly.

"I blew up the city once they were all inside." Josh said and the look of surprise was full and expected. "Of course I got all of my people out first, but that was the only thing I had time for once the attack began." Josh explained further. "We cannot do that here. You have no time to evacuate all of your people and I don't have time to make that much explosives. So we will need to do something different to help you." He said at last, actually assuming that their help would be accepted. Then Josh moved his point back to the action steps they had already discussed. "Captain, you need to draw your troops back sooner than later. They are in grave danger at the moment." He warned and the Captain looked at him with more respect. He turned away from the two of them and leaned out of his tent.

"Tell the men to withdraw from the wall and form a skirmish line at the second rally point." He ordered and when he turned back in he could visibly see Josh's relief that the order had been given.

"Thank you for that, it buys me time to come up with something that can save us all here." He said. The Captain just shook his head.

"Saving the city is my job. I need you to help get the people out of it. If that's the only way to avoid civilian casualties, then that's what we need to do." He said and Josh nodded; so did Erica. "How soon after they were blocked did the siege engines start?" He asked and Josh shook his head.

"I don't know. They were totally unexpected. I did not see them at all before the walls were going down around us. They have a really long range. I would expect them any time now." He replied and the Captain's face looked grim.

"Here, take this seal." The Captain said handing over a small metal bar with a crown on one end and a wax press on the other. "It will tell the people that you speak for the king in matters of their safety. I don't have the foggiest idea how you will be able to get everyone out, but I pray that you do." He said honestly. Josh could see the strain that the man was under and he fully sympathized with him. It was the same thing *he* had gone through in defense of their city.

"I will send word once it is done." He told the man, trying to help bolster his confidence. At this point he didn't know how they were going to move so many people so quickly, but he knew that they had no choice but to try. This kingdom, like their own, depended on him to work his miracles. It was just another example of how he had grown up in the past four years. With the talking over with, it was time for action. Josh waved goodbye to the Captain and he and Erica left the tent in a hurry.

They made it a few blocks and the task seemed overwhelming. The chaos and bedlam that was ensuing as the troops pulled back from the wall nearly had the populace panicked. Fortunately, the raining down of fire had not yet begun, so there was still a chance that they might succeed. They just needed to act quickly. Erica stopped and pulled Josh's arm.

"I can get a few people's attention, but we need something big if we are going to instruct a lot of people on what you want them to do." She said, almost panting, the panic around her was starting to fray her nerves. "Do you know what you want done?" She asked.

Josh glanced at her, but he was already examining the vast city. He needed a higher point in which to view it all. He looked around quickly and spotted a bell tower. "We need to go there first." He shouted to his sister and he pulled her along with him as they cut their way through the crowd. "I need to see what we're dealing with." He said to her as they traveled but the noise drowned it out fully. They reached the cathedral and Josh pressed his way inside and to the staircase that spiraled up the walls of the tower. He was still making good time even as they reached the top. He swept to one of the openings and swung his legs over the edge. Erica grabbed his shoulder in case he had gone crazy.

"What are you doing?" She asked, fighting her own panic long enough to test his.

"I need to see all of the city and this is the highest point available to us. If what I have in mind will work, we don't have much time to try it." He said. His eyes were scoping out the buildings. He was absorbing the details like a tremendous sponge. His temples began to ache with the effort and his eyes were drying out because he wasn't blinking. He checked cross streets and he counted buildings. The image was slowly forming in his mind. He pulled from his own memory as well. He had fought monsters by a lake once. He saw that lake now in his mind. He saw the buildings before him as if they had been built into the fine ground around the lake. He continued the image; he started to put even smaller details in. There was a barrel there, and a loose cobble here. There was a broken window on the house fourth from the end. He began to soak it all in. The breeze from the lake would be wonderfully cooling this time of year. He started to pull in the energy that would be required for this level of transference. This was not going to be easy. Erica grabbed his shoulders as he began to shudder. One wrong move would send him plummeting off of the bell tower. He was shaking badly as he pulled his own energy and then began draining that of his sister. She could feel the strange sensation. She yawned and loosened her grip, but did not let go of her brother. He continued to press on, against the impossible feeling of sleep and exhaustion, he forced himself ever onward. The lake was softly splashing the shore and the new village would have beachfront property to boast. He continued to add details to the image. The power was building to dangerous levels. He pressed on even more. He could feel his heartbeat starting to skip and slow. He knew that it was now or never. The enemy was about to attack. He was as certain of it as he was of anything in this crazy existence. He allowed the energy to flow out into his mental image. The buildings began to pop out of existence as he watched. They were being pulled to the last. This was not a copy, like he had done with his own city. This was more of a teleport. He was transporting the buildings to the lake front. The effort was enormous and the people were shocked and frightened as their homes began to disappear. Once the spell completed, the buildings were gone. The people were there, in the space that had once been their homes. Then, he did the last bit; he sent all of the people to the beach. His energy was spent; he and his sister fell back into the bell tower and fell fast asleep. A few minutes later, soldiers were storming up the spiral stairs. They found the two young royals and carried them away.

CHAPTER 8

The enemy was now blasting the church since it was suddenly the only building they could target. It was also why the Captain had dispatched his men to find the strangers. If all of the other buildings just vanished, then they had to be in the one that was left. It didn't really take a genius, and tactically, he was a genius. The soldiers made their best speed out of what was left of their city. The walls were still holding, but that would not last since the bombardment had started. Once the church was leveled, the wall and the gate would be next. Josh was floating in and out of consciousness as the refugees made their way out of the former city location and headed out into the wilderness. They spread out in squads so that they could not all be tracked at once. With the sounds of the church and the walls falling behind them, they made good their escape, at least for now. The enemy knew that the defenders had still been there when the buildings vanished. They were ultimately frustrated at having lost a good portion of their spoils. The blood they would have spilt had somehow eluded them. They were not happy. Their vengeance would need a victim and the wilderness would not protect the wandering soldiers for long.

In the Captain's mind, he was just buying time. These miraculous children had just saved his people. Well, at least he hoped that they had. He had no proof that they were saved, he just knew that they weren't in the invasion's way anymore. It was a technical point, he admitted to himself, but a valid technical point though. He stayed with the royals as they continued on into the night.

When Josh finally roused, his sister was drinking some hot mead from a tankard with a group of soldiers around a campfire. It was still dark, and they had long ago stopped hearing any sounds of pursuit. He rubbed the back of his neck as he tried to sit up. He was way too weak for that and he rolled halfway to at least try and see where he was. A voice called out next to him.

"Sir, he is awake." The guard that was watching him reported.

The voice of the Captain actually sounded quite amused. "Good, then let's have a look at our city's savior." He said with genuine respect in his voice. He made his way to where Josh was facing and he knelt down and smiled at the young man. "I think that we owe you an apology for our earlier doubts." He said as if he were more than one person. Since he was the leader of what people remained here, it sort of fit. Josh smiled back but was obviously still very weak. "You just rest, I'll have someone bring you some food when you look able to take it." He said and Josh actually managed to nod this time. "When you are feeling up to it, I'd like to know what exactly you did with my people." He said and there was only a trace of gruffness in his tone. "Your sister informs us that you probably moved them somewhere. I don't know how she could know what goes on in the mind of a magician, but there it is." He said and that same humor was back in his voice. "But don't worry about any of that now as long as my people are safe, I can wait." He looked closer at Josh. "They are safe aren't they?" He asked seriously.

"Yes." Josh croaked.

"Then I see no reason to bother you any more at this time. Get better and we'll talk later." The Captain said and he headed back to the campfire.

Erica stayed a bit longer. She knelt down next to her brother. "Where did you send those people?" She asked. Josh looked a question at her that he didn't have the strength to ask. Erica nodded and continued. "The sprites have sent a messenger to me asking what you did. They say that the hordes are searching for the missing people. Apparently, no place on this world is safe. Did you send them to someplace else?" She asked. The look of concern was genuine and Josh wondered if it was for his condition, or for those people that she didn't know. He hoped that it was a little of both.

He propped himself up on an elbow with an amazing act of sheer will. "They are by the lake." he managed to say. It looked clear to me." He said. Erica lifted a water pouch to his mouth and he drank. The cool water felt shocking working its way down his throat but he felt remarkably better. "I was careful about my choice, but I only had a couple of sites to choose from." He said, feeling his strength beginning to return. He began to get some real hope.

Erica did not move far from her brother's face. "Then they are still in danger since they are still on this world." She concluded and he nodded, although a bit weakly still.

"They are not in immediate danger, but I cannot take us to them for a while. I hope that I can recover soon, but right now I could not conjure us out of a paper bag." He said with only a hint of humor in it. "We may have to set out and find them ourselves." He added and Erica returned his nod with one of her own.

"I see, so we should provision up for a long trek across this enemy-ridden land with one very weak sorcerer in tow?" She asked. If she had wanted, she could have made that sting. This was more of an assessment of their situation. Unfortunately for Josh, he could find no fault in her analysis.

"I'm afraid so." He replied finally. "That Captain seems to be a good man. He will want to meet up with his people sooner rather than later." He paused. Erica was not sure if he were collecting his thoughts, or his energy. "We also have to deal with our own people. They are safely in another place, one that I created, but they have a limited amount of supplies. I cannot even visit them in my current condition." The thought bothered him more than he would have liked to admit. Erica seemed to sense that though. She always did.

"I'm sure they will be fine. This is just a minor setback for you. You will be up and around in no time." She said, trying to bolster Josh's confidence and morale. "Just don't go around moving any entire cities around again in the near future." She warned. She stood up to get a better attitude towards her brother. "You pushed yourself way too hard on this one. You even brought me down with you. If it weren't for the Captain's troops, then we would have been defenseless when the enemy breached the walls." She said. That church was the only building left when you finished so it was targeted right away. It was destroyed before the troops got us out beyond the city walls." She informed him and Josh lowered his chin.

"I knew that they were here to kill everyone, I didn't think they would destroy a church." He said with a hint of melancholy. "I just don't know what we are going to do for the rest of the world." He said and Erica's jaw dropped.

"The rest of the world?" She repeated. "Who do you think you are?" She started pacing around exasperated. "You cannot take on the entire world's safety as a personal quest. It is too much for anybody to do." She was building up steam and like a kettle on the burner, it was going to start whistling soon or it would simply explode from the pressure. The warrior queen turned on her brother. "How dare you assume that you were responsible for everybody's well-being?" Her elevated voice began to carry and the troops were looking at her now as she admonished her brother. "You sure have got a lot of nerve." She told him, in his weakened state, he was not following her rant anyway. "I should bust you one across the chops." She told him angrily. She made a final "Hmphff" sound and stomped off.

One of the medics, or at least what passed for one here, came over to check on the fallen wizard. "You okay young man?" He asked tentatively. Josh actually surprised him.

"Yeah, she's just mad because she could do nothing during the attack. She needed to vent and she chose me because I wouldn't fight back." He said and he actually smiled at the startled soldier. There were no specific wounds to check so this field medic was out of his comfort area.

"Well, if she bothers you again, I can have a guard posted to keep her away." He offered and Josh laughed.

"I wouldn't do that unless you want to be treating your guard for the bludgeoning he would take in response to that." He told the medic. "No, it's better to let her kill something to calm down. Maybe have the Captain send her out hunting. Then she can take out her aggression and get us a good meal at the same time." Josh offered and the medic seemed quite pleased with the suggestion. He began to walk away and stopped and looked back.

"Do you mind if I tell the Captain it was my idea to send her hunting?" He asked a bit timidly.

Josh waved him away. "Do what you want. I just need a few winks and something solid to put in my stomach." He replied and the man left almost hurriedly. Josh let his head fall back to the bedroll he was lying on. He was instantly back asleep.

The Guardian of Balance looked into his spyglass and he was not happy. The kingdoms were each doing what they could to try and hold off the enemy horde. Most all of the smaller villages had simply been wiped out. The crops were trampled and burned and the animals were slaughtered along with the people they served. The level of waste this constituted turned his stomach. He knew that the balance was shifting and that if something was not done soon, then things may well spiral out of control. He needed a new plan. He had talked to that young wizard and although the young man was impressive, he was still just one small man in a world under siege. The guardian would have to enlist some help in this task. He pulled up his own checklist and shook his head. He wondered how things had gone so far awry that he had to take direct action. He was angry at himself for letting things go this far. He should have done something much earlier. He could have done, but what? What could he have done to stop the encroaching armies from launching an all-out assault on the human race? No, this was a task for meddlers. He needed someone with enough power to do something and someone with few enough morals to actually do it. He needed to find more True Bloods. With that realization, he set about his task. He would contact the parents. They had interfered before and they would again. He was certain of it. At least this time it would be on *his* terms. He could control them, after all their children were at stake here. He could keep them on a short leash and let them do only what needed to be done. Yes, that would work. He convinced himself before he made the call...

The Dark Lord writhed in agony as his jailers continued to poke and prod everything that hurt. His vengeance upon them would be sweet. Of that he swore. His madness started to intrude upon his rage and terror flavored each new awareness. His body was broken and the fringes of his mind began to unravel. He needed to kill these pests and get back to the grand mission for which he had been specifically chosen. He would crush the human race. He would hand the world over to the master and he would reap the benefits for having done so. A corner of his mind turned cynical about his chances for accomplishing those lofty goals, but his willpower was something beyond legendary. A red hot poker came at him, again. He took the shot and then he recoiled. The poker flung back and struck one of his captors. The scream made his own aches almost cease entirely. He twisted on his broken limbs and burnt flesh and he lashed out again. Nobody had ever endured so much and still had the will to fight. It was part of the reason that his captors had become so complacent. He could smell their fear replacing his own as he found himself standing free. His limbs began that unholy regeneration that had for so long plagued him down here. He found a fresh strong arm and he pummeled the closest captor until its head caved in. Then he ran it through with the meat hooks that used to hold him up for inspection and further humiliation. The pain was searing and he recalled all of it. His mind was talking to itself now. His personality had fractured and now he was ready to begin anew the mission.

"Yes, the mission, we must do the mission." He said to himself as he looked around for something to throw on. He would fight his way out of this hellhole and he would retake his place at the head of the army he had harbored supplies for. He was ready to take his glory and shove it down the throats of anyone who would stand against him. His regeneration completed and all of his personalities could feel the raw power. They had placed a lot of faith in being able to escape, and now it looked as though they might actually succeed. He grabbed one of the torture rods for use as a weapon and he opened the ancient creaky door and stepped out into the dank musty hall. Looking both ways, he could smell the guards on this lower level. "Good, we will spill more blood before we find our freedom." He said to himself and he brandished the rod before him as he raced down the moldy hall. He was something of a sight, but he cared nothing for this. He wanted his vengeance and he would take it from anyone, even that upstart general that got into his way. This day would be his.

The General in question was having a strong day. He had leveled whole human settlements in the name of his evil master. His troops were being harassed by dragons from the skies and they had dropped several of them. The dead and bleeding carcasses littered the battlefield. Of course many of his troops were dead as well. He still had over five thousand of the constructs and at least two hundred of his demons left, but he had lost a lot. The pass, that insignificant piece of real estate still plagued him. The humans still held it and his troops could not advance. It was not a stalemate though, his siege engines were advancing and soon the sound of human cries would be heard and he listened intently to hear it. The next volley was aloft and he heard the report. Then, a piece of the mountainside rolled off as the explosion hit it. The pass was getting wider with each strike. Soon, his troops would overwhelm whatever was left up there and he would march into the human city beyond. There was nothing the humans could do now that would stop him. He was the commander of the end of the world. His glory was assured. Defeat was not an option. He was a major player in the demonic world and his own life could not end here on this plane. He was for all intents and purposes immortal here. He started forward, still craning to hear the cries of his victims. Another blast rocked the pass and this time there were humans thrown into the air for all to see. The war cry rose up from the troops and the General himself, heaved and pushed to get his troops into place to launch the final assault. They would crush each and every one of these people for the casualties that they had inflicted. It was a shame that their deaths would be so quick, but they were really only a distraction from the main killing frenzy to come. He would bathe in his victim's blood. Tonight, they would celebrate their victory in fire.

The Prince watched as the enemy advanced. They had held much longer than his original plan allowed for. Still, he had his people moving now. The front lines were taking a beating and the help they had received from Forraguth and his dragon friends had only slowed the enemy down, not blunt the assault as was hoped. Still, they had inflicted a lot of casualties on the enemy lines and everyone they took out would not be marching into the city when the time came.

The king had gone into hiding at the first note of fear. The enemy horde had been held back so the king, wherever he was, had nothing to do but wait. The Prince held nothing but contempt for the old man. Yes, he was his father and the ruler of this kingdom, but he had fallen from grace in his son's eyes. He had become lazy and greedy. The Prince would restore honor to the throne, if he was allowed to assume it. Right now, there was some question as to whether or not there would even be a throne left to be filled. However, he was the son of a once mighty king and his high morals and strong will had served him well in the past. They would do so again. The King had loyalists that would serve him, if he had simply shown himself, but they would not follow the prince. The Prince had people of his own. He called them Reformists. He would lead his followers into the bright future they so desired. The cobwebs of the past regime would be swept away in favor of new, bold decisive initiatives. He had his whole platform laid out in his mind. Of course if he had been found out by his father, he would have been tried for treason and the future of the kingdom would have been erased. Instead, this crisis seemed to be propelling the Prince into the public eye and he was not about to let this opportunity pass him by. People would support a savior and strong leader. He knew that he needed to pull a victory out of this somehow. He just didn't know exactly how to do that. His best laid plans had been successful, but only to a point. The enemy was still out there and they were advancing again. He knew that his meager defenses could not hold forever. He needed something more to change the situation. He almost said that aloud when a tap on his shoulder made him turn around.

"What?! Who are you?" He asked in surprise.

"Aww, have we been gone that long?" Dad asked in mild humor for the Prince's shock. Dad was there in his full hunter's outfit, complete with his trusty sword on his hip and those supple leather boots that allowed him to move silently across uneven ground. Mom was there too, and her getup was even more perplexing. She wore the mage cloak, but underneath she wore her everyday twentieth century housewife clothing. She also seemed to have been rushed into this situation. However, both of them saw the invading army and they both sprang into action. Dad charged into the main fray by heading out to the pass on foot, his sword held high as he ran.

Mom had taken a different approach. She had begun to visualize a dam across the pass. If she could get the wall established, it might buy them the time it will take to evacuate the city behind them. The only question that they did not have an answer for was where to relocate that many people to? She put that thought aside and continued to concentrate on the dam. She envisioned it huge, like the Hoover dam. It would tower over the mountain with all of that concrete and iron. She almost had the image solidified in her mind when Dad met the front line. He swept in with the full support of the ancients. They guided his arm as he slashed here and stabbed there. He was performing the dance of death and the human defenders rallied behind him. He dodged and thrust, parried and slashed. The enemy was falling away from his blade, but not fast enough. The advance still continued. He redoubled his efforts and sent even more of these evil creatures back into the abyss. Still they kept coming. His stamina had fallen off during his time back home and he was beginning to feel the fatigue catching up with him as he shoved three more bodies away. Most of these warriors were not even flesh. They were sticky mud, or clay things that had been enchanted to work like robots. He needed to find out who was controlling the robots so that they would become ineffective. He pressed again, looking over the fallen, trying to pick out someone who was paying too much attention to his fight. He spotted a demon thing in a suit of rusty armor and they made eye contact. The sudden realization of being found out brought fear to the demon's eyes. Dad now had a goal, he had a specific target and he began his attacks in earnest to reach it. Behind him, the dam began to form. The land was starting to buckle from the weight of the new construct and the rumbling in the ground made footing unstable. Dad continued on unabated by any of the little problems around him. He was gouged and nicked here and there but he was still on his feet and advancing on the hapless demon that seemed to have no clue to how to stop this madman from coming at him. There was a loud crash and everyone was knocked down. Dad rolled with the landing, kicked a hapless downed soldier and sprung up again with enhanced skill. He finally reached the demon he was looking for and he shouted in triumph as he drove his sword into its chest and then ripped up and out through the shoulder at the base of the neck. The demon thing died instantly in a spray of gore that would have made Dad sick if he had stopped to think about it. The huge lumbering thing coming at him did not allow for that thought though.

"You have interfered with me for the last time." The General said and he brought down a hideously large double-bladed axe. Dad sprung back just in time for the mighty blow to miss, but not by much and the force of impact with the ground knocked him off of his feet, rolling backwards. Archers began to riddle the General with arrows, but he didn't even seem to notice. His focus was now on Dad, and the fallen middle-aged man was too easy a target to pass up. The axe lifted up again and was held high over the general's head. Dad clambered to get up and the General swung again. The axe was well timed, but poorly aimed. It struck Dad with only a glancing blow. He managed to get hit by the side of the blade rather than the leading edge. However, that much force had to have some effect. This time it was a broken ankle. Dad cried out in pain and grabbed for his ankle even as the evil behemoth turned back to him. The General began to laugh as this moment. The thought of a personal kill, was one he had awaited since the plan had begun all those years ago. His senses were alert to record everything about this glorious moment. In fact, he was so intent on it that he failed to see the oddest thing that he could have imagined. What he missed was a Datsun pickup truck rolling off of the dam and falling ever so far directly towards the general. As vehicles went it was a small truck, white with rust over nearly a fifth of its body panels, but it still had weight and a long fall before impact. A shadow formed around the General and he looked up just at the point where it was too late to avoid. Instinctively he turned to the side to lessen the impact, but the truck crushed his shoulder and drove him and his broken body into the ground almost a foot. Dad drew himself away from the impact with help from the archers, but the scene was utter chaos now. The smoke and debris of the truck added to the sheer surprise of the attack and the humans successfully staged their retreat to the dam. They entered the massive gates that would have let water flow and then they sealed them afterward. The wall was complete. Up on the top of the damn, Mom threw a fist in the air.

"Yes!" She said as she pumped that arm in defiance. The guardian of Balance made a sound and she recovered her dignity, at least a little bit.

"It is time for both of you to go now. You need to get back to your world while this one sorts itself out." He said in an almost emotionless, nasally voice. He seemed like an annoying clerk at an underused government agency. His people skills were a bit lacking.

"Come on, I need to heal my husband before you send us back. Besides, these people probably still need our help." She added. They both looked out at the massive army that was held behind the enormous wall that she had conjured. "They are still under attack you know." She poked and the guardian seemed to deflate just a bit.

"You are going to be stubborn about this, aren't you?" He asked and Mom smiled back knowingly. "He sighed and turned around so that she couldn't see his face. His body language was enough to tell what she needed to know. He threw up his arms in the air and then his shoulders slumped and he waved her on dismissively. "Do what you need to do." He told her after the display.

Mom made her way down to Dad and the two of them hugged. The ankle caught Dad by surprise and he called out. She set to healing it with her magic and he was once again whole. They embraced again and she whispered into his ear. "It's been a long time since I've seen you in action, you've still got the moves kid." She told him and he smiled. The two of them were folded into the sea of humanity and they went to celebrate this temporary victory. Tomorrow may be another fight, but they had earned tonight. If Dad was too sore, she would put another spell on him. Mom would see to it that they both celebrated tonight.

Josh felt the bump as the makeshift cart jostled him yet again. They were traveling across some pretty rugged terrain, and even though he told them he could walk, the Captain would hear none of it. Erica had taken to hunting parties. It turned out to be a wonderful release for her. She hunted with a knife though and that caused a few of the soldiers a little concern. She had come back with kills, so she was obviously good enough at it to use that particular weapon, but she also seemed to enjoy the in-close kill. It was not what one considered normal for a monarch. Still, she was who she was and she was happy and jovial among the troops. She had several admirers, but none were bold enough to continue when she gave them a hard look. Josh had been fed regularly and tended to as if he were wounded. It was a policy among the troop and at first he didn't seem to mind. However, as his strength returned, he felt more and more confined by the 'standard treatment policy' that governed his release from the field medic and his one nurse. Josh ached to be able to walk around on his own. It was getting awkward here and he was not enjoying the ride at all. Plus, someone had to push the cart he was in. It didn't seem fair to him that someone had to be put out this way. Of course none of the various soldiers had complained. He hadn't expected them to. The shift changed every few miles and new faces greeted him warmly enough and then took the handles of his cart. They were usually exhausted by the time the shift changed again. Josh kept feeling bad for the men. He just couldn't see the need for all of this extra exertion on the part of the hapless soldiers that bore him across the rough terrain. He made up his mind to complain to the Captain when they stopped again to camp.

The day wore on and on. Josh felt himself getting angrier and angrier and having nowhere to vent it. He knew that it wasn't the most productive thing he could be doing. But then, neither was being carted across the open area while others toiled away. The sun was just starting to set when the order was given to halt. They had dealt with smaller skirmishes throughout the day. Small packs of enemy troops, well actually, one or two troops plus the clay constructs were out patrolling for any survivors. These small bands were no match for the Captain's trained soldiers. In fact, Erica was in her element here. She had taken out the first party that they had come across. She was an amazing hunter and she took out the two demons and let the clay constructs simply stand in place. More than one soldier felt just a little nervous around her, but it wasn't because she was so fearsome, but that she was so emotionless about the killing. She carried no anger against these enemies. She carried no resentment, or even grief. She was a cold killing machine with a determined face and lethal focus. Later, back at the campfires, she was her old self again. She would be happy and joking as they ate the day's game. Erica still hunted regularly with her knife. She also had the large steel sword, but it was for enemies she had told them. The noble beasts of the forest deserved more respect and thus she would not taint them with that soiled blade. The camaraderie was so good that most of them forgot about the thin circlet she wore that designated her queen. Of course nobody tried anything with her. If they had, she would have put them in their place quickly enough. That is, would have if the Captain didn't kill the man first. He kept a careful watch on his charges.

Josh gratefully climbed out of the cart and rubbed his sore posterior. The road had left more than its share of bruises on him and he would heal it later when he got the chance. He needed to talk with the Captain first. Josh patrolled around the encampment like a shark circling a school of fish looking for its prey. He knew that he would find the giant of a man sooner or later, but he would prefer to get the weight off of his chest now. He heard a bark of laughter and he knew which way to go now. He made a bee line towards the sound and when he reached the tent, there were two guards there to stop him.

"Let me through, I need to speak with the Captain." Josh stated in a tone that was almost a whine. He straightened his tunic and set his heels. "At least tell him that I am here requesting an audience." He ordered and the two guards looked at each other. One of them shrugged his shoulders and turned and vanished into the tent. The other watched Josh like a hawk, suddenly feeling awfully exposed to a magician with the other guard away. The missing guard returned and bowed to Josh.

"I'm sorry sir, please forgive my earlier reluctance. You see we were under orders..." He let the sentence trail off.

Josh nodded in acceptance. "Then may I enter now?" He asked and the guard blushed.

"Yes sir, please come in." The guard stammered. He pulled open the tent flap and Josh stepped through the seemingly impenetrable barrier. The inside of the tent was exactly as it had been when they were in the city. The floor was dirt instead of cobbles, but otherwise things were in exactly the same place. His mind was keyed to details like that and the level of detail here was impressive, almost staggering. Nothing was out of place at all. Even the picture that was hung had a slight tilt to it, the same tilt it had when Josh saw it last time. Josh began to suspect that something was amiss here. However, he still had that fire in his belly over being carted across this country.

The Captain sat in his chair, looking at maps on the table as Josh entered the tent and began to look around. He let the youngster continue his inspection. He pretty much knew what the boy was on about, but he let the scene play out in its own time instead of jumping to the next point. When Josh finished eying the room he turned to the Captain who took that as his cue.

"So young man, is there something you need?" He asked genially, always playing the good host. His smile almost made Josh's blood boil. There was still more here than met the eye.

"I am no longer going to be carted around like so much luggage." He said fiercely. The Captain's eyebrow rose ever so slightly in amusement.

"I see." He said and paused for Josh to continue.

"I have watched as man after man exhausts themselves pushing me around when I could perfectly well walk myself." He said, his indignation flaring. "There is no need for this to continue." He said, his voice starting to rise as his anger blew off steam. "I will walk from here on in." He said as his ire began to fade away. He had watched the Captain for reactions throughout his tirade and nothing came. The man was just cold stone.

The Captain stood up when it looked like Josh had petered out. "So, you think you are strong enough to trek across this land by yourself?" He asked. Josh felt that there was a trick in here somewhere, but he just couldn't see it.

"Yes sir, I can take care of myself." He answered. Josh was ready to test his strength on this giant of a man if he was pushed.

"I see." The Captain replied in a thinking way. "So you wish to deprive my soldiers of their exercise then?" He asked and Josh looked almost mortified.

"What?!" He cried out. "I was not exercise, I was only a burden." Josh cried, this time his voice was a whine.

"It's not a problem really, we'll just fill the cart with supplies and they will take turns wheeling it around like they did when you were in it." He said as Josh looked on blankly. "Don't worry about it anymore. You will just have to walk like the rest of us." He said and his amusement over Josh's reaction was starting to take its toll.

"Okay, at least that's settled." Josh said defiantly. His emotions were only barely in check. He would need much greater focus if he were to cast anything right now. Somehow the Captain knew that.

"You were looking at my tent rather intently, just what did you discover?" He asked, prodding the magician into making the conclusion that he needed.

"I noticed that it is exactly the way it was when you had us brought in to see you in the city." Josh replied and the Captain nodded.

"It is at that." He said almost casually. "You of all people should understand what that means." He said, a hint of danger altering his tone. "So tell me, what does it mean?" He asked directly.

Josh looked around once more. "It means that this tent and its contents are not transported from place to place, they are generated in place whenever you need them." Josh said, coming to the conclusion that had eluded him before.

The Captain looked at him and smiled wide. "That's close, real close. "No, what it means is that we have a sorcerer like you to conjure up what it is we need." He stated triumphantly. Josh's look of surprise was evident enough and the Captain laughed aloud. "Surely you didn't think you were the only magician in the world did you?" He asked, almost chidingly.

Josh shook his head. "No, I have met others; they were trying to take over the palace when I and my sister first arrived." Josh told him without preamble. "But they were using a different kind of magic and they were unaware of what I could do." He said honestly. The Captain nodded.

"Yes, I believe that's true. Still, you are a True Blood, and that is a pretty exclusive club, but you and your sister are not the *only* True Bloods around." He said and Josh looked just as surprised as he had before.

"Then why haven't they come forward when we were dealing with the kingdom's problems?" Josh cried. "It has been four years and we have not heard a whisper about others of our kind." Josh elaborated and the Captain just looked smug.

"If you knew what was going on at the palace, would you volunteer for daily duty and the sniveling refuse you have been dealing with every day?" He asked and Josh had to stop and think.

"You mean they probably heard the call and were afraid of the effort required and didn't answer?" Josh asked. It was his turn to have a little danger in his tone.

The Captain shrugged his shoulders. "I'm sure that's part of it. But I would not know for certain about that." He said. "But you have not asked me the next logical question young man." The Captain prompted.

Josh knew where he was going this time. "Who is your sorcerer?" He asked and the Captain nodded his approval.

"I am." The Captain replied. It was as Josh had felt, but was unsure enough not to ask. The Captain continued without regard for Josh's internal musings. "Although I must admit that I did not possess the power to move the entire city like that. I must admit that you are much more powerful than I am. Still, I think we can work together on getting us to our respective peoples." He suggested and Josh felt a real ray of hope flicker on.

"I have been getting stronger again, as you are well aware, but I admit that I cannot yet transport us to our people, even yours who are on this world." He said and he hated how it felt inside when he just wasn't *good* enough. Let alone, get to my people who are not even on this plane." Josh said and the Captain raised an eyebrow on that one, despite himself.

"Where did you send them? What do you mean not on this

plane?" He asked in a rush. The concern written on his face was very clear.

Josh took a deep breath. "I made a complete copy of my city and placed it in a limbo void. Then I aligned it to the real city and then transferred the people over to it." Josh said in explanation. The look of concern changed to one of puzzlement.

"What is this... limbo void thing you speak of?" He asked now more interested than concerned.

Josh took a seat for this looked to be a longer conversation than the one he had begun. "Well, basically, I made a bubble of existence. It is a place outside of the normal spaces where I can control everything about the environment. It has boundaries unlike that of the real world, but their impact can be minimized by clever placement of buildings and such." Josh continued, his listener was intrigued by now. "Once the void was setup I populated it with replicas of the buildings that existed in our fair city." He continued. "Then, at a designated moment, I ordered the people into their homes and they all shifted to the copies of their buildings. It took a lot less energy than the emergency transport we did for your people, but now I cannot get to them until more of my strength returns." He finished and the Captain whistled.

"I never even knew such things existed." He said at last. The weight of everything that Josh just told him seemed to make his mind hurt. "You actually made a fake world for your people to hide in while the enemy came to their doorsteps." He said and Josh nodded. "Amazing!" He said in a sudden boost of energy. He smiled hugely at the young man before him. "You are something special. I had heard stories of what you can do, but honestly I never gave them much credit. After all, who is that powerful? Who can do all of those things that you are supposed to have done?" He asked, not really expecting an answer.

Josh shrugged his shoulders. "I don't know what you've heard, but I have done a thing or two, mostly to improve the quality of life for my people." He said and the Captain looked at him squarely.

"Are you sure that you weren't doing it for the adulation of your people. Sometimes we do not realize that we are really working of ourselves when we say we are just helping others." The Captain warned.

Josh thought about it for a moment. "I, I don't think so. I mean, I don't get most of the credit anyway, my sister does. After all, she's the queen. I'm just a sorcerer." Josh said and the Captain's mouth fell open.

"Just a sorcerer?!" You have got to be joking. You are the rarest thing in this land. You are what allows our world to move forward instead of back into chaos. How can you think of yourself as anything but a god among regular people? None of them can do what you do with just a minor thought. You must consider this carefully for it is your destiny to become great. Your tales will be sung in all the lands when you eventually pass this plane. You are the important one, not your sister." The Captain said and his voice almost carried just a bit too far. He noticed it and immediately lowered it back down. "Remember my words." He told Josh as he waved a hand in dismissal.

Josh left the tent more confused than when he had entered it. He had just met another magician that used the same kind of magic he did. That seemed to be their only commonality though. The Captain seemed to be after power and prestige. Josh was after helping others. He was not always so, but it was the way his sister wanted it so he had adapted to it accordingly. He had to admit that it did feel good to help others. Yes, he did like when they thanked him, but was that really the goal? Had he done all of those things simply to hear them tell him how good and helpful he was? The doubts started to filter through his thoughts. Had he been thanked each time he had done something? Could he live without the praise? Josh walked away from the tent slowly, lost in his thoughts. He would do a lot of thinking about this, of that he was sure.

Erica was out on another hunt. Her small hunting party had managed to secure enough game for this night and with some of it jerked, they could easily make it through tomorrow as well. They were on their way back when a rustling in the brush caught their collective alert attention. Erica made a few hand gestures and the team fanned out and crouched down into the thicket. Whatever it was could have sensed the fresh game they were hauling. If so it meant that whatever was out there was carnivorous. That by itself was not so dangerous, but the fact that the mysterious creature was not afraid of a bunch of humans suggested that it was a major player in the food chain. That was dangerous.

Erica crouched down next to one of her comrades. He was a lean fellow with an accurate bow and a quick knife. Erica had liked him right away. His name was Fitch. Fitch, like all the other hunters, had left their loud and clunky armor behind at the camp. Erica had worn her supple leather armor so she was the best protected against assault. Because of this she usually took point on these outings. She nestled close to Fitch's ear. "What do you think we've got here?" She asked barely above a whisper.

Fitch shrugged his shoulders and when she nudged him he answered. "I dunno, but it is large. The entire brush over there is in motion. Either it is one large animal or several medium sized ones." He said, pushing the limits of Erica's hearing with the softness of his voice. It was Erica's turn to nod. She left him as she crept silently towards the moving plant life. Suddenly, a figure burst from the brush and it seemed to sense its danger and it turned away from the group and headed at full speed away from the band of humans. It was large, nearly the size of a horse. It had striped brown fur with black accents. Erica did not know what kind of animal it was but she was thankful that it didn't want to tussle with her. She looked down and saw the massive paw print in the mud. Her mind started to figure on the weight of the beast and she whistled. She stood up and turned back to her team.

"Emergency over men, let's get moving back to camp." She ordered and the massive arrow just missed her and plunged into the tree just in front of the startled warrior. The hunters all turned and saw that they had stumbled into a trap. The demon troops had somehow set this up. The clay constructs were forming a barrier that would prevent escape as the demons began to nock additional arrows into their bows

Erica felt the call of the ancients and she let herself go to their wishes. Her body became a killing machine. She moved like lightning. The first arrow was probably only a warning shot or she would have already been slain. It was the last mistake these ruffians would ever make. She raced in the direction from which that arrow had come. There was a demon there, trying to level his bow at her again. The look in his eyes was one of pure panic. She bellowed a battle cry that would have shaken the ground had she been on it. Erica had leapt an incredible amount forward and was rolling through the brush only to come up swinging her dagger and plunging it into the throat of her would-be attacker. His gurgled cries told the demons that the fight had begun and they each stepped forward, pinning the humans into an even smaller arena. The hunters had been working together since the last raid and they knew what each other's reactions would be. This allowed them to orchestrate their defense. This was something that the attacking band had not counted on. Even with daggers and swords, the humans managed to hold the demons at bay while Erica circled around and killed one after another of the suddenly frightened enemy. Her moves were clean and efficient. Her aim was perfect and her speed was almost superhuman. She reached and sliced another enemy demon across the shoulder even as it cried out a battle cry of its own. She heard a human cry out as one of the hunters was hit by one of those massive arrows. Others were now in melee combat and she was still on her rampage of death. A sudden stumble brought her face to face with a demon that had blood on his mind. He stabbed at her with a spear that creased a line of crimson across her thigh. Erica cried out as the poison began to burn in her veins. It was like her whole leg was on fire. The fight turned desperate at that point. The clay automatons were not even advancing. The demons had decided that an up-close and personal kill was more to their liking. Erica struggled to stand on a leg that just wouldn't support her anymore. It looked bright red from some form of heat. She killed the spear wielding demon by running him through with his own spear that she had deftly removed from his grip a mere moment before. She began to use it as a crutch to hobble over to the next assailant. She heard a weak battle cry from someone outside the circle and a young human plunged his own dagger into the neck of an unsuspecting demon. Erica fell over and the newcomer stood over her, defending her fallen body from the demons around them.

"To me!" He cried and the hunters obeyed as if they had heard it from the queen herself. The young fighter was unfamiliar to them, but he seemed to be working to defend the queen. That made him an ally and nobody wanted to explain to a wizard how his sister had been killed while they watched. They formed a tight circle around the fallen queen and the young man turned to her and knelt down.

"Josh told me this was only for emergencies, I think this time applies." He said and he actually smiled as Erica made dazed eye contact with him. "Stay with me your highness; we'll get you some help soon." He told her and her head fell over as she passed out. Mouse frowned, but he held the glowing rock close to his chest and said the ancient words that Josh had told him. There was a flash of light and the entire hunting party found themselves in their own encampment. The guards on duty called out and the whole camp came to life like a kicked bees nest. Erica lay motionless on the ground as the crowd began to form.

Mouse stood up. "Get me Josh now!" He screamed at the top of his lungs. A soldier immediately turned around and started running. In moments, he returned with the wizard in tow. To Mouse Josh looked older, more built and much more adult than he had before. There was a sudden realization that he had not identified himself to these people. He made eye contact with Josh and was relieved by the recognition.

"Mouse?" The startled young man asked aloud. Mouse nodded.

"I got there just in the nick of time. You've gotta help her, she's been poisoned." He said in a rush and Josh knelt down next to his sister. Instinctively he tried to send the healing to purge the poison from her system. He felt like someone had punched him in the stomach. Josh fell over backwards and lay on the ground doubled over. Erica was still weak and getting weaker. The poison was reaching a critical stage. The Captain knelt down and put his hand on her forehead. He spoke the words and drew into himself the power he needed. Erica began to glow the golden glow of a classic healing spell. This was old magic, not like the power Josh wielded. This was from the elder races. The Captain kept his eyes closed and the glow intensified until onlookers had to turn away. It died out just as quickly as it had begun. Erica gasped and returned to the living.

The Captain fell over and lay next to Josh and the two of them made eye contact.

"Thank you." Josh managed to mutter and the Captain smiled.

"So I am not useless just yet." He said as his vision began to tunnel. He had spent all of his energy at once. He knew that he would have to sleep and that his body would not allow him to decide where and when. He passed out. His soldiers carefully carried him to his tent and laid him down on the cot that was always there, in the same place, for him to rest on. They left him with a single guard to watch the door to the tent. Josh and Erica were whisked away with Mouse in tow and they were taken to another tent. For a temporary encampment, this was a first class facility. Mouse stayed with his charges until they awoke. He had hoped that Josh would awaken first and then they could catch up on events before his sister woke up and looked at him. Mouse was intimidated by the queen for he found her more than a little attractive. He did not hold any false beliefs that he had a chance with the monarch, but he was wise enough not to deny his feelings. He had done what was expected of him, he had brought her back in time to save her life. His service had meant something. He was important now. Mouse was important. He rolled the thought over in his mind. If felt good.

Much to his dismay, it was Erica who actually recovered consciousness first. She moaned and her blue eyes popped open to see Mouse standing there anxiously looking over her. She looked upon him as a stranger at first, but then recognition hit her. "Mouse?" She asked and he nodded to her. "What? What are you doing here?" She asked. His smile was a little too large, but at this point he didn't care.

"I had to save you." He replied simply. "I heard the scuffle you were in with your friends. Then I heard you cry out and I had to act. I moved in quickly and defended you when you went down. I couldn't see what had gotten a hold of you, but I knew that it was bad. So I used the locator stone your brother gave me and we all transported to him." Mouse paused for a brief moment and Erica's eyes seemed to replay the whole scene as she remembered it. Then she looked at her savior again.

"So I owe you my life?" She asked.

Mouse shook his head. "It was my duty to save you; there is no debt between us." Mouse said and he truly meant it. Although he admitted to himself that if the queen owed him something, he would spend as long as it took trying to argue her out of it as long as they could be together while doing that arguing. The thought made him smile again. He seemed to be doing that a lot lately. Maybe it was the contrast to the city he had seen destroyed. Here there was still hope. He remembered back only a few years ago when hope was something in very short supply. He had helped these two find their way into the palace to retake their thrones. It was truly amazing that they managed to do it. Now they were counted on by so many people for everything. He wondered if they knew that when they fought for their positions. None of that broke through his smile though so Erica was unaware of his musings.

"Don't give me that. You know that I was dying. You did something that brought us all back. The whole hunting party came back didn't they?" She asked, her voice suddenly taking on a hint of fear. "We didn't leave anybody out there did we?" She added, trying to get Mouse to answer her.

"As far as I know, everybody came back. One of your men died from his injuries. I do not know which one but I will find out for you. Your poison was healed by the Captain." He told her and Erica's eyes opened wide.

"The Captain!? Why didn't Josh do it?" She asked.

Mouse held up his hand to forestall any further questions so that he could answer her first one. "Josh made an attempt but he was too weak to do the healing and it recoiled on him. I guess that's how it was; I don't know about such things myself." He admitted. "Anyway, the Captain stepped up and performed an elf-style healing on you. It was beautiful until I had to turn away." Mouse said and he blushed just a bit. He had actually called her beautiful indirectly. Of course in his mind she was truly beautiful, but he could never tell her that. "Uh, anyways, you were healed and the Captain fell over. I am told that he is resting comfortably in his tent now." Mouse concluded for her.

"What about Josh?" Erica asked.

"What about me?" Josh's voice startled both of them as Josh approached from behind Mouse. He was rubbing his neck and shoulder. Apparently it had hurt more there than elsewhere. "I feel like I've been hit by a truck." He said and Mouse looked sideways at him.

"I don't understand." He said when his action failed to prompt Josh to explain.

Josh waved his hand dismissively. "Never mind, it's an earth phrase," He said and Mouse nodded, still not really understanding. That other world these kids come from was still a great mystery.

Erica propped herself up on an elbow. "I suppose that you were involved with that rescue attempt too?" She asked.

Josh shook his head. "I was just as surprised as everybody else when your hunting party materialized in the middle of the camp." Josh admitted. He looked at their old friend. "It must have been all Mouse." He added and Mouse bowed.

"I do what I can. I am sorry that I couldn't do more for my mission though." He said with regret flavoring his voice.

Josh rubbed his temple. "Yes, I recall that you told the grand High Elf to take his people north to avoid being slaughtered by the hordes." Josh said and Mouse blushed again.

"Yes your majesty, I did do that." Mouse said timidly. "I was told to." He added.

Josh smiled at the young man. "By the wolf?" He asked and Mouse looked surprised. Josh chuckled. "You don't think that we can find out what is going on around our kingdom? The High Elf told me that you were being ordered around by the wolf. It was the reason that I advised him the same as you and he took his people north." Josh paused and Mouse was going to speak up but Josh cut him off. "Yes, they survived. I must admit that he was put out at first, but he has seen the wisdom and he is not angry with you at all. He said that your dedication and commitment are astounding." Josh said and Mouse turned away.

"That was only part of my mission." He stubbed a toe on the dirt floor. "I'm afraid that my mission to help you has failed." Mouse admitted through a veil of pain.

Both of the royals looked more closely at him. Erica spoke up first. "Just what were you doing to help us?" She asked and Josh nodded that he agreed with the question.

"I was to ready the people for your call to form an army." Mouse said sorrowfully. "But I only got a hold of three of the ten people I was supposed to before the enemy attacked. The world may fall into darkness and it is all because I failed." Mouse whined. The weight of the world was not something he was accustomed to carrying around. He was not handling it all that well.

Josh looked surprised. "An army? Who said I was going to build an army?" Josh cried. He never wanted to be responsible for so many people with their lives in danger. The idea of hiding and waiting it out seemed so much more favorable.

Mouse looked hurt, but not directly. "It was the wolf that said you would make the call for the people to recruit them for a royal army. I was to get the people thinking correctly and looking for potential soldiers to assist in speeding up that process." Mouse said and Erica put a hand on his shoulder.

"It is true that we have discussed recruiting, but we never told anybody about it. How would the wolf know in advance of our own decision?" She asked and Mouse shrugged his shoulders.

"I don't know. I only know that the wolf told me a lot of things and they all came true. My guess is that he can see the future."

Josh looked a bit puzzled. "If the wolf saw what we needed and then helped us to get it, then he would be altering the future that he saw. It must mean that a royal army will fail as it is currently set in the time-line." Josh said aloud, his thoughts were racing ahead of his speech so it didn't sound all that coherent to anybody else. With the ability to see alternate time-lines, he was uniquely suited to this train of thought. "It must mean that we should not form a royal army." He concluded. If it is going to fail anyway, we had better use our resources in a more meaningful way."

Mouse looked at him as if he had just turned into a scary monster. "You mean, you're not going to raise an army then?" He asked, the lack of credulity was evident in his tone. "But don't you have to do it? I mean, it's your future isn't it?" He asked, trying to wrap his head around the complex problem.

Josh smiled at him. "No, we are not bound to a particular path. We can, and sometimes do, alter the course of events as we see them." Josh replied. However, it is always risky. I would even consider it if

161

things weren't so grave right now. We have villages and cities lost across the world. Whole kingdoms are being wiped out and the enemy has only been stopped in a couple of places. Most of the time, they are simply avoided. This is a war that we are losing right now. We need to find another way to handle it or the human race will cease to exist here." He paused as the scope of the problem set in. "For that matter, the elder races will perish as well. This is as real as it gets. We are in a world of hurt right now." He looked around at the faces in the tent. "It's time for another miracle." He said and his look was not the mischievous one he usually had when those words were said. No, this time he looked glum. That meant one thing; he didn't know what to do about the situation yet. That wasn't good news for the good guys. Josh paced a bit and then he looked at Erica and Mouse. "I need to do some thinking, could you do me a favor and find something to eat.

It was some time before the camp was ready to move again. The wounded were tended to and the fallen man was buried and remembered. It was a somber day among somber days. The world was crying as well as the soldiers. Dark smoke could be seen on the horizon, the razing was continuing. The timing was perfect for the invaders. Whole fields of unharvested produce were being destroyed. Anyone that survived the initial fighting would probably starve during the long winter that was soon to come. The outlook was bleak to be sure. All the hopes of the remaining humanity were resting upon the shoulders of the True Bloods. Magic would have to lead the way to salvation or it wasn't going to happen. Hopefully, they would find the answers.

CHAPTER 9

The Dark Lord gained strength with each kill he savored. His body was whole again and his mind was still fractured into shards with hate. Even the draining of fatigue no longer bothered him as he tore into demons and humans alike. It had not taken him long to find the fighting. He had simply followed his nose. The smell of death was sweet and satisfying. He knew that smell and he longed for it. Village after village was being shown his wrath. If a demon or a clay construct got in his way, they were shredded along with the victims. He no longer cared about what he killed, only that he killed. Indiscriminately he slaughtered everything in his path. It was just as the plan had required. He was still following the evil master's battle plan. The General had seen fit to give his own interpretation of the orders, but not the Dark Lord. He had done exactly as ordered. He had done the work for his preparations and now he was killing and killing as was the plan. Nothing would survive. That was the directive, the complete destruction of all life on this world. He felt his heart pounding in his chest as he overturned a wooden cart and then raked the cowering miniature humans he found beneath it. The smell of their fear excited him and the smell of their deaths brought a feeling of euphoria to his aching brain. His rampage would go on tirelessly as long as he continued to smell that smell. It drove him on like a drug. Nothing he could see could be considered a threat, so he continued unabated into the maelstrom that he and his fellow citizens of the dark realms had conjured. It was bedlam, it was chaos, and it was glorious. The Dark Lord bellowed to the sky in rage as he bounded forward to find another victim. This day would never end. This day was perfect. This was the reason he had been sent to this realm. He was living through his destiny. Nothing could stop him now.

The General made his move and his clay troops were all but decimated. He had about a hundred of his demons left, and they would have to do. The pass and that mountainous wall was behind him now and the city wall stretched out before him. It was much smaller than the one they had just destroyed and it felt good to have such small obstacles left. The costs had been so high that he had considered turning back. He had lost most of his army and although they would all fight until slain, he doubted that they could still take the entire city. Of course they didn't need to hold it, only to destroy it and anyone living inside of it. However, with the drastically reduced manpower, it was still going to be a stretch on his resources. He ordered his demon troops forward. The siege engines could not traverse this kind of terrain so they had been effectively neutralized by this infernal wall that had magically sprung up between them and their prey. Now they could only hit the area in front of the wall, they could no longer reach the stone they needed to crush. It would have to be done the hard way. He had ladder units and they were well trained at their jobs. He had bombs of various sizes that could be hurled over the walls, or maybe slammed into wooden structures to rip them apart. He was ready to lay siege to this human settlement and wipe it off of the map once and for all. He could feel that the time was at hand.

On the other side of the wall, the humans braced for the attack that they had calculated defense strategies for. The Prince led his loyal troops and the True Bloods were doing their best to fortify all the points that were identified as possible weaknesses. Of course there was way too much to do and nobody knew how much time they had before the attack came. The fever of combat would erase all of these pre-battle jitters, but for now, they would have to simply deal with them. The sounds in the distance of the crumbling concrete wall were impressive. The enemy had finally breached the outer defenses. The impromptu dam had actually worked far better than mom had thought it would. The battle behind them had cost them valuable allies. Now they had to fight this one on human terms. Archers were in the towers and spear-men were at the gate. They had no cavalry to speak of, but the grim determination of ground troops was enough to give any enemy pause. At least they hoped it did. Boiling oil and hot tar were also available in vats suspended over key places on the walls. Everyone was in readiness for the final battle to begin. Armor was cleaned and swords were sharpened. The enemy would be coming; there were no illusions about that. They had lost too much and fought too hard to stop now. The only real question was did they have any extra surprises up their undead sleeves? It was one thing to battle what you know is there, it is quite another to prepare for that something yet unseen. That was the real concern with the upcoming engagement.

Dad looked down from one of the arrow slots. He had a good look at the remaining forces. He could not see the metal carts that had destroyed his defense of the pass. They were either deployed elsewhere or they were unable to deploy through the ruins of the mighty dam that Mom had put up. In either case, they were not a factor in this new battle. Maybe they would be later, but for now, they were not. It gave Dad a minor sigh of relief over that one. After all, they were the current equivalent of a tank. They were just as deadly as any tank he had seen in the movies. God only knows where they got the idea from. He had his bow out and the arrows were arranged in a fan on the stone deck next to him. He would be able to grab them in sequence quickly without taking his eyes off of the targets. He was not new to this sort of engagement and he knew what to do. He also knew that Mom was trying to come up with something clever in order to save all of their collective hides. He had utter faith in her, but he also knew that Murphy's Law was the only law that still upheld when the fighting started.

The Prince had been busy too. He had brought more troops around to his side. The fact that the king had fled and left them to cover his posterior probably had a lot to do with it. It was also the fact that the Prince seemed to be unyielding in his defense. He would not let the city fall. It was the sort of dedication that earned the loyalty of seasoned veterans. This was exactly the type of men he wanted to add to his fighting force. Now he had enough to line the wall top and even more to reinforce the gates. They would not hold forever, but they would hold for quite some time. If he could find a solution for when those defenses finally fell, he might yet become a hero in the eyes of his people. Unfortunately, he had not yet been able to come up with that miracle answer that was so desperately needed. How can he defend the city once the gates fall? He couldn't possibly move all of his people, the city did not offer enough exits to accommodate the population the city supported. He would look into that truth later if anyone survived this assault. He vowed to make the public safety a higher concern in his government. He was frustrated and anxious at the same time and he needed to calm down in order to think clearly. A level head might carry the day; a confused one definitely would not. He paced the walls as he thought through his contingencies. He rejected plan after plan. He had already gone over this ground a number of times and had come up empty. He needed something new to think on. His mind was stuck in the well-worn ruts of negativity. It was then that something changed. He couldn't put his finger on it right away, but he could feel different. Then it spoke to him.

"Hello scum." The deep voice said from his own lips. "Are you ready for this city to fall?" It asked him, again from his own mouth. "I am just outside and I am coming. Prepare yourself to meet your maker, your time on this world is about up." He said and he looked around for the source. But he was the one who had spoken. Panic began to take him unbidden. They had somehow gotten inside his head. Who should he talk to? What should he do? What could he do? The Prince was nearly in panic and there was nobody around that could advise him on this. Honestly, who would even believe him? He decided to try defiance.

"Get out of my head!" He screamed. The voice inside laughed at him.

"You pitiful fool; you couldn't keep me out if you had a hundred minds. I am much more powerful than any puny human. Prepare to die." He said in that same voice that was not his own. He felt his body moving. He headed straight for a window. He knew what the beast had in mind. He knew that it was a long way down. He knew that he was about to die and he was powerless to even stop himself. He watched with curious horror as his hand reached up and unclasped the window guard. He watched even as his first leg swung over the sill and dangled perilously beyond the safety of the building. Then his second leg swung out and he was sitting on the ledge. His own fate spread out before him. He could see the wall and the gates from here. It was a truly amazing view. He saw the enemy army beyond those gates and there seemed to be more of them than he could remember. He watched all of this in fascination even as his own life dangled from the thinnest of threads. The General laughed again and made him look down. He could clearly see the cobbles so far below. He knew that he wouldn't survive the fall. His mind was detached, almost clinical about the whole thing. His emotions could not engage. If they had, he might have been able to stop through and adrenaline surge. Of course he didn't even know what adrenaline was. He sat that way for several long seconds. Then he felt his hands on the cold stone sill and he pushed off. The first thing he could sense was that feeling of exhilaration as his body raced through the wind. The roaring in his ears was from that wind. The ground was closing in fast and he tried to close his eyes before the impact. The general wouldn't even allow him to do that. Just as he was about to hit a scream distracted him from the side and he looked out at the source. Oddly, he had time to do that. The confusion that resulted seemed to take him. He looked around some more. People were coming around to see him. He was not dead. He didn't even hurt. Had he hit the ground? No. He was hanging impossibly in the air just a couple of hands above the ground. His mind started to clear as the General screamed in rage. The enemy mind left his and everything snapped back into focus.

Mom stood there, holding her hand out in a catching gesture. The cushion of air that held the Prince was controlled through this gesture. Dad helped him off of the spell and set his feet back on the ground.

"You'd better be more careful around those windows your

majesty." Dad said, trying to make light of what had just happened. The Prince blinked twice and looked at him almost in shock.

"What? I didn't fall on accident." He said and Mom and Dad both looked at him with worry on their faces. "I was pushed from inside." He said. The two True Bloods escorted the prince back to his quarters. The enemy would soon make their final attack and they needed the Prince to be himself when that happened, so they took him for some counseling before the public saw what had happened to him. His credibility would be shot if they found out.

"Okay young man." Dad said, trying to take the upper hand before the conversation could get away from him. "Why don't you just tell us what you meant by that?" He queried and the Prince looked at him again. This time there was more of the Prince behind the stare. It was a good sign.

The Prince looked around the room. It was the room he had just left out the window. It looked the same as it had, but it wasn't the same. He was not the same. He had just come into close contact with death and had miraculously survived. The whole world looked different now. He saw the two True Bloods before him and suddenly realized who they were. His mouth fell open as his brain processed this information.

He finally got up the nerve to speak. "Aren't you supposed to be dead?" He asked and Dad shook his head. He turned back to Mom.

"It had to happen sooner or later." He told her and he returned his attention to the Prince. "You have been contacted by the enemy haven't you?" He asked directly. The Prince tried to look away; he was bathing in shame for his weakness. Dad grabbed him by the shoulders. "Snap out of it man!" He yelled and the Prince cowered from the unexpected ferocity.

"Y-yes, I was talking with somebody, er something. I dunno. It's kind of foggy now." He admitted. I remember it was inside of my head. It told me that I was going to die and then I found myself sitting in the window and pushing off. I – I couldn't stop him." The Prince sobbed.

Dad released the Prince's shoulders and pulled his head up to force eye contact. "You were not weak. You did nothing wrong."

He said in a monotone voice as if he were trying to program the Prince.

"But I was taken over. I was… I was weak enough for him to do that." The Prince whined. He looked like a lost five year old, only with the responsibility of an adult to contend with.

"Yes, you were. It's a good thing we were here or you would have been lost to this world." Dad said and Mom nodded her agreement when the Prince looked to her for a way out of this uncomfortable conversation. There was no relief there. "The important thing is, you did survive and evil lost that battle. You need to focus on keeping your people alive and busy. The enemy is literally at the gates. It is only a matter of time before they begin their final assault." Dad continued. "Your people need you to lead them to victory. They will fall of you do not get it together for them." He scolded.

The Prince looked around the room again. It was still that same room. He knew it to be true. The differences he saw were that of perspective. He was the leader of this kingdom. He was a king!" His father had run when the trouble started and had abandoned the throne and its responsibilities. He had assumed command then, and had taken the throne at the same time without even knowing it. The realization struck him even in this moment of potential tragedy.

"I am king." He said softly at first. Mom smiled big at him.

"Yes, honey, you are." She said in a soothing voice that somehow gave the confidence to say it again.

"I am the king." He repeated. Dad stepped back from the former prince. "Was father also approached by the evil presence that possessed me?" He asked. Both Dad and Mom shrugged their shoulders.

"We have no way of knowing that, your majesty." Dad finally replied. "In fact, all that we know just now is that the enemy is at the gates and it won't be all that long before they attempt to break through to us."

"They seem to have been reinforcing during the hiatus." Mom reported. "I don't know from where they got their new troops, but they have also re initiated a full complement of the clay constructs. They will come in as a full army once again." She announced.. It was not the best of news.

The new King paced back and forth a bit. His mind was working on the problem, but neither of the True bloods could read his thoughts, so they just continued to watch him. Finally, he seemed to reach a conclusion and he stopped and turned to the two waiting visitors.

"We cannot repel a fully reinforced invasion." He announced with the finality that represented his royal nature. Once he made a decision, it was made, there was no looking back. "We need to get my people to safety. What can we do?" He asked, hoping that they had some kind of plan for him. It was then that he noticed a third individual standing behind the two True Bloods. "Who are you?" He asked.

The man behind them seemed surprised that he was seen. He straightened his tunic and stepped forward to address the king. "I am the Guardian of Balance." He proclaimed. The King, King Cedric Reginald Baldric the second, looked at him confused.

"The balance of what?" He asked the newcomer.

"Why, the universe of course." The guardian replied. "I maintain the balance between worlds." He elaborated, but it seemed to be just to stoke his own ego.

The King looked at him and decided that he was a non-issue. "Well you've let this world get pretty far out of whack." He said sternly. Then he turned to the True Bloods. "Do you have anything that can help us in the here and now?" He asked, still holding onto hope with his last grip strength.

Mom knelt before him. "Your majesty, we can try to help the people get out of the city, but where do you want them to go? The enemy army has access to the only ways in or out of the city. There is no escaping this predicament by normal means." She concluded and hearing it said out loud rang it so true to the king that he almost buckled.

He looked like a frightened child now. "You mean we've lost?" He asked desperately hoping to be wrong. There was a tear welling up in his eye. "How could we have come to this? My father should have protected us." He cried. He knew that it was unfair, but somehow he didn't care. He turned to the Guardian of Balance. "What can you do to help us?" He asked directly.

The Guardian looked stunned at first. "I cannot interfere." He said, his voice shaking with the enormity of the question he had just been asked. "It is forbidden." He added, trying to assert his confidence into the mix.

The King stepped forward and grabbed the Guardian by the collar. "Forbidden by whom?" He asked in a dangerous tone that suggested he knew more than his years.

The Guardian stammered. "Well, by forces in the universe that you cannot understand." He said lamely. He felt his own confidence slipping away as this young prince held him in an iron grip. "I am powerless to help in these circumstances." He said, trying to get off of this uncomfortable hook. It wasn't going to be that easy.

"Under what circumstances *can* you help?" King Cedric asked, still holding the Guardian in a grip that could not be broken.

It was the second time that the Guardian had felt like he was in a trap. He really needed to stop working directly with people. "I am in charge of maintaining balance. I can only act directly when the balance is threatened." He said, hoping to have been cryptic enough to avoid any further queries. Of course that was only a vain hope without much chance of success.

King Cedric pulled the Guardian even closer, their noses were almost touching. "I will destroy all the balance you cherish if my people are not saved before that enemy can get in here to slaughter them." He promised in a tone that held granite in it. "I will start by killing you. Do you understand?" The Prince said and there was not a trace of humor in his tone or mannerisms.

"I – I don't know how much I can do." The Guardian said, beginning to cave in to the ferocious demands of this tyrannical new king. "I mean, I can't move the people, or the city. That is something only the True Bloods seem to be able to do." He muttered. Even as he said it, he realized that he had given away too much.

Mom spoke up. "Move the city? Who can do that?" She asked. The King flashed her a look and then concentrated on the Guardian.

"I believe the lady asked you a question." He prompted.

The Guardian tried not to answer, but the grip on his collar shifted enough so that his throat was now being constricted as well. He found that breathing was becoming more of a bother. "No, I can't tell you more." He muttered under his strained breath.

Mom stepped alongside and beamed at the Guardian. "It is your fault that we are here in the first place; holding out now will not save anybody. If you didn't want our help, why did you bring us here?" She said and her look was far more dangerous than that of the king that already held him by the throat.

The Guardian seemed to think about it for a few agonizingly long seconds. Then he seemed to slump. "Release me and I will tell you what I know." He said. Cedric released him and he slumped to the floor in a rather undignified manner.

Mom knelt down next to the fallen man. "Well, I'm waiting." She pressed.

The Guardian shook his head. "Okay, it was your son who did these things. He made a duplicate city and then moved his people to it." He said and Mom looked shocked. "It must have taken him weeks to build the mental image necessary to form the entire city. It was perfect, I know, because he had placed me inside of it to prove that it could be done." The Guardian said. The indignity that this family had caused him just never seemed to end. Then he shifted. "He really is quite gifted you know." He said and Mom nodded.

"Yes, he is most resourceful." She paused and then brought the conversation back under her control. "You said he moved a city as well?" She pushed and the Guardian nodded.

"Yes, it was the most amazing thing that I have ever witnessed. After saving their own people your children went to help other kingdoms. They reached a fellow True Bloods kingdom unaware of his potential. Josh spent merely twenty minutes of acute study and moved the entire city, people and all, to somewhere else on this world. The enemy rolled in to find no buildings except the one that Josh was in. It would have been the end for him if the local militia hadn't spirited him away before the enemy destroyed that last building out of rage and frustration." He said and Mom sat back.

"I've never heard of magic that powerful." She said at last. She looked over at Dad. "Do you really think it's possible?" She asked and Dad shrugged his shoulders.

"Honey, I never know what miracle you are about to pull out of your hat. You also know that Josh has an even more structured mind than either of us. If anyone has the power to do these things, it would be him." He said with certainty. Then he turned to the king. "But knowing this, how does it help us?" He asked plainly.

Mom laughed. "Leave it to a fighter to think clearly about matters of power." She looked back at the guardian. "So, how does that help us? Why were you hesitant to tell us about Josh?" She asked and she was ready to do something nasty if she didn't like his response. Somehow she conveyed that readiness with a simple look. The Guardian shivered involuntarily.

"I think that working together you may be able to arrange the same feat. You have the same abilities as your children. It may not be that focused, but it is still there. I can sense it." He said almost wishing that he hadn't. "Furthermore, if this city falls and we're still in it, then we will be slain as well." He pointed out.

Mom shrugged that off. "Oh, I don't think you would risk your high and mighty posterior so easily." She laughed at the Guardian's raised eyebrows. "You have a way out at all times. You always have had one. You are no more nervous about being caught here than you were when were out in the woods. You can't fool me with that trap." She told him and he acknowledged the tip of the hat she had given him.

"Alright, you got me on that one. I can transport the three of us at any time." He admitted. "I brought you two here and you belong on the other side so it would be a matter of balance to take you away. I belong in the middle ground area between worlds in my lab so travel there would not break any rules either." He said.

Dad brightened at that last sentence. "So, you have an area that is outside of the normal balance of the two worlds?" He asked carefully.

The Guardian looked suspicious. "Yes." He replied intrepidly.

"Then can't you move the people to this temporary staging area until the threat has been immobilized? We can bring them all back once the problem has been dealt with." He suggested.

The Guardian shook his head violently. "That's out of the question!" He responded vehemently. "If I were to take so many people away from this world, the void here would cause incalculable risks to the balance of this world." He said and he set his jaw with a stubborn streak that was most commendable.

Mom seemed to catch the line of questioning and her mind was sharper than Dad's. "Yes, but it would not jeopardize the other world, or even your area of limbo where you reside." She stated, firmly backing Dad's idea. Then she took it to the next level. "Is there something there in your lab that could replace the mass of the people and thus maintain the balance and still save all those lives?" She asked and for a moment, the Guardian looked not to be listening at all. He had chosen this moment for his defiance and he was planning to stick to it. However, the idea held quite a bit of merit and he forced himself to reconsider.

"Well, I do have a few trinkets that I have collected over the millennia." He said at last, the tone was thoughtful, not defiant.

The King picked the Guardian up off of the floor. "Please, you must help me save my people. What kind of a king would I be if I let them die without expending everything at my disposal?" He asked. It was a solid and valid point. The Guardian looked none too happy about it either, but it just made so much sense.

Mom was still tied up in the logistics of the problem. "How much mass can you displace?" She asked and the guardian waved his hand dismissively.

"Please, let me be a moment. Preparations must be made and I have a lot to do." He said. "I thought your children were difficult to deal with but now I know where they get it from." He said with a "Humph."

Dad sensed that the victory was at hand and he was ready to grasp it and continue this campaign. "Okay, so if he takes care of the people, what do we do to stop this army?" He asked and both Cedric and Mom looked at him. In the argument to save the citizens, the idea of actually fighting this war seemed to have gotten lost. They stared at each other and they all realized that they had no plan. They had no ideas on how to defeat an army that could simply cast more soldiers and reinforce in such a short time. They would be relentless. That is, unless you took out the spell casters. With no more clay constructs, the army would be whittled down and eventually could be defeated. The real question was, how did you get through all of those constructs to strike at casters so far to the rear? So far, the only access they had was through the front and rear gates. That meant that whichever way they went it was into the teeth of the enemy front line. That just didn't seem so smart. If they held back some of the militia, and just sent away the civilian population, it would give them some support. But arrows did not hurt clay constructs. Swords could slash bits of them off but they kept attacking until destroyed. Hammers and maces did the best damage. However, they only had a limited supply of them and not nearly as much manpower as they needed to mount an effective front of their own. They had to rely on choke points to limit the number of enemy engaged at once. It was a bottleneck that served them and trapped them inside at the same time. That was not unlike the castle walls themselves. They were wonderful defensive fortifications, but you could not get out past them either it was a barrier from both sides of that same wall. They needed something different, something to tip the scales in their favor, and by a large degree. That was the problem that faced them as they sat or paced and thought.

All of this heavy thought was interrupted by a throat clearing. Everyone turned to the source. Standing there, looking all smug, the Guardian of Balance addressed them formally. "I am ready to complete the evacuation of the civilians as required of me. Do not be alarmed by strange objects appearing at random throughout the city, it is merely part of the displacement. I bid you farewell and good luck in your struggles." He said and in a flash, he vanished. Across the city, all of the civilian population vanished at exactly the same instant. Weird and curious objects were scattered about for that aforementioned displacement. The Guardian of Balance was apparently out of the equation now. He had done his bit and now it was left to King Cedric, Mom and Dad.

Mom stepped over to the window. It was the same window that Cedric had thrown himself out of and the king backed away from the window as the memory stung him anew. If not for these strangers, he would have perished. He held no doubts or misconceptions about that. They had saved his life. Mom looked out the window and started memorizing everything. She needed the troop locations, she needed tower locations. The archers could be posted where? The hills were arranged how outside the wall. She was seeing each and every detail. Her eyes didn't even blink for a long time. When she stepped away from the window, she was rubbing her eyes. She stepped into the middle of the room and stopped. The middle of this particular room was open with a large area rug in the center. The rug had intricate patterns woven throughout and the royal seal was the centerpiece. All of that detail was lost to Mom as she concentrated on the image in her mind. She saw a large wooden table and the city walls and outskirts as she had just seen them through the window. She held the image and focused it until it was solid. She reached out and touched the magic and wove it into the mental construct. Then she heard a gasp as she let the magic flow into and through her. In front of Mom was now a large oaken table with a three dimensional map of the city walls and surrounding area painstakingly recreated on it. The camps and troops were clearly visible and even the trees and grassy areas were displayed. The map was perfect. At least it was so good that the casual eye could not see the differences. The gasp had come from Cedric. Mom looked over at him and he nodded to her as a small form of apology. Dad let all of that parlay go unnoticed. He was already concentrating on the map before him.

"Good job honey." He said almost absently as his eyes probed the map looking for any weakness in the enemy formation. They seemed to have covered almost every square inch around the main city walls. This was still going to be a hard nut to crack, but they were obviously prepared with a large enough hammer to eventually do the job. The simple overpowering odds definitely put the edge squarely on the enemy. However, they did not have what the city defenders had, two people from another century, even another world. Dad had taken a handful of toothpicks from his pocket and placed them into the dirt on the model in various places. Mom just watched, not yet able to follow just where he was going with this. He was a brilliant tactician; she had to give him the credit where that was concerned. She was more of a spontaneous powerhouse that overpowered obstacles as they came. The two complemented each other well. Dad was moving around the map now, checking it from different angles. He seemed to reach the conclusion that he was satisfied and he stepped back to check one more time. Much to their credit, the other two waited for the explanation.

When it didn't come quite quickly enough, they both looked

stern at Dad. He noticed it and held up his hands in surrender. "All right, this is what I have figured out." He said and they relented, for now. "First of all, we need to eliminate the clay golems out there." He said and Mom nodded her agreement. They are made from clay and clay is hard to kill. So what we need to do is to make them a bit easier to destroy. The easiest way to soften up clay is to add water and turn it into mud." He said and Mom's eyes brightened. Her amazingly fast eyes swept the map and noted each of the toothpick locations. It was an amazing display of her abilities to assimilate data. Dad watched her for the briefest of moments, understanding exactly what she was doing. When her eyes returned to him, he continued. "I need a fire hydrant at each of these locations with a giant sized lawn watering appliance on each one." He said and Mom nodded again. The king was obviously lost, but he was content for now to let the wizard do all of the understanding.

Dad moved to the far side of the map. "Once the golems are mud, instead of clay, we need a waterfall to help wash them down this way." He indicated that they would travel down the main hill and towards the opening to the sea. "Once they are in the sea, they will dissolve and become a non-threat." He said triumphantly. "Then we need to focus on the demons that are controlling those golems." He said next. "They will be easier to kill than the clay monstrosities, but only by a small amount. Our archers can actually kill them with arrows. I suggest that we do a lot of that first, maybe we can augment the arrows with something to make them more effective. There are a lot of bad guys out there after all." He said with a grin that had less humor than it might have in other circumstances. Everyone at the table knew how dire the situation really was. Then Dad moved to the corner of the table that held the most dangerous part of the enemy forces. "Finally, we have the commander. I don't even know what he is but he is large and definitely in charge of those troops out there. He seems to hang back by the siege vehicles most of the time. For this group let's just call them what they are, tanks." He said and whatever trace of humor he had before was gone now. "They are by far the worst threat that the enemy can pose just now. Each of them seems to have the power to breech the walls. If they could have gotten them closer by now they would already be inside the city. We need to do something to keep them out of action. If the enemy can bring them up to support the rest of the troops, then we have lost." He said grimly. Then he looked up from the map that he had been studying and made eye contact with the other two in turn. "So, are there any suggestions?" He prompted with an almost child-like enthusiasm which was probably forced.

Mom looked at everything. Her mind had been ticking off points as he laid out his battle plan. She knew things that were not displayed. She hadn't held them back, it was just that she hadn't seen them directly and so could not picture them in her mind. She stepped forward. "I like what you have here." She began, trying not to crush her husband's ego. "The part about washing away the golems particularly sounds good to me." She added, further bolstering him before the shoe dropped. "However, I don't see how we can get to the tanks before they could fire. There is a wall there I am told and a crack unit of specialists that operate those monsters. We would have to eliminate almost all of them in order to have a chance at destroying the tanks themselves. The commander, whatever he is, would never let us get that close to them anyway." She said playing devil's advocate. She made a motion like tossing a crumpled piece of paper over her shoulder. "So let's focus on the parts of the plan that we *can* do something about." She said and all three of them leaned forward on the table as she laid out her specific idea concerning the plan as outlined. By the time she was done talking, there were no questions among the viewers. Her attention to detail and her thoroughness had once again won her the respect of others around her. She smiled sweetly at them as their minds tried to wrap around all that she had told them. She had even advanced the map to show them what would happen if this was used, or how long the gates would hold if this plan was used. It was amazing just how much could be extrapolated from the map as they had it before them. It was like watching a 3D movie on a table in front of you. If things hadn't been so desperate now, they might even have enjoyed the show. When all the scenarios were played out, they all agreed on which one they would use and then they split off to prepare their parts for its execution. With that solid plan in their minds, they left to defend the almost empty city from the dark horde of beings bent on annihilation. It was the final hour.

This was their big show. They had one chance to make this whole thing work. It was with that thought in mind that nothing was left to chance. As exhausting as the preparations were, none of them would have skipped a step. This was for all the marbles. The guardian would not even return to save them if this failed. It was all or nothing in the highest stakes game they had ever played. Once all of the preparation was done, all they could do was wait for the designated time. It was going to be a long next few hours.

The Dark Lord continued his own personal quest for vengeance. He had bloodied himself with his enemies so long that it was now one long adrenaline rush of rage and euphoria. His claws were sore and he ached all over. It was the price he paid for this power. He had killed humans and he had killed demons and he now stood upon a hill overlooking the destruction he had caused. There were bodies everywhere. The smoldering ruins that were once a thriving settlement brought pride to his stance. These humans would all perish by his hand. Then he would chase down the elder races and make them pay as well. Then, only then, would he kill the General for the disgrace that one had visited upon him. He panted as he stood there. His breath was short and labored. It would return soon enough and he would be on the move, looking for his next victim. Then the blood rage would be free again. He looked forward to that moment.

Josh had felt out of place among the militia before. They were not used to having a spell caster close by. That is, they didn't know that they had one close by. Now that their Captain had been revealed to them as a caster of some merit, their attitudes were shifting somewhat. Josh felt a warmer comradeship with these men and his own strength was returning more rapidly. He could sense the people in the other realm. They were asking questions. "Where have our leaders gone? How can we feed our children? How long must we stay here?" It was disturbing, and he longed to go and take care of them all. He would just as soon as he felt ready. He was careful not to try too soon. It was like charging a car battery, if you tried too soon, you would lose all of the charge that you had earned and would have to wait for it to start all over again. He didn't want that to happen. He needed to get there as soon as possible. In addition, there were more of the enemy troops here. He doubted that any had found the lake community yet, but it was only a matter of time. He needed to get there as well. The party had traveled for a couple of days and was getting closer, but they still had a lot of country to cover to get there by normal means. Josh had hoped to feel well enough to speed that process along. If he could at least put these soldiers with their people, then they could defend it if it was indeed located by the seemingly endless supply of demons that the enemy had to deploy.

On the bright side, he had watched as Erica came into her own. She was popular like she had been at home, but now she was able to hunt and exercise every day. She was strong now and her new strength and confidence made her attractive to more than one of the militia they were traveling with. Of course Josh frowned upon her fraternizing with them, but he did not voice that opinion. She was still a queen after all, they needed to show her at least that much respect. The fact that she was able to hunt and kill with such ease and grace only endeared her to them even more. Josh wished for his strength to return so that he could send these men on to their destination. So there was more than one reason for his wishes, that wasn't all bad was it?

The other thing that Josh had noticed was that he had not heard from any of his smaller friends lately. The sprites either could not find him, or more likely were afraid to reach him in the company of so many men at arms. Truthfully, he couldn't blame them for their caution. After all they had existed for far longer than humans because of their cautious nature. He wondered if they had existed at one time back home on Earth and had simply blinked out of existence as far as people were concerned. He sighed as he realized that he may never know about that. That world was now off limits to him. The delicate balance of the universe had been sorely tested. The stability was gone and he knew that travel back and forth would be not only a bad idea, but could very well destroy both worlds. It was a chance that he dared not take. He would die here rather than risk that much.

The group stopped again. It was one of the things that seemed to stick in Josh's craw was that they stopped all the time for this problem, or that break. It was amazing that any fighting force moved anywhere with these constant difficulties. At least he was no longer being carted around on all of this uneven ground. His foot strength had returned almost right away. He could walk all day without these breaks and he knew that he could have covered more ground than they had covered. It was just that if he did, could he do it while looking for enemy ambush at the same time. They had scouts out in front of the main group and support for those scouts could reach them quickly if they were jumped. Safety was not a luxury now and none of them took it for granted. The Captain had done nothing more with magic except to make his tent each night when they stopped for sleep. He was still something of a mystery to Josh. Who were his parents? Was there a connection between families? Does he know something more that Josh could learn?" They were all good questions. Of course he had not been 'summoned' to speak with the Captain for a few days now. He was beginning to wonder if he had been forgotten in the grand scheme of logistics that seemed to permeate every aspect of command. The regular routine was neatly falling into place and the camp was setup for the midday meal. The meat had already been cured and now it would be roasted over an open fire. They even had some flatbread that was made from locally harvested plant grains. Josh wondered if they even knew what a sandwich was. He would show them today. He looked forward to that.

A sound from beside him shook him from his thoughts. Josh turned to the new voice.

"Sir, if you'll follow me please. The Captain would like to speak with you." The soldier said. The summons was probably protocol, but it somehow seemed cold and distant. It seemed pretty bad from a man that Josh recognized and had walked with for days now.

"Of course" Josh replied and the two of them left for the now familiar tent that was recreated each time they stopped. The flap was slung open and they entered without any stopping at the entrance. The Captain was inside and he looked disturbed.

"I hope you are feeling strong today my friend." The Captain said and the hairs on Josh's neck stood on end. Something in his tone had sent chills. "We have a new problem." He continued as if Josh had prompted him with his very reaction; perhaps he had. "The scouts have reported a major force between us and the river." He added and Josh felt a small sigh of relief. At least this wasn't about his missing people. This was something they could tackle here and now together.

"What did you have in mind?" Josh asked, this time actually prompting the Captain to continue.

"Well, we'll need a diversion or maybe something better." He said cryptically. Then he pointed at the map on the table between them. It was always there, but it showed the area around the tent each day. It allowed him to plan the day's route accordingly. "This here is the main force." He said pointing at a large red splotch on the map." He then pointed out six smaller dots that were arranged in a semi-circle around the main force. "These are the guard posts."

Josh looked at the map. "I understand that we have a lot of monsters in the way, but can we go around them?" He asked. The Captain smiled.

"I was hoping you'd ask that question." He said and Erica, who had been standing in the background, snorted. Josh flashed an angry glance her way, and then turned back to the Captain. "What I propose is that we transport our meager troops to here." He said, pointing at a place on the map a good mile beyond the enemy encampment. "If we do this, then they will never even know that we went by them. It would maintain our element of stealth and surprise." He said, feeling rather smug about it.

Josh looked skeptical. "If I could transport our people, we'd already be at the city by the lake." He replied feeling a bit put out. The Captain shook his head.

"I understand that. The difference here is that I can help you with this transport. I have been on the other side of the river and I know what it looks like. Together, we can muster enough energy to accomplish this task." He said, a look of hope was on his face. He needed Josh on board with this plan.

Josh looked carefully into the captain's eyes. "Do you mean that we can link our powers to get this done?" He asked and the Captain seemed to think for a moment.

"Well, not exactly." He answered after that moment drew out a bit too long. "What I can do is transport our supplies and carts while you transport our people." He said, his triumphant face returning with that revelation.

Josh stopped for a second. "You cannot transport people?" He asked. "Why not?" He added, trying to see just what the Captain could do.

It was obviously something the Captain was not happy about. "No, I have been forbidden to transport people using my abilities." He said scornfully. "If I hadn't been, I could have helped you with the saving of the city." He said and his voice was hoarse, almost harsh. "I have been restricted since birth on things that I can and cannot do with my powers." He explained.

Josh blinked. "Who can do that?" He asked flatly.

The Captain did not make eye contact this time. "My father" He replied. He said father like it was a curse word. "We True Bloods are not all treated equal. Sometimes we get the short end of the stick and we muddle through as best we can." He said, hoping that explained everything.

Josh picked up on a particular thread and his mind was following it until he hit the next snag in the logic. "Then your father is still alive?" He asked and the Captain looked down at the desk and would not make eye contact.

"I do not know. I haven't seen or spoken with him for years." He admitted. "I was banished from our home when I asked why I couldn't be more than what I am. Why I couldn't do more than they were allowing me to do. My brothers and sisters were allowed to expand their influence all the time, and I was held back." He said. The memory was obviously causing him pain. "Can we leave it at that?" He asked and there was real hope in that question.

Josh felt the urge to ask further questions, but he also felt the pain he was causing, even if he was not the cause. "Sure, we can move on to the task at hand." Josh offered and the Captain nodded his thanks for the welcomed change. They both looked at the map and Josh looked up at the Captain again. "Can you transport only yourself?" The Captain looked unhappy first, as if they were heading back to the sore subject. Then he thought about it some more; then he became wary.

"Yes." He replied a bit timidly. "What are you thinking?" He asked, not sure he really wanted the answer. Josh smiled at him and Erica chuckled. The captain looked at her. "Do you know what he has in mind?" He asked her.

Erica shook her head. "No, but I know that look; he's definitely up to something." She told him with a smile that had just a hint of mischievousness in it. "I'd just go with it if I were you." She suggested and the Captain turned back to Josh.

Josh took the cue and brought his warm smile to the game. "I think we can do what you say, but not directly. We have a lot of material to move and you can do that I am assuming." He paused for the nod that the Captain gave him in acceptance. "Good. Then what we really need is to get you to see where we need to go." Josh said.

The Captain interrupted. "I told you that I have an image of the other side of the river." he said in an exasperated tone.

Josh smiled more evilly this time. "Yes you did, but that is not our destination." Josh replied and the Captain's eyes went wide. Josh pushed forward before he could protest. "I want you to survey the area where you arrive and prepare to transport all of the equipment to it. You can bring yourself back here once you have the image." He said and the Captain stood up quickly.

"Now just wait a damn minute!" He screamed. "Just where do intend to send me?" He asked indignantly.

Josh waved good bye and in seconds, the Captain found himself standing in an open patch of grass surrounded by trees on all sides. There were two paths leading into the woods in opposite directions. The patch was actually large enough to hold all of their belongings. The lack of fine details made this place easy to use as a target. The Captain felt a bit more respect for the young sorcerer. He immediately got to work memorizing the clearing. He had to get every minute detail. He spent a good two hours checking and rechecking his mental image to the real thing. When he felt he had it, he put that image away and then started working on his tent image. This time he wasn't going to create the tent, he was returning to it. Again, that youngster really knew how to make this easy. He already had this image so it would take no extra time for him to assimilate. In moments, he was standing back behind his desk where he had been. Josh was handing him a tankard.

"Here, take this, you will be a bit drained after that work-out. We will need to move fast to get this done before detection by that enemy force." He said in an all-business tone that suggested his abilities exceeded his age.

The Captain nodded and drank heavily from the tankard. He had thought that it would be ale, but he was wrong. His first instinct was to spit the vile liquid out, but a hand on his shoulder told him not to. Erica had a firm grip and a stern look.

"Drink it all, it will help you regain your strength for the transport." Josh said as he drank his own tankard. When the two men finished and set the tankards down, they both grimaced at the after taste.

"What was that?" The Captain asked, wiping his mouth and wishing he could spit.

Josh smiled, although weakly at this point. "It's a local concoction for building up your personal strength. I don't know what's in it. It is probably better that I don't, I need the strength." He said.

The Captain sat down at his desk. "So, just where did you send me?" He asked.

Josh looked concerned. "You've got the mental image right?" Josh asked seriously.

"Yes, it was an easy one to produce. You chose well, but where is it?" He asked again.

Josh relaxed a bit with the relief. "It's right around the corner from the lake and your people. I figured if we had to use magic anyway, then we should go all the way and get you home." He said with pride.

The Captain scratched his head. "You mean I could have seen my people and you let me come back here?" He asked. Then he thought some more. "Why didn't you send me directly to them?" He asked, feeling a bit put out.

"It was a much easier image I sent you to. You could have spent days trying to build the image where your city is. This way you were back in a couple of hours. We can move on to it sooner and a short

185

walk won't bother anyone in your troop. Not only that but your magic is somewhat of a secret among your people is it not?" He asked and the Captain nodded. "This way you can enter on foot and no one will be the wiser." Josh concluded and the Captain had to admit that it seemed sound enough. Then the real test came. "You need to start sending equipment over now. I don't know how long we can keep avoiding the patrols." Josh said; a sense of urgency was readily apparent in his voice.

"Patrols?!" You mean we have almost been discovered already?" He asked, his voice trailing up with the stress.

"Of course, you stopped us right next to the largest camp we have seen. There's an entire army out there and they patrol regularly around the area as part of their own security sweep. That's why we needed the tankards so that we can act immediately. The clock is ticking and nobody knows how long we've got." Josh said, trying to urge the Captain to get down to business.

"Wait, if we're that close, why didn't you just back the camp away from the enemy?" He asked, obviously not happy with the current situation.

"If I had then you would not have been able to come back. The tent would have disappeared, or been moved and you would not have found it. You know that it wouldn't work if I had moved it. Now let's begin the transfer." Josh said and he immediately went into that trance-like state where he was building the mental image he needed to perform this complex magic. His razor sharp mind pulled the people's faces to him and he grouped them like a class photo. He kept remembering and putting more and more faces into the shot until he had everybody. Then he placed a few other items in the shot as well, including the tent that they were currently standing in. Then he braced himself for the transfer even as he poured the magic on rapidly. The image solidified and grew in color and clarity. He continued to see the tiniest details and eventually, the group of people was standing before them just as he had pictured them. They were all standing in that clearing, off to the side of where the materials were just starting to appear. Josh watched as the cart that had caused him so much pain materialized in front of the crowd. When the last of it appeared, a cheer rose up and then the Captain himself appeared next to Josh and Erica. They had been successfully transferred.

Josh pointed out the path to the west. "That way lays your city as it appears now. You folks go on and see it. I'm sure your loved ones are waiting for you there." He said and the crowd began to file out of the clearing and into the woods.

The Captain clasped arms with Josh. "I definitely owe you a debt my friend." Then he, too, headed off in the indicated direction. Their long trek was over in just a few more steps. Erica swung by Josh. They had a place to go too. She hoped that he was up to it.

"So, can you take us to our people now?" Erica asked almost gingerly. Josh looked at her with a smug look. Erica held up a hand. "So just do it then." She commanded. After all, she was still the queen. The two of them disappeared from the clearing, not noticing the dark figure in the tree line watching them. The Dark Lord had traveled a long way to track the young sorcerer who had bested him. Now he had a magic trail to follow him to his hide-out. Things were going well for the dark one; he would have his revenge and still gain the admiration of the Master. Oh yes, his claws would bathe in blood again and he would have his revenge. Things were going quite well indeed.

In a flash Josh and Erica were standing on the cobblestone streets of the replica of their beloved city. It took a few moments for people to notice that their rulers had returned. When they did they started shouting to each other and flocking to the main square. The two True Bloods waited for the crowd to assemble before addressing them.

Josh stood up before the crowd; Erica stood back a few steps and awaited her introduction. "Good people, I bring you your queen fresh from fights in our home lands." He said and the crowd cheered. "Please be orderly as she has a few things to say and none of them will be easy." He warned and the cheering quieted down substantially. "So now I give you, your queen." He said and he waved at her with his outstretched arm and the crowd cheered again. Although he had just warned them, they were simply so happy to see her returned alive and well.

Erica stepped forward and Josh retreated. She held up her hands for quiet and the crowd humbly responded to her request. "I know that you have been worried." She said at first. "I know that news from the outside world has been non-existent." She added and there were nods scattered through the crowd. "I am here to tell you what has happened and what will happen to the best of my ability." She said and the sound of scuffling and uneasiness were evident in the crowd. Erica braced herself for the worst of it. She took a deep breath and made sure that she didn't put on a nervous smile. This was a serious announcement.

"Our city has fallen." The words were simple and powerful and they crushed the hopes of many that were assembled here. The buildings have been leveled and razed, the walls have been crumbled and the gates have been burned. Then, the whole area was scooped up off of the world in a fiery rage. Nothing but a large hole is left where we once lived." She explained and the crowd showed varying degrees of shock. "That is the bad news." She said almost unnecessarily. "The good news is that we still have you. We still have each other. Our city was not about buildings, it was about the people that lived in them. We have all survived the worst destructive force that anybody has ever heard of. We have lived to tell the tale. Believe me, this tale will be told. Everyone is important and we have a lot of work to do." Erica paused for all of that to sink in. "However, we still have a problem with the enemy threat." She told them and they sobered a bit more. "Yes, the army that attacked our city has been defeated to the last demon, but this war was not just against us. Other kingdoms have not been so lucky. Standing armies exist all across the world. We will have to defend ourselves against this ever-present threat. Running and hiding as we have done in this emergency will not help us in the long run. We need decisive action that will assure a victory for us and all of our kind." She heard the crowd erupt again as her words of motivation struck home. "It is in this thought that we have come to a difficult decision." Erica said and the roller coaster ride of emotions around her turned back downhill again. "We need to form a royal army." She said plainly. There were mutterings around the crowd. Some were of disbelief, and some were of rejection. This would be a hostile crowd. It had been a given that True Bloods did not have armies to prevent them from becoming too powerful. This was in direct violation of one of their oldest laws. The grumbling started to get louder and Erica held up her hands to forestall the objection she was sure was coming.

"I understand how you feel. I understand even more than you think I do." She added and it did nothing to ease the crowd. "What you are worried about I also worry about. I do not want to become some ruthless dictator with my own private army. That would be moving backwards, not forwards. What I propose is that the army be run by a general that is elected by the public." She paused to see if they were keeping up. Most of them were, but a worrisome number were already tuned out. "If you have representation in the army, then I or Josh, or any True Blood cannot exercise total power over you." She said and some heads turned at the direct and succinct way in which she had worded that. "We need to get started right away on this election and the training that will follow. Our need for defense is of paramount import at this time. I would like to hear suggestions on who should be our general." She said, opening the floor to the crowd to voice their opinions, in an orderly manner of course.

One of the citizens stepped forward. "I would like to try out for this general position of yours." He said boldly.

Erica shook his hand. "Great, now turn and tell the people why you should be the leader of our army." She prompted and he turned around and froze. The crowd before him was larger than he had ever spoken to before and the fear grabbed a hold of him in a death grip. He found himself unable to speak. Erica felt sorry for him, but he needed to be able to address people in order to issue orders. He needed to be able to keep a clear head as well. She tugged on his shoulder. "If you're not ready yet, you can step down and think about it for a bit. I'll call you back up here later." She offered and he smiled thinly and stepped down, a bit dejected.

The crowd was starting to laugh at the hapless volunteer but Erica silenced it with a stern look. She stepped forward once again. "I understand that change is a difficult thing to accept. Sure by now we have demonstrated that we look for changes that are good and beneficial to everyone, not just to the palace. Anyone who has an idea can feel free to express it. There is no shame in being told it won't work. If it will work, it may well be something that we have not thought of. Honestly, we don't know everything. Josh and I look forward to your input." Then she turned the attention back to the army they needed to raise. "Now, we need recruitment. The army will need to be formed even as we search for a general to lead it. I need volunteers to step forward and claim their right to fight for their kingdom. People who volunteer will receive training, armor and weapons, and compensation for their time. There will also be death benefits for the families of fallen heroes." She said and the last sentence brought it all home for the citizens. There was a real possibility of death while serving in an army. There were no delusions about that reality. However, if one's family were taken care of in their absence, it alleviated much of that burden for the prospective soldier.

It started as a slow trickle. One young man and then another volunteered. Soon, they were herding the recruits to the temporary palace where the barracks were set up. The outfitting and training would begin in earnest. It was a scenario where nobody knew how long they had to make ready, they only knew that it was not nearly long enough. The crowd dispersed with mixed emotions over this new change.

Josh was working feverishly on his mental image. It was the same one that he had used to create this city in this limbo realm. Now he was tasking himself with the image to restore as much of the real location as he could remember. He had added the landscape around the city as well. The fields and the farmhouses were there now and the roads leading into and out of the city. All of these things had been destroyed in the real world. They all needed rebuilding. He kept going and going. Hours he spent examining each facet of the image. He was wearing himself out again, but he knew that it was important. He would pull in as much magic as he needed for this one. Permanence is the key and whatever will not be recreated must be rebuilt by hand. Josh could feel that this would be his last major casting. The price was aging him prematurely. It was taking longer and longer to recover from each attempt. His body was strong, but his will was starting to ebb. The channels he needed to pull in the magic were worn and frayed. However, his stubbornness was still intact. He will get this done. The time for doubts was long past. The people needed him again. He thought about doing it in phases, taking pieces of the city back and then resting between. They just didn't have the luxury of that extra time. They needed the army and the city to defend back where it belonged. If Mouse was correct, then they would also have recruits from neighboring provinces. The logistics involved would be nightmarish, but he would manage them. There was still so much to do. He sat in concentration, his eyes closed to his surroundings and opened to his image. He had cleaned the city up as part of the rebuild, so that the other city-states could believe that it had been rebuilt. The crater that was currently there actually provided him with some added incentive. If any of the others saw it, the land could be disturbed enough to wonder how it had happened. It would be like introducing the atom bomb during the Roman Empire. Sure whoever got it would become powerful, but the rest of the world would suffer from it. This was not the legacy that Josh wanted to leave behind.

Josh wanted to be remembered for his kindness and power. His organization skills and sharp mind were already almost legend. He just needed to dot the i's and cross the t's in order to solidify his position in history. It was funny how he had never even considered such a thing before they came here. He was content to be the shunned kid at school. There were times when he wished he were back there, even now. Even with how much he and his sister had accomplished, he was still an outsider in this world. He had been raised back home with his parents, the former king and queen he reminded himself bitterly.

He pulled himself back to task and he found that the image was taking shape better than he had hoped. He smiled all too briefly and then he went back to it. It would not be long now and he would be ready to take his people home. He knew that they were counting on him to do it before anyone got hurt, or worse. Their food supply was running thin and the water was already gone. He needed to go as fast as possible without missing a thing. Everything had to be perfect. It was how he thought and it was how he worked. There were no points

191

for almost, and there were no cheers for second best. It would not be long now...

Mom had made all of her preparations and was just sitting down again when they all heard the crash. The enemy had come in full force. The main wall had a hole in it the size of three tanks. The clay constructs were pouring through the opening. They swept in trying to find people to kill. Mom drew upon her magic and the fire hydrants formed in the pre-selected locations and gushed huge streams of water into the clay golems. The initial reaction was to simply ignore the inconvenient ploy. However, with each second the clay construct were being doused, they were losing more material down the slope and out towards the sea. Dad was positioned with the archers and they began to pick off the casters. Most of them were still well out of range, but the ones controlling the leading force had to be in range in order to do their jobs. As the demon troops started to go down, more of the clay golems stopped their actions and just stood t here like lumps of dirt. The water continued to wash them away. Mom finished her spell and all of the hydrants were placed, that included three of them that were behind the forces. The General turned to see his siege machines doused by large streams of water. This was something no one had ever seen on this world. It took him a moment to understand exactly what it meant. The fires inside the machines had been doused and the troops that ran them were getting drenched to the point where they were beginning to drown inside the metal machines. The General ordered them out of the machines and they were only too happy to comply. The powerful attack machines had become death traps and they were happy to be free of them. The water did not stop with the evacuation of the siege vehicles. They pivoted in place and directed their streams at the rear guard and the other casters. It was a crazy maneuver but it had the desired result. It forced the army forward. The General raised his mighty arm and waved his troops forward into the battle.

Dad smiled as the rear line advanced into the range of his archers. The clay golems were already breaking up under the intense pressure of the water stream. The enemy was finding it difficult to locate a target. They could see archers on the walls every once in a while, but it would take a miraculous shot to hit one from down on the field below. Still, some stray shots did score hits. However, the ratio was definitely on the side of the defenders. The attackers outnumbered the meager defenders by so much that any losses on the defending side meant a possible victory for the invaders. All it would take was to get inside through that opening with enough forces to take the walls and the city would fall. Both sides knew this and the water streams were only the first line of defense. Mom had generated more than a few extra hydrants to cover the new hole in the wall and the concentrated spray was quite effective against the constructs, but did mostly nothing to the demon troops. They were making a run for it now, trying to force their way through their own front lines and into the city in order to stop the ranged assault from the walls above. Dad grabbed a rope and leaped off of the wall towards the interior of the city. His momentum carried him around in an arc as he slowly slid down the rope by one hand. He was quite thankful that it had been gloved with a special steel glove for this purpose. The glove had a hinged steel plate and allowed him to slow his descent by squeezing his grip. He hit the ground at a run and the swordsmen he had with him, less than thirty, entered the battle. The demon troops were attempting to storm the stairway leading to the upper ramparts. Their primary job was to kill the archers that were harassing their troops. The water streams had slowed them down quite a bit and now there were human fighters blocking their path. The fighting was fierce but the humans were tougher than the demons had expected.

Dad wove through the melee, the ancients guiding both hand and foot. He moved like a cat from one kill to another. His body twisted and whirled and struck like a snake. He was starting to breathe heavy, but the work still needed to be done. He continued on even as his shoulder ached from the strain. Another demon died, and another and now Dad was panting. He started to fight back towards the line. There were so many enemies now. He was not fully cut off, but it felt that way. He began to lose hope. His sword seemed to move of its own volition and another foe went down. His sword arm never stopped moving. He followed through the cut and sliced another enemy down. The wide arcs of open combat were less effective in this close quarters work, but he was using them anyway. Dad was confused, the ancients continued on unabated. Dad's arm was sore; he could feel each blow like a hammer on his nerves. He did not falter though. He could hear the screams of men. The sound almost made him drop to his knees. Had he failed? The screams did not die away as he thought they would. They were calling to him. A wedge of swordsmen was working their way to him. He could scarcely see them through the tumult before him, but his sword hand kept moving, killing things. He felt a stab in his lungs and he knew that he had driven himself too far. There was no wound, only the absolute loss of all energy that had gotten to him. He was getting on in years and he had to admit that he wasn't in as good of shape as he had been. He bent over and fell forward. The ground scraped his face as he went down. The demons tried to stab as one but something held them back. They looked at each other and then they turned to see the cause.

The Dark Lord stood there, lost in his insanity. "This one is mine." He told them and then he proceeded to slaughter the demons even as the humans backed away. Dad just lay there in his exhaustion. He was powerless to move, much less resist. The Dark Lord finished his grizzly work on the demons and then he hunched down over Dad and sniffed the air. "Strange, you smell like the one I want, but it is not you." He said, obviously confused. The battle raged on outside the wall but nobody from the outside wanted in where they saw the Dark Lord enter. He had effectively helped the humans defend the wall for at least the time being. The water cannons were still pouring away at the army and the whole landscape was eroding off into the sea. It would take a lot of work to restore it after the battle ended. That is, it would if the battle is successful and there is someone around to rebuild it.

King Cedric stood tall. He was still so much shorter than the Dark Lord, but his presence came as a total surprise to the evil demented creature. The fighter was on the ground helpless and the demonic lord was hovering over him. The time to act was now. "I hear that you have been searching for somebody." He shouted to the vile enemy leader. "I would like to know who you are after." He shouted when the Dark Lord did not turn to him.

The confusion was starting to turn to frustration, rage would be next. The Dark Lord turned to the new voice. "You are not the one I want either." He said disgustedly. I will kill you both of course along with this entire city, but I need to know where the sorcerer that hurt me is." He said, not sure why he was explaining to his prey. Cedric was nervous, but he did have a plan. Of course if he had told his plan to anybody they would have told him not to do it. That was primarily why he had not told anyone about it. All he had to do now is to hold this standoff out as long as he could, then he would initiate the next step, if he survived the first step of course.

"A sorcerer?" Cedric replied "I have but one mage here and she cannot be the one that you want either." He said as calmly as he could. In fact, his own voice almost surprised him with how calm it actually sounded. He had acrobatic butterflies fluttering around in his stomach as it was.

The Dark Lord stepped away from Dad and took a few steps towards the king. "You tell me that you have a caster, but it is not a man?" The Dark Lord asked. His veil of confusion was pulled back over his eyes. The hate and rage subsided as his mind tried to work it out. It was exactly as king Cedric had hoped. His hopes for a possible future were starting to return.

He decided to put on the next phase. "You have come to the wrong place." He said, trying to take the upper hand in this conversation. "You need to leave now." He said and the Dark Lord looked at him puzzled.

He scratched his head and cocked it to the side a bit. "You are ordering me out?" He asked. "Do you not see who I am?" He asked, feeling properly rebuked. "I am the destroyer of this world! I am the one who has brought humanity down. I am going to destroy all kingdoms and all inhabitants of this world! I am the only one that you should fear!" He screamed; working up a lather of spit as his emotions took over. He hunched forward and spread his claws. "I guess that a lesson in fear needs to be taught." He said angrily. The fire in his eyes flared and he began to lunge forward.

The hydrant had formed just behind King Cedric. This one would not shoot water. The Dark Lord made his charge and Cedric leaped backward over the hydrant just as Mom released it. The hydrant sprayed forth a large stream of acid. The smell was terrible. The Dark Lord had seen the harmless water sprays and so he was not concerned about this new one. It hit him full force in the chest and it hardly slowed him down. Then the pain began to register. He stuttered and slid to the side out of the stream. His chest was on fire. At least it felt that way. It was actually burning away in a chemical bath that he could not understand. The pain was all he had until the skin was gone. The acid was still burning him, but now there was no more pain. The gaping hole in his chest looked terrible. His healing ability was somehow not kicking in. A feeling of panic began to take him. The stream tacked to him like an automated turret.

"You cannot destroy me! I am immortal on this world! I can repair any damage! I am unstoppable!" He screamed as he fell over on his side trying to get back up. His ribs had eroded away and his beating heart could just be seen through the dripping muscle fibers. "I – I cannot be killed!" He screamed, but his lungs had trouble drawing the breath he had just spent. He fell over backwards and lay there, panting, trying to pull in even one more breath. He tried to keep the stream off of him by holding up his arm, but it dissolved to the elbow and he pulled it back again.

A new voice made everyone turn away from the gruesome scene. "You have done me a great service." The deep throaty voice said. The General stood centered in the hole in the wall. He was massive even when compared to the Dark Lord. "It is a pity that I must still destroy you when you have been so helpful." He said with a bit of an ironic chuckle. Dad was trying to push himself up off of the ground, but the General didn't even notice him. "I will grant you a temporary stay of execution." He said and everyone looked amazed. "I have orders to destroy all of the life on this planet. I will continue to do so and return for you later." He said. In his mind this was more than generous. "You cannot escape me, so do not waste what time I have given you with foolish ideas and strategies. I have already proven that no matter what you throw in front of me, my army will crush it and advance. There is no help for you and your kind. The Master wants this world purged. The final flame will cleanse anything that somehow escapes us. There is no recourse. You are all doomed. Enjoy yourselves with the time you have left. I will return." He said and he turned and stepped back out of the city through the hole. He held up his hands and all of the army stopped their advancement. They withdrew from the city and headed towards the next one. For now, the siege was over. Nobody understood what had just happened more than the King did. He visibly gulped as he considered how close they had come to annihilation. It seemed they were still not very far from it either. He needed a new plan. He could only hope that he and those he trusted were clever enough to come up with something, anything that they could do.

The Grand High Elf looked out at the field in flames before him. He could feel the hate rising within him. Yes, he had been angry when the humans cut down the trees to make their fields. However, he had relented when he saw that they were planting in them. They were food crops, but they were still using the materials that nature provided if in a more organized manner. This wanton destruction of everything was more than he could bear. The world he so loved was under direct assault from these invaders. His people could fight, but the enemy was so vast, so strong and the elves, fierce as they are, were few in number. The cloud of smoke the enemy left behind was actually hiding the elves from those same aggressors even now. Since their first flight from danger, the Grand High Elf had decided to take his people back to the forest where they could more easily defend their territory. They could also reinforce with help from some of the other older races. He was crouched down and the stench of the burning fields nearly choked him. He turned his head from the scene and wondered just how long the world could withstand this. If the humans, who had been so numerous and strong, could not defeat these monsters, then who could? The heat was beginning to die down since the foliage was now fully consumed. The high elf signaled and the column advanced again. With luck and a little guidance from the stars above, they would reach their homeland within a few days. He dedicated himself to holding the tree line. He had lost the city he had pledged to support. He would not lose his homeland as well!

The fall of the beast-men had signaled the beginning of the war. The council had been briefed and each elder race had decided to fend for themselves in order to play to the strengths of each particular race. The sprites had gone into hiding. Their role as information gatherers had been crucial, but now they were too small to fight. At least that was the general consensus. No one had seen any of them since they had been sent away. The remaining races had split off to do their best and hold as much ground as possible. The only ones who seemed not to care were the stone lords. After all, they could simply 'go deep' and rest out whatever occupation affected the surface dwellers. They considered themselves untouchable. The council had disbanded until the crisis was over. The long-time friends and fellow members bid a fond farewell to their mates. None of them knew if they would ever see each other again. This was the event that had been prophesied and it was believed that nothing could truly be done to prevent it. So the emotions in the conclave were grim, formal, even accepting. Fate had come to claim the elder races and if the upstart humans did not stop this threat, then the world was doomed.

The row of cadets stood at the ready, wooden swords in hand. Wooden shields were strapped to their off arm. They were unarmored and braced for the next beating they would receive. That was the life of a recruit. This was training that could save their lives. Nobody begrudged the way the Guard Captain taught it. He had a good track record of cranking out worthwhile troops. He would be tested this time though. They had given him more recruits than he had ever dealt with at one time. He had stepped up to the situation and faced it head on.

"All right you prairie scum!" He shouted at them to get their attention. "I want to see how well you can attack an unmoving little defenseless object." He said berratingly. The recruits looked at the combat dummy on the pole. It was basically a chest plate with straw stuffed into it and a burlap sack placed on top with a helmet on top of that. It looked ridiculous, but it was also intimidating. It had a wooden sword and a shield just as the recruits did. It was stationary now, but that was somewhat of an illusion. The post was a pivot point. The dummy could be manipulated to strike and block by pulling on ropes that were tied to it on an internal cross member. They knew that they would all have to attack the dummy and that more than one of them would find themselves sitting on the ground abruptly holding a new sore spot. It was better to get bruises here than to lose limbs on the battlefield. Although they technically agreed with the philosophy, it was still hard to muster up the courage to take the hits in practice.

Erica stood by the sideline watching the recruits eye the suspicious dummy and of course the two guards that were handling the ropes. They had been doing this all day and they seemed to know just what the other was thinking to help the dummy act with almost uncanny precision. Erica felt a stab of sympathy for the recruits. She had taken her share of lumps from this apparatus as well. Her thoughts were broken into by the Guard Captain.

"Well get to it!" He shouted and the first cadet in line advanced timidly at first towards the dummy. He held his shield up, sort of. It drooped just a bit to the left and the Guard Captain let him know it with a stream of shouted expletives.

The young man lunged and thought he would strike the dummy in the gut. The dummy ground and swung around so that the shield took the initial blow. The poor cadet's lunge carried him too close to the dummy and the wooden sword struck him on the temple as his weight fell forward. He rolled into the hay and slid back from the dummy as his comrades laughed. The Guard Captain shut them up with a glare and then picked up his troop.

"Do you know where you went wrong?" He asked almost gently.

"Yes sir, I was overbalanced forward." He replied and the Captain nodded.

"Good, how would you correct this?" He asked taking way more time than the cadet was comfortable with.

"I should strike from closer and not lean in like that." He said, hoping it was the right answer.

The Guard Captain looked back at the men working the dummy.

"He says he can take you if he can try again." He said aloud and the cadets cheered, except the one who had just been put on the spot. The Captain smirked as he pointed. "Go ahead son, give it a shot." He prodded.

The cadet dropped into his stance, concentrating on where his feet were, and where his center of gravity was. He approached the dummy and this time it was already moving. The challenged guards were determined to put this cadet back on his seat. He lunged again, this time as a feint. The dummy swung around to strike but he had already retreated just enough to make that swing miss. He swung a backhand swing towards the dummy's head and it pivoted wildly to avoid the unexpected strike. The top of the shield barely deflected the blow. More determined now, the cadet slid a step to the right and drew the dummy out of position with a double stab that would have missed anyway. The shield of the dummy was attached well, but the wooden sword was supposed to be able to be knocked off. The cadet brought his sword down hard on the hilt of the dummy's sword. There was an audible crack as the dummy's sword broke. It could no longer strike back. The cadet then started poking and prodding, and eventually struck the unprotected side of the dummy. The Guard Captain called the exercise to a halt amidst the cheers of the fellow cadets.

The Guard Captain smiled, it was only slightly less intimidating than his glare. "Nicely done" He said and then he pointed the cadet down to the next test. Then he switched his attention to the next cadet in line. "Well, what are you waiting for?" He asked. While they had been cheering, a replacement wooden sword had already been affixed to the dummy. The guards that had just been beaten had a new determined look on their face. The young man stepped forward as he gulped…

Erica had seen enough to know that the cadets were in good hands. She needed to see to other matters of state. She was relatively happy to shed her armor for a more comfortable set of leathers. Her crown was not heavy; it was practically a small loop of gold with only a hint of ornate engravings on it. It was not endowed with multiple sparkling gems like the ones in the movies. She wore it with pride though. She was making her way to the kitchens next. With limited supplies, the daily fare had been slipping. This was to be expected. However, the cooks had done wonders with what they did have to work with. The palace was feeding more than a hundred extra people each day. Erica had seen to the 'soup line' personally. She would have helped with the distribution of food, but she tired quickly of being bowed to repeatedly. It was tiresome to be smiling all the time. She loved her people, but when work needed to be done, she'd rather be doing that. Her motivation was not as strong as Josh's but she had done remarkably well since they found out that this was their permanent home. It had brought a new level of dedication to her normal personality. In short it had made her a better queen. The kitchens were abuzz with activity. The next meal was only forty minutes away and tremendous batches of some amazingly good smelling foods were in evidence. She nodded her approval and made a really quick tour through the kitchen. The cooks had long ago stopped pandering to the queen since she had forbidden it in the kitchen. As a result, they were much more relaxed around her and she was able to sample bits here and there as she made her way across. Everything was perfect of course. They would not have offered anything less or the head chef would have their heads in a basket, figuratively speaking of course.

The queen completed her brief, but enjoyable inspection and made her exit on the far side of the kitchen. The dining hall was situated a short distance away for obvious reasons. The servers were placing flatware and cloths out in preparation for the next meal. They stopped and bowed to her and she nodded to each one in turn and smiled. She left them in a hurry afterwards before others could walk in on them and make her repeat those unsettling actions. She was due to check in on her brother. Josh would work and work until he dropped if someone didn't keep an eye on him. She understood this, even though it seemed strange. She also knew that the whole city needed his efforts now. The supplies of food and water were running low and they needed to return to the real world. This stasis he had constructed was a remarkable feat of magical engineering, but it would not sustain them forever. In all honesty it had never been meant to. This was like a temporary storage locker for an entire city population. She couldn't even imagine how he had come up with this idea in the first place, but he had and it had worked! Their people were still alive. Unfortunately not every kingdom could say the same. Erica reflected upon when they first arrived with the palace under siege from rival dukes trying to usurp the throne. It was a different age then, and so were they. Looking back they were only kids when all of that happened. Josh had started using his magic at age twelve and she had ruled a kingdom at fourteen. She shook her head at the memory. They truly knew nothing about what they were doing back then. They only had a deep desire to help others. It had been enough to endear them to their public, but they paid a high price for that. They were basically shut-ins in their own home. The palace was the only place they could control what went on around them. They held daily courts that settled disputes and listened to people's problems. She was just thinking of how much trouble that had been to establish when she reached the door she wanted. The realization broke her strand of thought and she stopped a moment to collect herself before knocking on the door.

The room beyond was Josh's study. It was nearly as large as their quarters were, but he had privacy there like no other place in the kingdom. He had worked out his plans in here. Erica knocked on the door three times, paused for two seconds and knocked twice more. The door opened with a loud creaking sound. In fact, it was not coming from the door. Josh had rigged up a sound box and it made various sounds for him at certain events. His twisted mind had brought that right out of the Saturday night horror movie fest they had watched as kids. The musical box had a lot of pieces of their history in it through sound samples. It was truly convenient that he could record them into the box from his own memories. Erica stepped into the room. The room was big, she had expected that. It was also full. That was new to her. She looked startled at first at the sight. She suddenly felt like a giant. She was standing in one of the many market squares in their city. Her feet were almost big enough to fill the entire square. She was looking out at all of the uneven roofs. The streets of cobble were laid out before her and she could even see the fires in the fireplaces through the second story windows. She looked off into the distance and she saw Josh sitting in a meadow just outside of the cultivated lands surrounding the city. He was staring at a tree that was shading a good portion of his meadow. It all looked so real that it didn't look like a model. She turned around in place and looked at the door again. It had not shrunk for her new size, so she hadn't been turned into a giant. It really was a small city and surrounding lands in this room.

Erica turned back to her brother who was still staring at that tree. "Ahem," she said and he didn't even flinch. "Ahem!!!" She said louder, adding a clearing of the throat to give it emphasis.

Josh did look up this time, he looked surprised at first and then he looked irritated. "What is it?" He asked as he turned back to his tree.

Erica could not see a path to him so she stood in place and tried to use her authority voice. "How long has it been since you ate anything?" She asked, almost shouting. She saw Josh flinch, shake his head, and then not respond to her. She was starting to get miffed. "You will listen to your queen!" She shouted and he looked at her with rage in his eyes. It was most frightening. Then he turned back to his tree.

Erica felt like raising the stakes, but was unsure how. Josh seemed to be able to tune her out whenever he needed to. She was not going to take that this time. Feeling a little like Gulliver, she carefully stepped over a row of buildings to plant her left foot onto the next street. The absolute level of detail was staggering. She could see the hay in the stalls at the livery stable. She could see the cobbles and pebbles around the city well. The clay shingles on the roofs looked authentic as well. They were beautifully reproduced, just in miniature. Any modeler would have paid a fortune for just one of these buildings. Josh had built a whole city. She eyed the terrain for her next step and found it. Carefully she stretched her right foot over the part of the industrial district. There was a foundry there and even the smoke from the smokestack resembled the billowy black soot that normally pumped out of that chimney. There were storage barrels and rain barrels and canvas awnings. She could see no flaws in any of the construction. The only difference that she could spot from the original was that everything was perfectly preserved. There was no deterioration of the buildings. It was if the entire city had just been built. Of course a city this size was built a piece at a time in reality so this tiny replica could never have existed. Some structures simply aged while the others waited construction. It was the natural order of such things. Erica took another step and this time it was over the city wall. Her foot planted solidly onto the grassy plain beyond. She could now see the city gates. The mechanism that pulled the gates up using heavy ropes and a counterbalance was something she had seen firsthand. That mechanism was perfect here as well. She took a few more steps and made her way to where Josh was squatting, eying the tree with that same exacting eye. Something had him bothered about that tree. That much was plain, but what could have disturbed him so? She decided to ask him.

"Why so much trouble with one little tree?" She asked and he glared at her briefly and then stared back at the tree.

"This one tree seemed to lose its shape when I look away from it." Josh said irritation in his voice. "I can't get it to stabilize so that I can finish." He complained. Erica knelt down next to her brother and looked at the tree. The branches were flawless; the leaves were rustling in a breeze she could not feel. There were even birds nestled in those branches. As she watched, Josh looked away and sure enough, the tree shifted. She gasped.

"Why does it do that?" She asked and he shook his head. She looked closer. "Is there someone else's will involved? Could someone be trying to make it a different way and both of you are struggling to force your image onto the tree?" She asked and Josh sat back, letting the tree revert to its other state.

He seemed much calmer now, though. "I – I don't know. It didn't occur to me that someone could be getting in the way of this cast." He admitted. Then he turned speculative. "Who would gain from me not completing this spell?" He asked aloud.

Erica sighed. "Is it that difficult to understand?" She asked him. "The enemy would benefit the most from any delay to keep you out of the action. They keep you locked in this room, trying desperately to correct a tree that probably shouldn't even be there. Then they have successfully nullified your influence in the events that they are causing in our world. We need to get back there and fight this war.

You know that, that is why you have been working so hard on this." She looked around at the amazing diorama before her. "I half expect to see horses coming out of the gate at any time on your model here. It looks so real." She added. Then she turned to lock eyes with her brother. "We need to get back there with our people now." The army will not form until we return. We cannot sustain the people here in this realm much longer." She concluded.

Josh shook his head. "I know all that." He looked at his map and almost blushed. "The image is pretty complete, huh?" He asked almost sheepishly. Erica slapped him and his look of shock was priceless.

"How could you even ask such a thing?" Erica threw her arms into the air. "Just get us back home. I need to do some serious training with the new recruits and we need a practice field for that." She demanded and Josh nodded, more seriously this time. His resolve slipped back into place.

"I--" Erica cut him off. "Oh no you don't; you will eat first and get some rest, then you can cast this mighty spell of yours." She ordered. He started to protest and she gave him a stern look that would have made the villagers shake. "I don't want to hear another word. Go and get some food by royal order of the queen." She added to prevent any further hemming and hawing. Then she turned back the way she had come. The trip back was going to be treacherous, but she had to get back to her duties. She stepped over the wall again and made her way cautiously back. When she reached the door, she was relieved to find Josh working his way through the model towards the door as well. He was gifted, powerful, and brilliant, and she loved him dearly, but he could be so daft sometimes. "It's a good thing you have me to look after you." She said as she left the room.

Josh completed his journey as well and soon was in the kitchen where the young ladies fawned over him and heaped all sorts of delicious food on a plate for him. If he had been resistant to come here, he could no longer remember why. This was amazing and he was soon satiated, and then some. He left them and their smiles with grateful thanks. He yawned and realized that his sister had been right all along. He had worked too hard and too long and the spell would have been faulty if he had attempted it too soon. He was suddenly glad that he had waited, and equally glad that Erica had warned him not to even try it. He headed off to his quarters for that much needed rest.

CHAPTER 10

The General headed away from the city where he had just lost a lot of his troops. He had promised to return to that one last. He wondered why he had done such a thing, but being rid of that Dark Lord was enough to make him feel much better. The humans had managed what he had believed was impossible. They had killed a lesser devil with regenerative properties. They had somehow stopped his regenerating from happening and then applied so much damage that he could not recover. Surely, if given enough time, he could maybe begin to dry out and recover, but he didn't believe that the humans were stupid enough to let him do that. They would keep pouring on that fire water they had until there was nothing left to regenerate. It was a stroke of genius for his enemies. Still, they had done him such a great service, that he was prepared to cut them a little slack. The Master would be coming soon and he needed to have as much of this world conquered as possible when that happened. He needed to hand over the planet to his master and then bow and become the prime subordinate in the new regime. He would enjoy a position of power and authority as long as he kept his master pleased. Those that did not would simply disappear. It was the reality of it all that he accepted. It just was, there was no arguing, or negotiations. He would have the power soon. He licked his lips in anticipation. His campaign had been littered with failures as well as successes.

He needed to apply more force and more power to get this job done before it was too late. At least he no longer had a rival for the Master's attention. This had become a good day and he was not about to let it die out now. He would continue to march his troops and destroy settlement after settlement. The human race was officially extinct; all he had to do was to bring it about. He checked on his casters and the few that remained were indeed bringing more of his clay infantry into existence. He was quite pleased. With enough little victories, the big one would not be all that far off. He would regroup for a few hours more, and then they would march. This glorious day would be followed by an even more glorious night. He vowed that to himself and to his troops. They would rend the souls and destroy the bodies of these upstarts and they would all feel the rage and the blood lust that came with such a grand adventure. None of them could wait.

Mom cut off the acid bath. The body of the fallen evil creature had dissolved completely. The color ichor that was left of it flowed out to sea with the rest of the hydrant flush. This allowed the land to be used again by people. Of course it would be some time before anything grew there, but for now they could live with that. It had been too close. They had almost fallen to this dark demon creature. Of course they had been given a temporary stay of execution for the city. It was not much, but it did offer hope. If they could negotiate with this devil, then maybe they could wrest continual existence from his grips. They needed to try. All could not be lost now; they had been through so much already. Dad was taken to the infirmary and there he was being seen to by the equivalent of a field nurse. His injuries were rather extensive, but he yet lived. Mom went in to check on him. She made her way through the other casualties, looking for that familiar face. When she saw him she paled.

"Does it really look that bad?" Dad asked weakly. He would have laughed, but he had so little energy and the pain in his lungs was intense.

"I… I… No, it's not so bad as all that." She lied trying to keep up appearances for her husband.

This time Dad did chuckle, but it was followed by a nasty rasping cough that basically put him in stitches of pain. He winced with each convulsion. When it all settled down to a dull roar, he actually smiled at her. "Kind of wish they had Morphine here." He joked and she shook her head.

Mom looked grave. "I can go and get help. Another wizard could heal you." She offered. She lowered her head. "I don't know how." She admitted sorrowfully.

"That's all right dear." Dad said; the energy level in his voice had dropped noticeably.

"Don't talk, save your strength. Promise me that you will still be here when I get back." She implored him.

He remembered not to speak, he simply nodded to her and she left in haste. Mom made her way to King Cedric. "Your Majesty, is there a healer left in the city?" She asked, almost whining like a puppy.

Cedric shook his head as he considered the question. "I'm afraid that my healers were all helping the citizens of my city when your Guardian of balance took them away. We have been working with no better than a nurse for the fighting men." He replied. It was what she had guessed, but she had not really wanted to believe it. Now she had no choice.

"I need to get to a healer and bring him back here." She said. "My husband is badly wounded and he will not last long enough for this to get over with. I need to move now." She said in a rush.

King Cedric raised his hands. "I will not prevent you from leaving, you are free to come and go as you please, we owe you a debt. However, the countryside is not the safest place to be just now and where would you go? The next closest kingdom has already been wiped out. The neighboring villages suffered the same fate. There is nobody close enough to help that still lives. We are cut off from any aid from any human source." He said flatly. It was obvious that he had thought about summoning aid as well. The news was crushing. Then Mom caught on a particular word.

"You said any *human* source." She repeated. "I may be able to contact a non-human source of help." She paused, obviously putting her thoughts together. "Thank you your majesty." She said and she whirled and left him standing there with his mouth half open. Even though she had just committed an offense against him by breaking proper protocols, he smiled.

Mom returned to Dad. He was looking even worse, if that was indeed possible. His strength had been drained away like a sponge. She knelt down beside him and whispered in his ear. "Try to relax, hold on, I have an idea." She said and his eyes opened very briefly and then closed again. Mom pulled herself away with difficulty, but it was the only thing she could do. She headed to the wall. The outside world had been decimated and she knew that this was a long shot. She sat down cross-legged on the top of the wall and she concentrated. Her body became an antenna for her thoughts. She began to broadcast her S.O.S. to whoever was listening. It was a desperate act, but one she was more than willing to take. These were desperate times after all. She would continue until she was exhausted. She could think of nothing else.

The dark figures passed by closely as the wolf laid in hiding. It had come far to try and aid the True Bloods. In truth, it had sent that other human to do some of its assigned task, but somehow that plan had failed. The enemy had attacked before the human army could be raised. There were burnt out cities and towns everywhere. It was a catastrophe of global scale. The wolf was unsure of how it could be of service any longer, but duty forced it to try. If only it could continue to evade these mindless invaders, it might actually be able to help somewhere. The Wolf's ears perked up as it sensed another presence. A voice was calling from far away. It was a familiar voice, but one that could not be real. That voice was of someone he knew was dead. Had he died? Was he hearing the call from beyond the grave? He hoped not. After all, he still had a mission to perform. His work on this plane was not done. He would need more than forgiveness to ascend if he died now. The voice repeated and the message was slightly different. He sniffed in the direction it had come from, but the source was too far away to smell. The voice sounded desperate and the message was even more so. A True Blood was dying. This could not be allowed to happen. The Wolf would bring help. It was a simple task, but a long one. If only the human could hold out for long enough, he might be helpful and that would at least allow him to earn some points towards his eventual ascension. He decided that the risk was worth the pay-off and he bolted from his underbrush hiding spot. The demon troops spotted him immediately, but they were slow and lethargic compared to his power and grace. He made his way quickly through their ranks and soon he was clear of them. He had a long way to go and he didn't know how often he could rest. This was going to be one of those journeys worthy of legend. His smile looked more like a snarl on his wolfen face. His powerful legs drove him further onward. He knew who to contact, he knew who to bring. If he was fast enough, they might just save the day. He pushed himself even harder at the thought and the ground seemed to become a blur. "Hold on your majesty, hold on." He thought back to the voice. "I'm on my way."

Back at the top of the wall, Mom sat there sending her message. A tickle in her brain told her that someone was answering. Hope began to flicker and she smiled, but kept right on sending her thoughts. She added "Please hurry!" to her existing message. She was partially satisfied that she had made a contact, but it had been too weak to come in clearly. She had no idea who it was and what their intentions were. At this point, any help was better than no help. She held onto her hope like a vice. She would not; could not fail.

Josh had gotten his required rest. He had made his way to the kitchen twice before finally returning to his study. The city was there, just as he had left it. He gazed out upon it and nodded in approval. It was finally ready, so long as he did not include that tree. It was still there, trying to spiral the wrong way. He banished it from the scene and it obediently disappeared. He was ready to cast the actual spell now but he was going to take more precautions this time. He was not going to do this alone. The young man stood at the base of his creation and held up his arms. The whole display slipped out of view and back into his mind. The mental image was practically perfect. It would save them so much time on the rebuilding of their city. Of course there were always things that didn't get caught, and they would deal with them once everyone was back where they belonged.

Erica found her way into the room and Josh turned to note her arrival. Then he sat down just as his mother was doing and suddenly the message filled his mind.

"...must help, my husband is dying and we cannot heal him. We need magical help right away or it will be too late. Please hurry!" There was a pause, and then the voice started over again. Josh's eyes opened wide in surprise. He looked at Erica who had that surprised look of 'what is it now?' written plainly on her face.

"Mom and Dad are here and they are in trouble." Josh said without preamble. Erica stepped forward and Josh held up his hand to stop her. We need to go to her as soon as we can. Dad is near death." He said and Erica's look turned frightened. Josh was ready to go and he knew that running off at this critical stage was the wrong thing to do. He looked at his sister with sorrow in his eyes. "I need to take us all home first, and then we can go if I have the strength left to travel." He said. The grim tone told his sister that this decision was not a light one. She knew that he was right too. It didn't make it any easier to take, but they had to keep the safety of their people in the forefront of their minds.

Erica seemed to reach the same conclusion. "You had better get on with it then. Take us home and then we'll see." She said. A single tear rolled down her cheek. She was glad that her brother had to make the decision though. She was not so sure that she could have chosen correctly this time. He was so much stronger then she remembered him being before. She let the thought go for now. They both had to concentrate to pull this off. Josh slipped into his trance where he began to examine his mental image. The snapshot of their humble kingdom spread out before him like a watercolor on canvas. Then it began to sharpen and details began to fill in. It was an amazing process and it was not all that long until he told Erica that he was ready. She knew that he was not looking at her, but at the image so she responded verbally. "Do it then." She was sending him all that she could. Her mind was filled with good cheer, hope, and wishing that everything went as planned. It was the supportive role that he needed at this difficult time. Josh began to pour the magic into the image. Like pottery clay, the image began to take substance and form. The grass started blowing in the breeze and the shingles on the roofs began to glisten in the sun. They were still forming and taking on their final shape when he pulled himself back ever so slightly to peruse it. Then, he thrust himself in fully and the magic swept across the image like a wave of color and light. The slightly three dimensional view became a hard reality. The energy unleashed was massive and Josh cried out as it took its due from him. Erica stepped forward and grabbed his shoulders. The power began to consume her as well. The streets were laid and the buildings were placed and the grass and trees, minus the one that had been omitted, were sprouted and blossomed. Then, as a final act, the people that had been sequestered away were placed back into their homes. It had been a bit of a shock, but it was a welcome one. The two young rulers were lying on the grassy hill overlooking their city. The power had drained them almost fully. Their kingdom was back where it belonged. A familiar form stepped out of the tree line and trotted easily across the field towards them.

"Ah, I have found you." The wolf said. He snuggled next to Josh and offered his support. He nuzzled the young man but Josh did not move. The Wolf's body language altered from happy and supportive to worried and protective. "What has happened here?" He said as loudly as he could. It was Erica that was shaking the cobwebs out of her head. She was rubbing her eyes and when she opened them she started.

"Oh, it's you!" She exclaimed and the Wolf bowed.

"It is good to see you again your majesty." The Wolf said formally. "I believe that there is something wrong with Joshua." The Wolf said and the tone of worry somehow was transmitted through the telepathic speech. In fact, almost all emotions were broadcastable through that amazing form of communications.

"He's just really tired. He just built that city with his magic and put our people back into it." Erica said as if describing a shopping list. The Wolf found that it was his turn to be surprised.

"He's that powerful?" He asked of the unconscious wizard on the ground.

Erica simply nodded. Then she looked at the Wolf with concern. "He heard that our parents are in trouble. We need to get to them as quickly as possible." She said, the urgency returning to her face. The Wolf was happy with this change.

"Actually, that is why I have come here. I received the same message and was on my way here to retrieve you for this task. Well, actually to retrieve Joshua. He has the healing gift." He said, the hope in his tone was unmistakable. Then he flicked his ears in annoyance. "When will he be ready?" He asked the queen.

Erica shook her head. "I don't know. It took him over a week last time to recover. It is an enormous undertaking that he has put himself through more than once now." She explained. "It was the only way to save our people and to defeat the dark horde." She said and the wolf bowed.

"The evil army you speak of is not defeated; they spread across the countryside like a plague. They kill everything they find. They burn what can't be killed. If they go unchecked, there will be no world to live in. The forests will slow them down some, but if we lose that resource, the world is doomed to live in darkness. The light will not come if the life is not here to draw it to us." He said and he was being more serious than usual.

Erica sighed. "I knew that the entire army was not destroyed, but the group that attacked us was wiped out." She replied. "Of course we had to destroy the entire city with them in it to accomplish that feat." She added. Then she remembered the cadets. "We have started to gather an army as well. It is a small thing now, but it will grow now that we are back here in the world." She said; hope trying to push its way through the dark cloud around them.

The Wolf smiled; it didn't look all that pleasant. "That is partly my doing, but it came too late to be of real value. The enemy attacked before the forces could be raised to stop it. Mouse was helping me with that." He said and Erica nodded in response.

"Mouse came to us by way of a teleport spell that Josh had given him. He told us of the plan and how he felt he had failed. Poor kid. "I told him that he had survived to fight and that was a victory in itself." She said in a rush. The wolf tossed his head.

"Time is running out, we need to move soon, please try to wake your brother." He ordered and Erica drew herself up with a visible effort. She was bone tired and she knew that Josh had bore the brunt of the spell. He must have been decimated physically.

"I'll do what I can." She answered truthfully. She dragged her weary self over and tugged on his arm. "Josh." She said. He was limp. She plopped to the ground next to him. "Josh!" She yelled at him, next to his ear. There was still no movement. Worry started to creep in. She rolled him over and slapped his face. "Pull yourself together little brother, I need you now!" She shouted and hit him again. The side of his face was pinker than the scars that were always there. It made her feel guilty. He still had not moved. She noted the rise and fall of his chest, he was still breathing. She gave thanks for that. "Come on Josh, we've got to save Dad." She whined and the Wolf came in close as well.

"The young queen speaks true milord; your presence is requested now." The wolf added. Josh began to stir, a groan escaped his lips. Erica looked at the wolf.

"Your thought speech is getting through where his ears aren't; try again." She urged and the wolf nodded and flicked his ears.

"Your father is in grave peril and you are the only one who can save him. Get up now and do your duty!" The Wolf shouted and Erica put her fingers in her ears, but it was of no use. She wasn't hearing the words; they were just in her mind.

Josh flung an arm up in a dismissive gesture. "I'm not going to school today." He muttered as if far away. "Just a few minutes more sleep Mom." He said and Erica almost laughed. She grabbed him by his tunic and hoisted him upright. His eyes were still closed for most of that. She slapped him across the face hard and they popped open in shock.

"Better." She said and he looked suddenly angry. "We need to go, are you ready?" She asked him and his mind was whirling around. Josh could not seem to focus.

"What?" He finally asked when no sense could be made of it all. "What are we late for?" He asked.

Erica sighed, but she had him back now. "We need to go and save Dad. Mom sounded desperate for medical aid." She told him slowly so that it would all sink in. He was obviously still shaken from that spell. "We need you to transport us to them and then you will have to heal him." She made him look directly into her eyes. "Are you ready to do that?" She asked and she had never been more serious. Josh nodded. She let go of him and he somehow managed not to fall over. In fact she somehow managed the same miraculous feat with her own level of energy loss. "Then let's go!" She shouted.

Josh pictured Mom. He still could see her clearly. His mind had latched onto a tickle in the back of his brain. She was calling to him even now. He let his mind follow that tickle. "Mom, are you there?" He asked aloud. His mind also sent the question and Mom answered immediately.

"You're here! We need you so badly!" She cried. "Come to us, I am sending the image." She said and Josh felt the tickle begin to pour into his mind. He saw a castle wall with bodies strewn about and Mom sitting Indian style in the middle it with her eyes closed. He closed his eyes to concentrate on the image. He needed to be sure what he was doing. He saw himself and Erica, and the wolf there. The image looked a little out of place, but that did not bother him. They were going to go help. He could feel the fatigue pulling him away from the image, begging him to stop. He let the magic come. It came slowly at first, his reserves were dry. He pulled it from around him. It began to do its job and the image solidified in his mind. Then that loud crack that bothered the ears and they were all three standing around Mom. She looked up from her meditation and smiled at them.

"My, how you've grown!" She exclaimed. Then the urgency she had been trying to portray returned to her. "We've got no time to lose, let's go!" She said, sprinting along the wall and down a flight of hazardous stone steps. The children did their best to keep up and the Wolf ran along happy to be moving again. The scene was grizzly. The bodies were strewn about all over the place. There were a few men here helping to tend the wounded, but there were no civilians around. Many of the bodies were that of demons. There were also bits of clay here and there. Josh knew what those had been. He had no real time to survey the area though, they were moving at a sprint right until Mom dove into a building. They all emerged in the make-shift infirmary that had been set up. Dad was there along with other wounded. He looked like he was already dead. His skin was pale and his breathing was very shallow. Erica stepped back and Mom and Josh knelt down close. Josh had seen things like this before, but it hadn't been a member of his own family. He suddenly got very nervous.

"What if I can't do this?" He asked and the fear in his eyes was almost absolute.

Mom looked at him and her empathy for him was only partly tinged by the concern for her husband. "You'll do fine, we're right here to help you. You can do this." She said supportingly.

Josh pulled the image from his memory. He saw Dad as he was when they had last left home. He was sparring with Erica and they had donned their hunting outfits. It made more sense than the stuff he had on now. Of course there was so much blood on it that he couldn't have identified the shirt or pants anyway. Josh brought the image to the forefront of his mind and a bright spotlight began to trace through the details. He started regenerating wounds. The magic came again, this time it was quicker, but more costly. Josh took in a sharp breath as he felt the stab of weakness. Erica held one of his hands tightly and Mom held the other. They were offering their strength to help him do what he needed to do. Josh suddenly felt the warmth around him and the magic came and smothered Dad in its blinding light. The whole spell lasted only for less than a minute but in that minute a lot of things happened.

Dad had been fully restored. His wounds were healed and he was sleeping quietly now. Mom had given even more of herself than Erica had and she had collapsed to the floor. A field nurse put her on a cot. Erica had released her grip on Dad and had caught Josh as he crumpled. She laid him down next to Mom and then she sat down as her head began to swim. The wolf had ushered everyone out of the room after that and then he stood guard on the only entrance. It had been a really busy minute.

The Guardian of Balance.

Here is the concept art for the Guardian of Balance, with his holier than thou attitude.

Word of the miraculous healing began to spread throughout the nearly abandoned city. The soldiers that they had left were eager to meet with this wizard that had done this. The Wolf had made sure that nobody bothered the royal family. Even King Cedric had not been allowed entrance. It was with the utmost of respect that the Wolf had refused him, but it was equally as hard as iron that the human king would not get through the protector. In fact, there was only one visitor who did manage to see the family reunion, the Guardian of Balance popped in like an uncle on Bewitched. He looked at the sleeping family and smiled. The Wolf noticed him and made a threatening advance, but then thought better of making a real scene here.

The Guardian held up a hand in supplication. "Don't worry about me; I'm not here to harm them." He said and the wolf's ears twitched in annoyance.

"I know who you are, meddler." He said with venom in his tone.

The Guardian stopped and looked mildly surprised. "Meddler? Me? I think you have me confused with someone else." He said with all of the arrogance of an untouchable aristocrat. "I maintain the balance of the universe." He added for credibility.

The wolf made a sound that was almost a snort. "I know exactly who you are and what you have done to this world. I will be watching you closely. Do not interfere with these people or I cannot be held responsible." The Wolf warned.

The Guardian waved a hand dismissively. "As I said, I mean them no harm." He repeated. "In fact, if there are meddlers here, it is them." He added to help strengthen his own position.

The Wolf was getting tired of his banter since he had so little patience for it. "So, if you are not here to harm them, why are you here?" He asked directly.

The Guardian of Balance looked at his fingernails as if they were suddenly in need of his attention. "I have a number of people inhabiting my realm and I'd like to put them back. I came to see when I can do that." He replied, the Wolf got the feeling that he was explaining to a child, or a simpleton. It was another personal affront and he was ready to tell this Guardian to get lost.

"I would suggest that you hold on to them, I don't think that this city is safe just yet." He said to the Guardian in hopes he would just leave.

The stuffy man looked around as if noticing the palace for the first time. "Yes, the place looks dreadful, doesn't it. You'd think they would clean up at least a little bit for the royal family." He said with annoyance of his own.

The Wolf stepped closer and his posture was more threatening. "You need to leave now. When they awaken, you can return and ask them your questions." He offered and the Guardian still looked miffed. He pouted for just a second and then he disappeared. There was no sound, or no magical residue, or even any visible arm waving or incantations, he simply was gone. As magic went, it was quite impressive. The Wolf went back to his post to guard the family. He lay down in the doorway and waited with the patience of an immortal.

The Master had watched his troops destroy countless smaller villages. He had witnessed the blind and enraged Dark Lord even as he met his demise. He had watched as humans and demons died with only a slight interest. Somehow, his army had to win this world without him. There was a barrier that he could not cross until victory was achieved. He was ready to step through the veil and punish those that were responsible for the setbacks that they had suffered. The destruction of so many of his demons had brought a rather nasty taste to his mouth and he was certain to pass that coppery feeling on to his subordinates for their less than stellar performance. His current quandary though was the simple fact that his army was moving away from a takeable city. The humans were so few in number that victory at this location was assured, but the General had let them go. He had shown weakness and weakness deserved to be punished. The veil between realms was weakened and it will continue to weaken until his claws could tear through and soon, very soon, he would emerge on the other side and his wrath would be insatiable. His blood lust would be so as well. The world had never known torment before this and it would never know anything else afterward. He was ready to begin his own personal conquest. The minor skirmishes he was watching were but a foreshadowing of things to come. Darkness was coming and it will sweep all that is good before it.

Mom awoke and looked around. She had been placed on a cot and her family was nearby, also resting. Her eyes were beginning to adjust when they saw the Wolf on the corner. "How long?" She asked and she was surprised by the hoarseness of her own voice.

The Wolf trotted over to her and she petted his head as she would a loyal lapdog. "Your majesty, it has been three days." He replied and for a brief flash, Mom looked alarmed.

"Have there been any changes?" She asked. The wolf had not been outside of the room so he knew nothing about the goings of the humans in the city. Nor did he care about them. His interest was in the True Bloods and he had done his duty. He had brought them together and he had witnessed their remarkable abilities yet again. The world was still in peril, but he had done his best to make sure that good had at least a fighting chance in this lopsided war.

"I do not know about changes outside your grace." He replied honestly. He somehow managed to portray his lack of interest in that short sentence. "I must leave you now." He added. "There are things that I must see to. Your army is still in its infancy and I must do all that I can to push it along." He said and Mom just looked confused. The wolf chuckled, or at least he came as close as he could to it. "Your children have changed a lot. I suggest you get to know them. I promise you it is worth it." He said and with that he trotted out of the room and once again, out of their lives.

A guard, a human guard, had been posted outside of the room with orders to check in on the guests as soon as it was possible. When he saw the Wolf leave, he knew that his opportunity was at hand. He made his way purposefully to the doorway. Once there, he witnessed what he had been sent to see. The family of True Bloods was awakening. This was exactly what King Cedric had been waiting for. He left to report the event immediately. It was not long before the King himself was at that very same doorway.

"Ah, I see that you are awake now." He announced to them

unnecessarily. "Maybe you can tell me what we are going to do next time the enemy army invades." He said flatly. He had prepared his speech for when they were back with him, but somehow it didn't feel right. Yes, they were wizards and fighters of legendary skill, but they were also just people. They were frail and scared and just as clueless in the grand scheme of things as he was. It was somehow disturbing to realize that truth. It also made the deeds of these people even more impressive. "I have arranged for you to be cleaned and fed before you have to do anything else today." He continued, breaking himself out of his thoughts. "We can talk later." He added, trying to get his own agenda on their plate before anything else could get in the way. "So for now, I shall leave you." He said in an unusual flash of pomp and then he departed. Dad was stirring now and Mom shook the two kids awake. When they realized that they were all together, there were hugs and kisses around.

Dad pulled back from an embrace and looked down at himself. "Woah, how did I get into these old clothes?" He asked and everyone chuckled.

Mom looked at him with a twinkle in her eye. "Oh, that was just part of the service." She said and then her tone turned serious. "How much can you remember?" She asked.

Dad rubbed his temple. "Not too much. I remember that I was fighting and trying to hold my own against way too many numbers. The ancients were taking control and my hands were not my own anymore. I seem to get lost just after that." He said.

Mom drew close to him. "Honey, you were almost dead. If Josh and Erica hadn't shown up when they did, I would be a widow by now." She said and Dad looked at his children with renewed pride.

He stepped over to Josh. "Let me take a look at you. My, how you've both grown up." He said appreciatively. Then he turned a bit more serious as well. "We've been hearing tales about your exploits. It seems you've been quite busy working on your magical skills over here." He said and Josh blushed.

Mom interrupted and took Dad's side of the conversation. "From what we've heard, you have moved an entire city with your magic!" She exclaimed. "How on Earth did you do that?" She added. Josh shrugged his shoulders and Erica took the ball from him.

"Yes, and he did more than that." Erica said. "He made sure that our people were safe by creating a replica of the city in a 'out of bounds' area and then bringing them back once the fighting was over." She said. Before either parent could react, she rushed forward to get it all said. "Then, we went to help another kingdom and he moved the whole city for them to the lake in a matter of hours." She said. She looked at Josh and his eyes were on the floor. He was obviously uncomfortable with how this conversation was going. Erica decided to lighten it up a bit. "He has done so well, you'd both be as proud of him as I am." She said and her smile radiated warmth and confidence.

Both parents looked at her in mild surprise. "You've grown up too young lady." Dad said. "I can see none of the flippant casual attitude you used to sport. Now you are responsible and dedicated. You've really grown up." He said and it was Erica's turn to be uncomfortable.

Josh broke in now. "Yes, she has helped the people realize that they have purpose and meaning. They almost worship her for her benevolence and they love her for who she is, not for the crown she wears." He said and Erica shot him a dirty look, but honestly, she had it coming. But Josh was not completely done yet either. "She's also been practicing her art. She is pretty good with sword and hammer." He said and Dad's eyes widened.

"A hammer?" He said incredibly. "How do you have the strength to use one of those?" He asked and Erica looked like she wanted to kill Josh. The hammers had taken her to one of those moments in life you would rather have completely forgotten. Even so, she had been good with them. It was then that Dad noticed her sword. He whistled. "Wow! that is one fine sword. How long is it?" He asked and Erica drew it to show him its full length. He whistled again. "That thing is over half of your height. How can you be nimble with that thing?" He asked and Erica smiled at him. She turned and with one smooth motion, she sliced an apple on the table in half without nicking the table beneath it. Then she wiped the blade clean and re-sheathed it. Dad looked startled at first, but then he got control again. "Forget I asked." He said and it looked like they were going to be catching up on the past few years when a throat clearing brought them all out of their reverie.

"If you please, it is time that we all had a good talk." King Cedric said. He had been watching and listening, from just outside the room. He had waited what, in his mind, was the right amount of time for them to get reacquainted, but he had a kingdom to save and the enemy was going to come back. It was not a question of if, but rather a question of when.

Erica stepped forward. "Excuse me, but I don't think we've been properly introduced." She said and she held out her hand for a firm handshake. King Cedric was taken so far by surprise that he shook the hand, even though it broke with traditional protocols.

"Forgive me." He said, bowing after the handshake was released. He did notice just how strong that slim young woman was, it was remarkable to say the least. "I am King Cedric, your mother and father, I have already met. You are...?" He asked in return.

Erica beamed at him. For his station he looked quite young, much like her. "I am Queen Erica of the True Blood nation." She turned to Josh. "This is my brother, Joshua." She said and Josh bowed accordingly. "We've been summoned to help our parents in their time of need. However, we also need to get back to our people. I have a fledgling army to train and the threat to all of our lands is still very real." She said, and her all business tone caught Cedric a little by surprise. She was beautiful and smart too. It was a combination that went unnoticed too often.

"I understand your need for it is also mine." He said clearly. "I need to protect my city from the impending attack. We know that they are coming to destroy this city. According to the enemy commander, he promises to come here last." He said and it was Erica's turn to be surprised.

"Really, how did you manage to negotiate that?" She asked.

Cedric shrugged his shoulders. "It wasn't me who did this. It was your parents who brought this about. Apparently there was some infighting amongst the enemy leaders and when they destroyed one of them, the remaining one gave us all a concession for the effort." He explained.

Mom and Dad did not respond to the quick glance that Erica gave them. Then she returned her attention to the young king before her. "So if you believe what this enemy commander told you, then all we have to do is defeat this army at another location and they will never come back here again." She said logically. Cedric scratched his chin.

"Yes, I suppose that makes sense. Mind you, I wouldn't risk my people on the word of the enemy leader, but the logic is sound." He admitted. Then he eyed Erica suspiciously. "What are you thinking?" He asked.

Josh spoke up before Erica could answer. "She's thinking about putting together our armies and stopping the enemy cold at some neutral location." He said triumphantly. Everyone turned to him. "Come on, you've got to admit that if the enemy can be defeated, then defeating it outside of any of our cities is quite preferable to fighting them in one. The collateral damage alone destroyed our city entirely." He said and Mom and Dad gasped. Josh turned to them. "Don't worry, I rebuilt it and nobody was home when it went up." He explained briefly.

King Cedric felt out of place here. These people had done so much and all he had done was to manage other people doing the actual fighting. This Josh had built an entire city while saving the people who were supposed to live in it. He was only a few years younger than he was. It was a major feat. He had managed the same through help, but it seemed so hollow a victory to him now. "What do you suggest that we do next?" He asked when nobody spoke up for too long.

Erica took the ball again. "We need to combine our armies just as Josh said." She replied. "Of course we need to do more than that. My army is so small it would be insignificant when compared to the enemy forces. We need to do some heavy drafting and get enough bodies to fill the gear we have stowed away. There will be a unified defense force if we can muster enough personnel to fill it out. Then, maybe we can drive this enemy out of all of our lands." She said and the words sounded grander from her lips than they would have from Cedric's. He was certain of that.

"So how many troops do you have so far?" He asked and Erica's face went ashen. "I – I don't know, we left in such a hurry that I don't have an accurate count. I know that it is not that many yet. More are still trickling in all the time, but they need to be trained into a cohesive force before they can actually be counted on for defense." She answered honestly. "I have a lot of work to do yet." She shifted gears a bit. "How many troops do you have?" She asked and Cedric felt a twinge of panic.

"I have the palace guard, they number about two hundred minus any wounded we still have down at this time. I have the archers which count as another thirty men." He said and Erica felt the disillusionment that came with the overwhelming numbers they faced.

"That's all? We really do have our work cut out for us. "How many civilians do you have to recruit from? Maybe we can gather our recruits together for mass training." She asked, trying to sail to a different tack.

King Cedric lowered his eyes to the floor. "None." He replied softly.

"What?! None? How can that be?" Erica said, her voice rising in stress as she continued.

Mom interjected on the young king's behalf. "Now honey, his people are not here, but they are still alive." She told her exasperated daughter. "The Guardian of Balance took them to his realm for safe keeping until this crisis is over." She added, trying her best to be helpful.

Josh stepped forward, his ire obviously rising. "So the 'I'm not involved except that I created this mess' guy was here too?" He said and it sounded like a curse.

Mom and Dad both piped up this time. "That's why we're even here. He brought us here to help out this kingdom." They said together. "He was forced by Cedric into taking the civilians away while we fought the fight he brought us here for." Mom continued.

Josh shook his head. "Yeah, it's like when he stole the Spirit tree and put a fountain in its place." Josh almost whined. "He does things without concern for whomever he is hurting in order to maintain his precious balance." He said and everyone thought he was going to spit, he didn't. Instead Josh began to pace the floor as his mind started working on the problem. Then he stopped and made a quick turn to Dad. "Do you have a way of getting a hold of the Guardian?" He asked directly.

There was a response, but it was not Dad who spoke. "All you have to do is ask." The Guardian said and everyone jumped and turned to the new speaker. He had materialized a couple of feet away and was sitting on one of the cots that had recently held a family member. It was most unsettling. Josh was the quickest to recover.

"We need those people back." He said and the Guardian nodded. Josh held up a finger. "But not just yet, there is more." He added and the Guardian raised an eyebrow in question. "We need to enlarge our training facility and then pull the people in to be trained. Can you ask them who among them is willing to fight for their homes?" He asked and the inconvenience level of the question was like a personal affront the Guardian.

"I am not your messenger, boy!" He said with venom in his voice. He pointed back at Josh. "You have always been demanding and unsupportive of my work." He said and his look was piercing.

Josh brushed the verbal assault aside with effortless ease. "You have his people and we have our people. We need for them to work together and we need to get them trained to do so in an extraordinarily short time. We do not have time to bicker and banter with you. Put his people in the open field outside of our new kingdom. I will take care of the rest." Josh ordered and the Guardian of Balance looked miffed, but he also realized that he would no longer have to babysit these people if they were returned. He nodded his acceptance.

"It is done." He announced.

King Cedric blinked twice. "You mean, just like that? All it takes is a thought for you to move all of my civilians from one realm to another?" He asked and the outrageousness of the idea came through in his elevated stress levels.

The Guardian looked at him with a sideways glance. "Of course I also took back my objects so that the balance of this world was not upset by the transfer." He replied as if that explained everything. Then he turned back to Josh and Erica. "So if you have no further need of me, I'll be going on my way then." He said and his look suggested that even if they weren't done with him, he was gone. The delay was only a couple of seconds, but then he vanished right before their eyes.

Mom shook her head. "That man is flighty, that's for sure." There were nods of agreement around the room. Then she turned to Josh. "So, where is this new kingdom, I'd like to see it." She said almost whimsically.

Josh felt the situation slipping away from him. He worried that his parents might be seen and then his own grip on the throne would be challenged. He and Erica had put a lot of work into it, so they were not all that enthusiastic about losing control of it all now. His concern must have registered on his face.

"Oh, don't worry; I'll stay out of trouble." Mom said reassuringly. She reached out and put a hand on his shoulder. "I'll even help with the magic." She offered. He did feel grateful for that much.

Josh turned to Cedric. "Please get all of your men assembled in the courtyard; we'll all go at once." He said and the King turned to his aide.

"You heard the wizard, get my men assembled." He ordered and the aide left the room at an almost respectful run. Then he turned back to Erica. His eyes locked with hers yet again and his mind started to float a bit. He reigned himself in again. "How do you propose to combine our forces here?" he asked. The look on her face suggested that she had not thought all of it through yet. "My men are loyal to me, and yours are no doubt loyal to you. Do you think any transition will be smooth or even peaceful?" He asked and Erica took his meaning to heart.

Her smile beamed. "Oh, I don't think that will be too much of a problem." She said and it was Cedric's turn to look confused.

"And why would that be?" He asked when she didn't elaborate right away.

Erica's smile turned mischievous. "Because we will join houses." She said and all faces turned to her in shock.

"What?!!" King Cedric blurted out. "How do you imagine that will happen?" He asked, feeling the beginnings of a trap surrounding him.

"Isn't it obvious? Erica asked, we're going to get married." She said as if it had been a matter of fact. Cedric's initial response was one of rejection. Then he began to think about it.

"So, you mean a royal marriage? One of those made out of duty and obligation?" He asked. Erica looked hurt.

"Is that how you see me?" She asked, almost sobbing. "Someone you'd only marry if you had to save your kingdom?" Mom and Dad were still in shock about this conversation. They said nothing as this all transpired. Josh, on the other hand, had been there when the Sprite King told her she would have to marry.

Josh would have spoken up in defense of his sister, but he didn't have to. Cedric held up his hands. "No, it's not that at all." He said hastily. "Please don't misunderstand me. I was only thinking that this is so sudden that maybe you felt that way." He said and Erica sniffed once and then her anger flared.

"So you think that I am the kind of girl that would marry you for your connections?" She said and her tone was dangerous. Cedric already knew that he was in too deep, and he could see no way out that could save him.

"No, please." He said and he used his most moderating tone to try and diffuse this situation. "I am flattered that you would even suggest this. In fact, it is so flattering that it doesn't seem real to me." He paused, as if selecting his next words carefully. "You... you interest me." He said almost cryptically. "You seem to care so deeply about everybody that I figured there was no room for a personal relationship like that. I find you attractive; that could not be questioned. I, I just don't know if I'm ready. I mean, I just became king a few days ago." He concluded lamely.

Erica was a flood of emotions. "We need to unite our peoples. If you need to use that crutch to make you commit, then I can live with that. I had hoped that you were stronger than that." She said challengingly. "I can work on your strength later, when we have more time." She offered.

Cedric started to get angry; this young woman was taking him to the mat about his feelings and his manhood. It was not the most comfortable thing he had ever lived through. "You do me a disservice." He said, his defiant mood slipping into place. "I am certainly strong enough to marry you. I am strong enough to rule both of our kingdoms with you. I am man enough to bring peace and prosperity to the land once the threat has been eliminated." He stated boldly. "I'm just a little bit scared of you." He said and Erica looked a bit startled.

"You… you're afraid of me?" She asked almost timidly.

Cedric nodded quickly. "You are a warrior, and a damn good one I suspect. You are bold and adventurous. You are bold enough to ask me to marry you. That is not something that I am not used to to say the least." He explained. "In fact, I am terrified by your commitment and I admit that freely. I also admit that something about all of that excites me as well. I feel a bit guilty about that. You are all of the things that a heroine of legend has to have." He paused for a second and when it looked like Erica was going to protest, he plunged on. "How can I, the son of a king that fled his people in their time of need, compare to any of that?" He said self depreciatingly.

Erica had an answer for that. "You are more of a hero than I am." She responded. His face turned pale and he started to object. She would hear none of it. "You stayed behind to help your people after your father fled. You made arrangements with the Guardian of balance to have your people secreted away into safety when the enemy came knocking on your doors. You have done all of this and you have acted honorably. Can you doubt any of the things that I have said?" She asked in conclusion to her statements.

Mom was that one that answered up this time. "No, he is everything that you said. He is the hero of his people, just as you are to yours. He has done all of the things you give him credit for and more I am sure." She said and Cedric actually blushed. "He is a good match for you and your father and I approve of this choice." She said glancing at Dad just long enough to see his nod of agreement. Then she turned back to her daughter. Your timing is a bit odd, but your logic is sound and it is obvious to everyone here that you two are quite enamored with each other." This was what she had wanted when she first laid eyes on the young king. He would make her daughter happy. She slid over and pressed Cedric to Erica. They both blushed with the simple contact. Mom actually sighed. "You see, it's not just a mother's wish. This is real."

Dad stepped up and gave a stern look at Mom. "Hold your horses dear, they haven't actually said it yet. I have not heard either of them actually ask the other one to marry them." He pointed out and as everyone reflected on that, they all realized that it was true.

Cedric took the ball here. "I had always thought that my father would tell me whom I was to marry. I was sure that it would be for the good of the kingdom. I – I don't really understand what is going on here." He admitted. Dad stepped in close and put his arm around Cedric's shoulders.

"I understand, it's a big decision that we're all talking about here. I know that it can be scary. After all, my own marriage had been arranged by my parents. Actually finding somebody to marry had not been my responsibility. Your father left when everything hit the fan, er got out of control." He released the hold on the young man and backed away towards a more equal footing. "Just know that even though we are not always around, we have not abandoned our children. If you marry into the family, we will not abandon you either." He said being supportive. Then he backed away.

Cedric shook his head. "This is all happening so fast." He said out loud, with more than a trace of frustration in it. "I need my advisers, I need my court, I need…" He trailed off. He looked at each of the expectant faces in the room. "I need to rely on myself a bit more." He finished. It was a shift that boded well for both kingdoms. He turned to Erica who was watching him closely, wondering what he would do next. He got the image of a deer ready to bound away and it make him laugh. Then, of course this was no deer; this was a predatory cat that stood before him with her dazzling blue eyes, pony tail and warm smile. "This wasn't how I expected this moment to be." He said at last. "I.. I … Will?" He stammered.

Erica took his hand and he suddenly found the courage he needed so desperately. He smiled at her and they shared a moment of just being near one another. Then he looked startled when she winked at him. Erica found the words first. "Will you, King Cedric, marry me?" She asked in the most sincere tone he had ever heard. Her eyes were boring straight into him and he found it so self-revealing. He pulled her closer to him and saw her lip twitch expectantly.

"Yes, Queen Erica of the True Bloods, I will marry you." He replied and they kissed. The moment seemed to last forever until Mom realized that Josh had done something to the time. It could last practically forever. He winked at Mom and she rolled her eyes. Then he let it go and the two freshly engaged royals parted.

Dad was the first to speak up, probably because he had not realized what Josh had just done. "Well that sounds like a celebration is in order." He said with laughing eyes and a good-natured roll to the tongue. "We will have to make arrangements." He warned.

It was Josh that brought the impromptu festivities to an early close. "Look people!" He said in a somber, but forceful tone. "Cedric, your civilian population is currently wandering an open field next to our kingdom's walls. We need to get there and reassure them that they have not gone insane. We need to make an announcement to our combined peoples." Josh paused; his steam was beginning to fade. He had used up so much of his personal energy that he was sure that it would never fully recover again. It made him doubly glad that he had worked out so hard when he did. He would have come up short if he had not. Then his mind began to turn back to the problems at hand. "We will need to add to our kingdom to make it big enough for the extra personnel we just acquired. Our training facility will need to be expanded as well. We have to build up an army and do it fast. The evil horde is still out there. They will be back to try and eliminate all of us. We need to get our people organized and informed. Most of all, we need to start doing this now!" He stated with finality that could not be argued with. Of course the faces around him agreed with what he had just said. Then Josh let his anger die down a bit. "So, let's get your troops and go." He suggested and all of them filed out of the room that was the place where history was being made. The union of two great houses was an event rarely seen in this world.

The group of royals and their respective followers made their way to the assembly that was just about complete. The men were all in formation, at least the ones that were uninjured, or only lightly injured were. The others were in cots or carts next to the assembly. The orders had been interpreted correctly and the logistical geniuses that Cedric had for aides had done exactly what he *meant*, as opposed to exactly what he had ordered. It was definitely a good sign of what was to come. The group all viewed the assembly and they were in turn scrutinized with the minor restriction of the eyes-front rule, the standard of all formations. The men would have cheered their leader if they were allowed to. Instead, they remained silent and proud.

Cedric made his way to the reviewing area and Erica was beside him. Her armor was dented and scratched and her huge sword nearly scraped the ground behind her. Her smile was warm and comforting though. The king looked out at his men and a feeling of belonging hit him squarely. He looked out at his commanders and the pride they held in their men was obvious. He let his gaze follow the line of men and he had to admit that he felt that same pride. They had done all that he had asked of them. Some of them had done even more than that. He smiled and cleared his throat.

"You men have fought hard against an enemy that outnumbered us greatly." He began and each of them felt the weight of those words. "We still stand here today as a testament to your courage and strength." He continued. He let his hands gesture to take in the city around them. "These walls are still standing, and the people that normally live here are safe and alive." He said and there was a bit of a cheer, but the discipline quickly silenced it. "You have done me and yourselves proud this day." He told them and he might, just might, have had a tear in his eye. "Today we do something difficult. We are going to have to leave this place. We are going to abandon this city and go to a new place where our loved ones await us." He said. There was a single cry out in anguish.

"No, we cannot leave!" The voice said again even as his squad leader stepped over to administer a small amount of discipline in the gut.

King Cedric found the whole ordeal a bit unnerving. "Do not feel sad over this change. There is a bright future before us. I stand before you now, an engaged man." He said and there were several surprised shouts. The leaders tried to quash it, but the news was too extraordinary. The troops won and they became a cheering crowd. When it died down a bit, Cedric brought Erica forward. "Meet Erica, queen of the True Blood nation to the west." He told them and the cheering began again as her cheeks turned just a little bit rosy from the attention.

Erica took the lead. "I would like to thank you for protecting and serving my betrothed." She said clearly and with a melody that soothed the soul. "I am here as an ambassador for my people. I gladly accept the ambassadorial role for you as well. If there is something you need, you have but to ask and I shall see if it can be done." She paused for a moment, collecting her thoughts. "The enemy is still

233

out there. We will need to form a unified army to defend ourselves against it. You are battle-hardened and seasoned troops. You are also the teachers of the next wave of soldiers. Your experience and knowledge will be invaluable in the new battle. I urge each of you to find a squad and to begin the training just as soon as we are all on the same soil." She said. You are all valuable, just as my people are. Everyone is important." She looked at all the confused faces and she knew that the education process would be slow. We are preparing to transport you back to your families and recruits. Do not be afraid by this, we will tell you when it will happen and you will have no need to fear." She said, trying to pave the way for Josh's contribution. "In the mean time, we will provide some nourishment and a toast to the happy couple." She said. Her eyes were twinkling with that last sentence. She turned to Josh. "If you would, brother, please take it from here." She instructed and Josh nodded. He stepped forward and bowed to the assembled troops.

"I am Joshua." He began simply. "I will be transporting you to the open field where your families have already been deposited. Do not be alarmed by this. This is only a temporary holding place until I can get the proper buildings erected to support you. Do not despair, it will not take long." He told them. There were sounds coming from the crowd that were of disbelief. He smiled at them.

"So, are we all ready to go now?" He asked them and the men all looked at each other. Even the group behind him did the same. Then he grinned childishly at them. "Then we go." He said. He closed his eyes and the image that he had been forming while he talked began to take shape, but on the hillside that he had previously created. There was a sudden shift, as if the world had been tilted for a brief second, and then the whole assembly, wounded and all were in the same field along with a crowd of civilians. The enormous walls of the True Blood kingdom were off in the distance. They were once again home.

Just as Josh had described it, there were clumps of people wandering around on the hillsides. The green grass was looking rather trampled. There were also many people who had found their way to the city gates and were now shopping and wandering through the kingdom proper. Mom and Dad looked at the new city and were instantly impressed.

"Whew! You did that son?" Dad asked when nobody said anything about the splendor they were all witnessing.

Erica saved Josh the embarrassment by fielding the question herself. "He worked on that image for days." She volunteered. "It is truly remarkable the detailed model he had made in preparation for this casting." She added.

Mom nodded her head. "I would have liked to have seen that." She said. The scale of the work before her had her awestruck. She knew that Josh had a unique mind. He had practically been born to play the part he was playing. With this new example of his work, there was really no choice but to admit that fully. "How far does this go?" She asked, feeling more of the technical aspect of this amazing scene.

Josh smiled. "It goes all the way." He replied.

Mom looked startled. "Really? all the way?" She repeated.

The others did not understand why the words were so amazing to Mom. She realized that and turned to see them. "What you don't know about the magic is that it has limitations. The power required to create a city wall drains you and many magicians use shortcuts by limiting the distance from which an object can be viewed. Or they show only the necessary things and other items will later need to be filled in. It's like a video game designer placing objects in a scene. The only difference is that these objects are hard and physical manifestations of the caster's mind. To create something this real requires more thought and energy than I can even imagine. For Josh to tell me that it has no limits, no stopping points, meant that he thought all the way to the shoreline and placed every object. He left nothing to chance. He left nothing out. Every detail you see had to be envisioned and fleshed out and then cast. A large group of sorcerers would have to work together to make this much stone and that many buildings. It is not something that can be taken lightly." She turned back to Josh. "How do you feel? Her motherly instincts knew that he was in trouble. She knew what he had done and now she fretted over the cost he had paid.

"Mom, I'm fine. I am just so tired." He said and she pulled him close to her and hugged him.

"I'm here now, you will be fine. Just don't try to do anything like that again. The price... is just too high." She admonished.

Josh pushed her away. "I have to. We need the extra room." He said and Mom started to object. He looked at her and his eyes were sad. "I have to..." He said. He closed his eyes and Mom started to scream.

"NO! Don't do it!" She screamed and the others were startled by her outburst. Josh slumped to the ground and he lay there, eyes still closed. As he lay there, buildings started popping up all over the field. They looked like extensions of the one that made up the city proper. The walls extended around the new area and all of the streets became cobble as well. Josh's mind was still functioning as he lay there unable to move. Mom and Dad each held him and they could feel the drain on themselves as well. Erica knew what this was about and she stepped up to help too. It probably looked very strange to those that were watching. A whole family huddled around a fallen young man and the world changing around them. The entire process took about thirty minutes and by that time, all of them were exhausted. The new addition to the kingdom was remarkably complete. Stables, docks, even a courtyard. There was also a new palace. It was as if Josh had simply duplicated his original image and attached it to the existing one. Actually, that wasn't far from the truth. When it was all done and everyone leaned back from Josh, you could see light streaks of gray in his hair. The casting had been so strong, so powerful, that it had aged him again.

King Cedric ordered that the family be brought to the new palace. They would soon be his family as well. They had just sacrificed of themselves to make his people have a place to live. He could not turn his back on them now. He was amazed as he walked through streets that he had just seen be built through magic. The cobbles were perfectly aligned and none of them shifted as he walked on them. The shops and houses were fully furnished as well. His people were being placed into homes and the merchants that he had were finding shops to sell their wares. Those shops seemed to already be filled with stock. They had lost nothing to the war. Their needs were met fully by the one wizard who had made all of this possible. Cedric greeted his people as they met him in the streets. They were thanking him and praising him for their deliverance. He smiled, nodded, shook hands, and he told them that things were going to be all right. He only hoped that it was so.

He made his way to his new palace and he had to admit that it was more impressive than the one he had left behind. Prince Josh knew what made a structure look grand. His guards were leading the way, making sure that everything was safe. They took their jobs very seriously. When the palace was cleared, they allowed the king to visit with the True Blood family that was now under the close watchful eye of the court healers. There were teas and salves and root to be chewed. All of these things were used to help the drained people get their personal energy back. Erica and Dad were doing fine. Other than their obvious concern for the others, they had fully recovered. Mom was still down and her features were a little bit sunken. Josh, however, was white as a sheet and his breathing was very shallow. He had lost the most and he had already been tired beyond the normal sense of the word before the casting. His road to recovery would be a long one. Hopefully, they had the time. There were still a lot of problems out there and they needed to get that army up and trained. The entire kingdom, as grand as it was, was still vulnerable if the enemy came now. King Cedric understood this and he was ready to take the steps required to address it. Of course he would need Erica's support, but he was certain that she would give it.

The Grand High Elf had gotten all of his people to relative safety in the woods. The arduous trek had cost them quite a bit, but they had finally made it. His people were even now digging in and placing their sentries so that the enemy could not enter the woods. He breathed a tired sigh of relief at the thought. He wondered how the humans had done with their defense. He knew that the enemy had hit them and hit them hard. He hoped for good news, although he admitted to himself that informing him would be a seriously low priority for the new king. Then his thoughts turned to the other elder races. He had not heard anything from any of them since the war had begun. Initially he figured that they were simply too busy to contact anyone else. The defense of each group would be the paramount worry. He could understand that clearly enough. He had done the same. He had even fled with his people when the warning came. He also knew that he needed to thank the young human who had done that. The boy had been so amazingly sure of himself. Then, the confirmation from Josh had sealed the deal. That was one powerful and startlingly well informed wizard. If he believed the young man, then it was good enough for the Grand High Elf.

The water began to boil and he pulled the kettle from the fire and poured some of it into his teacup. He had not had teas for other than medicinal uses before spending time with the humans. He found that he was rather fond of the practice. They were remarkably good teas with rich flavors that he had lived alongside without experiencing before. It made him appreciate the woodlands even more. These miraculous plants were growing wild and who knew what else was out there to be discovered? It was yet another reason to keep the enemy out of the woods.

No matter how he distracted himself, the thought of the enemy always resurfaced. It bothered him all day long and then his dreams would torment him further. It was fortune that had saved him from the fate he saw in those nightmarish dreams. He couldn't shake that thought from his mind either. That wolf had sent the human to him and it had been right. His bony hand grasped the teacup and the warmth felt good. The thin line of steam rising from the cup brought the aromatic flavors to his nostrils and he breathed it in deep. His aged body sucked in the air and let it out again, he had produced another sigh, but this one was more of pleasure than the exhaustion one he had done last. A knock on his tree caused him to look away, and broke his train of thought. He wondered briefly if he should thank whoever it was for the distraction.

"Sir, we have completed the outer perimeter defenses and are working on the inner perimeter." The younger elf reported. He was dressed in Captain's hunting dress and the Blue and white straps on his brown tunic represented a clan. Yes, the elves were based on a clan structure and the Grand High Elf was fortunate enough to be above that level. He did not have to deal with the pettiness that resulted from one clan's inability to coexist with another. He was who he was and his job was to safeguard all of his people. It was true that he might lose some of them if a physical defense of the woods was necessary, but the loss of the woods would be a lot worse. The report stood there unanswered, and the elf who brought it stood there patiently awaiting that response. The seconds strung together in a seemingly endless line of delays. Then, as if on some unseen cue, the Grand High Elf pulled himself back from the report.

"Very well, inform your commander that I am pleased, for now." He said cryptically. "Make certain that we have active sentries at all times. We will be setting up a more permanent solution soon." He said and the soldier elf lifted his hand to his heart and then dropped it again.

"Yes sir." He practically barked. Then the elf left the Grand High Elf to his business. The High elf felt the passing of time slowly. He could sit for hours as if it were a couple of minutes for anybody else. However, these times were almost desperate and he did no such thing now. Instead, he decided to check on the progress of the enemy, and if he could, discern the status of the human city that he had fled. He pulled the ancient bowl out from its leather wrapping. The weathered object was made entirely of one piece of wood and it had been grown in its current shape. It was a process that took centuries to perfect and this bowl would be handed down to the next high elf upon his eventual passing. He placed the bowl gingerly on the small table that he had grown in his room. The bowl set there perfectly. It truly had been a perfect growing and he treasured the vessel highly. It also helped him with his magic. He poured the water into it as he had done so many times before. This was a distant scrying so he decided to use wet sand as the pigmentation. He poured the three primary colors of sand into the bowl, one at a time in equal amounts. They looked like little mounds of sand under the water. He looked into the bowl and was satisfied by what he saw. Then he waved his boney hand over the bowl and started to say the words of the incantation that would bring the sand to life. The water looked calm at first. There was scarcely a ripple on the surface. He continued to recite the words and the sand began to stir at the bottom. The surface rippled ever so slightly and then the sand became a murky solution of vibrant colors. It was a swirl and then it was chaos. The High elf thought of the enemy and the sand began to organize. In seconds the image of a burning field with black dots in the bowl. It was even shifting and moving as he watched. The bowl remained perfectly still, but the images inside of it were moving. He was watching a movie of a distant place. The field could have been anywhere though. He willed it to back away from the scene and to pan out to see where they were. He caught the edge of a river on his image as the bowl followed his command. The image pulled away more and mountains could be seen in the distance. It pulled back more and then the ruins of a city could be seen. The smoke was climbing from burning buildings. He felt a lump in his throat as he realized the devastation of the scene he was viewing. It was not the city he was supposed to be defending. He knew that from the burning standards that were trying to hold on even as the wind fanned the flames that were destroying them. This was the southern city near the vast southern ocean. The rivers that fed into the southern ocean had created a perfect place for a large city and this was one of the largest, or at least it had been. The image was so disturbing that he swept it away. It had been awful, but it meant that the enemy was nowhere near his people and the beloved forest.

Now he turned his attention to the prince who had become king. The city he had pledged to defend. The one he had abandoned. It still made him feel terrible. He decided to check in on that city. The bowl began to form the image and he watched closely as the damaged, but not destroyed, walls came into view. There was smoke here and there. There were wash marks where large amounts of water had been used to wash away something, presumably enemy troops. There were no people here though. He pulled back the image to encompass more of the city. The major population center was intact and no one appeared to be present. He scratched his head and panned around the scene. Yes, a major skirmish had happened here. The nearby mountains had been changed. The passes had been filled in and the front gates had been destroyed. Yet, the city still stood. It made no sense. He had yet to see anybody in the city as well. Where could they all be? He pulled back, determined to catch a glimpse of somebody. The outlying fields had been burnt and the farmhouses had been razed. There was nothing left as far as city support. Food would be a serious problem by the time winter came. He still saw no one. He pulled back far enough that a person would be indistinguishable from the background and still there was no movement, no movement at all. He swept away the image in frustration. Then he chose to focus on the prince himself.

The bowl started to form the image of a crowned figure and immediately the High Elf recognized his friend. A wave of relief swept across his face as he realized that the human leader was safe. The surroundings were unknown to him. The walls of the buildings near the new king were pristine. It was as if they had just been built, or at least had recently been maintained. There were cobbled streets and people moving to and fro. It was as if there was no war going on. It was a strange sight, nearly as strange to him as the empty city had been. He needed to know more. He pulled back the image to find out where on this world he was. The image became more complex as it pulled back. The walls that were perfect belonged to a massive city. The pull out continued and it was now obvious that the entire city was brand new. He didn't know how this was possible, but it was right there before his own eyes. There was no denying it. The pull out continued and he could see that the city seemed to stretch on up the hill and off into the distance. It was much larger than any city he had ever seen before. The architecture was even grand. Here there were people bustling about on their business. This was an active city. He couldn't even guess at the population of it. It was simply incredible. As he pulled out he caught sight of the ocean front view. This was the western city! This was the kingdom of the True Bloods! How had his prince come to be here? It was obvious that strange things were afoot among the human settlements. The lesser settlements were gone. The only thing that remained was this massive city. It was such a wonder that the Grand High Elf continued to look at it until the spell ended. When the bowl turned all murky and then became unwatchable, he actually felt cheated somehow. It was as if watching this city made him a part of it. Perhaps it did. He decided that a visit to this place was in order. He wasn't sure when he would get around to it, but he now felt the need to see this fantastic place first hand.

The Master found himself surrounded by his underlings. His transference to this world had gone off without a hitch and he was ready to take his place at the head of his armies. The sunlight burnt his flesh. He waved an arm and the clouds came in to cover up the offending ball of flame. He stood there, hunched over and steaming. His red claws really stood out in the diminished light. He took in a lungful of the local air and its sweetness turned his stomach. He put that on his list of things to fix in this world. Gone were the ever-present smells of sulfur and tar. It was cold here as well. He started to pull on his armor. His red skin was only further highlighted by the armor that was made from bone. His weapon of choice was a mighty scythe. Once he was ready, the masses around him parted and revealed the way out of this small area and out into the open. The first real sign of his work was that the fields were now ash. The closest city had been burnt to the ground and there were bodies strewn about everywhere.

"Ah, it is like home." He said with a low chuckle. "Let us bring our hospitality to the rest of this little world." He said and the surrounding mass that was his personal army fell into step. They were each armed and armored much as he was. They were substantially smaller than the mighty devil, but they looked just as gruesome and horrifying. This was the day that they had awaited. The shock troops had done well in places, but they were incompetent when faced with a sizable resistance. This army was much better suited to the slaughter that this mission required. They were deep in the southern portion of the continent and the southern ocean could be heard in the background. He was facing away from it. The conquest was not in the water, it was on the land so his enemies were all before him now. He licked his lips in anticipation. Now that he was here, the real battle would begin. With a mighty leap forward, he launched out into the burning fields and arrowed towards the northeast. He would take the next city himself. Nothing could withstand his might. He looked forward to the fun. His troops leapt into action as well. Even though they were much smaller, they were agile and the wall of red flesh moved as one towards the unsuspecting city. The sounds of thundering feet could be heard from quite a distance off. It would strike fear into the enemy even before they could see his army. They had no chance to defend against him. He was the Master!

The City of Greensborough sat amidst a series of rolling hills. The main tributary from the mountains to the north fed a good sized river right past the human city and out to the eastern sea. The trade routes to the western and southern cities were over land. They did not trade with the northerners. The bandits and other low-lifes were too thick in that direction. No sane merchant would dare risk his investment in that direction. Even with all of that, the city was prosperous. The surrounding hills held a great bounty in tradable goods. They had silkworm farms and orchards of ripening fruit trees. They had fresh honey from bee hives that were staggeringly large. They also had craftsmen that could take these materials and produce some of the finest quality goods available anywhere. They were so far removed from the normal trade routes that the war had not yet come to them. So blissfully unaware, they continued on with their normal lives, not knowing that a rude awakening was coming just over the horizon.

King Cedric looked at his fiancé and smiled. The seriousness of the moment was somewhat lessened by her smile. Still, they had work to do and he knew it. They were on their way to the training grounds. The proclamation had gone out looking for defenders of the realm and many young men and women answered the call. The training grounds were full. It was a sight for weary eyes. There were formations of recruits learning their craft. The sounds of training, barking orders, and cadences was music to the ears. Exercises and weapon-craft were taking place all around them. It was a source of great pride. They continued on and behind a wall were the archers. There were a hundred archers practicing behind that wall. They were working feverishly to be ready when the enemy came. Unlike their sister city to the east, they *knew* that the enemy was coming. Time was not a luxury they had to waste. The targets were riddled with arrows and the tables behind them were heaped with even more. There were more people to take up the bows when these people finished their turn. Two kingdoms worth of volunteers added up to a lot of troops. The mess hall was running around the clock and supplies were being brought in from storage houses that Josh had included into his original design. Without those storehouses, the whole project would have been in jeopardy. There were literally tens of thousands of arrows and hundreds of bows available. There were swords, hammers, axes, and even slings aplenty. Armor of varying weights and sizes were also present. Cedric had not known about these supplies at first, but when his own scout stumbled across a storage house, the report was a welcome one. The walls had small raised towers with archer slots scattered throughout. Nothing seems to have been left to chance. The army, such as it was, was still growing. People were still coming in when they heard about the massive buildup and the wondrous training. All of Cedric's original fighters were now instructors. They had each selected prize pupils to help in the logistics of supplying information. Those pupils became squad leaders. The individual recruits were then supervised at the squad level and periodic testing was done to ensure that no squad would fall short of the expected goals. There had never been a quicker mobilization of manpower. It was so vast that the ban on female warriors was lifted. A second barracks had been provided by the amazing foresight of the young sorcerer. The women were training just as hard as the men were. It was a concerto of blood and sweat.

The two royals completed their survey and they could tell that both of them were pleased. Erica's guard captain strolled up with a huge sword over his shoulder. The two leaders stopped to allow him to catch up with them. They both smiled as he approached.

"Ah your majesties, I had heard that you were here. Are you missing out on all this fun?" He asked them. Cedric laughed, but Erica took the challenge seriously.

"Not missing it enough to let you get away with that." She replied hotly. The Guard Captain smiled.

"I thought not." He replied and then he handed her the massive sword. He drew his own and the two of them stepped aside to one of the many sparring areas that had been cordoned off. King Cedric found that he was amused and he sat back to watch the display. He really didn't know what to expect, but he was ready to be entertained. The look on his face when Erica did move was classic.

Erica checked the balance of the weapon and found it to her liking. She dropped into stance and she and The Guard Captain began to circle, testing each other's defense. Erica began her first move. The four foot sword swung down and to the side as she stepped forward. This allowed her right side to be unprotected. The Captain saw the opportunity and knew that it was a trap. He held his stance a bit longer, an imperceptible heartbeat and then he moved to the left. It would have exposed Erica's flank if she did what he was expecting her to do. Somehow, these two had sparred for so long that Erica knew what his reaction would be and had planned for it as well. The sweep she had started was supposed to have swept back and covered the exposed area and pulled her opponent out of position. Now she was faced with a head on charge because they had aligned to each other. The Captain knew what her move was, so he was not concerned about the sword tip. He should have been.

Erica did not sweep back as anticipated, she dug the tip of her massive sword into the ground and used it as a pivot point to launch herself forcibly at the Captain. She brought both feet up and kicked him squarely in the chest as he swung, taking him off balance. The Guard Captain went sprawling, his own sword flinging from his grasp as he was dumped unceremoniously on his back. The look on his face was priceless. It was full of shock. Erica smiled sweetly at him; her breathing was slow and regular. Cedric just gaped open-mouthed at the young girl who had bested a man at arms without breaking a sweat.

Erica pulled her sword to the side and reached out a hand to help the Guard Captain up. His first look of shock turned into a look of joy. She helped him up and he did not release her hand.

"Tell me your majesty; did you use the ancients for that one?" He asked and his eyes were sincere.

Erica blushed, but her smile did not fade. "Nope, that was all me." She replied proudly. Then her tone changed to thoughtful. "Of course it would only work against you. We have sparred so many times that we know each other's moves. Because of that I was able to predict your response and then do something unexpected." She said and he nodded his agreement.

The Guard Captain was smiling now. "As your instructor, I am proud of your progress and I applaud your dedication to the craft." He said with admiration. Erica pulled away from him and found her Fiancé close by.

He looked at her in a different light. "They told me you were a fighter." He began; his mind seemed to be replaying what he had just seen. "They didn't tell me how good you were." He added. "That was an astounding display of skill." He turned back to the sword that Erica had been using. "I thought he had given you that sword because it was too heavy for you and he wanted an edge." Erica started to protest, but Cedric held up a hand. "However, I was completely wrong. I can see that he is a great teacher and that you, as his student, have surpassed his expectations." He smiled at his bride to be. "It matches the other things that I have heard about you." He said and Erica gave him a sideways glance.

"Who have you been asking about me?" She asked him outright.

Cedric felt the trap he was about to be caught in and gracefully pulled back. "Look, it is obvious that your people love you. It goes beyond their being loyal to the throne. They would live and die for you. They count on you for everything and you deliver whenever asked. Your connection to the commoners is unheard of within the royal ranks. You are something very special. I only hope that you realize how much that is so." He hoped that would suffice to appease her.

Erica winked at him. "Oh I'm not that uncommon." She teased. "After all, I rely heavily upon my brother to take care of many of the things that I decree." She stated honestly. "We are a pair that was designed to help the people. We are not at all alike except for our interest in making our people's lives better." She said without pride, it was simply a matter of fact to her.

Cedric laughed. "Yes, that was exactly what I was talking about." He put his arm around her as they walked. It was so slick of a move that Erica didn't even realize he had done it and that she had leaned into him. "You are somewhat of a mystery to the rest of us royals."

He said without any malice. "I must admit that you think quite differently from every queen or princess that I have ever met." They stopped walking for a brief second. "Don't get me wrong, I mean that in the nicest of ways. I find the fact that you are different most intriguing." He added as they resumed their casual walk. The training was still going on around them.

The Guard Captain had taken his leave of them since it was obvious to him that they needed some time alone. It had seemed like an odd place to attempt it, but he did not want to bring that up for fear of reprisals. The new king had her majesty spellbound with his charms. In all honesty, he was thankful for it. If she produced an heir, then the line would continue and the people could continue to enjoy her rein without the heavy clouds of doubt hanging overhead. The clouds on the horizon were dark enough already. That enemy army was still out there. It would eventually find them. That's what all this training was about after all. He just hoped that they had enough time before the attack came. They needed to be ready, for the next fight would be the last one. It didn't take a master tactician to understand that. There were duties to be performed and the good Captain had squandered enough time on his favorite student. It was time he got back to business. He nodded to himself as he cleared the wall and headed down to the armory. He would oversee the maintenance on the weapons. He was still needed, and that felt good.

CHAPTER 11

Sarvir Kinden sat atop his wagon. The tired old horse that he had owned for six winters now trudged ahead at his miserly slow, but steady pace. The grasses were tall and the thought of a bandit raid crossed Sarvir's mind more than once. He had a crossbow on his lap just in case somebody tried something. Mr. Kinden was a merchant. There were a lot of merchants in the Eastern City of Greensborough, but he was one of the more successful merchants that did a blisteringly profitable trade by using some of the questionable roads and getting to his somewhat disreputable customers ahead of schedule. Yes, he was a legal merchant, but only just so. The sounds of the wagon wheels, grinding heavily in the well-worn ruts of the road were the only sound he could make out. That and the clop clop clop of the horse hooves that suggested that they were still moving. The darkness here was almost a physical thing. That last hour before dawn was always dark, but here, shadowed in the foothills of the majestic mountain peaks above. It was almost pitch black. His nerves were starting to wear thin. He wished that it were dawn already so that he could see a bit more. It would still be dark here, but not blindingly so. A noise in the distance to his right made him look closely. The dark was just that, dark. He could see nothing. He strained his ears to hear something, anything more. There were no more sounds. At least there were no sounds that he could hear over the wagon. He decided to spur the horse on a bit more with a light slap on the reins. The horse seemed to take it as a personal affront, but begrudgingly started to pick up the pace. Of course this just made the wagon louder. The chance of hearing anything else was remarkably low. He continued on and hoped that there were no surprises in store for him further up the trail. He was almost to his destination and the small village of cutthroats and thieves were waiting for his delivery. He was hauling two casks of ale and one of wine. The wagon rode heavily with that much cargo aboard, and it made his trek seem longer than it actually was. He found that he was very close to his destination. He breathed a sigh of relief even as the scout watched him from the comfort and safety of the shadows. Even the cutthroats and thieve were unaware that they were being watched. These scouts were stealthy and they gave away no sounds of life, not even breathing, since they were long dead.

Sarvir brought his wagon into the small village and he pulled around to the guards. The competitive nature of thieves in these parts meant that there was always someone on watch. In fact, if any of the rival factions had known Sarvir's cargo, he would never have been able to complete the trip. He knew this and he had purchased extras bolts of cloth and other minor pieces of finery to explain his presence in the countryside. The casks were well hidden from casual view. He reined up and smiled at the guard who had the disposition of one who was not supposed to be doing guard duty today. That didn't bode well for the hapless merchant. Still, business was business.

Sarvir let the guard take the reins of his wagon near the horse's snout and then he was led to the staging area of the small village. This was procedure and was no cause for alarm. He tried to keep his nerves in check even as daylight began to finally make a showing. When the wagon finally reached its parking spot, Sarvir got down from the seat. He tied off the horse's reins and he gave his best disarming smile to the guard.

"I have a delivery for your leader." He announced and the guard rolled his eyes.

"Of course you do or you would be dead now." The guard barked and Sarvir hoped that he was joking, he wasn't. "What did you bring?" The guard prompted when Sarvir failed to understand the previous statement. It was a known fact that merchants were not the brightest breed in the hills.

Sarvir started. "Oh, sorry, I brought ale and wine." He replied hastily, hoping not to further earn this man's ire. Apparently it had been the right thing to say.

"Well why didn't you say so?" The guard asked in a much friendlier demeanor. "I'll help you with the offload and get the boss." He offered and Sarvir nodded and thanked him. In moments the casks were setting on the ground and the boss, a surly looking ruffian with a scar on one shoulder, was greeting him with a mostly toothless smile.

"It seems that you have arrived none too soon my friend." He told the brave little merchant. The area that he had driven to bring these goods was infested with bandits and thieves. Of course these men were more of the same, but the bounty he had brought them was more precious than gems in these parts. "I am grateful for you efforts." He added and he handed over the coins that were the agreed upon payment. Then his smiled faded just a bit. "We hear rumors of strangers in these parts; watch yourself carefully as you head out of here. We wouldn't want to lose our favorite merchant friend." He told Sarvir.

The merchant thanked him for his business and the advice and he turned his wagon around. It would not be long now and he would be heading across those same lands in the daylight. He would be much more comfortable then. These deals always made him edgy; perhaps that was why he took them in the first place. His father had taught him long ago that no real reward was worth anything unless the risk involved was just as great. Those words and served him well and he was smiling when his wagon came around the bend that had him so afraid last time. The sound of something whizzing through the air made him pause and he looked up just to see the arrow sticking out of his chest. He had not felt the impact due to shock, but now it was beginning to hurt. A second arrow sailed in and added to the problems his chest was having. The first one had punctured a lung and blood was beginning to fill that one up. Breathing was getting increasingly difficult and he tried to call out. A third arrow caught him in the throat. His cries came out as a gurgling sound and he fell off of the wagon. The wheels of the wagon rolled over his legs and he was already too far gone to notice. The wagon was aflame in seconds and the demons slaughtered the horse in truly nasty style. The carcass was spread over a fairly wide area and then the group moved in towards the human settlement this wagon had just left. What the demons had not counted on was that the wagon had another *hidden* cargo. The gunpowder that had been lining the lower bed was below the rest of the wagon so it did not ignite until the wagon was almost completely engulfed. The explosion ripped the flaming embers apart and startled the demons. It also sent a warning to the thieves that Sarvir had just visited.

The camp came to life as the smoke rose in the not too far distance. The explosion had shaken the ground and nobody could have ignored the repercussions of a fire and explosion this close to their hideout. The boss looked in the direction and his head bowed down. He knew that the merchant was now dead. It was a shame since he had just warned the smallish man. Still, they had this warning and if they wasted it, it would mean that the merchant had died for nothing. So, even though he was a thief and an outlaw, he was also an honorable man. He strapped on his sheath and armor and prepared to do battle. He already knew that his look-outs would be on full alert. If any of them weren't then they were all dead. His rage was such that he would haunt whoever survived and make sure that they suffered for their hand in this if he died. A grim smile crossed his lips as he prepared to face the unknown. He left his tent and made his way to the horses. This would be a grand fight. He would make whoever had killed the merchant pay. He swore this to his gods, uncertain and uncaring of whether or not they were listening. His men did hear him though, and they reflected his mood back at him. They all wanted justice and bloodshed, today they would get it.

The spirit tree had shown the Sprite king so many things that his head ached. There were so many things going on at once and the tree had limits to its ability to portray them. He had watched such insignificant things that seemed to be a waste of time until he saw other things that linked back to it. He knew that the Spirit Tree was wise and all-seeing. He also knew that it had all eternity to make its point, even if he didn't live long enough to hear it. However, these images were disturbing enough that he had to pay attention to them. He couldn't even look away. Then he saw the eastern city and he realized that he had made a mistake. He had not sent a messenger to warn them of the invasion. Initially he had figured that they were too far removed to be in danger. Now it looked as though the enemy force was heading directly at it. Worse yet, they were clearing the path along the way. Anywhere there were signs of civilization or even organization, they destroyed. Orchards were burnt and villages were wiped out. Cattle and sheep were also slain. Nothing was allowed to live in their wake. They even killed all the bird using some sling device that seemed to be a competitive sport for them. The enemy was destroying not only the peoples of this world, but the world's ability to sustain them. This was not a war over territory or rights. This was simply genocide. No quarter would be given for surrender. No lives will be spared due to negotiations. They would sweep across and kill everything and everybody. The images froze for a moment as he digested that. He asked the tree to wait just a bit longer. The images were hurting him and he wanted a bit more rest. The tree paused for the briefest of times and then told him that they needed to finish. He had no choice but to listen to his god tell him of how the world was coming to an end. The final image was the most disturbing. He witnessed the Spirit Tree burning as the bodies of brave sprites lay scattered about. The image froze and the Sprite King could not pull his eyes away from it. This was tortuous.

"Please, Great Spirit Tree, allow me to divert my eyes." He cried out and the Tree did drop the image from his mind. However, the memory was already there. He would remember that image for the rest of his life. The enemy was closing in on those poor unaware humans and he could see no way to stop the images from coming true. He would need help, and a lot of it.

If he had been able to look back at the images, he would realize that other things were happening that would show the first signs of hope in this agonizing war. He would have seen the new kingdom that combined both Erica's and Cedric's influences. He would have seen the army that they were building. After Mom talked with Erica about what Josh had done in his first city defense, she had been busily casting the scarecrows that were his expendable defensive troops. The natural boundaries, coupled with a few surprise defenses would allow them to hold off the enemy for quite some time. But that hope was lost to the Sprite King. He was lost in his despair. He knew that he needed to contact someone, anyone that could help the eastern city. His main problem now was that he knew nobody that could even get there before the image became fact. Even his very fleet-of-foot scouts were unable to travel that far. He was sullen and withdrawn. There had to be a way. He continued to go over ideas in his head that he had already rejected. The few sprites that were around him remained silent but they were concerned. They had just as few choices on helping him as he had of helping the war effort. This was not the best of times for the sprite community.

A chime sounded and everyone looked up. It was not a familiar sound and it made no sense. The sprites' initial reaction to something unknown was to flee or hide. They were so small and fragile after all. However, the chime seemed to hold their interest and they swarmed out of their hiding places to see what was coming. There was nothing but surprise for what they found when they all looked up.

Mouse rode in on a bicycle. This was no ordinary bicycle though; he was flying it using the magic that Josh had once before put into it. He was coming in to land and his own confidence seemed to waver just a bit as he neared the ground. The chime sounded again, 'bring bring'. His front wheel touched down and the back one followed quickly thereafter. Mouse brought the vehicle to a stop by placing it sideways and the back tire slid in an arc, draining the remaining speed. The human got off of the strange vehicle and looked around. The sprites were still all there, huddle around him and he smiled at them.

"I'm sorry to bother you folks, but is the Sprite King here?" He asked and the looks of shock swept the assembly like the wave at a sports stadium. Mouse maintained his genial smile even though he could feel the tension rise at his request.

"I am king." A Sprite said and the little green faces all turned to see the Sprite King standing on a branch, nearly eye level with Mouse. "I have seen you before, haven't I young man?" He asked and Mouse looked embarrassed.

"That may be your highness, since we have mutual friends in Josh and Erica." He replied and the Sprite King looked as startled as his people now.

Mouse found the courage to continue in the face of all of the attention. "In fact, that is why I am here. Josh needs your help." He said and the Sprite King looked concerned.

"What has happened?" The Sprite King asked and Mouse leaned in closer.

"To be honest your majesty, I don't know." Mouse replied and then he shook his head. "No, I'm not crazy. I have been sent here to find you and to enlist your aid for Josh at this time. I am only a messenger here." Mouse explained.

The Sprite King seemed to think this over. "So who are you delivering a message for?"

Mouse dropped his eye contact. "I am delivering a message for you from the Wolf." He said and the entire group looked even more nervous. "It's not exactly like you think. There is no evil in this wolf. I have been doing his bidding for weeks now and everything he has told me has come to pass. All of the instructions that he made me memorize have been crucial to the recipients." Mouse continued. "I'm afraid that I cannot tell you more than this, I simply don't know what is going on, I only have my messages to deliver. In fact yours is the last one I have." He said and his relief at having completed his mission was obvious.

The Sprite King took in all of this and he thought about it carefully. "I do remember Joshua speaking of a wolf that helped him to understand his power when he first arrived in this world. It is possible that we are talking about the same one. It is a mystical beast after all." The small green monarch scratched his chin in contemplation. "I believe that you have been completely honest with us and that you believe that Josh is in trouble. With what is going on right now in the world, it could hardly be otherwise. We need to go and help our friend. He saved us before and that debt can never be fully repaid." He turned to his people. "Do what you can to find out where Joshua is and what sort of trouble he is in. I shall prepare to go and meet him as soon as I have a destination from you." He stood in a majestic pose as if considering the horizon. "I am counting on all of you. Let us be the ones who tip the scales to the side of good. Fly fast and free my brothers and sisters." He said and all of the sprites took flight. They spread out like a water ripple in a pond. Satisfied, the Sprite King turned back to Mouse. "You may stay a while if you like. I would like to hear more about your affiliation with the True Bloods." He suggested and Mouse smiled and knelt down.

"It would by my honor your majesty." He said and the two of them proceeded to get comfortable for the story telling that was to come.

The eastern city was not a fortress, but they did post guards at the entrances due to bandit activity in the area. Their city militia was top notch due to the constant deployment and rigorous practice and maintenance of the troops deployed there. So it was normal to see guards at the gate. The lone thief was wounded and weak as he staggered towards the city. The guards spotted him almost immediately and dispatched a team out to investigate. The man collapsed right as they arrived, the feeling that he had actually made it took too much for him to continue.

"What's this about then?" The guard asked in a burly voice that spoke more of impatience than anything else. A lone thief was not a threat to the city.

The thief looked into the guard's eyes. "We were attacked by demons. They are coming here soon, you must..." He faltered and almost passed out. The guard shook him violently and his eyes popped open again. "You must close the city and prepare to defend it. These were scouts only. I think there's a larger force on its way here." He said and his strength was pretty much gone. "Please hurry." He said as he slipped from consciousness.

The guards hoisted the fallen man up and took him back to the gate. Then, because it is better to err on the side of caution, the guard called an alert and the city gates were closed. Then, two guards took the thief to the Officer of the day.

The officer of the day was a lowly Lieutenant today. He was not pleased with having the duty either. His temper was such that he was in trouble often, and so he drew the duty as a form of punishment.

Although they didn't call it that, they called it disciplinary training. He was sitting at his duty desk when the two guards carried in a wounded man and he was ready to go off on the breech in protocols alone.

"Why do you bring me this wounded, stinking man?" He asked in a brazen tone of anger and hostility.

"Sir, he brought a report of an impending attack on the city." The guard replied who had ordered the alert. Apparently the alert had been ignored at this desk. "I have had the gates closed and an alert called." He added, trying to show his initiative to a superior officer. He shouldn't have bothered.

"So this possible drunkard, wounded and all, told you that we are under attack so you close us all up?" His voice hinted at incredulity.

"Yes sir." The guard replied, ignoring the slight and hoping just to get out of this with his stripes intact. "He said that demons attacked him and that they were only scouts. He said that a larger force was probably on its way here." The guard elaborated.

"That's even better!" The officer screamed. "He tells you that demons exist and are attacking weary travelers and that we happen to be in their way. Then he tells you that there are more of them!" The Lieutenant looked disgusted. "Have his wounds seen to and have him washed. When he is ready, bring to me for questioning." He ordered and the guards carried the man out of the Lieutenant's office as quickly as they could without looking like they were hurrying. It was a novel job of acting on their part. They had just dodged the spear and they were both rather relieved that they had successfully done it. Now they rushed to comply with the man's orders. There was no sense in tempting fate twice in one day. They wanted nothing more than to put this little episode behind them for good. Once they dropped this guy off, they would just disappear into the woodwork again. Just to complicate things for them, the patient started babbling in his sleep.

"They're coming, look out everyone." He said mumbling. Then he screamed "Boss NO!" The sound rattled the windows in the small room. The nurse stood over the wounded man with leaves and salves. His wounds were soon dressed, but the babbling and tortured dreams continued. The poor man tossed and turned in his restless sleep. The nurse had to report on his progress the next morning and she told them the tale of this troubled man in that report.

It was a new day and the Officer of the Day today was a powerfully muscled Captain in the local militia. He had a handlebar mustache and keen gray eyes that caught everything. He also carried the scars from more battles than most men ever heard of. Still, with all of that, he was still agile and definitely in shape. He looked at the report and found it to be interesting. He strapped on his sword belt and put on his hat. Then he headed out to visit the medical building.

The sun was shining out and the shadows were getting steadily shorter as midday approached. He had a good spring to his step and he whistled as he walked across the compound towards his target building. The city proper was inside the double wall, here were only crews' quarters and militia barracks and support buildings. He found the door he was looking for and knocked heartily on it. A smiling face met his eyes as the door slid aside.

"I hear you have a mysterious man here." He stated with anticipation and the nurse backed away from the doorway to allow him entry into the cramped space.

"Quite so, sir." The nurse responded as she beckoned the good Captain towards the bed. There, the prisoner, or refugee, or whatever he was lay perfectly still. If not for the rise and fall of his chest, one would think he had already passed.

"You there!" The armed Officer barked and the man on the bed startled. "I think you need to do some explaining." He said a bit briskly.

The man looked around, as if confused. Of course that might be because they had brought him to this place at night, or even that they had moved him once he was no longer conscious. "Whe... Where am I?" He asked, trying to get his bearings.

"You are in the medical wing of the western gate of Greensborough." The Officer replied. "Perhaps you could tell me what you were doing outside our gates and with wounds like that on you?" He prompted and he tried to portray a sense of urgency to the fallen man.

"We were attacked." The thief said plainly.

"Yeah, I got that. Why don't you start from the beginning?" The officer prompted.

"Okay. I am a member of the Thribold clan. Before you say anything about that, I must add that I am a relatively new member, and that being in a clan is one of the only ways to survive out there in the wilderness. But none of that matters now. The clan has been wiped out except for me." He paused as the sadness tried to overtake him.

"Get on with it. What happened?" The Officer prodded. His patience was a little strained.

"We had just received a merchant shipment of ale and wine and were about to celebrate our good fortune when an explosion went off just outside of camp. We came to full alert and waited for the enemy, whoever it was, to come for us. The explosion was way too close to have been a coincidence." There was another pause. It was uncertain if it was because of the grief connected to the next memory, or if he was searching for the right words. He continued again without the nudging this time. "They came in a wave. There were not many of them, only twelve, but they fought like demons. In fact, someone said that they were demons!" His eyes went huge at the memory. "They killed and killed and burnt everything. The Boss sent me out early on or I would have been killed too. What I did see scared me half to death. Cold steel plunged into them, and they laughed at it. They continued to fight with wounds that a normal man would have fallen to. I saw one of them lose an arm and he picked up the sword in his other one and continued to attack. I did see one of the demons die, though, when his head came off. But the Boss had only killed one and then he fell too." Another pause, this one was definitely for the grief. But he took a deep breath and then pushed on. "I was hit a couple of times and had fallen during my flight. The demons were killing even the fallen men and I scrambled for all I was worth into the underbrush while they were distracted. The fear inside me made me keep moving. I realized that these demons were going to kill everybody. I had to warn the city. At the least you needed to know to take their heads to stop them. There were only twelve of them, it was a scouting force. There would be more to come. The Boss was certain of it before he died." With that last statement, the thief had lost most of his energy. His emotions were taking a huge toll and now he had to be worried over whether or not he was believed. If they ignored his warnings, then he would die along with them when the demons came. It was almost too much for one man to bear. Still, if he died, then it would stop hurting. He was suffering from survivor's guilt. It would be quite some time before he felt anything like normal again.

"Well, you've given me a lot to think about. I shall take your warning under advisement." The Officer said. There was a hint of interest in his tone and that tiny spark of chance brought hope to the fallen thief. For whatever reason, he felt that he had somehow succeeded and maybe, just maybe, he and this city would survive the upcoming attack. The Officer of the day nodded and left the recuperating man to do a little investigation of his own. There were regular patrols and it would only be prudent to at least prove that this man was not telling the truth. If they discovered a real threat during that process, then the city would get the confirmation it sought. He headed to the stables to dispatch a patrol into the vicinity of the Thribold clan. He would know one way or the other in less than a day. Who could ask for a more rapid response than that?

Mom was still holding a vigil over Josh. He was so far gone this time that she was always worried. Dad had done his best to console her and to tell her what a good job he had done, but it was not what she wanted to hear. She wanted to hear that her little boy was fine. Nobody was telling her that. She even considered taking him to the emergency room of the hospital at home. Her motherly instincts were powerful and even though she knew of the damage that might cause, she was ready to risk it. If not for Dad's cautioning, it would already have been done. In the back of her mind she wondered what that blasted Guardian of Balance thought of that. She shook her head to clear it of the memory. Instead she turned her attention back to her son. He was still laying just the way she had left him. In fact, he had not even moved a muscle. She had thought that people in a coma could move a little bit every so often in order to make sure their attendants were paying attention. Of course that had been wrong. Mom tried to join minds with him using the call of the ancients, but Josh could not respond. Or at least he did not respond. He was lost to her at least for now. He looked so peaceful now. His skin was a bit wrinkled and he had streaks of gray hair now. The spell had been absolutely massive. She had tried to stop him at the last minute, but his determination had carried him through it. He had fallen early and they had all given of their own strength to help him finish. Without that small amount of aid, he may have died. Nobody had ever done that much magic in one shot. Josh's work was the stuff of legends.

Mom and Dad both had to lay low when dealing with the civilian population. They were supposed to be dead so that their children could hold the seat of political power. It had created a small amount of grief when the Sprites had learned of the deception. However, they had understood the reasoning behind it and had actually helped to keep the secrets of the True Bloods. Mom jerked upright as her mind latched onto that thought. She blurted out two words. "The Sprites!" She said aloud, almost in a shout.

Dad shook his head as if to clear it. "What?" He asked almost lazily. He had taken the night watch and was still pretty tired. He noticed the look of excitement on his wife's face. "What is it?" He repeated.

Mom was almost beaming. "The Sprite King! We can call on him and he can help us with Josh!" She said in a rush. She continued on, making sure that she couldn't be interrupted. "They have that healing and natural magic. The sprites have long been friends of us True Bloods and from what we've been told Josh has a direct connection with them. It *has* to work!" She seemed to have finished her head of steam and Dad looked at her with a sideways glance.

"Okay, how do we contact the Sprite King?" He asked, trying to follow her logically and make sure this was not a false hope.

Mom looked around and found what she was looking for. "In our world, I would use a mirror, but the most reflective surface we have is water." She explained. Her hands were moving feverishly fast as she made the preparations for the spell. "I need to remember exactly how he looks and then we'll need just a bit of luck." She said, her voice trailing off with her concentration on the bowl. The water in it was now perfectly still. Dad felt himself feeling a mixture of emotions. There was hope and relief that they were able to try something, anything. There was also suspicion that this was yet another dead end. There were so many 'what-if's' that his mind kept throwing at him. He kept shoving them aside in order to remain calm. Inside he was panicking though. The only outward sign of his personal struggle was the clenching of his right fist. Mom did not notice it at all in her busy work.

She had the image in her mind and she applied the magic. The thought that she was able to do this again filled her with personal glee. This power had been denied her back home. It would only have caused trouble over there anyway. Now she needed it to work flawlessly. Nobody knew how much time they had to complete this. Josh was immobile and unresponsive. She needed to do something now. The bowl started to shimmer with the image and ripples began to churn the water and within seconds, the image was of a green man in royal dress with a human male talking. This was not exactly what she expected, but she did not dare argue, or try again. She felt the link begin to snake its way through the ether to the target. Once it connected, she saw the difference immediately in her bowl. The Sprite king blinked twice and then turned to face the bowl. He was looking right out of the reflection at her.

"Ah, so both of you are alive." He said and there was some joviality in his voice. "What is so important that you need to contact me from the other world?" He asked and Mom's serious tone made him lose his smile.

"We are not in the other world, we are here. Josh is in trouble and we need you to help him as soon as you can get here." She said and her surprise was evident when the human male spoke back.

"That's what I told him." Mouse said. "They have been looking for you for a couple of hours. Tell them where you are." He instructed and Mom replied, not sure how this young man knew about this call even before she placed it. She sent the mental image though.

"Do I know you?" Mom asked, trying to place this strange young man.

Mouse smiled back warmly. "I am Mouse. Josh and Erica know me." Mouse's eyes lit up. "You're their mother aren't you?" He asked excitedly.

Mom was still off balance. "Well, yes, actually." She replied, wondering when she had lost control of this conversation. She decided to return to topic. "How soon can we expect aid?" She asked seriously.

Mouse looked at the Sprite King and the small green ruler made several gestures and spoke softly to the human. When Mouse turned back his face was more relaxed. "He says that he is re-routing his people to you as we speak. The first ones should be arriving within the hour. He will be there a bit later, but rest assured that he is coming. They are just trying to figure out how to get me there. I told them not to worry, I will get there first." His smile was huge now. "I look forward to meeting you personally your majesty." He said and he grinned at her. "Turn around." He said.

Mom whirled around and startled Dad and the others that were attending to Josh. As she watched, the air shimmered and Mouse appeared in the room. He held out a ring that had done the magic for him. He was not a caster himself.

"Please stop your spell your majesty." Mouse said with another big smile. "The Sprite King is on his way and others will be here shortly." Mouse repeated. He bent over Josh and shook his head. "What has he done now?" Mouse asked no one in particular.

Mom did as she was told and dispelled the bowl. Then she turned all of her attention to the young man who had just appeared among them. "How did you get here so fast?" She asked and Mouse handed her the ring.

"Josh gave me this and he charged it for me. It allows me to come to him from anywhere. But it can only be used once and then it must be recharged. This is the second time that I have used it." Mouse explained. Mouse opened a small pouch and took out some leaves. They were from different plants and he laid them out carefully over top of each other in layers. Then he placed the entire stack of them onto Josh's forehead. There were questions all around him and he ignored them until this task was complete. Then he turned to Mom. The Sprite king told me to do this; I do not know what it does. I only know that he said it would give him more time to work." He said truthfully. Mom simply sighed.

"Things sure happen strangely in this world." She said aloud and Dad nodded his agreement. How long do you expect the Sprite King to take?" She asked and Mouse shrugged his shoulders.

"I'm only a messenger. I am only told enough to do my job. I'm sorry that I don't know more." He said. Then he looked down as if trying not to make eye contact. "Is there a chance that you have a working kitchen around here? I have been traveling and I am quite hungry." He said feeling embarrassed.

Mom smiled at the young man. With all the problems they were dealing with, feeding this young man was such a small request. "I will have some food brought to you." Then she shifted gears. "Is there anything that you can do for Josh?" She asked, a flicker of hope was behind those eyes.

Mouse looked down at the fallen man he had come to trust. "No, I'm sorry. I truly wish that there were. The Sprite King will know what to do. If the Wolf comes by, I will ask him as well." Mouse offered.

It was a remarkably short time later that a servant woman brought Mouse a tray of food. The young man must have been hungrier than he had let on. He was scarfing down the food at an alarming rate. Mom just watched him, fascinated by the whole display. He just kept going. It reminded her of Josh when he came home from school. The memory triggered a pang of pain and she looked over at her son again. He still hadn't moved. He looked peaceful. The sound of the doors to the chamber opening drew her attention away.

"Mouse!" Erica cried. Mouse dropped the food he was eating back on the tray and stood up. Erica left her fiancé and trotted over to give Mouse a big bear hug. She nearly bowled him over. "It's good to see you again." She remarked as she let him go. He took a step back and straightened his tunic then he bowed to her.

"It is good to see that you are well your majesty." He replied formally.

"You're lucky I like you or I would cuff you for getting so serious on me like that." She warned and Mouse smiled back at her a bit defiantly.

Mom interjected. "Never mind his good manners." She said and all eyes shifted to her. "He has brought us news." She continued when she was sure she had their attention. "The Sprite King is coming here." She announced and there were a mixture of reactions around the room at that. The guards were annoyed by the incoming

263

dignitary. It would make arrangements for security that much harder to maintain. Erica and Mouse were all smiles and Cedric had more of a look of shock. It was king Cedric who recovered the most quickly and responded.

He turned to Erica. "You sure do travel in strange circles milady." He said with a half-bow that he knew would get on her nerves. It was just a gentle reminder of who he was and that he enjoyed seeing her in action.

Erica explained to Cedric. "The Sprite King is a friend; we have known him almost as long as we know Mouse here." She flashed Mouse a quick grin. "He has helped us in the past and we have returned the favor whenever it was possible. The entire Sprite community was in peril once and Josh saved them. Now the two of them meet periodically for advice. The Sprite King is very knowledgeable and he has a warm place in his heart for us." She concluded.

Mom looked at Erica and nodded she understood about the Sprite King. "Honey, how do you know Mouse?" She asked, obviously still confused.

Erica paused for a second. "Mouse was the one that helped Josh and I get into our palace when we first got here. Without him we would never have regained our thrones." She turned back to Mouse again. "Josh told me that you were out adventuring. Isn't that our job?" She asked and Mouse bowed again.

"Your majesty, I was placed on crusade in your behalf by the Wolf." He replied in explanation.

Erica thought back for a while. "Is that the wolf that helped Josh figure out his powers? It would be good to see that wolf again. I still have a few questions that need answering sooner or later." She said and her tone was not as ominous as her words were. Then her mind latched onto an idea. She turned all serious as she addressed Mouse again. "Can you summon the Wolf?" She asked and Mouse looked shocked at first. He thought about her question and how his uncertain relationship with the wolf might be perceived by others. This took a few moments and Erica was becoming impatient.

"I cannot just call on the wolf to appear." He said apologetically. "I also do not know if this is the same wolf that helped Josh in the beginning, although I would guess that it is." Mouse seemed to fidget as if something more was being held back. "I… I…" He said and before Erica could reach him a familiar voice echoed through the chamber. The new voice was high-pitched and contained age and wisdom.

"He does not know who the wolf is; he simply follows his orders without question." The Sprite King told the startled assemblage of people present. The wise old little green man with wings winked at Erica and then he flew to hover before King Cedric. "You've made a fine choice in this one." He told Erica as he sized the human up. "There is a lot of good here, just like you have inside." He said and then he whisked away from Cedric and landed on Erica's shoulder. "Let's see if we can help your brother shall we?" He said gently into her ear and Erica nodded enthusiastically.

"Yes please." She blurted out and then she knelt down by the fallen young sorcerer. This allowed the Sprite King to look from a sort of bird's eye view while not being too far away. Erica sat there a long time, waiting. Mom and Dad moved in a bit closer, but not so close as to get in the way of the professional.

"Hmmm." The Sprite King said after a lengthy pause. "We have a problem with his energies here." He said at last. "We need to restart his energy flow before he can begin to recharge." The Sprite king flew from Erica's shoulder to Josh's chest. He moved his staff around in a varying ellipse as he spoke words that could not be remembered. Once they were said, they disappeared. The room began to glow and Josh's body began to radiate light and warmth. There was another pause as the brightness slowly climbed. Suddenly the Sprite King shouted. "There it is!" He called out and the light vanished. The warmth returned to normal. Josh groaned. It was the first sound or movement he had made since he collapsed and everyone seemed to be holding their breath.

Josh lifted a hand up and covered his eyes. "Did anyone get the license on that truck?" He mumbled and Mom, Dad, and Erica all laughed. The truck reference just confused the others. Josh had awakened. He was going to be sore and badly in need of energy, but he was back.

The Master looked out at his massive army. The denizens of this little world had no idea what he was about to bring for them. They had destroyed everything in their path and now the city was in sight. The original scouts to this area had encountered some resistance so it was expected that casualties here would be high. However, they were bringing so much firepower to bear that no human settlement could resist them. From the commander down to the first troop in line, the battle lust was upon them. They wanted to smell blood and they wanted to kill. Once the charge had been sounded, there would be no turning back. This was going to be a berserker attack of epic proportions. The Master stood up to his full height and peered off into the distance. His superhuman eyesight allowed him to see the humans that were manning the tops of the walls. They had bows and one or two of them had mechanical bows, crossbows the silly humans called them. These weapons would be all but useless against his terror troops. He licked his lips and noticed that he had bit it until it bled. The coppery taste of it nearly drove him into the killing frenzy. He settled back into stance and he held forth his mighty scythe. It was the move that the entire force was waiting for. The front line quivered in anticipation, their adrenaline was spiked and they were ready to charge. The Master brought down the weapon and the charge sounded from the horns in the back. As one the wave of demons and lesser devils swept forward shouting and screaming. The city before them was the piece of fruit to be plucked and juiced. They saw it in red only. They were now in full blood lust.

On the walls, the archers watched. The enemy force had stopped just in sight about two hours ago. Nobody knew what they were waiting for since there were no siege engines visible in the formation. What they did have was a lot of troops. In fact there were way too many to count. The Eastern city boasted some of the best natural defenses of any of the major cities. The northern wall was a cliff face nearly two hundred feet high with a sharp drop off to the sea on the far side. The eastern side was a protected bay that could possibly be attacked by smaller shipping, but larger ships were unable to cross the multiple natural sand bars that regulated the waves in the bay. The southern face of the city was covered in heavy thicket. The trees that supported the massive root structure were thousands of years old. Then there was the western side of the city. This was where the main gates were placed. Since it was the weakest natural barrier, the architects had compensated by making it the strongest structurally. The massive wall was built like a very steep pyramid; the massive base blocks would support the upper wall easily even if they had sustained major damage. It was also done in sections that were staggered. No one section of wall presented itself as a weak point to aggressors. The wall themselves had arrow slits, and higher elevation windows that were designed for the best field of view while maintaining that same defensive posture. There were also mounted crossbow ballistae and other fine traps that had been added as a deterrent to the marauders that had regularly tested the defenses hoping to find some chink in the impenetrable armor of the city. The area before the western gate had been cleared to build the main road and to allow for maximum visibility to the only true entrance to the city. The archers sat atop the wall and waited for the enemy to come into range.

Across the way the charge had been sounded and the wave of enemies was steadily growing closer. The arrows were nocked and the strings were drawn, arm muscles tensed with the strain as the keen eyes sized up their selected targets. The order had not yet been given, but everyone knew that it would come soon. The anticipation was like a thick blanket of suppressed terror. Battle jitters always had some effect.

The commander of the gate stood up and counted to three; he drew in a deep breath and shouted. "Archers Fire!" The twang sound of fifty bowstrings sounded at once and the second wave stepped up to follow the first. A small cloud of arrows swept out from the top of the wall and each of these had been aimed. The front row of demons lost a lot of speed as the arrows drove home and punctured legs and took out eyes. Some of them bounced harmlessly off of armor, but many of them scored good hard hits. The enemy bellowed out its renewed battle cry and there was some magic intertwined into the call. Many of the archers were swept by a wave of fear. About a third of the men began to cower, or run from the unseen fear. The ones who stayed were firing slower. They were still afraid, but their determination allowed them to continue fighting. The commander took another deep breath. "Ballistae fire!" He shouted and this time a dozen of the giant crossbows sent three trunk sized arrows into the onrushing crowd. One of them scored a direct hit and skewered four of the demons onto the one shaft. All of them hit something. There were too many of the enemy for the shots to miss. However, there were way too many for this defense to hold. The commander saw this too, but he still was tasked with whittling down the enemy as far as he could before falling back.

The first demons hit the walls and the gates and they began hacking at the wood and mortar. It seemed like a silly thing to do, the odds of them actually hacking through with hand tools was so low it was laughable. Pots of hot oil were poured over the lead enemy and then torches lit the group. Burning flailing bodies fell for they had nowhere to go. The pressure from behind them was too great for them to escape. The next wave of defenders threw rocks and the heads of the attackers took a beating. There were bodies fallen all around, but many of them were simply getting back up. The demoralizing effect of this was substantial. Then the commander remembered the report from that thief. He prepared to bellow again. "Take their heads! It's the only way!" He screamed and they did what would have been considered a suicidal action, they opened the gates.

The leading line of the invaders was surprised no longer have a barrier before them. They rushed forward only to be impaled and then beheaded by the soldiers defending the recently opened gate. Large poleaxes were the weapon of choice for the ground troops of the city of Greensborough. They were in a tight formation that allowed them to advance or retreat and cover their flanks at the same time. This was a practiced maneuver and they were the best the city had to offer. The demons were rushing through the gates and they were falling at an alarming rate, but not fast enough. A trickle of survivors managed to get past the first defenses and they were finding their way out into open streets where more, easier targets would present themselves. Containment was failing at an exponential rate. This was possibly the end of the city's defenses.

Atop his tower, the Prince of Greensborough, Alahan Ghengis Douherm watched with frustration in his eyes. He wanted to be down there fighting for his people. Well, more accurately for the glory of defending his people. His vanity would not allow him to fight if it was not for the glory. He needed to distinguish himself from the other fighters in this city of trained professionals. However, his father had already told him that he was not allowed to go. This fight would go on without the heir to the throne.

"It's not fair!" He told himself for the tenth time since the gates were opened. He could just make out the fighting at the gates. He could also see the stragglers that were getting through. He tried to tell someone, but no one would listen to him. The ones that were around the prince were assigned to guard him bodily from the enemy. The security of the city was someone else's concern. The Prince's frustration was only growing and his sharp mind would find a way around the order before too long. His guards knew that as well. They were ready to cuff the royal brat and make sure that he didn't wander off to find fame and fortune. After all, this was not one of those tales told in court, this was real. The prince watched as the standard swordsmen foot soldiers engaged the stragglers. For the moment, the balance was maintained and the city was not yet ready to give up. He didn't know how long the militia could hold them off, and he had to admit that one more sword down in that mess wouldn't make all that much difference. However, his presence as the prince would bolster morale and that could be huge in the later hours. So, he waited to hear from his father. Surely the man would acquiesce sooner or later. He just hoped that there would be something left to save by the time his stubborn old man decided that the prince had been right after all.

Josh was feeling quite a bit better. The regular food and exercise was doing wonders to increasing his blood flow and thus restore his personal energy field. He had seen so many visitors that he could not remember them all. There were two kingdoms worth of people who wanted to wish him well for their deliverance from the enemy that had been at their doorstep. He had allowed visitors, but only under the close supervision of either Mom or Dad. He had been grateful that they were there, but for them to see him so weak was something of a blow to his ego. He wanted to be strong. No, he needed to be strong.

He held the hopes and dreams of two kingdoms on his shoulders. It was an incredible burden to bear and he did it without hesitation or complaint. Now the visitors had all gone but two. He smiled at both of them since it was now obvious that they were a couple.

"Well sis, what do you think about the new place?" He asked jokingly. It wasn't Erica who answered though, it was King Cedric.

"I have to tell you that what you have done here is a marvel. The lengths that you went through just to make sure that both peoples had everything they needed was without question the most selfless thing I have ever witnessed. In addition, you put storehouses of armor and weapons and food that have become so important that I cannot overstate how important that they are. In short, you have provided us with nothing short of a miracle." Cedric concluded. Josh looked embarrassed, but he said nothing. The silence in the room began to stretch out uncomfortably.

It was Erica who broke the ice that was forming. "Yeah, it's really neat how you got training areas and practice fields for the troops we needed." She added, trying to lighten the mood a bit. Then she looked at her brother intently. "The shops were fully stocked and people that thought they had lost everything, had everything they needed again." There was a tear in her eye. "I don't know exactly what it cost you to do that, but know that the people are more than pleased with your efforts. You have impacted everyone's life in a way that no one could have foreseen. Well, no one but you of course." She added and she smiled hugely at him. Her eyes stared directly into Josh's. "I know that you did all of this for the people. You almost lost your life to this spell. It was way too much, and you know it." She admonished.

Josh felt his indignation flare. "It needed to be done!" We had one shot at this. The enemy is still out there and we will need to fight it again. I didn't want a repeat of last time. You know all of this. Why am I explaining it to you?" He asked, frustration spilling over and not knowing where to go. "I... I had to do it." He said softly.

Erica put a gentle hand on his shoulder. "I know you did." She said and he nodded. Tears were running down his cheek. "Next time you think of doing something so big, get help. Mom could have done some of this and the Captain from the City by the lake could have helped as well. You didn't need to do it all by yourself."

She said, trying to keep from hurting him anymore, but also trying to keep him from hurting himself anymore. She pulled him towards her and squared off his shoulders. "Look, I love you and I don't want anything like that to happen again. I almost lost you and I need you in order to do my job. I can't rule this place by myself. Without your powers, how would I help so many people?" She asked, it sounded almost pleading.

Cedric put his hands on both of their shoulders. "You are two special people. I know that you will both be fine. You will be revered by your people and mine. Do not worry about anything for now, just rest and regain your strength. I will push the army and soon we will be able to withstand another attack. Then we can talk about how to rule with or without magic." He said and the two siblings nodded solemnly. Cedric sighed. "I was raised to be a prince, and thus to be a king. You two seem to have stumbled upon your thrones and therefore you have different attitudes. This is a good and bad thing. I will help both of you to understand what it is you need to do and then you can decide for yourselves exactly what your role is." He was not much older than either of them, but he seemed so much wiser just now. "Like I said before, we'll talk about this later. Just get some rest and we can bring in a future that all of us can be proud of together." He said and his smile was infectious. He had unwittingly applied a great big dose of hope and its effects would reverberate to everyone who saw the royal family. It was a good thing for hope had been in such short supply recently.

The Eastern City had fought and fought and its warriors were weary, those that had not already fallen. The enemy seemed relentless. The only ones that stayed down were the ones who no longer possessed their heads. Every other type was wound appeared to be non-lethal. Unfortunately that was not true of the human defenders. The city gates were ablaze and the walls were crumbled in a couple of spots. The torrent of violence had spilled over into the streets and many a civilian had fled in terror only to be brought down by the merciless invaders. The defense had been strong until its organization fell. A lucky arrow shot had silenced the commander and the squad level control had held for a bit longer. However, the casualties had taken too much of a toll on the command structure and with fewer defenders, the area of coverage grew. It was more a matter of when they would all fall. Still, they fought bravely and they exacted a high price for what they had given up.

Just when they all thought it was the darkest, a tall figure stood in the crumbled wall entrance to the city. He stood so much taller than anyone else that he was visible even from the rear of the defense line. He stood there grinning evilly at them with a massive scythe dancing in his hands. His bright red skin and gigantic horns made it clear who and what he was. This was no demon, this was a devil. Immortal souls were now at risk as well as earthbound bodies and lifeblood. The scythe cut a swath through the defenders and attacker alike. The attackers had the benefit of getting back up, the defenders were not so lucky. A victory shout rose from the Master and the demons surged forth with renewed strength. His very voice was dripping with magic and it was all dark and evil. The weaker of the men simply withered and fell in place. Then the scythe came in vertically and it crashed down and split the ground right there in the streets. Fire erupted from the new crevice and more demons began to spill out of the opening. Nobody from the Eastern City could have imagined such a demonic sight. Hell had formed around them and the buildings caught fire from the radiated heat and sulfur. The very ground shook as it if it tried to ease its own pain. The fires were uniting and the human defenders were no match for the evil that had brought this destruction upon them. The people that had fled were now faced with an ocean view in front of them and hell behind them. It was motivation enough for many of them to plunge into the sea and take their chances there.

The Master laughed aloud and he held up his claws in victory. His bellow made a shock wave that further decimated the buildings as the city burned around him. It was glorious! His army would do this to every remaining human settlement and then it would finish off any of the elder races who dared to survive his initial shock troops. They would curse their own births before he was done. The force of his shouts was causing large bits of the cliff faces to collapse in on the city as well. Those that had chosen to cower within the shadow of the mountains had paid the price for their decision. They would remain crushed beneath the monstrous rocks.

Only one boat had gotten free. Oddly, it was the king's boat. Forty men and one thief were aboard and they had all hands working the sails vigorously. Escape was the obvious objective. In fact, the prince had barely made the trip himself, and it happened to be his fault that the thief had come aboard. The boat was tacking properly and was almost twenty degrees into the wind. They were making their best speed away from the smoldering ruin of their home. Unfortunately, nobody had the time to look back and see what was left of their beloved city. Perhaps that was for the better since the smoke billowing above the ruins was black as soot. The crumbling rock only played even more debris into view and nobody could have confused the dismal scene as anything but a complete loss. None of the people that were left behind would survive either. That grim knowledge was the seed of guilt and self doubt. The only thing driving them on now is fear. They would get away. The king had to survive.

The Master eyed the ship and his lip curled in disgust. "The human leaders have fled and left their charges behind for the slaughter. That kind of cowardice is criminal." He spat and the spittle sizzled on the blackened ground. "I will have to make sure that they do not get away." He said in a matter-of-fact tone. Then he began the spell that would complete his task for this place.

Out on the water the boat continued to slice through the shallow waves of the bay. The shoreline was becoming more distant and its color had faded somewhat to blue. An occasional glance back was all that anyone was willing to risk. They were still making excellent time and it was hoped that they could make the distant island of Mesallond where they could find provisions and enough land to hide in. In time they would return, but for now they would run and hide.

The blue-green water began to churn around them and the sail went slack. It was as if someone had swept the wind away from the boat and it slowed down to a glide as the water became more and more violent. The men furled the sail and began to row the boat along. The drummer pounded out an aggressive cadence and they were still making okay time. The water seemed to be pushing them off course. There was no suitable explanation for it, but the water seemed to be dancing around them. They continued to pull hard on the oars and it looked as if they might actually get away with this. Then the unthinkable happened. The water rose up like a living thing and slammed the boat from both sides at once. The men were tossed around like a child's toys on the slippery deck. Then the monster wave rose up and crashed down upon the boat. Splintering wood and screaming men announced the onset of damage. The water was filling up the boat and bailing seemed to be less important than abandoning the accursed ship. Then all dove into the water and the giant waved crashed down on them, driving them deep under the waves. By the time any bodies surfaced, they were long dead. It was a total loss.

The Master smiled cruelly and his troops began their celebration. The city was in flames and the inhabitants were slain. This was a victory well worth the wait he had suffered. Now he would extend his conquest to the rest of this pitiful world and all would know fear before they died. His bloodlust was not quenched, only fanned into full bloom. He sniffed the air and knew where he wanted to go next. There was a massive human infestation to the far west. It would be a long journey, but he would destroy everything across the land along the way. Then, after all of this menial work was done, he would get to his generals and they would suffer for not handing him this planet already conquered. He looked forward to that. He led his troops out of the smoldering ruins and they headed for the far coast. This had been a good day.

The Guardian of Balance sat in his chair behind his desk and watched on the monitor as the Eastern City fell. He sat there with mouth open and his fists clenched. The loss of life and total destruction were such a powerful image that he was unable to look away. When the army departed he switched off the monitor. He rubbed his temples and sighed deeply. A tear rolled down one cheek and he knew that the balance had been disrupted a great deal today. He needed to act and act quickly. The tides were shifting in his neutral area, and that was always a bad sign. If the balance shifted too much, he might be unable to counter it and the whole system could come crashing down. This was the universal balance, not just the balance of this little world.

It was really amazing to him how such a small place could create so much trouble. Still, he sort of had agents in the field there already. He had brought two extra True Bloods into the equation in order to help him maintain the balance against the chaos that threatened it. He hated involving them because they were almost as chaotic as the enemy, but now he had little choice. The real question now was what can they do to help? How can they affect a change in the balance to help stabilize a region that was spiraling out of control? He needed a plan, and he needed help to implement it. He picked up his stylus and began scribbling notes. In order to create any plan, he needed to outline his objectives. He would start there. Surely there would be enough time for him to release his own genius. If only he hadn't been so busy with those blasted magicians to notice when this all started, he might have nipped it all in the bud. He sighed and pushed that thought away. The problem had not been circumvented and he had to deal with it now. That much was certain fact. He scratched his head and then concentrated on the page in front of him. Then, as his mind popped his ideas he scribbled again. His determination would be put to the test this time, but he would not fail.

The arrow was perfect, and the shooter was equally so. The Elf looked down that flawless arrow shaft, aiming at the demonic troop that was attempting to breach the security of the forest. This was not going to be a random shot by some inexperienced archer; this was going to be a called shot and placed expertly into some vital spot on the unsuspecting enemy troop. The tall thin man had the patience of a god and he had slowed his breathing to make certain that there were no variances in the shot. The demon was swinging at a bunch of underbrush, trying to cut its way through the thicket that the elves had grown there for their first line of defense. The arrow was still perfectly aligned and with the precision of a top notch marksman, the arrow took flight and caught the demon behind the right ear and the barbed tip tore its way through the hind quarter of the creature's brain. There was no sound as the demon went down. It was an instant kill. The other troops had not yet noticed their downed comrade. So sudden had been the attack that it went on unnoticed for quite some time. Another went down a few moments later and it was suspected that the alarm would be sounded amongst the enemy. However, this kill had been equally placed and the woods remained silent. How long could their good fortune last? Another front line soldier of the vile enemy fell and this time, his gear was noisy. He rolled on the uneven ground and the elfin archer cursed under his breath for not taking the terrain into consideration when planning his shot. Other than that, it had been just as flawless as the first two. The dead demon rolled to a stop and his fellows bellowed out an alarm and the sounds of voices, many voices, broke through the calm of the forest.

Now was no longer the time for snipers, so the archers switched to standard arrows and prepared to blunt the new assault. They had long sword equipped troops of their own should the ranged attacker falter. Each of them held a grim face as they prepared to hand out death at a wholesale rate.

The demon troops had been told to clear the forest. Everywhere they went the fire would not burn. Confusion had them second guessing their orders and when they got not better results from a blade they started to wonder what other unseen forces were at work here. This was not a full invasion force, they were members of two squads that had been sent ahead to map out the land and clear any resistance that could warn the elves that the main force was coming. They had actually thought that they could sneak up on the ancient race in their own backyard. It was a mistake that would cost this quad their lives. It is true that demons had a good measure of regeneration, but their heads were their weakness. If the brain was damaged, then the regeneration process would halt entirely. It was a natural defense against brain damaged troops populating the evil army. Still, the one weakness was rather inconvenient. The squad commander was just a little bit older and tougher than his subordinates, and he was only slightly smarter. It is entirely possible that he was unprepared for what was about to happen to his command. The alarm sounded and he sent all of his thirty troops to investigate what had happened. He was running along behind them when an arrow zinged out of those accursed woods and plunged into his throat. He could not cry out, or even give an order. His hand instinctively clutched at the arrow and he pulled it free. This had been yet another mistake. Not only did it hurt more than anything he could ever remember, it showered the front of him with blood, his own blood. His body began to heal and he was almost ready to bark an order when a second arrow entered his brain through the eye. He was hurtled backwards and he skidded to a stop. His limbs twitched a couple of times, but he was already dead. The troops carried on without their commander. In fact, they were unaware that he was no longer with them. The skillful elves took them out before they could even bring melee weapons to bear on them. The squad was defeated. They would fail to report back in their two week deadline, so eventually more trouble was certain to find the woodland elves, but for now they were safe.

    The General had returned to the former site of the massive kingdom that Josh had moved. The walls were there and the buildings were there, but there were no people. The entire place had been abandoned. They hadn't even taken any supplies with them. Everything was in place, just like it had been when he was here last. The spot where the Dark Lord had fallen was of particular interest to him and he studied it carefully. This was definitely the place, but where had they gone? Some of his troops would have seen that many humans moving overland to a new location. If they had been slain by another of the invading force, there would have been bodies littering the grounds. Here were no signs that they had gotten away beside the fact that they were not here. His rage began to boil over as he realized that he had been all too generous with these humans. They had no honor evidently. He was more than ready to kill them all and be free of them forever. In fact, those were his specific orders. He was supposed to be killing all of them. It was very frustrating to him to have been denied this particular jewel. He had so wanted to present this and all of his other victories to the master and thus bargain for his own continued existence. Now he had very few cards to play. He sent scouts throughout the abandoned city to find clues, any clues as to where the humans had gone. His patience had run out and he was ready to slaughter something or somebody. All he needed now was a target.

Josh had been feeling much better and Erica had agreed to let him view the army in training that was the primary focus of each day here in the secondary kingdom. The news of the engagement had traveled to both kingdoms quickly since they were physically linked now. The overall feeling was one of hope and optimism. Everywhere the royal couple went, they were surrounded by citizens who were eager to see them and to wish them well. In Erica's case they were also throwing on praise. It made her a bit uncomfortable but Cedric was pleased with her public's support and he was surprised how well she handled all the attention. He had come to study her closely. Every time he thought he knew how she was going to react to something, she surprised him yet again. She was giving and kind. She was strong and fearless, at least on the surface. She was smart and sneaky. She was also the most loved ruler that he had ever seen. There were onlookers everywhere in the city that wanted to get a glimpse of their beloved queen. All of this adulation still persisted even with the threat of war at any time on their doorstep. They understood what was happening in the world because the royals had told them what was going on. That level of education was unheard of among the general population. That same information had been the driving force behind the amazing rate of enlistment into the royal army. The thing that was missing was the formal dinners, the dress balls that royal engagements usually contained. They met people in counsel; they visited with important merchants and military commanders over quick food or even at the sparring ring. Erica was 'just one of the guys' when it came to the martial arts. She was good with hammer and sword and hand to hand combat. More than one man mentioned something about 'ancients' helping her but Cedric had not seen anything like that so far. Mostly it seemed to be some sort of excuse for losing to the smaller and in some cases stronger opponent. Cedric had his own skills and soon the royal couple was talking with tradesmen and artists and Cedric took the conversation in ways that honestly Erica had never even dreamed of.

They had this beautiful new city, complete with a massive population and enough stores to survive the next winter without worrying about planting and harvesting this season. That meant that there were a lot of people with extra time on their hands. Cedric had come up with a plan to employ artisans to decorate the city and they would sub contract the menial labor from the farmers. It allowed both groups of people to be useful and also to earn some extra coin. It was a foregone conclusion that trade with other kingdoms was pretty much over with until the end of the war and a massive rebuilding takes place. That meant that everyone needed to find buyers for their wares in house as it were. This new plan had alleviated some of that tension and allowed many people to resume normal life without the threat of imposed poverty. Overall, the people were still happy.

Erica had stopped by a shop and she marveled at a material on the bolt of a weaver she had not met before. The weaver bowed to the royal couple and then the twinkle in his eye of a potential sale put him in business mode. The material was a royal blue background with shimmering metal tabs sewn into it. It looked kind of like small scales and they shimmered off the sunlight as the fabric moved. It was obvious that she had no real use for the fabric, but it had captured her attention so well that she had difficulty looking away from it. Cedric noticed her quandary.

"Do you want this?" He asked her directly. She shook her head and looked at him.

"What?" She asked as he made his way closer and he ran a hand over the scales.

"It is nice; it would make a fine dress for you." He said and Erica blushed.

"I don't wear dresses." She said a little perturbed.

"Really, you would look so good in them." Cedric replied. He stayed just out of swinging range in case he upset her too much.

"The world is in danger and you want me to buy material for a dress?" She asked, letting some of her pent up anger out.

Cedric nodded enthusiastically. "Yes, I think it's exactly what the people need to see you doing. You know that the enemy is still out there, and so do they. They also watch you to see how you are handling the crisis before making their own mind up on how they feel about it. If they see you fretting and worrying, then they will worry too. That sort of worry could start a general panic that could undermine the people's safety. If they see you doing something normal, like buying a dress, then they feel like they can return to their normal activities and the general feeling will be much more positive." He explained logically. "Remember, the people are extension of you." He reminded her.

Erica felt the trap she was in. She did like the material, but she could not honestly see herself ever wearing it. Josh always made her clothes through magic. The thought of her carrying the morale of the whole kingdom felt like a huge burden to bear. "It's not fair." She said at last. Cedric took that as a good sign, she had accepted his explanation and they were going to be buying the material.

He turned to the merchant. "We'll take the bolt." He said and he handed over more coinage than it was probably worth. The merchant's huge grin verified that opinion and they left with instruction on where to deliver the cloth.

Erica basically put the uncomfortable situation behind her. There were more important things for her to be worrying about. They were in the middle of a rebuild and the enemy was still going to find them, eventually. Nobody knew how long they had. Josh was working on defenses, but it was Mom who was doing the actual casting. Josh had been forbidden from it until his recovery is complete. Dad was helping with the training of the troops and all of her former guards and various military men were assisting in that training. They had many more troops than they used to. Thanks to Josh they were fed and well equipped. The straw constructs were a possibility as well. Mom had added a few ideas of her own to that plan. The general feeling was that they stood a good chance of fending off the enemy when it came. She hoped that it was true and not just a product of wishful thinking. The posters in the city were all requests for ideas. The general population was free to voice their opinions and ideas about the upcoming confrontation and several good suggestions had come in as a result.

This was a concept that was foreign to Cedric, but Erica took to it right away when Josh made the recommendation. They were adding outer defenses and lookout posts to spot the siege engines before they could engage the walls. There were moats of oil and tar that had been covered up to slow down ground assaults. Spiked sticks dotted the landscape in grids as well. The city was bustling with activity and the economy of the city was booming. Of course the foreign trade was non-existent, but the local economy was thriving. Later on, the loss of the trade from outside the city would hurt, but with the goods that Josh had provided and the goods being made by the artisans now, the economy would be good at least for the short term foreseeable future.

Erica found herself wishing that she were back in the training grounds again. Her frustration levels were easily dealt with there. Well, easily from her point of view. The maintenance crew felt otherwise as did anyone who happened to need a sparring partner at the wrong time. She turned to Cedric and her eyes told the story. He had not known her that long, but he was beginning to note her emotions well.

"You go ahead and thump some poor unfortunates. I can wrap up here." He told her and the happy eyes that lit up her face told him that he had been correct. She left him and made her way through the crowd like a shark. He watched her go, admiring her figure as she did so. "I am a lucky man." He said to himself under his breath. Then he went to complete the marketing. He had a few surprises to arrange, so his fiancé's absence was actually fortuitous. It was at least a couple of hours before he returned to the castle.

King Cedric

**This is the concept art for King Cedric, formerly Prince
Cedric, shown here without his crown.**

The general had been sending his troops forward and killing everything in his view. He had somehow lost an entire city of humans and he knew that he would somehow pay for that loss. He also knew that what he had accomplished should buy him some small measure of relief. At least he hoped that it would. With the Master, there really was no way to be sure. He had no choice but to continue the campaign and hope that he had enough victories under his belt to advance his career.

"Bring my troops around the backside of this ridge." He ordered and the Lieutenants around him scrambled to comply. The scouts had picked up a human settlement where it had not existed before. It was by a lake and there were no signs of the construction materials here to account for it. He wondered if he had just found his lost city. The initial size reports were off, but he still had hope that they had simply misjudged the size. This ridge was the closest natural boundary that could hide his troops before they would be seen by the as yet unsuspecting enemy.

The General made his way to the edge of the ridge himself. He had a looking glass and he was ready to find out for himself if the lost humans were here. He took care to note the sun's position so that there would be no glare from the lens of his glass. They had been cautious up until now; he didn't want to blow it this close to another victory. He raised the glass and peered into the eyepiece. The city, such as it was, was nestled into a hillside right next to the lake. There were no roads leading into or out of this city. That was strange enough, but it got worse. There were no fields around the settlement to suggest that the humans were able to feed themselves. Of course they could be fishing in order to fulfill those needs, but there were no signs of boats or nets either. It was obviously a quandary that he was not able to answer for. He knew one thing beyond all the questions, these were humans and he was supposed to eliminate all of them. So he started studying the countryside, planning for his attack. He did know one thing for certain; he would not strike until dark. The element of surprise had burnt him before; he was not ready to give the humans a chance to recover when he came down on them. This victory had to be absolute.

283

The Captain stood at the guard post. He had decided that a routine inspection of the sentries had been in order. The wildlife had been acting peculiar lately and only the very dull or completely incompetent ignored changes in the environment around them. To be honest, the whole idea of hiding out the war had him on edge. They were hidden from all of the main roads, that was for sure, but they were still a city. It was not the largest city that humanity had ever built, but it was much bigger than what could remain hidden indefinitely. They had no earthen works dug for protection. Their main defense was camouflage. If that failed them, all they had was the fighting force the Captain maintained. With the previous battles, there were not as many of them around as he would like. It gave him the constant feeling of vulnerability. He just couldn't shake it.

Off in the distance, a small group of birds took flight as if they had been startled. In the wild this sort of thing happened all the time. However, The Captain's paranoia was in full bloom and he stared into the direction of the disturbance. His keen eyes could make out nothing as yet. The brush was moving, but winds off of the lake could easily explain that. The birds had flown from somewhere behind the tree line. That was even more disturbing. He could not see that far effectively. He knew that he was probably just being worrisome over a minor thing, but somehow it would not let him go. His mind was latched onto this and he wanted desperately to investigate it. He had more than his eyes available for such surveillance. He was a wizard. He sent a spiritual bird out from his mind. Their minds were linked enough for him to see through the bird's eyes as long as he concentrated on it. The bird was sailing out over the water and it banked towards the direction that the Captain wanted to see. The trees were coming in close as the bird flew unflinchingly towards them. The hill sloped up away from the lake and it suddenly dropped off at a ridgeline. What the bird saw chilled his heart. There were enemy troops there. The siege engines were nestled back even farther and he could see the General there, looking through a spyglass towards his position! It was amazing, they were watching each other. Hopefully, the General did not know this. He dispelled the bird and he passed the word to sound the alert – quietly. He wanted to make ready without the enemy being aware that he had done so. If he could not gain some element of surprise, then their defense would fall. The enemy was still too numerous for them to defeat. He did not have the power to move the city as Josh had done. He had to rely on more normal means to defend his people. He wondered if he could get help here in time. The troops had not looked like they were advancing. In his opinion, they were waiting for the city to go to sleep. The way his nerves were feeling right now, nobody would be sleeping tonight.

The Master had watched village after village destroyed. With each of these small victories, his hunger for the ripe plum of a major city became stronger. He wanted this to be done, but not too soon. He would savor the moment that the human race fell. He would savor when each subordinate species fell to his minions. His power will be absolute. It will be here the way it is in hell. His word will not be questioned. Any resistance at all will be crushed and an example will be made. He strode along stepping on the remains of yet another settlement and it only fed his fire. The billowing smoke and the coppery smell of blood filled the air. For him it was sweet. He took in a good lungful of the sweetness and let it out grudgingly. His scythe took down a tree with one mighty swing and the flames licked at it as they spread. All that would be left behind was blackened soot. The very ground would be wounded and things would not grow there. He would make sure of that. This land will no longer be for the living, it will be for the dead. The smell of life still emanated from the west and he knew that his goal was getting closer. He did not know how far this accursed land went, but it mattered little to him. He would kill and kill until there was nothing left. This was his purpose and this was his campaign. He marched on, looking forward to the next target. Hopefully it would not be too much longer.

Josh had done amazing things with the help of his mother. They had come up with a new construct that could withstand more damage before it fell apart. It was a mixture of materials. One of the new materials was concrete. The stone golems of old could not compare to a concrete creation complete with the iron rods that supported them against the massive stresses of combat. There were other things mixed in as well. This new construct was the most advanced sorcery ever produced. They were making them at a few an hour so far. As the magic got used to the new pattern, it would take form faster. It's like a copier. The more originals you had, the more copies you could produce at once. That is, so long as the strength of the caster and the magic available held out. These were concepts that Josh was well aware of, but that Mom was only just beginning to fully understand. They had about twenty of them so far by the next casting would double that. They would soon need a place to store their creations until they were needed. There were so many logistical problems to such a casting. Of course nobody had ever imagined that so many castings could be made by just one person. Josh had raised the bar a thousand fold. It had cost him some of his own life force to accomplish what he had, but he had done it gladly, knowingly. The next casting was due and he and Mom were already bringing the image into their minds. They had a pool of energy building between them. It was as if they were both putting magic into a bowl and the spell would soak up the amount that it needed. In fact, it was a lot like that. The pool of energy would prevent the spell from taking it directly from the casters. Mom knew that she couldn't let Josh cast something so massive again. The last one had put him in a coma. Her fears were evident even as she let the energy spill into the spell. The twenty golems became forty. The spell completed and they stood there in formation awaiting orders. They looked like a squad. Josh smiled at Mom.

"I think we need to hurry up with this." He said almost out of the blue. Her look of concern turned almost panicky when he winked at her.

"Don't you try anything!" She warned. "You don't have the strength for anything adventurous." She reminded him. Mom put a hand on Josh's shoulder and made him lay back down with only the slightest of pressure. It demonstrated two things, her power over him, and his lack of physical strength to resist her. Both messages rang home to Josh.

"Okay okay, I get it, but something has me worried and I know we'll need these guys sooner than we expect." He said and Mom looked at him sort of sideways.

"What makes you say that?" She asked, concern for him turning into concern for the city itself. "Can you see or hear anything?" She asked and Josh shrugged his shoulders.

"No, I can't see or hear anything, it's more of a feeling." He replied, not sure where the feeling was coming from. "I just know that it is essential that we get as many of these up and running in a hurry." He added. The look on Mom's face was dubious. "Look, I'm sorry I can't say more. I've become accustomed to listening to my feelings, especially when they come in this strong." He explained.

Mom knelt down beside him as he lie there. "How strong is this impression you are having?" She asked and his eyes gave away more than he had wanted to reveal. He was frightened.

"I... I feel it all over. There is a sense of impending doom and dread. What's worse is I don't feel it here. It's somewhere else." He explained. Mom's brow furrowed.

"How could you know that?" She asked, this time not batting aside his proposal, only trying to get an explanation for how it was so.

"I am uncertain. Maybe it's somebody I know that's in trouble. Maybe it's something I did. I am connected to it somehow though, I am sure of it. I can feel fear from an outside source. Someone is very afraid and they need our golems to save them." He said all in a rush as it occurred to him. "That's why we need more of them. We need them as fast as we can make them." He pleaded and Mom was a little more on his side than she was.

"We need a larger pool of energy then. We will need to pool resources from more than just ourselves. Where do you suggest we get it from?" She asked, trying to facilitate the seemingly impossible suggestion he was making.

"Perhaps I can help with that." A small voice said behind Mom and she started terribly. "Please forgive my intrusion, but I could not help noticing you are in a bit of a quandary here. I think my people can help you with the energy." The Sprite King said. He bowed deeply, and for him that was almost three inches. "We can call upon the spirits of the tree to ask for energy." He explained and Mom looked more pleased than startled now.

"Wait. I thought you left." Mom said as the realization hit her.

The Sprite king smiled revealing a perfect set of teeth. "I am never far from my best friend." He replied and he looked over at Josh. "He is frail and strong at the same time. He needs us from time to time." The little ruler explained. "He also has a big heart." He added as an afterthought.

Mom looked at the small king closely to try and ascertain if he were being truthful. Everything seemed to be on the up and up. "Then what do we do to make this happen?" She asked, getting back down to business.

The Sprite king held up his hand. "Relax, things are already in motion. In fact, I know why you need to do this. I can provide this information to you as we wait." He said.

It was Josh who took notice of this first. "Who is in trouble?" He asked and the Sprite king nodded to the young sorcerer.

"Your instincts are correct once again. It is uncanny how often that happens." The king explained. "You have a deep connection with the imperiled group because you put them there." He said cryptically.

Josh's eyes popped open wide. "The city by the lake?" He asked, fearing the response he was certain he would hear.

The Sprite King almost laughed, but the mood was way too serious. "Of course it is. Your instincts needed only the tiniest of prods to make the connection yourself. Your friend does not know how he will defeat the enemy army that is lying in wait for darkness to spring upon him. He has laid out his defenses as well as can be expected, and he was intelligent enough not to tip off the enemy that he was aware of their existence, but his city is doomed without external support. Part of their hiding meant that they simply couldn't build standard defenses. It would have drawn way too much attention to them and they would not have lived this long." The king explained even before anyone could ask.

"Okay, so we are supposed to cast these golems and send them to help the Captain." He said in a matter of fact voice. "How long do we have before the attack you spoke of?" He asked the small king and trusted confidant.

The Sprite King lowered his head. "Not long now, the sun sets earlier here than there but the shadows will stretch across them soon enough." He replied and Josh pushed himself up on an elbow and Mom instinctively pressed him back down.

"Relax son, they are still gathering the energy we need. We will be doing this as soon as possible." She tried to console the troubled young man that she had become so proud of. Of course with Josh's mind, he just couldn't let it go like that. She was aware of that as well, but she hoped that he would have the decency to at least pretend for her. As it turns out, he did have that much decency.

In Josh's mind, he did the math and he did it again and again. He was not going to make forty more, or eighty more golems. He was already envisioning the multitudes he would need to defend the city by the lake. If any of the constructs survived, they would be helpful used to defend their current location. There would be no waste on this casting, but it would be difficult and costly. He knew that already. He started to make those calculations as well. The images in his mind were taking on a real life of their own. He would submit the image as soon as it was ready. He hoped that they pooled enough energy. This one was going to be huge.

"You are going to make this difficult for me, aren't you?" Asked the Sprite King. Josh blinked twice upon realizing that he had just been spoken to. The king winked at him. "I know how you think. You are not going to be satisfied with the duplication technique that has been used so far. You are doing the copying in your head." The Sprite king said as if he had been reading the young man's thoughts. "That is a dangerous shortcut that may cost you much more than it gains." The small king warned. "How much do you think we can help you?" He asked seriously.

Josh scratched his head. "How much energy can you provide?" He asked in response.

The Sprite King took a turn at scratching his head as he thought about the power that was available to him. "Actually, I have no way to explain a quantity, but I do have deep connections and we will be able to channel a great deal of energy into you when the time comes."

He said, feeling confident that it would suffice. The look on Josh's face made him reconsider that feeling.

"How many of these constructs do you mean to create at once?" He asked, feeling his own estimates were about to be smashed to bits.

Josh felt the eyes of the people around him; they were all intently waiting on his response. "I will create five hundred and twelve of them in the first wave. If that is successful and we can do it again, then one thousand and twenty four will follow it closely." He replied and Mom's mouth fell open. The Sprite King shook his head and his eyes were larger than normal.

"How much energy will that require?" The king managed to ask through his shock.

Josh smiled at the surprised little man before him. "We will pool your energy into the lake itself. The lake will amplify it and make it strong enough to do the castings all at once." Josh looked at the startled faces around him. "We need to hurry though, we haven't much time." He said and nobody bothered to argue with the powerful sorcerer. "In fact, we need to contact the Captain as soon as possible in order to coordinate our arrival with his defenses." Josh said logically.

Mom was the first to speak up this time. "If it's a war conference you need, then we need the rest of our group in on the call." She said and Josh nodded his acceptance. She immediately dispatched a messenger to retrieve Dad, Erica and King Cedric.

The Sprite King flitted about, trying to figure out what was important and what wasn't. The comings and goings of humans sometimes got the better of him. "You are going to contact this leader of humans then?" He asked and Josh answered in the affirmative. "Is that not a risky prospect?" He asked. "If the enemy can somehow eavesdrop on that conversation, then the whole plan could be compromised." He said and Josh paused to think about that. "If there is a way to get you into the city by the lake and tell him yourself undetected, that would be much better." He suggested.

Josh thought a moment further. "Yes, it would, but do we have enough access to the lake in order to perform the casting we need?" He asked. The Sprite King took a moment to visualize the area. He had not been there himself but his people had scouted it, if only briefly. He had to admit to himself that he didn't know as much about the area as Josh probably did.

"I do not know the answer to that." He admitted finally. "I am sure that your knowledge of the area is greater than mine." He pointed out.

Josh seemed to be taking a visual survey within his own mind. A few moments passed while everyone waited for him to finish it. When his eyes opened again, everyone waited for his next words. "We can make it work, but again, we have to move quickly. Can you have your spirits meet us at the lake or will they have to transport with us?" He asked and the Sprite King smiled.

"They are already en route to the lake. Since they are in spirit form, they will not tip off the enemy that you are coming. I suggest that the transport be quickly though. The spirits are skittish without us there to reassure them." He told them and Josh surprised everyone by standing up. He had tapped some reserve strength somewhere, he looked fit and trim and actually energetic. His stride was one of confidence and determination. He was ready to do this. Mom stepped directly to his side. They looked at each other and her concern for him was evident on her face.

"Don't worry Mom, I can handle this much." He told her and it only eased her mind slightly. He turned to the entrance of the room and sure enough Erica and Cedric were walking in with Dad and a small contingent of personal bodyguards in tow. It was exactly as Josh had hoped. "Now that we are all here, it is time to get things done." He announced and Erica looked worried suddenly.

"What needs done?" She asked. The messenger had not briefed the two royals on what had gone on in this room. Josh shook away her question as he went into that trance of concentration that allowed him to use his magic so well. The entire room seemed to shift ever so slightly. The door behind them seemed to shimmer and in moments, the view outside the door was that of a lake. Josh had placed them onto the edge of the city and also onto the shore of the lake. Unless someone was looking when the room materialized, no one would notice one more building on the end of the city tucked away into the woods.

The Sprite King was the first to recover and he was smiling from ear to ear. "Your skills are most impressive sir." He told Josh and Josh bowed.

"Thank you your majesty." He replied and the Sprite King gave him a sour look.

Then the spirits began to become visible. There were hundreds of them hovering just over the surface of the lake. The glow that emanated from them was drifting down into the water and it was starting to change as well as it absorbed the magical energy. It was quite beautiful.

The power was collecting and all the casters around could feel it. The Captain was busily preparing his defenses when he felt the surge of power. He stopped what he was doing and headed out at a run towards the lake shore. He noted that the sun was just about to set and he stopped cold in his tracks when he saw the surface of the lake. It was glowing with a blueish green hue and a whole lot of spirits seemed to be pouring energy into the water. He scanned the area and almost immediately noted the new room. The architecture was exactly the same as his city so he knew in an instant just who had come. He had to admit to himself that it was a welcome sight. He started off at a trot towards the new building. As he approached, he saw several people inside. There were a lot of royals here. The Sprite King was in attendance, King Cedric was there and Queen Erica was also there. Mom and Dad had been king and queen here and they were also staring back at the dumbfounded Captain.

Josh blew past all of that brass and broke through the Captain's stupor. "Well there you are! I was wondering how long it would take you to notice us." He said a bit jovially. Then Josh's expression turned serious. "We were none too soon." He said with a hint of alarm in his voice.

"It is really good to see you." The Captain blurted out. He would have hugged the sorcerer if there had not been so many imposing people around. "What's the plan?" He asked in a direct tone. The tension of his predicament was quite evident in his body language.

Josh stepped forward and clapped him on the shoulder. "We're going to build you an army." He replied and the boyish face actually smiled at him. The Captain shook his head.

"And just how are you going to do that?" He pointed out at the lake. "Is that light show something to do with it?" He asked and Josh led the way out of the room and onto the beach.

"It is a very important part of the preparations, yes." Josh replied. There was a hint of something more in his tone. The Captain couldn't tell if it was worry or fear. "We will stage the army here." He said, pointing up and down the beach. "Then they will march directly at your enemy and we will watch the whole thing from here." Then Josh turned to his old friend. "You will need to help me with the spell though. I need you to pull all the energy you can and dump it into the water like the spirits are doing." He instructed. It was a very unorthodox move and the Captain had no idea why they would do this, but he was not about to upset the man who had come to save him and his people.

The lake continued to glow and that glow was now overpowering the wavering light of day. The dusk had come and the lake was now illuminating the lower part of the sky. The energy was refracting and combining and becoming stronger and stronger as it interacted with the water. Then Josh began his spell. The glowing lake shimmered as the power began to resonate and be used even as it was still increasing. Josh closed his eyes and pulled up the mental image. He saw the army, all of the army, in exact detail. He had worked on this image so long that it was almost easy now to do this. He tentatively began to channel some of the water's energy into it and the leading edge of the troops began to take on substance. Josh stepped forward until his feet were in the water and the energy from the water swirled around him like a tornado of blue and white light. It pulled at his short hair and his clothes seemed to be lifted as if by static electricity just before a lightning strike. He held the image in his mind and Mom and the Captain were still pouring energy into the lake. The spirits were eager to see what was going to happen but they kept pouring it in as well. Josh felt the pull as his own energy began to tap. He knew that he didn't have that much left, but the warmth of the power from the water soothed him as he continued. The army was about half way formed and there was a gasp as they popped into existence all along the beach. Josh clenched his fists and he pushed to complete the spell. The army of stone stood ready for action and the final wisps of power fluttered away. Josh felt the water reach out to him, calling him into its depths. He resisted the urge and stepped back onto the beach. He had done it! The army was there! The Captain swore and he smiled hugely.

"How do you do that?" He asked, wishing he had that sort of command. However it was done, the young man had done it and The Captain was satisfied with Josh's silence. He turned towards the city and called his troops forward. There were whoops and shouts of celebration as they realized just what had happened out here. Their discipline was good though and they formed ranks upon command.

Compared to the army that just materialized on their doorstep, it was a small group. However, with a renewed determination and the resurgence of hope, they were going to be a force to be reckoned with. The glow of the lake was gone now and it was only a matter of time before the enemy army came over that ridge to attack the city. With the new army in place the defenders were finally ready for it.

CHAPTER 12

T he preparations for battle were being made as quietly as possible. The swords, axes and armor were being wiped down a bit and the demons were busily building up their energy for the attack. The General watched it all closely. This was going to be a tough nut to crack, but he was overseeing it all personally. He wanted this victory to add to his chain. He would take the head of whoever was in charge over there as a trophy. His troops looked ready to spill blood. He admitted to himself that the blood lust was not far from his mind either. He was a killer after all. That was why he was here in the first place. A voice sounded from up on the ridge and the General turned to see what was going on. The signals were muffled due to their proximity to the enemy, but the gesture to 'come here' was clear enough anyone could have understood it. So the General sighed and trudged his way up the embankment to the back side of the ridge. He knelt down so as not to stand above the edge and thus be seen by the unsuspecting enemy sentries. When he got to the top of the ridge, he stopped quickly. The lake appeared to be on fire with blue light. He couldn't tell much more than that from here, but it was definitely bright now that the sun had fully set. The shadows were taking over the countryside and he was finally getting back into his own element. This glowing lake thing caused him a bit of distress. If the humans had found a way to light the lake, then maybe they would be able to detect his troops when they advanced. He dropped back from the ridge so that the blue light would not show his face to the enemy. Then he started giving orders. He wanted his troops in motion now. They could not allow the humans to get dug in, they would take them quickly now. Glowing lake or no, he needed to get this underway fast. His demons were forming a column that would follow the natural ridge for quite a distance before it emptied out by the city. If all went well, they would be storming the buildings without much more than a couple of guards to slow them down. Victory was at hand. The thought brought the blood lust to the fore and his smile brought the same to his troops. This was why they were here. The killing time was now. The glory was theirs for the taking. They wanted that glory and they wanted the recognition that would come with it form the Master. It was for him that they all toiled and no one was stupid enough to think that they were not expendable. The column moved forward in an orderly step and the sound they made was thankfully hidden mostly by the natural barrier. The adrenaline spike would hit just as soon as they cleared. It would be a mad rush into the heart of the enemy settlement and then the real killing would begin. The eager faces of his troops told the general that they were feeling just the same as he was. He smiled and lowered his head.

"We shall be victorious." He said aloud and his troops nodded, rather than give away their position with the cheer that would normally burst forth in the throes of a victory. However, they all reflected his emotion and it felt really good. The moment couldn't come quickly enough, but they were in range now. Just a little bit more…

The stone army deployed a staggered skirmish line. The opening the enemy would be coming through was covered five units deep. The constructs could not use bow and arrow, but they did have pikes and spears. The secondary forces had swords and shields. Each of these groups was overseen by a human soldier from the city's defense forces. The captain was in charge of the entire battle plan. He still had no idea of what the destructive power of these constructs would be, but he trusted Josh to bring adequate firepower to the fight. Mom and

Dad had hung back to protect the civilian populace and the Sprite King had disappeared into the wilderness once he decided that the humans had the situation well in hand. The General did have siege engines that could loft deadly accurate fire a very long distance, but they were deployed quite far to the rear of the column that was advancing on the city. Josh had special plans for those anyway. The lead line of demons cleared the opening and the front row of constructs lunged forward with pikes. The front row of demons was skewered and they flopped around helplessly on the end of those pikes when faced with the enormous strength of the new golems. The second row of each force then tried to get around the first in order to engage. This created a somewhat less orderly cluster of combat in the middle of the opening. Because of this, the column had stopped its advance. The remaining forces were unable to step up to support the lead elements. In effect, they entire formation had bottle-necked itself into this small area and they were unable to break through.

Several rows of demonic troops fell without any hope of success. Then the whole problem was realized by the formation and they broke to climb the ridge themselves. It looked like somebody kicked an ant colony and there was movement everywhere. The entire force of demons and troops began to swarm around the stone golems and they were having only marginally better success with them. The new re-bar supported stone golems were tough and very difficult to break. They had amazing strength that would allow them to crush an enemy if they got their stone hands on it. It was like watching two sets of monsters go at it. However, one of the sides was defending and one was attacking. The wave of enemies was limited by the lakeshore as well. This was a natural funnel into the city and the human archers were taking advantage of this. The melee was getting intense on the front, but the archers were able to pick and choose their targets at leisure. There was simply no pressure on them to rush a shot. It was not going well for the demons when the General ordered a strategic change. The siege engines fired. They were not close enough to strike any buildings yet, but they were advancing and the first rounds struck friend and foe alike. The massive shots were hitting the front lines of both sides. Much to their credit, the stone constructs continued to fight even when they were struck. Large pieces of them had been pulverized, but they continued to fight at a reduced effectiveness. The iron bars were visible in the broken constructs, it looked very surreal.

The siege weapon salvo was something that Josh had been waiting for. He closed his eyes and pulled up the image he wanted. It was a much simpler image than the golems had been and it only took seconds before he was ready. Mom grabbed his hand to offer her strength to his as he let the magic seep into the image. Above the front line of defenders, a large net, like a circus safety net appeared suspended across the entire front line. It was on an angle and it was not merely a net, but a giant 'pitch-back'. The next siege weapon round was already inbound when the net went up and it hit the net and the net flexed and threw the round back towards the vehicle that fired it. The screaming sound of the shot caused the demons in the siege vehicle to panic and run. At least that is what they tried to do. The round went unerringly to the place it had come from. The siege vehicle was crushed and the thunderous wave of spent energy swept the troops on the ground off their feet. The attack came as a complete surprise this far back from the front lines. The siege commanders continued to launch thinking that first hit to be a fluke. However, the shots hit the net and reflected back at perfect angles. The siege vehicles were effectively out of the fight after they fired one time. Their only hope now was that they fired on the move. Then the shot would miss when it came back. This was only marginally better since their destructive force was obviously not touching the enemy at all. With each failed shot, another commander took his weapon off line. Now the ground troops were without their support and they pressed harder into the golems. If they failed the push now, they would be caught outside the city where they could still be targeted by those blasted archers. The shafts were still pinging here and there, each one taking out its target with lethal accuracy. The demons needed to get into range to take the irritating humans out.

The General had been advancing along with his troops. He had been about in the middle of the formation in the beginning; he was much closer to the front now. This sort of devastation was familiar. He knew that he had found the missing humans that had evaded him before. He couldn't see them yet, but was sure that they were here. He raised his double bladed axe and charged over the ridge and into the melee. His larger size made him a good target and he drew arrow fire from pretty much everywhere. His self healing kept them from causing any real damage and his thicker armor deflected many of them anyway. He was slicing through the stone constructs and his axe was shaking his arms with each hit. They were sore now. "What are these things made of?" He asked himself as his axe drove through three more of them. He could feel the ache in his arms begin to stretch across his back. He was beginning to feel drained and there were more and more of these stone things coming at him. He had to admit that this army was impressive. Of course he would have to destroy it utterly and then kill everything behind it in order for his victory to complete. He lowered his head and drove into the fight even deeper. He was battering his way through the constructs. They were hitting him, and he was taking damage, but he seemed to shrug it off as if he healed it as fast as it accumulated. He bellowed in rage as the blood lust took him. He struck left and right and cleaved stone golems with each pass of his mighty axe. His arms were aching badly now but his rage made him go on. He made a path through the middle of the defenses and his demons were falling in behind him to ensure that it did not close off. The archers were having trouble picking targets now. The melee was so interposed that no clear shots presented themselves. They began switching to sword and shield and waited for the melee to reach them.

Erica and Dad were ready to throw in their swords as well, but Josh had warned them to stay back. He still had other plans for this invasion and he would let nobody, not even Mom, know what he was up to. He had asked for more energy to be fed into the lake and without the spirits' help, they weren't going to be able to do much with it. Mom and the Captain still did what they could and there was a glow to it after all. It was nowhere near as bright as it had been, but it was there nonetheless. Josh was running calculations in his mind. He had the distances before him and he was working out the exact moment to deploy whatever it was that he was going to deploy. No one bothered or interrupted him either. He had already done so much, save so many lives, that nobody dared to interfere. He seemed to be counting in a soft voice. Then he smiled. That was when he was at his most dangerous.

Josh threw up his hands in the air and shouted to the skies. There were no words, only guttural sounds and raw energy. He had envisioned his construct and now he was giving it the final spark, that piece of life that would make it real. He had tapped the water again and he had thrown all of himself in it as well. The enemy army was caught between two ranks of stone golems and they had no idea what this meant for them. They were about to find out. Josh pulled his arms out to the side and then he brought them together in front of him with a loud clap that could not be explained from just his hands. The wave of sound went forth from him in a thirty degree arc that would encompass the entire melee area. The stone golems began to melt and reshape. The oozing and pulsating golems made the demons pause to view them in horror. Then the unspeakable happened, they melted together into one large construct. They combined from both sides to encase the entire invading force in concrete and iron. Mom whistled as she realized what he had just done. The golems were now a stretch of highway. The demons and even the General were trapped almost waist deep in the concrete and their lower bodies were crushed under the immense weight. It was horrible and a relief at the same time. However, Josh was still not done. He had planned every detail of this engagement and they had stuck to his plan almost to the letter. He removed the netting over the scene by dropping in onto the ground. The problem was that it was no longer supple like the net it had been. Now it was sharp. It cut the enemy troops into squares of flesh that fell over and steamed on the fresh concrete. Then they burst into flame and were gone. This battle was over. Josh breathed a sigh of relief as he fell forward into the water. Erica's cry out brought everyone's attention to what was going on and they fished him out of the water before he could drown. He had used up everything this time. It was The Captain who carried him to the city and hopefully some medical help. They needed a healer fast.

Josh felt himself drifting away. He hovered above his body and he had to admit that he felt more peaceful than he had for quite some time. He had fallen over into the water and Erica shouted. He drifted there looking at all the faces. He had saved these people. He felt a sense of accomplishment for that and he was filled with warmth. The Captain carried him from the water and headed to the city he had just saved. It was touching. There were other spirits here, some were hovering over the lake and others were moving gently around him. They were asking him questions. He could only make out parts of what they were saying. His attention was still on the battle and the subsequent struggles to save him. Mom and Dad were crying and the healers were shaking their heads. Was he really gone? Had they given up on him now? He couldn't tell. He did know that the pull to his body was much less now than the pull to the other spirits. He felt lost. An uncontrollable feeling of loss began to overwhelm him and he fought to shove it aside. Dad was performing CPR and Mom was counting off the presses as he watched with almost a distracted interest. Then a voice he recognized came from behind him.

"You know it would be so much easier for me to just let this go." The Guardian of Balance said and his smile was almost melancholy. "But that wouldn't be right either, I can feel that." He said. He was somehow floating there with Josh. They could not touch each other for at this point neither had a body, but they could understand each other well enough. "You really are a brave young man." He told the distraught royal. "It would be a shame to lose you like this." He said and he reached out and slapped Josh across the face. It actually stung. Josh was startled.

"How did you do that?" He asked and the Guardian swept in very close.

"Stay focused on me. I need to show you something." He said and the two of them flew away like the wind. They were heading away from the world and up into the sky. Everything looked differently from the spirit point of view. The colors were all off and the sky did not have clouds, it had moving wisps of ether. As they approached they could see that the wisps were converging on a single point. It was a tear, a jagged looking rip in the fabric of the universe. Josh looked at it and felt fear. The Guardian seemed to notice Josh's reaction and he chuckled. "You were never meant to be here. You do not understand what it is you see." There was a pause as if the Guardian were deciding

301

just how much he could tell the newly deceased Josh. "This was caused by the Master." He said at last. "He was the one that started this war and he is someone you have not yet seen. He is looking for your people though. He is the one who wants every last living thing extinguished." There was another pause, this one seemed more self-reflective. "I should have seen this coming long before I did. I'm sorry." The Guardian said in a rare moment of emotional outburst. "It is this rift that you should be concerned about. I can close it, but not until the balance has been restored. You need to know that all spirits can cross from the spirit realm to this world as long as this tear persists. You will have to return to your body now and prepare for the final battle." He said and Josh started again.

"You mean I'm not dead?" He asked, unsure if he believed it or not.

"Of course you're dead. However, you have not crossed over, and there is still a short amount of time left for you to return. You need to hurry." The Guardian urged. The two spirits wisped back even more quickly than they had come. There was Dad, exhausted and Mom still counting as Erica performed the CPR. If he had still been in his body, he would have cried.

"Okay, what do I do now?" He asked and the Guardian grabbed him and shoved him down towards his body. The pull began to catch and like static electricity, he felt the 'cling' begin to align him with his body. Then, snap! As if he was clicked into place. There was suddenly pain in his chest. His eyes opened and he tried to cry out. Erica jumped back, started as her face lit up with excitement. Josh coughed a few times and it hurt terribly. He knew he had broken ribs.

"You're back!" Erica exclaimed. You're really back!" She cried. There were tears everywhere, even the Captain could not hold back. There was such a sense of relief in the room that it could not be avoided.

Josh lifted his head up a little, it was difficult, but he felt that it was important. "We have a new problem." He said and Erica shifted from jovial to concern with eye-blink swiftness. "I'll... I'll tell you later." He managed to say and she simply nodded. "We need to get home." He told her and she smiled.

"Do you mean home to Earth, or home to the palace?" She

asked and it was Josh's turn to smile, although he did it with much less energy. "The palace" He replied weakly. "We need to hurry." He added and then what little strength he had left him and he passed out.

Above the scene, seen by no one, the Guardian of Balance nodded his agreement. "You are quite the impressive young man." He said to Josh, knowing full well that he couldn't be heard. "Most impressive." He said as he faded back into his body in the other realm. It had taxed him greatly to perform this miracle of incalculable risk, but he had believed in what he was doing and he paid that price willingly. He had time to recover; he hoped that Josh did too. For whatever it was worth, he hoped that the sorcerer was successful. He hoped that all the clues he had dropped would be figured out. The boy was quite clever, hopefully he was clever enough. The Guardian smiled as he gave in to his own exhaustion and fell asleep.

The Master had felt the loss when the other army was destroyed all at one time. The tremor he felt had been... disturbing. What had the power to destroy an army in one blow? Was there a power on this little world that could rival his own? He began to get self doubts. However, his will was strong enough to carry him forward. He would complete this mission and assume his role as the supreme ruler of this world and nobody would be alive to complain. He would rule all of his undead minions. This realm would become just like home. His influence would grow and then he would launch a similar attack against another world. It was a good thing that the universe had so many playthings in it to keep him occupied. He was enjoying this world; he looked forward to finding out what was in the next one.

The army with him continued to march on relentlessly. Since none of his troops were living beings, they did not require rest or food or... well anything. They were obedient and tireless. They would cross this continent and then search the next if need be to accomplish the primary goal. He had underestimated his enemy in the past and he was dead certain not to do it this time. He felt the reassurance of his army's feet marching along. The clink of armor and the tread of foot accompanied him and soothed his nerves. They were the mightiest fighting force that this world had ever seen, and if his nose was not playing tricks on him, they were close to another human settlement. He would let the distraction lure him away from his doubts and fears. He was suddenly angry with himself for the moment of weakness. He was the Master! He was to be feared! Those who see him will know his wrath before they die. Then he will savor their deaths as he basks in the blood and glory of the kill. He scanned the horizon and he smiled wickedly. Oh yes, the glory would be his.

The healers witnessed the miracle of a recovery from what appeared to be death. They could not even say that magic had been used to accomplish this. They looked at the True Bloods with new fear and respect. The relief on the faces of the chosen ones was enough to know that they were not to be bothered just now. But, if these skills could be taught... Well there was no telling what other things they knew. This was a source of knowledge that had remained untapped, and they were eager to find out more about it. However, with emotions running so high just now they would have to wait.

Mom had done her best to contain herself, but she had failed. Her emotional roller coaster had cost her greatly. She needed to take them back to their own city and two kingdoms worth of people to defend. She knew this intellectually, but her body had not the strength to do the deed. She could at least work on the mental image required for the transfer. The Captain had offered to help, but he had not seen the new kingdom and thus could not build the image they needed. She would have to do that herself. She wished that she had Josh's raw talent. He had done things that no one else had even thought to try. She was so terribly proud of him, and yet she worried all the time. She pushed that aside for now. The mental image was her first priority. She would get it done.

Erica had taken to being a nurse. She had administered to her brother before. He seemed to always be pushing himself too hard, doing things that no one else would or could do. She knew that he suffered each time he did this, and yet he still did it again. It was selfless and noble, but not particularly bright from her point of view. If he had passed on, how would she rule the people? She was just a bit angry with herself for worrying about her own needs while her brother lay there on the brink of death, but it was how she felt. Cedric was a remarkable young man as well, but she held no illusions that he could do what Josh had done. He knew things she needed though. Perhaps they could rule together and make their kingdom great. She hoped that it was so. She also hoped that Josh would still be there to see it. His hair was almost white now. It looked odd on him. It was not very long, but it looked out of place on his young face. Still, he had channeled so much energy through him that there had to be some consequences. She was glad it was only that. His scars were particularly bright when his personal energy was low. He had suffered before and he carried the marks to prove it. The thought of him back in that dungeon those years ago made her angry. She had been unable to help him then. Now she was feeling almost as helpless. She had seen his energy raise and lower by using others. She was unaware of how this was done or she would give him some energy to wake up again. His breathing was slow and shallow, but he was breathing. It was a definite improvement over what he was doing not all that long ago. It made her think of what he had seen when he died. She knew about the ancients, they were spirits that could help her. Had he become a spirit as well? She looked forward to talking to him about it when she got the chance.

Cedric found himself looking on sort of from the outside. He was new to this family. In fact, he had not yet really joined it. He liked Erica's parents and he was taken by Erica herself. Her brother was a frighteningly powerful young man and he was not sure how to feel about the events he had just witnessed. They had pounded on his chest and blown into his mouth when he was dead and suddenly he was alive again! It was the talk of something unnatural. It really bothered him that they had powers that were not based in magic. Magic he could understand, he did not have any of it, but he could grasp the connections and he understood what was happening when it was done. Any son of a king should know these things. However, what he had just seen was more on the line of a miracle. Nobody

305

among them seemed to even think twice about this and it was slowly getting on his nerves. He had made eye contact with the healers and they seemed to share his concern. He looked at the aged warrior seated next to his son, fully exhausted from the miracle he had helped to create. Was that how it worked? You gave your own self to make the miracle happen? He was not sure. His will was strong and his stubbornness was almost legendary. He would find out what he wanted to know. He steamed and steamed over it until he was ready to burst. Finally, he could take it no more.

"What did you do to bring him back from the dead?" He asked Mom directly. The healers were in shock, but they were watching and listening intently for the answer. Mom looked more surprised than anything else.

"What?" She asked him when he did not continue to speak.

"When Josh died, you did something to him to bring him back. What did you do?" He asked again. His ire was rising steadily. He would know this secret that could restore lives.

Mom shook her head. Then she realized what he was asking and she began to think about why he was asking it and she blushed. "Sorry, I guess I take things for granted sometimes." She explained lamely. "What we did was a live-saving technique we learned from our other home. It is called CPR." She replied. She purposefully did not confuse him with the words that the letters represented; they would not have made sense to him anyway. "Basically what you do when you perform it is breathe for the person and pump the blood in their heart for them until they can do it again themselves." She said and the healers seemed to nod and confer very quietly. They were still watching intently in case she said something else.

The Captain had been sit ting back on the sidelines and watching the whole scene take place. He chose now to interject. "I was interested in what you did too, but I am only happy that Josh, our personal savior, has been brought back to us. If you can teach this skill to us then maybe we can use it to help others when they fall." He suggested. Mom looked thoughtful. "Now granted, I don't understand what you just said about what you did, but I can mimic the movements in order to make the same thing happen." He added trying to be helpful.

"It's not as easy as that, but we can teach you the skills needed to do what we just did." Mom said with a happy lilt to her voice that had not been heard for some time.

The captain bowed to her. "I promise to learn what you teach." He told her in the style of a noble knight. Mom smiled at him.

"That will have to wait for now. We will need to get ourselves back to our kingdom in order to ensure that it is safe from attack. We know that the General has been defeated, so it is possible that the threat has been neutralized, but none of us wish to risk our people's lives on that." She said in a sober tone.

The Captain bowed again. "Your wisdom is a shining example for all of us to follow." He said almost regally and he stepped back to leave them to their preparations. "Let me know when you are ready for my help in this casting." He offered and Mom thanked him.

"Don't worry; it will not be long now." She said. She was still working on the image and it was almost done. The current conversation had slowed her down a bit, but not overly so. "Just a few minutes more." She added her voice distant as she concentrated on a place far away from the lake. Dad and Erica picked up Josh; he was just waking up when Mom was finished. The group all huddled together to make a smaller package to deliver and Mom and The Captain added their magic to the spell and then they were back in the palace. Josh felt woozy, but he kept his feet under him. Other than that, they were all fine. The sounds of training outside were now familiar and Erica was glad to hear them. A young boy was cleaning the floor with a sponge when they appeared and he started briefly and then came to his senses.

"You… Your majesties, it is good that you have returned. I must tell the Guard Captain that you have arrived." He said in a rush and he bowed and left at almost a run. Cedric looked around. He was getting used to traveling without even taking a step.

"You True Bloods sure have shortened the distances." He remarked almost off-handedly. "I'm sure that a ride in the country is well beneath you now." He said and there was a smirk behind it. Erica thumped him on the shoulder and he rubbed it making a face at her. Actually, it really did hurt, but he wasn't going to tell her that. He looked for a way out of the room. "I need to check in with the troops." He said and it sounded a bit hollow. Erica's eyes lit up.

"OOO, Can I come along?" She asked and she put on that sweet face that he was already learning not to resist.

"Of course my dear" He said holding out his arm and she put her arm in it and the two love birds left the rest to their business.

Josh was looking around. He knew that he needed to say some things. He wasn't sure who needed to hear them. He had just lost two of the potential royal ears and he was not too happy about that. "Mom" He said wearily. He still needed a lot of rest before he would be anything close to normal. His ribs hurt badly as well. He winced when he tried to shift his weight. Mom stepped over quickly. Her face was lined with worry. He couldn't blame her for that. He just wished that he weren't the cause of all that worry. "We are still in danger." He said and Mom helped him to lie down. Every movement and every breath seemed to stab at him. "The veil between this world and the spirit world has been torn." He said and her look of worry turned to speculation and then back to worry.

"You should rest honey." She told him softly. "You're injured and very weak. Don't strain yourself. We'll talk about this later." She said and he was powerless to resist her. Even with his own mind screaming to speak, he found his eyes closing. He drifted off to sleep against his own will.

Dad strolled over to see what was going on. "Poor kid, he's so tired." He said and Mom glared at him.

"No, he was just dead. He has seen the other side. He knows that there is something wrong and we can't let him tell us about it yet because it will get him all riled up and he needs to rest." She scolded her husband. "That's why I just put him to sleep." She concluded and Dad's eyes went wide.

"What? You cast a spell on our boy?" He asked his voice dripping with incredulity. "How could you do that in this time of need?" He asked. It was more of an accusation than anything else. Mom knew that this would be Dad's reaction. He was a fighter and now informed in the intricacies of magic and the power struggles that go along with that. He was a straight forward, hit-it-head-on sort of guy and such tactics would be completely beyond him.

"Know that we still have trouble on the horizon. We will need him to be strong later. Right now he needs to heal and rest. If what he just said is true then we have more to deal with than some random demon or lesser devil." She said and Dad took notice to that. "We will be facing someone capable of tearing the veil between worlds. Someone with that sort of power can easily defeat us all." Mom looked thoughtful as she considered something else. She turned back to Dad. "I'm not even sure if the Guardian could help us against this foe." She said almost pleading for him to disagree, unfortunately he didn't.

Dad did stop and thought about what was said though. "You mean that there is something bigger and badder coming and we need to get ready for it." He started. It was basically just repeating what she had said and she nodded. "You also think that we cannot defeat this new threat." He said in a tone that was almost a question. "Then we need to find better weapons to combat this foe with." He said as any fighter would have. Mom rolled her eyes at him. Then she thought about the statement and suddenly found that she agreed with him.

"You're right about that." She said and she winked at Dad. He was startled by the sudden change. He became suspicious at once but his point had been made and he intended to get on with his part of it immediately.

"Let me know when Josh awakes." He said and Mom sighed. "I will be working on some new weapons with the smith." He told her and he left the two sorcerers to their complicated magic business. In truth, he understood more than he was letting on, but he couldn't let his wife know that. He had a few ideas swirling around in his mind and he needed to check with a specialist on the feasibility of them.

It was not long before the lad that had gone to deliver his message returned. He picked up the broom and then continued his assigned task. He ignored Mom and Josh completely. Perhaps that had been a part of his instructions as well; she neither knew, nor cared at this point. She was tired, very tired and some rest would be just the thing to make her mind work a little sharper. She would need that if her suspicions were correct. If Josh was right, then they would need every asset they could get their hands on. It was with that troubling thought she drifted off to sleep. She tossed and turned in that restless slumber.

The Master had covered a lot of ground with his army. There was still a long way to go until he could reach the far shore, but he had the smaller villages and outposts to help satiate his hunger along the way. In fact his army had diminished only slightly since that first encounter. Only a select few humans had discovered his troops' only weakness. Now that they were dead, he was relatively unopposed as he swept across the unready countryside. The scorched earth behind him was the final sign of the devastation that he was causing. He turned back to see it again. It was wonderful. The smoke still trailed up into the sky here and there and the ground was black soot. Nothing was alive there at all. They had killed even the insects that would normally have been buzzing about. The feeling of pride was profound. This world now belonged to the undead. He had claimed it and all that was left was a little mopping up. His fine sense of smell told him that there were more humans to the west. They were heading that way, sort of. They stopped to kill anything that moved along the way and that took some serious time. His impatience would not override his desire for the successful completion of his mission. He had assigned this mission after all. It was his bidding that had caused his delays. He would use the anger that generated to drive the fearful quivering vermin before him into dust. There would be more of them; they seemed to reproduce surprisingly quickly. They infested the entire world. There were pockets of them everywhere. He had to clear out from even the smallest glade to be sure that he got them all. If he left just a few, they would be back. He knew this and he was ready to make sure that it didn't happen. The human race would fall and be forgotten. He swore that in the beginning and he swore it again now.

The troops had been worried when word circulated that the True Bloods had left the kingdom to defend another one. Such things caused great concern for the general safety of the populace. What if they had died out there and could not defend us? It was that sort of unrest that had the potential to cause mass hysteria and undue mayhem. The palace guards and the new army did wonders to subdue the uprising even before it had a chance to mature. This was a good sign of independence for the young kingdom. It was also a sign that Josh and Erica might be able to take a short vacation without bedlam being the result. However, the news that they had returned had such a positive impact that it was not to be believed. Their return meant that they were here to defend this city. It also meant that they had successfully defended the other one. Such a victory did so much for public opinion and the general morale of the populace that the True Bloods seemed like gods. Well, maybe not gods, but at least angels of god. Of course, if they had been told that, they would have strictly denounced the idea immediately. And that would make the people believe it even more. The reign of Erica and Josh had only been four years, but they had done so many things that everyone knew who they were and what they were and nothing could shake their beliefs. Strictly speaking, this was dangerous as far and dependence goes, but now they were seeing that it was a terminal condition. If the people could see the government as their protector, then Josh didn't have to do it all himself. The concept was perhaps a bit beyond the average citizen, but it was a keystone of thought among the royals. Erica would have to deliver a speech now that they had returned. The people wanted to know what had happened out there in the other land. They would want to know if the enemy had been utterly defeated. They wanted to know a lot of things, but the primary question was the same on everybody's lips. "Are we safe?"

Erica and Cedric had made their way down to the training fields and it was obvious that Erica was tired. She had been worried and scared and even sad in the last few hours and she had not yet rested. It was something that showed on her face and in her lack of bounce in her step. She knew that she shouldn't be out here in public like this, but the troops wanted to see that she had returned intact. She would show them that and then she would get the needed rest and show them that she was still who they thought she was, Queen. Everyone she saw gave her the utmost respect and they all seemed to be beaming smiles at her. All of their hopes rested upon their queen and she could feel the burden of it accumulating as she saw more and more of those jubilant faces. It began to wear heavily upon her and Cedric noticed it and cut the walk short.

"My lady, you need to get that rest sooner than later." He said, trying to say it lightly. Erica started to argue, but then her own fatigue began to tell her not to. She simply nodded and they headed back to the palace. As they got nearer and nearer, Erica felt the weight of the world upon her. She could barely stand up anymore when they got inside. Dad had been in the same boat and he was asleep already. Mom led Cedric to his room and Erica to hers. She told each of them to have a good rest and then she made her way to the kitchen. The cooks were there and they were ready to offer up anything that Mom wished. All she was coming for was some broth and they looked disappointed. Mom lessened their depression by informing them that a celebration was coming soon and that they would need to be their most creative to feed the guests when it came. A challenge was always the best way to get a kitchen firing on all cylinders. Mom knew that; she had been royalty long before the kids were. She was feeling the edge of exhaustion herself. There had been a lot of support casting and basic worry and it was beginning to take its toll on her. She headed back to her room with a bowl of the broth and a couple of biscuits. They wished her well as she headed back down the hallway to her quarters. She was thinking back on what she had witnessed recently. It had been an amazing couple of days. She shook her head and headed to bed. The warm broth in her lap and the biscuits dipping brought soothing warmth to her body and she was asleep shortly after it was gone. She didn't even notice the young girl taking away the dishes. She was that far gone. The new day would see her more refreshed.

The scouts reached the site of a massive battle. Well, at least it must have been a massive battle to take down an entire army of demons and constructs. The two shadow demons moved silently through the trees as they surveyed the final resting place of the General. A human population was nearby and that must have been the fallen commander's objective. They would report this holdout when they got back to the Master. The army was nowhere to be seen. There were no bodies strewn about and the countryside was blemished by a massive stone passageway into the city beyond. It had strange white and yellow markings on it and some metal railings on the outside to keep wagons from falling off of it. The construction was impressive. The surface looked to be totally smooth and flat. It also looked brand new. There were no signs of wear and tear on this passage. They were not sure if it were important so they decided to report this too. There were definitely humans in that settlement still, that report was going to be the most important. There were too many of them to count, that was not a good sign. They slipped away unnoticed and began the journey to give their report to their leader. The Master would be pleased with them for their loyalty. That was how to survive under their leader, you had to impress him all the time or you were disposed of. They would make all haste.

Life in the newly unified kingdom pretty much returned to normal. The shops were open, the people were happy. The green grass outside the walls was being ploughed under for cultivation. It was too late this season to actually grow anything useful, but the fields were being staked out and assigned to the farmers that would work them later. The city had stores enough to last until the spring so there was not a lot of pressure on this activity. However, the process had begun. The sun was shining and the light breeze from the ocean front was cool and welcoming. The work was not labored, but celebratory. The sounds of gulls could be heard off in the distance and the sounds of hammers in the smithy were ringing through the crisp air. The only thing missing was the trade that would have come from other cities. Those places were gone. At least no one had heard from any of the other cities except the one that was somehow by a lake. Humanity had taken a huge loss. The people could not see that for themselves yet, so it didn't seem real. It would only be a matter of time before it sunk in, but for now things were rosy and happy.

That same shining sun cast its light through the windows of the palace. The small flecks of dust danced in the bright light as Josh watched them. His ribs still hurt badly and he knew that healing himself was out of the question. He had simply gone through too much of his personal energy to be able to cast for quite some time. It made him feel a bit lost, or even helpless. All he could do now was lie there and try not to breathe too deeply. He hoped that someone would take pity on him and at least heal these ribs. He could still think, he could still be useful. He was going to tire of lying around quickly. He had never been one for sitting around when something needed doing. He didn't expect that to change anytime soon; at least he hoped that it wouldn't. He had watched as his family got up and started their day. Servants had brought him breakfast and he immediately noticed a change in their demeanor. He used to joke around with them and he had eventually gotten them to loosen up a bit around him. It eased the tension in the room drastically to have them be happy around him. Now they looked upon him as their savior. He had accomplished one miraculous thing after another and he had saved everyone's life. That sort of thing built up barriers that in his weakened state he could not tear down. For Josh it meant that they would scuttle away just as soon as he had finished eating. They would make no conversation with him. They would respond if he addressed them directly, but they wouldn't even make eye contact. They darted away like shadows after they cleared his plate. Josh was miserable. He knew that he would need to bathe soon as well; he didn't look forward to that. He wished that they had a shower like he had in the old house, but of course they didn't. A hot bath normally calmed him. It would not this time and he knew it. The people that brought the water and refreshed it for him would be the same silent people that had brought him the breakfast. His normally jovial nature was not going to help him for a while. He needed a plan to fix this. He started working on those plans when his thoughts were disturbed by Mom.

"Hi honey, how's my little hero?" She asked in a slightly taunting tone and her smile faded when she noticed the mood that Josh was in.

"Mom, it's just not fair." He said finally as she sat next to him on the narrow bed. She stroked his hair as he stared up at the wooden ceiling. "The staff treats me like a china doll. They won't even talk to me anymore." He complained. He tried to raise his voice but the pain in his ribs cut that short. He winced with the effort.

"You have done things that they cannot understand." She told the frustrated sorcerer. "You have to give them time to get to know you again. What people don't understand, they fear. They need to see you doing normal things for a bit so that they can realize that you are normal too." She offered and Josh looked thoughtful.

"We had already done those things. I am the same person I was when this war began." He said in anguish, holding his side as another wrack of pain hit him.

Mom looked sternly at him. "No, you're not." She turned to make direct eye contact with him and he did his best to return it. "You have changed quite a bit. Let's not forget what you did and how you did it. You even died to save people. The palace staff knows this. The rumor mill have painted a picture of you that would be impossible for a normal person to fill, and yet you did all of those things." She added, building her case. "You have to face that fact that you are a hero. You don't have super strength, or the ability to fly, but you have the capacity for good and the will to overcome impossible odds." She said, a tear began to well up in her eye as she spoke. "I've never been prouder of you than I am right now." She stood up again and looked down at her son. "I need you to rest, no we all need you to rest. You are not to get out of bed for any reason. Is that clear?" She asked. Her tone suggested that there would be no debate on this point.

Josh saw that he was trapped. "Yes." He said weakly. His will was not completely broken, but it was very subdued.

Mom bent over and kissed his cheek. She spoke much more softly now. "Good, then you can have this…" She said and she put a hand on his ribs and the sharp pain caught his breath and then the magic flowed into it. The bones began to knit back together and the redness went down with the loss of swelling. In moments he was able to take his first full breath in a long time. "Remember your promise, get some real rest and then we will talk." She told him. Then she walked away and Josh laid there, thinking for quite some time before his mind let him fall asleep.

The army of demons advanced slowly, killing and burning everything. Of course this method of travel gave each human settlement plenty of advance notice that they were coming before they actually arrived. With their ability to heal and their sheer numbers, this was not even a consideration for them. No matter what the humans did, the outcome was always the same. They would take a few casualties and those casualties would get back up and rejoin the fight. The humans had no such ability and thus the morale of the enemy would fall when they saw it. A broken morale made the fight go so much quicker. This army had been assembled for this ability. The Master had held back the best troops for his own use. The General's troops had been good, and his squad captains had been able to regenerate as well, but he had used siege engines to engage the enemy without coming in to close contact with them. This was not the way of the warrior and the Master spit at the thought. He had gotten to where he was by in close slaughter and the feeling of rending flesh on his claws. That was something the General had lacked. That commander had been a thinker. His instincts were not savage. His intellectual approach had obviously failed him. In truth, the Master was actually surprised by that. He had thought that all of those tactics and plans had to have made him at least formidable on this world. It had not been enough to save him when it came right down to it. So the Master had deduced that intelligence was a sign of weakness. He would make sure that any commanders he used in the future were more animal in nature, and less sophisticated. He felt more comfortable that way and besides, then none of them would be bright enough to challenge his authority. "This small village has going to fall quickly." He thought to himself as he killed the cow that was unfortunate enough to be in his way. Burning the outlying fields was one sure way to make sure that the enemy was ready to resist when you arrived. He wanted a good fight. He was growing tired of all these sheep. He needed to face a true warrior and then savor his victory. His eyes scanned the small village and his hopes began to fade. This place was too small to have a real fight in it. He would console himself with the rising death toll. He could still smell a large settlement to the west; in fact it was the largest one he had ever smelled. It would be the ripe plum that he would pick and crush in his own claws. It would not be too long now.

Life in the True Blood kingdom continued on for another day uninterrupted by the threat of war. That did not mean that training was suspended, in fact it had still been going at full steam. No, it simply meant that the enemy had not yet found them. Erica and Cedric had been running around giving speeches and informing the general public of their precarious position. They were also making preparations for a royal wedding. The sparkles in the people's eyes were a testament to just how deeply they loved their queen. Erica enjoyed a spotless reputation for being generous, fair and just, and open minded. It was a combination that still made Cedric marvel at his fiancé. The people were prepared to defend their new homes, but they were just as ready, eager even, to watch their queen wed a king and thus combine the two kingdoms. They were already together physically, the local laws applied to all and the prosperity that came with that belonged to everybody as well. There had been no real uprisings over being absorbed into the True Blood kingdom. In fact, if there had been, it would have been from Erica's side, not wanting to share their queen with 'outsiders'. The fact that Erica was always seen with Cedric had eased a lot of those sentiments. Politically, it could have gone far worse. The weather was even cooperating and many of the speeches were delivered outside in the streets. That way more people could hear what they had to say. The security detachment that was always accompanying the royal couple maintained an ever vigilant surveillance. Of course it was only a precaution. Erica was so loved that she could have brought home just about anybody and the public would have accepted them. Now if Cedric were seen hurting Erica, then that same support for him would turn into something far uglier. It was a fine line that Cedric was walking and Erica felt a little bad for him. She could feel all the stares as she made her way through the busy streets to their next destination. Erica found her footing nice and solid upon the box that the servants had just laid down before her. The people gathered around quickly. News that the queen was out on the streets always seemed to travel fast. She sent out a beaming smile and the crowd cheered for her.

"Please quiet down a moment." She ordered and the crowd did quiet down a little. The clapping continued on for another couple of minutes. "Okay, please allow me to tell you what I know." She said and the sound level in the crowd dropped drastically. It was not pin drop quiet, but something fairly close to it. "I have been telling all of you for a few days now that we are still in danger. King Cedric and I have been warning all that trouble is on the horizon. We are taking the following steps to try to ensure that your safety is maintained. This is what we plan…"

The speech was the same one she had given some five times now. She knew how to judge the timing and she knew when to wait on the crowd for their reaction. In the four years that she had been queen, dealing with public speaking had become less of a problem for her.

Josh awoke and it was mid-morning according to the location of the beam of bright sunlight that was glaring across his face. He yawned and stretched and suddenly remembered that his ribs were not broken anymore. It was wonderful. He sat up in bed, careful not to get out of it. He had made a promise and he knew that someone was watching him to make sure he complied. It might not be Mom, but there was always somebody. He saw the young girl standing by the door to this chamber. She was carrying a towel and a set of clothes for him. He looked at her directly and she lowered her head.

"Are you here for a specific purpose?" He asked her in a tone that let none of his disappointment in her reaction show.

She did a neat curtsy and cleared her throat ever so quietly. "Yes milord, I am here to escort you to your bath." She said, her timid tone was probably because she was so young, she must have been about nine years old.

Josh shook his head to shake the cobwebs from it. "Does that mean I can get out of bed?" He asked and the little girl giggled.

"You don't have to ask me for permission to do anything sire." She said, the familiarity was coming back slowly. "The queen is busy giving speeches in the city proper and the older queen told me to make sure that you were washed up before you ate anything." The small girl replied.

The mention of food made Josh's stomach growl. He wondered when he had eaten last. He could not remember. "Well, the food sounds good." He said. He stood up and found that his legs were still wobbly. The young girl was at him in a flash. She steadied the sorcerer and handed him his towel.

"You are still quite weak." She said needlessly. "May be I should call for some more help." She said and Josh hushed her.

"No, I think we can manage to get to the next room." Josh said. He was not sure of the fact himself, but he didn't want to appear as weak as to not be able to walk anymore. "How long have you been waiting for me to wake up?" He asked as his mind grasped the new idea.

The girl giggled again. "Sire, I have waited my turn for two days now. We have a schedule to watch you and it was my turn when you woke up." She explained.

Josh started. "Two days?" He looked around the room, nothing looked different. "Have I really been asleep two days?" He asked, amazed at the fact.

"No sire, you have been asleep four days, but the older. More experienced servants got tired of waiting for you and they set up our schedule two days ago." She said in that tone that suggested that 'you should know all of this, it's about you; you know'. But those words did not find her lips.

Josh made his way across the stone floor and found that the tub was where he expected it to be. There were several men filling it up with steaming hot water. The young girl stopped at the doorway and laid Josh's clothes down on the chair by the door.

"is there anything else you need?" She asked and Josh thanked her and told her no. The men completed the filling of the tub and then they withdrew leaving Josh to take care of business. He was rather relieved about that. He had always had problems being naked in front of people. The rest of the bath went off without a hitch. Josh was dressed and feeling much better when he stepped out into the hallway. There was a small table there with pastries on it and his stomach reminded him that he was more than hungry. He grabbed one and almost swallowed it whole. He chewed and chewed as he grabbed a second one and then headed down to the dining hall. He knew that someone was tracking his movements through the palace and he was also sure that there would be a meal there waiting for him when he arrived. It had always been that way. He wasn't even sure how they managed it, but he was grateful for it today. The guard opened the large oak door and the smells of a country breakfast hit his nose. His stomach clenched in anticipation. He tried not to let it show, but it must have anyway. The serving girls were there and they smiled warmly at him as he made his way to the table. He sat down and let his eyes take in the impressive spread. There were eggs and bacon and freshly baked breads. Some sort of cinnamon roll and even freshly squeezed juice from a local fruit plant. He sat forward and started to fill his plate. In the back of his mind he knew that if he was over-hungry, then eating too much would only hurt him. He did his best to limit himself, but he still probably grabbed too much. He shrugged his shoulders at his own mental warning and then began eating. He was almost half-way through the plate when Mom entered the room.

"I see your appetite has returned, that's a good sign." She told him and she nodded to one of the servers. In moments they had a plate before her that looked like a low calorie selection from the IHOP at home. It was pretty, but it would not have been enough food for Josh. Mom nibbled at the plate even as Josh finished his. He wanted more, surely he did, but he knew that it would be a mistake. He had to give himself time to work his strength back up. Then he was surprised when Cedric and Erica entered the room. He had not seen them in days and the two were so obviously a couple now that it took him a bit by surprise.

"You two look very happy." He remarked and they glowed with the energy of young love. Josh almost snorted, holding back his amusement, almost. He grabbed a piece of bread and shoved it into his mouth to make sure that he behaved.

"Oh Josh, it's so good to have you back with us." Erica said. Her voice was almost singsong with her mood being so good. "You missed some glorious weather outside." She added almost as an afterthought.

The group got bigger when Dad came in. The Guard Captain followed him closely. The table was filling up. Josh greeted each one as they wished him well. The last one to come into the room was the most surprising one of all. The Guardian of Balance stepped into the room and had a seat as well. Nobody else seemed to be surprised by his presence so Josh just went with the flow on this one. They were all seated at the table now and the servants took away the food at a rate that was almost magical. The table was wiped down quickly and then the servants all departed. The doors were closed and the guard on the other side would make sure that no one was eavesdropping on the assembly. Josh looked around the table, wondering who had called this meeting that he had been lured to. He didn't have to wait long.

The Guardian swept his hand in a welcoming gesture and took the floor. "I am glad that we could all make it to this meeting." He began with a flippant tone that seemed out of place here. "The news about the enemy has come from multiple sources. They are coming and they will be here soon." He said without preamble. Josh felt his eyes open a bit wider. His indignation flared.

"Why am I not hearing about this until now?" He asked and the Guardian rolled his eyes.

"You have been asleep for days, young man." He replied and there was just a twinge of nastiness in that. "You have been lying idly by while we have been making the preparations for the defense of this kingdom." He further explained. It was not fair, but it was actual fact. Knowing that didn't make it any better for Josh.

"When I saw you last it was in the spirit world. You know that I was dead then. What did you expect from me?" Josh asked, his hurt showed in his voice.

The Guardian held up his hand to forestall any protest from the table. "Now now, that is not what we are gathered to discuss. You are here now, and we shall take advantage of that. However, it is generally understood that magic from you will not be possible in the upcoming battle." He said and Josh felt like he was stabbed. If he could not cast during the time his people needed him most, he had become a liability in their protection. That meant that his purpose here had been lost. It was a crushing blow.

Josh looked down at the table, he felt as empty as it looked. "So I am useless." He said quietly. The Guardian of Balance flew across the table and slapped Josh across the face, just as he had done in spirit form those long days ago.

"I will not listen to that sort of talk!" He said sternly. The rest of the family seemed to be in shock at what just happened. "You are an important part of the defenses even without your magic. You are the defensive coordinator. Your tactical mind is far superior to anyone else here and that makes you quite valuable indeed." He further explained. "There will be no more talk of uselessness. I want you to focus instead on what you *do* bring to the table. Can you manage that?" He asked and Josh nodded numbly.

Then, as if nothing had transpired between them at all, the Guardian picked up where he left off. "It is obvious that the previous defensive plans will be ineffective here. The army that marches on us now are demons and devils, not the constructs that came at us before. There are at least a few differences that should be noted in that classification." The Guardian paused to make sure that his audience was attentive and ready for him to proceed. Once he was satisfied that they were, he plowed on into his recitation. "The first notable difference is that demons can call up lesser demons like the troops that you have faced before. That means that *any* enemy troop can summon a squad around him if he feels cut off or trapped. It allows the army to march without the logistical need for provisions for the extra troops. Secondly, the main force is commanded by a devil that goes by the name of The Master." He paused as everyone noted his words. "The Master is a devil, and not just one of those lesser devils, he rules a good portion of hell. He had brought his own flavor of hell here for us to enjoy. He won't be happy until all life on this world has been wiped out. He will not leave so much as a swarm of insects alive if he has his way. He is destroying villages completely. The people, the animals, the crops, even the grass has been burned. He is methodical and exact. It is this that has delayed his arrival this long. He has had to kill everything from here to the Eastern city to get here and that takes a long time." The Guardian said as if rattling off the stats of a war long ago fought and mostly forgotten. His lack of passion was disturbing to the listeners.

Mom was the first to react to it. "You mean that nobody in this world between here and there are alive anymore?" She asked, her tone suggested his answer had better be better thought out than his announcement had been.

The Guardian missed her warning entirely. "Of course, that is what I have been telling you. He is trying to eradicate the species, well all species on this world. He will go after the harder to find races once he has finished with humans." He said and his tone of annoyance at the question almost sealed his fate with Mom. She was steaming.

"Listen up you arrogant, thoughtless, insensitive bastard!" She began and Dad put a hand on her arm to try and calm her down. She shrugged it away. "Just who do you think you are telling us that now? We could have saved at least some of those people if we had been told sooner." She was letting her rage show now and the pitch of her voice was getting higher as the danger rose. She was ready to explode. "You had better have a damn good reason why you are telling us this now when it is too late." She warned and some of it actually seeped in. The Guardian looked at all the unhappy faces around the table.

"I did not tell you earlier because there was nothing you could do about it. If I had told you and you ran off to fight this force, you would have been destroyed and this kingdom would be left defenseless." He turned to Josh. "The fact that you were successful at the lake was a miracle. I was adequately surprised over that even though it did cost you your life." He said and Mom was still steaming. Only the influence of Dad kept her from jumping up and striking the Guardian of Balance repeatedly. The oblivious man rambled on nonetheless. "You were quite inventive out there and it is that sort of thing that I want to capitalize on now." He said and Josh threw up his hands in the air.

"You told me that I cannot use magic, how can I help in that way then?" He asked exasperated and just as upset as Mom was.

"You do not have to do the magic," was the simple reply. "You can tell other sorcerers what to do and then they can do it. You have the unique ability to visualize things more than a few steps ahead of the problem and plan for them. It is very... I don't know the word for it, but it is good." He said, lost in the thought.

Dad spoke up next. "Proactive is the word you were missing." He put in and the Guardian nodded his approval. "We need a full plan, and Josh has only just gotten up. The enemy is at the doorstep, at least figuratively, and you tell us that everyone else is dead. How do you suggest that we overcome all of that?" He asked. A fighter was not equipped to handle difficulties of this scale. Both he and Erica were feeling the weight of it all and they weren't very happy about it either.

The Guardian looked upset at having been interrupted. "Unless you have a squadron of bombers in your pocket, we need to organize a ground attack." He said with a bit of a huff.

Josh's face lit up. "Bombers?" All eyes turned to the young sorcerer. "I didn't think of that." He said thoughtfully. His eyes began that far-away look, the one he got when he was crafting something in his mind. "Yes, I think that will do nicely." He said at last. Everyone was still watching him closely, more patiently than they would like to admit.

Nobody spoke for several long moments. Finally, Erica could take it no more. "What will do nicely?" She asked; her exasperation clearly on display.

Josh blinked twice. It was like he was noticing the people in the room for the first time, again. "Oh, I think we can do bombers, just not the kind you were thinking of. We cannot magically produce airplanes, they are much too difficult, but zeppelins, that we can do." He stated and the Guardian sat back down heavily.

"I…" He started to say and then he corrected himself. "You never cease to amaze me." The Guardian admitted to Josh. Josh smiled back at him, but it was clear that he was working on something else as well. They had started a chain reaction of ideas in him and he was following them through in his head. All anyone else could do now was to wait and see what surfaced.

Josh sat there, almost motionless, running through all kinds of thoughts in his head. He would pull up an idea, reject it, and move on to the next one. It was like lightning dancing around firing neurons in there. Who knew where it would strike next. Then Josh startled the whole room by slamming his hand on the table. "That's it!" He shouted. He looked around and saw expectant and hopeful faces. This time he continued before they had to prompt him to do so.

"The solution is not a military one, although how to bring it about is." Josh said and a few eyebrows furrowed at the complex logic behind that. "We cannot hope to defeat these demons with ground forces or even the bombers I have in mind and keep our own casualties down." There were various nods of ascent around the room. "We need to get them off of this world entirely." He said and the confused faces met him as he looked around. Josh turned directly to the Guardian. "You told me that you can seal the tear if we can restore the balance between worlds. Every one of the demons and devils out there belong on the other side. That means that this world wants to flush them out. They are using either will power or magic to override that balance. Everything they destroy here makes that shift even worse. If they succeed in eliminating all of us, then the world will be so out of balance that it cannot ever be corrected." He explained and the Guardian nodded, all of the others looked confused still. "Okay, so we need to get all of the demons and devils back through that opening." He said coming around to his point. "In order to do this, we need to release their hold on this world and then the natural balance will suck them out." He said and light bulbs started lighting over his audience.

Mom seemed to grasp the concept best. "What do you want to do to lessen their grip?" She asked plainly. Josh paused in thought.

"The first thing we need to do is to get them to stop focusing on us. We need them to be thinking of where they came from. The direct concentration of the army is helping them to stay here." Josh explained. "If we can get them thinking about hell, or wherever it is they came from, then that hold will be gone." Josh stood up and paced around a bit. "Next, we need to get them off of the ground. Physical contact with this world gives them a foundation that it is real and it is helping them to maintain their hold." He told the startled group.

Cedric snorted. "Let me get this straight… You want to make the army that is coming to destroy us think of home and you want to somehow get them to stop touching our world?" He asked. His tone suggested how ludicrous it all seemed to him.

Josh looked at Cedric and the two had a tiny battle of wills which Josh won. "Yes, actually, that is exactly what I am saying. We are tethered to this world because we were born here. You were too so you have that as well. They were born of the other world and so they are tethered to it." Josh explained for those who had not yet caught up with him. "Right now that tether is stretched very thin and the pull on it is rather extreme. If we can make it snap back, then the whole army would snap back into their world and leave ours." He said triumphantly.

Again Cedric was the fly in the ointment. "Okay, say you're correct about this tether, whatever that is, and that they are struggling to stay here." He said and Josh nodded. "That still leaves you with the problem of changing what they are thinking and making sure that they can't touch the ground." He said. "If you can't do that, then none of this other stuff even matters." He put as succinctly as he could.

Josh accepted his point. "You're right about that. That is why I have a plan to do those things, but it will take a lot of fast work. We'll need to get started right away." Then Josh turned back to the Guardian of Balance. "You are sure you can seal up the hole once they are on the far side?" he asked and the Guardian nodded grimly to him. "Good." Josh said. "That was the lynchpin to this whole operation." He chuckled as everybody watched him leave the room. "Come on people, we've got work to do and I will tell each of you what you need to do." He said and they all filed in behind him, wondering just what crazy thing he had dreamt up this time. For all of his complaining, the Guardian really did wonder what Josh had cooked up. He had to admit that even though the young man was a pain in the neck, the universe was less boring with him in it.

The Master could feel the humans now. They were so close and he was so thirsty for their blood. The scouts had reported that there was another city to the northeast, but he was so close to the western city, the largest one left, that he had to take it down first. After that, he would go and cleanse that final city of human infestation. His troops were tireless and he had to admit that he was actually a bit proud of them. This world never knew what hit it. The occasional lucky decapitation had been all of the casualties that he had suffered. His army was at least eighty percent strong and he knew that it was going to be strong enough to take down this fortified city. He had placed scouts outside of the place and he had to admit that what they described sounded impressive. He would enjoy undoing all that they had accomplished here. He could still feel the pull of hell, but he had so much yet to accomplish here that he simply ignored it. He would be attacking those human built walls soon. He would do it without the siege engines that the General had once used. He would not be so cowardly as to employ those. He wanted to see the look on his victim's face when he tore through their guts and pulled out their organs. This world would be his soon. Once the last living thing was destroyed, there would be no resistance and he would reign supreme, just as he had done on other worlds. He was making his final preparations and it felt good. His body did not suffer from fatigue or weakness, he was immortal and he was clad in darkness. There was nothing on this world that could harm him and he knew it. It gave him a superiority complex that could not be denied. He wiped some vile meat from his last kill off of his chest plate and then he turned to see he troops.

He leaped up onto a fallen stump as the flames burned the area around him. The flames licked at him and reminded him briefly of home. Then he gazed out at all of those demons and lesser devils and he smiled an evil smile that would make a man shiver. "We are about to face our most serious obstacle!" He shouted to the assemblage of monstrosities. "We are about to take down the biggest enemy stronghold on the world and we are about to do it without any special weapons or aid. Your strength lies not in those gadgets, but in the sinew of your backs and arms and legs. You are the machine that will crush these human vermin once and for all!" He shouted at them and a cheer lifted up over it all in response. "When we are done, there will be nothing but bones and ashes." He said and there were grunts and nods of agreement as he gazed out at the mass of warrior before him. "Let us go and take this world for ourselves." He said and the whole assembly started the march to the final holdout, the large human city. The final conflict had begun.

The group of royals followed Josh through the corridors of the palace. The pace was fast, very fast, and it was amazing that someone so recently close to death was moving this briskly. Josh was on a mission. He had put together some kind of plan and there was no time to waste in him explaining it to them. The standard defenses were already in place. The archers were on the wall and the pits had already been dug. The front gates were sealed, and by sealed we mean that Mom had made them just another part of the walls. There were no longer any access gates. Mom was casting zeppelins that carried baskets of explosives. Dad was checking all the weapons and armor, making sure that the defense force was ready to face this enemy. Cedric, commander of this army, was in the tactical station where he could view the entire battle. Through the miracle of something called a walkie-talkie, he could actually talk with his field commanders down at the front. In truth, the walkie-talkies only looked like electronic devices, Mom had managed to fashion them from a spell called magic ear and another called powerful voice. The result was the same except that the range seemed to be almost limitless. The lookout reported the mass of bodies in the distance and the alarm was sounded. Erica was ready to hit the front, but Cedric stopped her.

"Dear, you don't expect to go into battle unarmed do you? " He asked and she looked at him sideways.

"I'll grab a sword down there; I will not go in empty-handed." She retorted but there was something in his eyes that gave her pause.

Cedric motioned for a servant that Erica had not even noticed to step forward. The servant was a smith's apprentice and he bore a box with a fancy cloth covering it. He presented it to Erica at Cedric's direction and she pulled the cloth off delicately. The box was as ornate as the cloth had been and it looked fabulous. She opened the clasp and pulled back the leather straps. The lid opened silently and inside was two axes. They had similar handles to the hammers she had used before. They were meant to be used with one hand each so that she could be doubly lethal, especially close up. They were even etched with the royal seal and they had a blue hue to them, like a glow. The golden grips were wrapped in leather with jewels studded in the end. The blades were long and sharp and had holes in them in the pattern of a dragon, they looked exquisite. Erica smiled hugely as she picked them up carefully out of the box. They fit her hands perfectly. The balance was amazing for such awkward looking weapons. She stepped back and hefted them to test their stability, and then she spun and did a series of moves that made the apprentice's jaw drop.

"They're perfect!" She proclaimed and Cedric folded his arms.

"I'm glad. I wouldn't want my queen to be in battle with a normal sword. I had talked with your Guard Captain and he told me that you had a problem with hammers. So I was sure not to get those for you. I noticed earlier that you wielded a large sword almost with one hand. That meant to me that two handed weapons would be a waste for you. You needed two weapons to wield at a time. Swords are okay for that, but nothing matches the bite of an axe." He said and he was smiling as well. "Consider this a peace offering for my betrothed." He said at last and Erica set the axes down to give him a hug. They embraced for a few seconds longer than was comfortable and then Erica backed away to retrieve her weapons again. She headed down to the front. She would help to repel anyone who made it to the top of the wall.

Josh turned from his tirade when he heard the alarms go off. They were out of time, he knew this intellectually, but he also knew that they had no choice but to proceed. He had no personal energy yet, so he could not cast anything. He hoped that the Guardian would be up to the task.

"Are you ready for this?" He asked and the Guardian simply nodded. Josh pulled up the image that he wanted. It was not overly complex because he knew that someone else was going to cast it. This was not the solid construction he had overtaxed himself with either; they were going for illusion now. He wanted the demons and devils to think of home. This was going to be tricky and the timing would have to be perfect. "Okay, I'm going to send you the image now." He announced and the Guardian opened his mind.

The image that came into his head was startling. There were fires burning everywhere. The entire countryside was in flames and the strong acrid smell of sulfur permeated everything. Smell was such a powerful aide in getting the mind to follow a specific thought process. Josh had planted hell just outside of the walls. He hoped that it would trigger the memories that would break the devil's hold on this world. Or, failing that, it needed to weaken that hold to the point where something else could finish the job. This was all guesswork; it might or might not work. He knew that and he also knew that they were out of options. Without him being able to bring up another army, this was all that they had to offer. It would be down to the fighters after this.

The Guardian studied the image closely and he was once again impressed at how such a thing could be viewed so simply. The countryside and the fire were perfect, but they were only lights. They would be easier to control than actual fire. There was even warmth from a centralized point and of course the smells that had been included. It was another piece of masterful art that a very few could have appreciated. He was one of those that could. Josh pulled him from his thoughts.

"Okay, I will need you to cast this just before the enemy makes contact with the city wall. We don't want them touching something solid when they see their home around them." He warned. The Guardian understood this and told Josh so. Satisfied, Josh left the man to his preparations. The enemy was on the field, they needed a presence there as well or all of this would come too late. The gates no longer existed so sending actual troops out there would have been next to impossible and more than likely it would also have been suicidal. There would have been no retreat possible without an entrance. Josh went to work on his next phase by rushing down towards the wall at an impressive speed. He could feel that his personal energy was still low, very low, but he had adrenaline for now, hopefully it would last long enough to carry him. If not, then his involvement in the plan would cease prematurely. That would be catastrophic. He shoved the thought aside and ran.

CHAPTER 13

T he Master looked at the city walls. They were indeed impressive as his scouts had told him. This was the jewel of the human infestation and he was ready to pluck the heart from it and eat it. He was ready to assume the throne of this world and he was ready for all of this to be behind him. The grass fields before him made him sick. The clean walls of the city and palace beyond were something of an enigma. Humans did not normally create things to perfect, so beautiful. Normally things were run down or dirty, or both. He looked forward to tearing these walls down. He scanned the wall looking for the city gates. He scanned the entire length of the wall again. There were no city gates! What fool built a wall with no way in or out of it? How did they get the people in their in the first place? There had to be a secret entrance. He turned and dispatched several scouts to go and find it. Human cities relied heavily on the surrounding countryside for sustenance. It was one of their primary weaknesses. This one seemed to be self-contained. He would see how they did that once he was inside this crazy city, tearing up everything he could find. His main force was ready, but he held them back until the entrance could be found. He would send an elite group through that vulnerable spot even as he coordinated the primary attack at the middle of the wall. If they weren't going to give him a gate to smash, he would simply make his own. He licked his lips. "I have been waiting for this fight for quite some time. I don't want to miss a second of it." He said aloud to himself. His sentiments were echoed by his troops and they all knew that the order to march would come soon. They were getting antsy to go. He understood that, but tactics were tactics. He needed to wait just a bit longer, but soon they would be unleashing their frenzy upon these hapless vermin. His blood raced at the thought. Hold on just a bit more...

The zeppelins were finished and Mom had even managed to keep them tethered by thin cords that were easily slashed with sword so that they could be launched by anybody, not just a spell caster. The basket loads were directly from Josh's image and they looked lethal enough. They looked like modeling clay, packed in cylinders and surrounded by rows and rows of razor blades. When these went off, they would launch all of that steel out in all directions. They promised to be really messy. Mom had cast fifteen of these airborne attackers and she was ready for her next task. She headed towards Josh.

The Guardian sat waiting for his cue. There was little more that he could do except that. He was so far away from the fight that all he had was a tiny window from which to cast the illusion spell. At least he would be well protected when the fighting started. He was feeling a bit put out just now, but he knew that his part was important, so he swallowed his pride, for now.

Josh had reached his destination. Cedric still had his loft post and that was where Josh would witness the culmination of all his plans. It would be a glorious battle that hopefully none of them would have to fight. He watched as his sister made her way to the front lines. The middle of the wall was the most likely place they would attack since there was no visible gate to be targeted. The main defensive force seemed to be favoring the spot. Josh wondered if that wasn't a weakness in the defense all by itself. He considered having Cedric spread them out a bit more, but thought better of second guessing him just before a battle.

The enemy line was advancing across his beautiful grass fields. They were stomping and trudging it all up and he knew it was just the beginning of the destruction that they had planned. The first zeppelin sailed out over the wall. It had been launched a bit prematurely, but Josh didn't mind. He was anxious to see how well they worked anyway. The large aircraft sailed out silently over the field, casting its shadow on the untouched green grass, heading out towards the enemy horde. The demons looked up in amazement at the thing and one of the commanders took aim with his bow. The zeppelin was halfway to the lead enemy line when the string twanged and the arrow took flight. It was a barbed arrow for tearing through flesh. It tore into the balloon just as easily and the zeppelin began to lose altitude. A cheer rose up from the demons on the field for they had scored their first kill. The zeppelin dropped slowly and kept moving forward. The front line advanced to it to see just what this human thing was. The basket was almost to the ground when it detonated. Thirty or so of the lead line went down from the blast. The steel blades tore them to shreds. Others, a bit back from the blast took shrapnel damage and went down as well. The cheer from the horde was now echoed from the human side. The demons began healing except for the nine of them which had lost their heads in the blast. The human cheer died out quickly when the enemy troops pushed themselves back up off the ground to continue to advance.

Josh had watched the whole thing and he felt sick to his stomach at the blood and gore on the field. Then, when the troops got back up he felt even sicker. The bodies that lay on the ground were the ones he was interested in. He looked closely using his wizard sight and he discovered the one true weakness of these demons. He picked up the walkie-talkie. "Alert the troops, you must take their heads for them to stay down." He said into the unit twice. He wanted to be sure the message got through. He got the reply that he was understood and he sat back to watch as the next part of the battle unfolded. He gave the signal that the Guardian had been waiting for.

The grass fields were suddenly transformed into hills of molten and shifting lava with fires everywhere and the strong smell of sulfur everywhere. The demons stopped and looked around. The Master stepped forward and took in a lungful of that sweet smell and then he advanced even farther. The ground rippled and danced before him as he knelt down to touch it. The heat was wrong. He knew it right away. He looked around at his confused troops and he laughed.

"You fools! It is but illusion!" He screamed and he sent out a wave of disruption that shattered the fiery image and the green grass was blown about in it. The troops renewed their advance and Josh shrugged his shoulders.

"Well, it was a long shot." He explained off-handedly as Cedric looked at him. "At least they thought of home instead of us for a bit, hopefully we can use that." He said optimistically. The walls were still out of arrow range for the attackers. That was not the case from the heights of the amazingly tall walls looking down. Here and there an arrow picked off one or another demon. Of course the arrows only slowed them down a small amount. The creatures healed from just about everything. The reason they were firing at all was to make sure that the enemy did not know that the humans knew their one weakness. The enemy continued to advance. The order to take heads seemed counterintuitive to the soldiers waiting on the top of the walls. Basically it meant that they were supposed to wait for the enemy to breech the wall and then they could strike them down. At least that was how it felt. They would kill a few more with the zeppelins, but otherwise it was a waiting game for the human resistance. Well, it was for all but one.

Erica held tight to the rope as she swung her axe to cut free the zeppelin. It sailed into the air and headed out over the wall with her dangling from the tether line. She had one of her axes in hand and the other on her back, waiting for her to free her other arm. The enemy started firing at the balloon right away and it started losing altitude just as the other one had. Erica dropped off and dove away when the zeppelin dropped to about twenty feet from the ground. Her ability to crouch and roll had saved her from injury, but she was too close to the thing and it was about to go off. Erica engaged the enemy. She had both axes out now and they were cutting arcs through the hapless necks of demons all about her. She counted to six as the shadow crossed her position and then she grabbed a demon and threw herself to the ground with the vile beast on top of her. The basket exploded and blew apart many of the demons again. There were even more that were beheaded this time because the basket was at the correct height when it detonated. The body on top of Erica was thrown clear. She felt the blast and she tried to cower away from the massive force of it.

She got up and looked at the carnage around her. She had a couple of scrapes from the fall and a trickle of blood from a near miss on her shoulder. The demons were still getting their bearings as she was hacking at them. A dozen swordsmen from the walls started sliding down lines shot from crossbows. Mom had fashioned a low-tech zip line in a hurry and had deployed them as quickly as possible to save her daughter from the sure death she seemed destined to chase.

Erica was in the dance. Her blades were slicing through flesh and bone with hardly any resistance. These were no normal axes. She pivoted here and cut one and then dodged there with another slice for that one. She took heads whenever possible. If she couldn't, then she took the sword arm. Then the troop would have to regenerate to cause her any harm. The melee was getting intense. Erica had the power of adrenaline and the countless hours of practice that she had invested in her art. In addition, she had these amazing axes and they really seemed to be a part of her as she tore through demon after demon. The problem was that there were always more of them. She was surrounded now by the attacking and fallen demons. Her steps were calculated and she was almost cut off completely when the small troop of swordsmen cut their way to her. Then, as if on cue, the whole unit wedged back until they were back at the leading edge of enemy activity. All of them were cut here and there and bruised by repeated blows. They were good, the best that could be taught in the limited time they had had, but they were only a few against so many. Erica began to feel her strength ebb when she stuck her arm to slay another demon only to find a ghostly arm already doing it. The group of fighters paused as a wave of spirits joined the melee. Erica realized that surprise was on their side and she pressed further into the enemy. These ghosts were warriors, old and powerful. She sensed from them nothing but good and helpfulness. It was most unsettling. Then it hit her, these were the ancients! They had helped her ever since she arrived in this world. Now they were fighting alongside her and she felt invigorated by that. She decided that they needed to regroup before they lost their momentum and many lives as well. She called a retreat and the spirits pulled the humans back to the safe side of the wall by pulling right through it. Erica felt drained, but happy. Her scores of injuries were minor next to what she had dealt out. The ancients stood before her and she bowed to them. They returned the bow.

"You really are here." She said almost unnecessarily. "How can this be?" She asked and it was Josh who answered her. He had come at a run when he saw the ancients appear. He was winded now, but managed to speak between pants.

They came through the tear." He replied. He had bent over to try and get more air into his lungs. He was still pretty weak apparently. "They can actually be here just like the demons and devils that we face." He said, trying to add to his explanation. "My guess is that they feel the pull to the other world as well though." He cautioned and the ancients looked at him. One of them looked particularly interested in the young man. He slid forward without walking the way only a ghost can.

"Yes, you are right about that." He said in an old voice that had been silenced many ages before Josh had been born. We are not of this world, just as that army out there is not. When we were called, we came. It is the first time that we have been able to respond this way instead of sending some skills through the link. We do not know how long we can remain here though. Our world is pulling us harder and harder as time goes by."

Josh nodded his understanding. "Then the demons and devils should have the same problem. The pull is getting stronger all the time." He concluded. He picked up his walkie-talkie and spoke into it quickly. "Guardian, get ready on that illusion spell again. We need to increase the pull." He said. The immediate reply was a sigh, but then there was acceptance from the other end. Josh decided to continue. "Hit that as soon as you can, if they bring the spell down again, do it again. Do your best to keep it active as long as you can. We want them to believe that their world is taking over this one. Then their pull on this one will be greatly diminished. Oh and also be ready to close that rift once they are sent back." He added and this time the response was quicker.

"I'll try." Was the humbling response from one of the most powerful beings in the universe. He had been tasked with a tall order, but not any taller than the one Josh had laid before him. The young sorcerer turned back to the ancients who were waiting expectantly for him to address them again.

"Do you think you can help us to take the demons and devils back to where they belong?" He asked directly. The lead spirit smiled crookedly at him.

"I think we can do that, so long as you understand the costs involved." He said and Josh looked worried.

"What are the costs then?" He asked, not sure he wanted to hear the answer. Erica was listening intently as well. After all, they were *her* ancients.

The eldest spirit kept his smile in place as he started to explain. "The power for us to return to this plane comes from the True Bloods, your sister to be exact. If we link ourselves to the demons and carry them back over the threshold into our realm, then you will not be able to call upon us any longer. If you do, they we, and our demons will respond with less than desirable results." The spirit explained. Erica turned pale, not as pale as the ghosts they stood among, but paler than usual.

"I... I can't lose the spirits." She sobbed. "They are what make me special. They are the source of my power." She continued and Josh shook his head.

The spirit turned to face her directly. "You must hear this and listen well." He said and she looked at him with fear in her eyes. "You are special because of who you are, not because of who you can summon. Any old tyrant can build an army and rule with fear, you did it with love. Your power comes from the people you serve and the ones who serve you." He said, it looked like it pained him to say it. "Have you not noticed how few times you have called upon us recently?" He asked when Erica shook her head. "You no longer need us to protect you; you have others that will help if you are in need. You need us to take away this enemy to save your world. It is how we can best serve you." He concluded and Erica had to admit that it made sense.

Erica rubbed her eyes. "Can I still talk to you then?" She asked and the spirit looked thoughtful. "I mean, I understand that you cannot help me anymore once this has happened, but can we still talk? I can learn a lot from you still." She said almost whining.

The spirit looked troubled. "I do not know the answer to that. If we can get free of our link on the far side, then maybe in time you will be able to talk with us. I cannot foresee if this will be a truth in your lifetime though. Be prepared to lose us and our support when this deed is done." He said with finality that would take no more discussion. Erica looked like she was going to break down and for a moment; the spirit looked like it hurt him to see her that way. Then he shrugged and moved back to Josh. "Your sister is brave and sometimes foolish, much like yourself. You will need to take care of each other better." The spirit scolded and Josh nodded solemnly.

"I can take some of the responsibility for that as well." Cedric said and he entered the conversation. He had heard that the spirits of the ancients were conferring with the True Bloods and he was sure that he didn't want to miss that.

The spirit eyed Cedric closely. "Yes, I have heard about you and the things I hear are promising. Know that you have chosen very well so far. We will be watching you, hoping that you can continue this trend."

Josh pulled the main topic back to the discussion table with an interruption of his own. "So what do we need to do to get started with this?" He asked directly. The spirit flashed a look of annoyance and then relented.

"You are quite right; we need to take care of this threat soon. Even now, they attempt to scale your walls. The damage that they have done is extensive and it will take quite some time to put things to right." Then the ghost drew his ghostly sword and held it into the air. "We have demons and devils to defeat men! Let's get to it!" He screamed and all of the ancients sailed from the humans through the wall and out onto the converted battlefield. The field looked like a day in hell again. Some of the vast army had already lost its grip on this world and had vanished into the ether. The spirits began taking demons and devils with them as they raced for the tear. The shrieking and wailing of the demons showed that they were not ready to give up so easily. The Master looked out at the fields that reminded him of home and for an instant, he was happy. Then he realized what was happening and his rage flared. He sent pillar of fire and smoke to try and prevent the spiritual fight before him. His demons were being taken from him and he could see the tendrils drawing them back into the void. He knew that his own tendril was also being stretched. He had much more presence of will however, and such a tactic would not work to dispel him from this world he was about to conquer! The ancients were many, but the horde was greater still. The ancients realized the imbalance and tried to snare two at once as they sailed back to the void. This worked for a time, but the devils began to organize. The element of surprise slipped away as full realization came. Over half of his army was gone, but the spirits were now too few to pull stronger than he could. He would keep the remaining troops. His smile as the last of the ghosts were banished could not be mistaken.

The Master held up his weapon and he shouted at the wall. "It was a valiant effort, but you have lost!" He said and his troops began once again to scale the walls. The illusion of the fire went away as the Guardian realized that the tactic was no longer needed. These troops were here for the final fight. Even with their numbers halved, they were still a formidable force. The only question was how many heads they could take before the defenders went down.

The demons, what there was of them, hit the top of the wall with a battle cry as they found themselves overmatched by defending troops. The swords and axes were flying and all of them were aimed at the heads of the demons as they crested the wall. The demon bodies either fell off the wall or were kicked off. They careened down, knocking some of their fellows off the wall as well. The human army was well positioned and they had the high ground at each stage of the battle. They also had instant communications with their leader in the high tower. From his view, he could direct with amazing accuracy and the defense was going better than either side would have predicted. There were casualties of course, but there were a lot more on the invaders' side than on the defenders.

Josh had run out of tricks. He had watched helplessly as Erica lead one group into a bottleneck to hold back the invaders even as Dad did the same thing on the far side. Mom was sending fire and ice at the attackers and that just left him standing there. He grabbed a sword from a fallen soldier and headed in to join the line. If he could not cast, he could still fight. The steel felt awkward in his grip, but he knew that it could kill. He hefted it as well as he could and when he joined the line, the men around him protected him as he protected them. They were hacking away at the enemy in an organized group of parries and thrusts. He had not even considered this type of fighting before. It was quite eye-opening.

The feeling of battle was something that he had not expected. His nerves were on end and the onslaught of enemy troops was overwhelming. They were using the terrain to maximum effect, but the fight still seemed desperate. The wall tops were now filled with combatants and the inner courtyard started to see stragglers that somehow managed to get through. This was where Josh's line was. They were finishing off the few that made it by the main force.

An explosion ripped through the wall and sent several people flying. The Master stepped through the smoking hole and began his own attacks. His weapon swept and when it hit it killed. The fight on the walls was now chaos. The enemy was coming up the stairs behind the defenders and cutting them off. It was not looking good. The archers had been pulled back from the walls since they could not behead a target. They could, however, pin one to a wall so that someone else could do the job. That is, if the wall was not made of stone. The inner buildings afforded them this opportunity. Cedric had pulled them back to do just that. It was hoped that civilian casualties could be kept to a minimum. The Master commanded everyone's attention in the inner courtyard of the main walls. His mighty swings were killing humans faster than any attack had so far in this battle. He was taking hits from arrows and swords alike and they seemed to heal as quickly as they hit. He was actually laughing as he swept the crowd once more and was rewarded by more cries of pain and death. Josh had fallen from the blast and had thus been on the ground when the Master stepped into the melee. He was looking for his opportunity now. He needed to get a good grip on the devil in order to try the impossible thing he had in mind. This was not going to be easy. Josh dropped the sword and stood up. Somehow, in the middle of all of that chaos and carnage, the Master sensed that something was up and he stared straight at the young sorcerer.

"What have we here little one?" He asked in an arrogant and presumptuous tone.

Josh stood as tall as he could. He was much shorter and smaller than the Master, there was nothing he could do about that. But he stuck to his plan. "I have seen where you come from." Josh said and somehow his voice carried to the Master. "I have seen how it calls to you." He said and the Master scoffed at him.

"No pull can overpower my will; I am stronger than any mortal." He boasted and Josh smirked at him.

"Really? Any mortal?" Josh prompted and the Master looked angry. He lifted up his massive weapon and prepared to bring it down on the defenseless young human before him.

"It is time to finish you and then kill this city you protect." The Master said and he started his downward swing. Josh was still there as the blade came down, but he had moved one step to the right. It should not have saved him, but it did allow him to do what he wanted. He grabbed hold of the Master's hand and the contact sent spasms of pain through them both. Josh had left a piece of himself behind when he came back from the other side. He could see the tether that was pulling the Master and he grabbed it. It was like grabbing a live wire and both of them were being electrocuted by the feedback between them. Mom screamed as she witnessed her son die again. Both Josh and the Master fell over and then they both vanished. The tether that held The Master returned him to his domain and Josh was linked and pulled along. The two individuals were thrown directly into the fiery pits of hell and they were deposited roughly and lay sprawled. The landing was actually rough enough to separate the two and Josh lay there, panting in the sulfuric wasteland. The Master was shaken beyond anything that he could have imagined.

He shook his massive head and sat up. The human wizard lay there, just a few feet away. The dark one looked around and realized that he was home. In truth he was much more comfortable there and the pull that he had learned to resist was non-existent here. He drew himself up to his feet and he stepped over to the human. What a pitifully small and fragile thing it was and yet, somehow, it had brought him back here. There was something even odder about this situation. This human boy was alive. He did not belong here at all. Ironically he was tethered back to the other world. It was possibly a link that he could use to return, but that would take more days than this young one had. If he left the human here, it would be a constant reminder to him and his followers of their failure. That could seriously undermine his authority and that sort of thing he could not afford. So it was with great difficulty that he came to his decision to send Josh back home. He looked up at the tear and it was stitching back together, he needed to hurry or this human would be stuck here forever. He picked up the young man and hefted him into the breach. He watched with keen interest as Josh's body flew up and up and hit the opening almost exactly right. The tear sealed them in once the body cleared it. Someone from the other side had managed to repair the damage that had taken him so long to cause. He shook his head once more. Next time, he would take more care. Next time, he would pick a world that had less defenses. Next time, well it would be a long time from now. He sat back and brooded. He had lost so many of his followers in that last battle that he wondered if there would even be a next time.

◆ ◆ ◆

Josh felt the pull as he was hurled across a vast expanse. The Guardian of Balance held him closely as he brought him back to the world he had died defending. Josh felt the wind as they traveled and he felt that strange. Last time there had been no wind, or even the feeling of acceleration. This time he felt a bit queasy. He realized that he was flying with the Guardian. They landed back at the point where Josh had been pulled away and the Guardian set him down gently and then vanished. He needed to get back to his body in the tower. Josh felt a rush of sounds around him as he slowly climbed back towards conscious. There were faces looking at him from above when his eyes finally obeyed his command to open. Some of them he recognized, others he didn't. The smell of carnage was everywhere and his stomach still hadn't recovered from the flight he turned and lost his lunch and the curious people jumped back. He was thankful for a bit of room. They were just starting to crowd around him again when he heard the Guardian's voice approaching.

"Let him be! Give him some room!" He was shouting as he approached. He stooped down next to Josh as the crowd receded and made him drink some blue liquid from a vessel. "This will help you regain your strength." He told the young man. Josh drank it and it was sour, really sour, but he did feel better. He sipped some more and then he got over the sourness and downed the bottle. He could feel his inner self gaining in strength by the minute.

"You're gonna have to tell me what that stuff is and where I can get it." He said almost jokingly. The Guardian looked into his eyes.

"Yeah, I think that's enough of the stuff for now." He warned. "The side effects can be nasty." He said and then he sat back and looked at the young hero. "You are the luckiest, bravest person I have ever met." He said finally and Erica, who had been one of the people standing over Josh, knelt down next to her brother.

"I second that one." She put in and Josh looked at her with a grin. "What exactly did you do?" She asked him.

Josh looked at the crowd that was awaiting his answer eagerly. "I pulled his tether." He said simply. The looks around him looked rather confused except for those special few who understood what he meant. Mom, Erica, Dad, and the Guardian of Balance made up that elite group. "I… I wasn't sure what would happen, but I hoped that if he were focused on it, then his hold on this world would be broken." He said in explanation.

The Guardian nodded. "You were right about that. In fact, since you managed to make all of the rest of the enemy follow him through the tear, balance was almost restored. Once you came back from the other side, and I'm not sure how you managed that, then balance was fully restored and I could close the tear up like we had planned before." He said triumphantly.

Josh managed to sit up and he felt better than he had for some time. "How bad were our casualties?" He asked and it was time for someone else to respond. The Guard Captain stepped forward. His arm was in a sling and he had cuts and bruises in a lot of places. It reminded Josh of his scars.

"Sir, we have taken our share of casualties, but I am happy to report that no civilian casualties have been reported. In a word sir, we held them." He said and his pride was obvious, even in his battered state.

"Well done." Josh said and then he stood up. "Well done to everybody!" He shouted and a cheer rose up in the filthy courtyard.

A second cheer rose from the city beyond and it spread further back like the wave at a sports stadium. Josh turned to Mom. "Can you help me to heal as many as we can? The human race has lost so many members recently that we cannot afford to lose a single one more." He explained and Mom gave him a big hug.

"Of course honey, I will do all that I can." She replied and she let him go. Then Josh looked around at the bodies strewn about and all the blood and gore.

"We need to get this cleaned up as well. I will not have my new city tainted like this." He said sternly and there was laughter in the crowd. However, the cleaning was already under way. Then Josh turned to his sister. "You had better go and get cleaned up as well. You have a wedding to get ready for." He reminded her and she blushed. The crowd abruptly burst into cheers and applause that echoed back along the streets as well. It was the first sign that life would go on. The queen had found a king and not even a war with devils and demons had been able to separate them. This was truly a time for celebration. The group made their way back to the palace. It was slow going with all of the well-wishers lining the streets, but they did make it. The palace guards were more than relieved to see them approach and the staff was a blur of motion. They saw to every need. The city was in a time of change and they knew what the cause was. Cedric joined them as well. He had participated in a celebration further into the city since he had been stationed in the tower. Public opinion of the royal group had reached a new high. The trade guilds would complain later when they found out that there were no other cities to trade with. The small places had been wiped out as well. That meant that colonization of the world could begin anew. Of course the land would need to be worked quite a bit. The rest of the world would be in ash. At least that was the original thought. It was hoped that there were still some survivors out there. There was also a bit of worry about the elder races. If they had not survived, then this world had lost a great asset. As if to underscore that thought, Josh heard a familiar voice behind him and he turned quickly.

"Your majesty!" He cried as he stepped up to the Sprite King. "You don't know how good it is to see you. We have all feared the worst." Josh said in a rush. The Sprite King usually held his emotions in check. This time, he let loose a rare hug as he flew up to Josh's shoulder and hugged the side of his head.

"You have done so well." He said behind a flow of tears. Then he sobered and flew back to his regal position. "The world has taken a bad beating these past few weeks. Many, many people were lost; and of all types." There was a pause as those serious words sank in.

Josh looked into his saddened eyes. "Who is left?" He asked through tears of his own.

The Sprite King looked around the room. Cedric seemed just as eager to find out as Josh was. "Well, one good thing for us elder races is that the enemy seemed to concentrate on humans. Of course that is bad news for humans as you already know. There were three major factions of elves in the world before the attack. We have only heard from one of them since. The whole world knows of your victory here, it was felt right away when the evil was banished. I will want to hear how that was accomplished by the way." He paused again to make sure that they understood his request. Satisfied, he plowed on. "The beast-men are gone. None of them survived. There will be a memorial for them as soon as we can get everyone together. The Stone lords went deep and simply waited out the battle, so their society is intact. The dwarves and Dragons each took losses, but they kept their women and children safe, so they will continue." He said and there was at least that much good news on this day. "From what we have been able to tell, and we have not explored everything yet, you are the largest concentration of humanity left. There is only one other city that we found and you know which one that is, you put it there. The areas that we have looked at don't even contain livestock anymore. The evil killed and burned everything along their way. Farms, villages, fields, everything was gone." He lowered his head. "I grieve for you losses." He said solemnly.

Josh had nothing to say to that. He shook his head partly in denial. "How did your people fare?" He asked when his throat cleared enough to allow speech.

"We have been spread out so far in our efforts to maintain communications in this war. We will not know how many have been lost until we have the grand conclave meeting in two weeks from now. However, the field that we used to hold it in has been destroyed.

We were wondering if we could hold it here, in your fields." He said and there was something else in his tone. Josh could not identify it.

"Of course you can use the fields." Josh replied. "We are still allies are we not?" He asked and the Sprite King smiled hugely at him.

"There are fewer allies of late so I cherish the ones that remain." He said and he did a short dance as the moment took him, then he sobered yet again. The Sprite looked at Cedric. "The Grand High Elf wanted you to know just how sad and angry he was that he had to abandon your city to the attackers. I'm sure he told you himself, but he sees this act as a life debt to you. If it wasn't for Josh, your people would be gone from this world like so many others." He said and Josh tried to look away, Cedric wouldn't let him.

"I know that fully well. Joshua of the True Bloods has saved any hope that humanity had left. He had help, to be sure, but the plan, and even the final blow were his. There is no way to ever repay him fully for his service to my kingdom." He said and then he got a smirk on his face. "In fact, the only thing I can do is go ahead and marry his sister." He said and the Sprite King smirked back.

"We talked about this before you know that you have made a wise choice." He said and it was Erica's turn to look away. Then the two kings seemed to huddle closer to make some arrangements. They had suddenly become wedding planners. Josh and Erica left them to it. Mom and Dad had already retreated. A good hot bath and some food would do wonders and they all wanted at least some bit of civilization back in their hectic lives. By the time they returned, it seemed that the wedding plans had been completed. Cedric and the Sprite King looked rather smug.

"The wedding will happen in four weeks." Cedric announced. Erica's jaw dropped. He turned to her directly. "We will work on the guest list together. It will be perfect." He said and she shook her head.

Erica thought about it for a while and then she smiled. "Good, then we will see how well you handle logistics then." She said surprising both kings in the room and making Josh laugh. Mom and Dad came in wearing normal clothes. They looked seriously out of place here, but that didn't bother their children. "Mom, you are coming to the wedding aren't you?" She asked and Mom and Dad looked at each other, and then back at Erica.

"Honey, we just had a long talk with the Guardian, and he says that he would never hear the end of it if we missed that." She said, allowing her smile to warm her face. The two girls hugged and Dad cleared his throat for attention.

"You do realize that if we are visible here then we would probably give you a problem where governing is concerned?" He asked, being the wet blanket that prudence demanded of him. The four True Bloods looked at each other and it was Cedric who startled them all be responding.

"I don't see why that should be a problem. You all just saved everybody here and they are so happy to see Erica get married. They won't give you any trouble at all. In fact, sir, you will just have to give her away at the ceremony." He said, lifting his chin high.

Dad gave a sideways glance to Cedric. "You wouldn't have stopped me from doing that young man." He said sternly. "However, the chain of succession has a chink in it. I believe that you are correct and that the people will accept the situation without too much grumbling. However, there is always a faction that wants everything done by the book and to the letter. Those people may give you a hard time." He said without any ill feelings at all.

Cedric made a dismissing gesture. "I don't think that will be a problem. Your public opinion is so high that nothing can tarnish it. You practically glow like angels in their eyes." He said and he could tell that his own enthusiasm was not carrying this conversation. He let it go for now. "If you like, though, I can ask my advisors what they think about the political situation. They may not be as versed in public relations as you seem to be, but they have not given me bad advice yet." He said in qualification.

Dad relented on this point. "Fine" He said. There were still so many other things to think about. They had a world to recover and nobody knew how long they would be here to help. He knew now that it would be at least four weeks. He was determined not to let them go to waste. "Now let's get down to business." He said, leaning the conversation back to work. "There is a lot of damage out there and you will need those crops next year to sustain the people that you have left." He said bringing the whole situation back into focus. "What do you plan to do about that?" He asked Josh in particular.

Josh started to reply but Erica was the one who jumped in. "First of all, we will go over who we gave land grants to in the old kingdom. Those people will be issued parcels based on the size of lot they had before. Next, we will have to look at the people that were farmers in the other kingdom and address their needs as well. We suddenly have a lot more land than we have people to populate them. We need to make the grounds usable again, and that will most likely fall to Josh. However, once that has been done, then we have the ability to do it in an orderly manner and our visitation chamber will be reopened to the public." She said and Dad looked at her sort of sideways.

"So you handled this before?" He asked her and she nodded.

"We did. We had to. There were so many claims against the lands around our city and it was Josh who organized all the claims and produced a map. This is what we will have to do again." She said feeling pretty secure in the answer.

King Cedric interjected here. "The system you have seems to be based upon requests for land. What do you have in place for people that were born to land? What if there is a hereditary claim?" He asked and Josh smiled at him.

"We have not handled hereditary claims because they are invalid. The land will go to people who are willing to work them. If those same people who would have inherited the land are willing to apply, I will surely grant them a parcel to work. A family who is willing to continue to work their land will hold their grant until such time as they can no longer do so. If they are too old and feeble, then they should be in the city where they can be properly cared for anyway." He said and Cedric shook his head.

"What you are saying will upset some of my people." He told them. "That's just not how my kingdom was run. There were political rivals and power struggles. There were families that had garnered heavy support and thus earned discounts and trade agreements using their political pull. Are you saying that there is no such thing in your kingdom?" He asked skeptically.

Erica looked at him now. "We treat everyone as equals." She said flatly. "The only way to raise your own status is to work for it and demonstrate your ability to do more and thus earn more." She said. Our system is probably quite a bit different from any other you've seen, but it works. With everyone producing more to make their own lives better, the whole city will prosper better. We look after our sick and old. We feed and house our hungry and homeless. We take responsibility for our people. In return, we require that those who can make a difference do so." She paused to check Cedric's reactions. "Does it sound *that* different?" She asked almost tentatively.

Cedric shook his head and rubbed his chin. "Actually, it does." He saw Erica's ire flare. "Don't get me wrong, it doesn't sound bad. It just sounds different." He added, forestalling the tirade he almost brought down on himself. "You've got to admit that it doesn't sound like anything else around here that you've ever heard of." He told her and she had to admit that she was unaware of how any other kingdom worked. She knew about classes and politics due to Social Studies in school. She knew enough about them to know that she wanted none of that in *her* kingdom. She tried desperately to avoid people abusing the system she and her brother had laid down. It was a component of her rule that endeared her to the general populace.

Erica felt that the uneasiness of the moment could be stopped by getting back to Dad's question. "So you can see that we will distribute the land wealth as necessary to ensure that the city is properly cared for and that those that are settled are compensated for their services appropriately." She said and all of them switched their focus back to topic willingly.

King Cedric smiled at his fiancé. "I am so glad that we met." He said and Erica cocked her head at him. "If I had heard anyone with that much conviction as a child, I might have turned out to be a much better man. As it is I seem to have a lot of catching up to do." He said and Erica blushed. "If you'll be patient with me, I'll do my best not to disappoint you." He told her and she was ready to hit him as a reaction to her own discomfort.

"We'll talk about that later. I think we need to be seen by the public now." She said and nobody argued with her. "They need reassurances that things will be okay once everything is cleaned up and running again." She said as if someone had asked her why.

Cedric took her arm. "Good idea, we still need a few things for our wedding darling." He said and Erica rolled her eyes. "After all, what is more normal than shopping?" He asked and Josh smiled. Erica looked like she wanted to lash out at him, or ask him to free her from this madness. Instead she put on her most regal face and surprised all of them. "I think a walk and some good shopping will do me good." She said and Cedric was oblivious to how out of character that statement was. His lack of knowledge became funny for the rest of the family and he must have thought that they were crazy when they laughed the couple out the door.

The shops were just beginning to open when the royal couple and their security entourage made their way to the main square. They looked at lavish fabrics and jewels. They looked at finery of all types. It all seemed to fragile or gaudy to the young queen, but she did her best to look interested in everything that was offered. Cedric seemed to be in his element, being waited on like this. Of course he had grown up in a palace where the hierarchy was his father, and then him in the power ladder. He had always been waited on. It made his current status more remarkable. He was loose with the coin and the merchants were eager to please. Erica wanted to duck out of it, but she had a responsibility to her people to show them that she was happy and alive and ready to move forward with her life. The public notices had already set the stage for her royal wedding and there was no one that wanted to be left out of the guest list. Of course not everybody could be there, but that would not keep them from wanting to be there. Cedric would have his hands full taking care of the arrangements. That thought made her smile a bit more genuine. The poor man still had no idea who they knew and how important they had become to the elder races. All of that was in addition to the Wolf. She hoped that the mighty beast still lived. The world had changed so much. She wondered what it would be like in another hundred years. This kingdom was now the major power in the world, at least the human population of it. That was another point. With so many fewer humans, it was possible that the elder races could get more area as well. The future was definitely a big question mark now. The past had been rather complacent and now the present had been forcibly changed forever. Now it was for the dreamers and architects to make the future what it would be. She was happy for her part in all of that, but she had to admit that Josh was much more pivotal in that respect. He had saved the only remaining human cities and he was the one who had stopped the war. He was the reason that there was a future. His gray hair was only the outward sign of what it had cost him. He looked older than her now. It was strange, but it was also true. He had lost some of his life in the transition between worlds. His spells had cost him even more. There was so much more out there that she had not yet seen. She was a little envious of his understanding of the Sprites as well. They viewed him as a savior. She had been listed as 'helpful' when they talked of her. Part of that was that she was queen where Josh had no real rank. Looking back, that had probably been a mistake. Since he had no rank or title, he had been forced to earn the respect that he deserved. The people loved him like they did her, but they also feared his powers. It was a fine line that he had to tread all the time. She had witnessed his frustration when the staff changed their perception of him. She knew that it hurt him.

"So this, your highness, is the best that they have to offer." Cedric said, holding up a very expensive looking scarf and smiling. He had pulled her from her thoughts and she realized just how long she had been slipping away. In truth, she didn't want a scarf. She had not been comfortable in them. This wasn't even for warmth. It was so light and airy that it fluttered in the slightest of breezes. It made her wonder what its purpose was. Even so, it looked extravagant and the gems that were stitched into it made it sparkle in the sun. It was dazzling. She tried it on and it was again obvious that she didn't understand its purpose. The merchant stepped around the counter and helped her to put it on. When it was all done, her bright blue eyes were peeking out from behind a dazzling field of gems suspended under her chin and draped over her shoulder. Cedric looked on approvingly.

"You are gorgeous my dear, and that scarf merely accentuates your natural beauty." He said and the merchant nodded enthusiastically. They purchased the scarf and Erica wore it as they walked away.

Erica leaned in close to Cedric and whispered in his ear. "Thank you for the scarf, but I need to get back to the palace. I shall await you there." She told him and he bowed deeply to the queen.

"Of course, I shall be counting the moments." He said and it was only partially playful. Then Cedric turned and dove into some serious shopping. He had agreed to arrange the wedding and now that he had a time table, the pressure was on. Erica shook her head as she watched him go. Then she wrapped the scarf up to carry it more carefully, it had been expensive. Then she headed off to the palace again. There were duties to get back to. She knew it even as she dreaded the drudgery of it. Still, it was her calling and she would answer it obediently.

News of the end of the war spread like the fires that had destroyed so much of the countryside. The survivors, what there was of them, were making their way to the last known city. It was a scattered pilgrimage and no one would be turned away. Along with that news, the royal wedding notices were posted and special invitations had gone out to a select few dignitaries. This would be the healing event that the world demanded. It would be the first real sign that life was going to continue. It was the cause of great celebration. The date was set and preparations were underway. The Grand High Elf got his invitation and he immediately gathered his traveling party to make the trip to the western seaboard. All of this was going on, even as Josh was busily repairing fields for cultivation. He was doing his best not to overtax himself, but there was so much to do. He concentrated yet again and when he opened his eyes, he breathed a sigh of relief at the field of grass that he had just put back. You couldn't even smell the ash anymore that had taken over this stretch of land next to the main road into town. The first time he had done this casting, he had done all of the support lands at once. He now knew what that sort of thing had cost him and was a bit wary about trying it again. He had left Mom behind because he knew that she would just worry. She was good with the magic, but she couldn't see everything that Josh was doing. He was not only putting grass in the field, he was putting nitrogen in the soil, and insects and bacteria that were vital to supporting the kind of life they needed now more than ever. It was like this piece of the world was being reset to its original condition. The concentration needed for this was extraordinary but he was doing it. Josh knew that the farmers would not understand what he had done, but he knew inside that he was giving them their best chance at survival. He sat down after the spell completed. He was winded from the effort and he knew that he needed to back off again for a while. It saddened him that he was so limited. Of course for him limited was such a relative term. He had moved entire cities. He had created a null realm to hide his own city inside. Now he was struggling with a piece of dirt about twenty acres across. Part of him was angry for that weakness, but part of him was actually grateful that he had learned this lesson. He was older now, not so much that he was ready for the grave, but he was actually visibly older now. It had been a long road. He took a sip from the bladder he carried water in. It was both cool and refreshing and he felt the warmth of the sun on his face as he looked up at the blue sky. The light breeze was bringing the smell of the grass to him and he sampled it deeply and he knew that he had gotten it right. Soon, there would be birds singing again. He had that on his to do list. The songs of the birds and the calls of the insects had been startlingly gone. He had not seen so much as a bee when he journeyed out here. He hadn't realized just how comforting those sounds had been until they were gone.

He lifted himself up and nodded to his protector. The soldier had been assigned to him by King Cedric. Josh didn't even know the man's name. He was all "yes sir" and "no sir" and ready to get in the way if anything came. Josh was grateful that the man was that dedicated, but it did make him rather boring. They did not chit chat, or even tell stories. Josh had some good ones too. Instead the two men moved along the road towards the next land grant. They had just three more today and then they could go home and eat and rest. Of course out here he was away from the hustle and bustle and the preparations for the royal wedding. He was sure that he couldn't dodge that one forever, but he was glad to be out in the countryside for now. The two ambled on down until they saw a stream, it looked really bad with all the soot in it, but they stopped anyway. The next parcel of land was just beyond it. In fact, this stream crossed a part of it. Josh sat down on the narrow bank and hung his feet out over the polluted water.

"It really is a shame you know." He said and his guard simply nodded. Josh tried again to engage the soldier. "Do you realize just how refreshing a bubbling spring can be?" He asked and there was that nod again. This time though there was a glimmer of agreement in his eyes as well. Josh felt the grass in his hands as he laid them palms down on the ground. He closed his eyes and dreamt of the stream in its former glory. He could even see small fish darting around to and fro. He was lost in the image. He had not intended to keep it in his mind this long. A voice startled him out of his dream.

"That never ceases to amaze sir." The guard said and Josh's eyes blinked open. The stream was just how he had dreamt it. He had somehow flowed the magic into it without realizing that he had done it. The stream was just as he had seen it. The soldier was dipping his helmet into it to retrieve some fresh, clear water. "It's cold, just like you said." He added and Josh simply smiled at him.

"Well, we have only a few to go and then we can head back. The farmers will be anxious to hear that we have done our jobs." Josh replied, trying to get back to business and knowing that this little stream could keep him occupied for hours if he let it. The soldier frowned.

"Of course I will go along with anything you say sir, but you seemed to need this relaxation." He said and Josh suddenly got suspicious of the soldier that was guarding him.

"Did Erica put you up to that?" He asked speculatively.

The soldier drank from his helmet and then splashed the cold water over his face before dumping the rest on the grass and putting his helmet back on. "Oh no sir, it's just that you talk about how wonderful the stream would be and then you make it that way. I figured that was what you either wanted or needed." He said and then his face slipped back into professional mode and Josh knew that the conversation was over. As amazing as this man's self control was, the fact that he was right was little comfort. Josh leaned back and listened to the babbling of the little stream. He was happy now, whatever the future brought. He had done his part to save this world and these moments were his to share with everyone that was left. It brought him a sense of fulfillment that could hardly be described. A few minutes later he pushed himself up. His back was a bit sore from the way he was laying, but he pushed that discomfort aside like so many before it.

"I guess we really need to get going, much as I'd like to stay. The work won't get done by itself." He said cheerfully and the soldier nodded curtly as he stood and headed back to the road.

"Yes sir." He said and Josh sighed.

King Cedric had done one of the wisest things any ruler had ever done; he handed off some of the wedding details to Mom. Not only did this give Mom a direct connection into the wedding plans, it ensured that Cedric was liked by his new mother-in-law. He had done his part during the past unpleasantness, and his affection for Erica was evident enough, but he had yet to win the hearts of her parents over. This was the first real advance towards that goal. She was moving with dizzying speed, setting up floral arrangements and placing specific food orders for the royal wedding dinner. Then the tailors were called in to make the clothes required for the grand event. She had musicians, they were the standard court musicians and Josh had given them more updated music to play. Mom had somehow managed to mix up the music with both period and contemporary tunes that somehow complimented each other. Before Cedric could even blink at what she had done so far, she was on to decorations and the palace staff would be working overtime to get this all done. Still, they were happy and the work was something of a healing thing for the palace and the kingdom in general. He had to wonder how she did it all so easily. He had fretted over the choice of dress materials. This woman seemed to have a grasp of everything in her mind even before it happened. Perhaps that was why she was a mage. With the planning stage almost completed, the actual work to make it all happen could commence and Cedric was glad of that. He had been more worried than he would like to admit. Mom somehow seemed to sense it as well, but she had the decency not to mention it. The guest quarters were being freshened up for the important dignitaries that would be arriving soon. The staff was aware of the expanded meal requirements and they had set out their plans to handle it as well. The palace took this new workload in stride. It was a source of pride among the staff and Mom smiled warmly at them when she met them. She looked down at her notes and sighed.

"Well, that's all that we can do for now." She said resignedly. "Tomorrow we shall start talking with the troops. We will need an honor guard for the entrance into the cathedral. The priests will want to do something as well. We should give them as much notice as we can to avoid stepping on anybody's toes." She warned and Cedric only nodded. This project had been so far over his head that he was unaware of just how badly. Now he was more than grateful for Mom's professional help. He wondered if Erica knew what she was getting out of when he had agreed to take on the responsibility. He would make it a point to ask her later. At least it would mean that they would have time enough together to at least talk. Both of them had been so busy lately.

Trumpets sounded as the first carriage arrived. The roads had been cleaned up for quite a distance thanks to Josh's handiwork. Thus travel to and from the western kingdom was now an easy matter. The guards at the city gates happily waved the carriage through after a quick, but thorough visual inspection was completed. The carriage rolled straight up to the palace entrance which was currently bedecked for the occasion. The red carpet had been rolled out and the carriage driver dismounted the carriage as a livery manager grabbed the reigns and began stroking the horses to make sure that they stayed calm. A footman, clad in royal blue with gold trim leggings stepped down to the door, paused as if for some unseen cue, and then opened the carriage door. The trumpets sounded again as the Grand High elf stepped out of the carriage along with three other elves. They were dressed in finery that consisted of crystals and vines. It was an elaborate pattern of life and family that was weaved into the wonderful cloaks they wore. The newcomers were greeted by a short man with puffy leggings and a gold inlaid tunic. His frilly shirt was puffed out at the sleeves and his hat was worn somewhat lopsided on purpose. He smiled at the arrivals and put on his warmest smile.

"My lords, it is wonderful to have you here. We have made arrangements for your accommodations and you will have an audience with the king and queen after you have had the chance to freshen up from your journey." He paused to make sure that his message had been received. Then he plowed on. "If there is anything that you require, please inform any of the staff and it shall be seen to. He turned ever so slightly to indicate the stairs. "If you will please follow me..." He said and then he led the way up those grand stairs as the trumpets played a song that none of them had heard before, but it reflected upon the rolling hills outside and the crashing of the waves on the western seashore. It was actually quite fitting for the elder race most devoted to being in touch with nature. As a small crowd watched, the dignitaries disappeared into the palace and the moment was over. The carriage was pulled around to the stables and the horses were tended to. These people knew their jobs.

Erica had been holding open court for the purposes of land grants. She had made a couple of minor errors that Josh had managed to catch before they got out of hand. Other than that, it had gone remarkably smoothly considering the differences in attitude concerning land and who should get it. Erica's fair and open minded approach was winning over even the staunchest of opposition. A messenger came into the room and quietly whispered into her ear. She nodded and thanked him as he backed away, bowing to her.

Erica looked at the line of people and she stood up. All faces turned to her as she broke her normal protocols. "Good people, I am most sorry, but I have important visitors to grant an audience to. We will take your names and you will be able to plead your cases for land tomorrow. Please accept my apologies for this inconvenience." She said and then she stepped down from her dais. The crowd watched her go and nobody said a word. Soon after she was gone, the steward took down the names of the applicants as the queen had promised and all of the applicants were then ushered out with the promise that business would reconvene tomorrow.

Erica made her way to her quarters and she felt a bit giddy. She had always respected the elves and their leader had just arrived to see her. She remembered thinking about all the myths and legends she had heard back home. She remembered Santa's elves and Keebler elves and D&D elves. When she finally met a real one, they were nothing like she had imagined. They were quiet and powerful. They were tall and thin, and their eyes could bore right through you. At least they had on the few individuals she had met. They represented an intelligence that could quite possibly be beyond her understanding. Of course a degree of arrogance came with that package. They had been around much longer than humans had so perhaps some smugness was justified. Even this flaw did nothing to deter her interest. The dressing girls were there and they smiled at the young queen. In truth, they were not much younger than she was, yet they were called girls and she was not. Of course if they had seen her swinging two axes on the field of battle, they would never have called her a girl either. They had chosen a gown. Erica rolled her eyes at the choice. She had been forced to wear dresses more and more lately. She was not as comfortable in them as she was in a good leather tunic and pants. Still, duties were duties and she had the suspicion that they were slowly weeding her off of those old garments as part of her being a queen. She couldn't call them on it, what with no real proof, but she suspected it more and more.

She got changed with the assistance of the two girls and they were spraying a mist of perfume around her. She almost gagged at the stench. Was all of this necessary? Again, the scent of pine needles and fresh soil were much more to her favor. The smell of the ocean outside would also do, but that was not to be the case this time. She washed her face off a bit using the bowl of water on the bureau then she toweled off and smiled at the polished steel mirror. In her opinion, she looked ghastly in that reflection, but they had yet to make a real mirror and she was not about to show them how to make the glass work that way. Much as she would have liked a decent mirror, there was danger in introducing technology faster than it would normally be discovered. At least she assumed there was. Josh had warned her about that before. She trusted him enough not to question it. After all the primping and nitpicking was over, she drew herself up and then headed to her reviewing chamber. She hoped that Josh would be there already. He usually was, it somehow took him a lot less time to get ready than it did her. She wondered if there were less things a boy had to do to get ready than a girl. She shrugged her shoulders in an uncharacteristic move for a royal and she stepped into the chamber. Pages flanked her on either side and they escorted her to her throne. The reviewing stands were full of spectators and circles before the throne had been carpeted with a rich, deep throw rug that depicted a wolf howling at the moon. It was quite striking and she wondered why she had never seen it before. She sat down on her throne as all eyes tracked with her. She could feel them like tiny bugs crawling on her skin and did her best to keep from scratching. It was not an easy battle. Once in place, Erica turned to the speaker and he nodded that they were ready to proceed. Josh was in his throne just as she had hoped. He was dressed up and he looked like he felt silly. She would have chuckled over that if this wasn't such an important meeting. Cedric was in a third throne that was easily bigger than the first two, but due to its location was somehow subordinate. He was dressed in some of the finest regalia ever produced. He had rings and gold chains and silks about him. His crown was polished and the gemstones encrusted in it were sparkling along with the gold ring. He simply smiled at the other two. He was obviously the most comfortable of the three of them. There were three raps of the mighty staff that the door man held. The speaker bellowed out his announcement of who was coming in and all eyes turned to the door.

The Grand High Elf strolled in effortlessly. His advanced age was not in evidence for this visit. His entourage followed him in a diamond formation at a respectful distance. His robes brushed the floor lightly, but his movements were fluid. If Josh hadn't known better, he would have guessed that the Elf was using a conveyor belt to approach. The very old man stopped at the appropriate distance from the lead throne. He took in all three of the royals before him and he bowed collectively.

"Your majesties;" He began. "I must congratulate you on your victory in these troubling times." He said plainly and there was an edge to it that spoke volumes more. "Those congratulations and many thanks come from all of my people. We do understand what you did and what it cost you in order to save what was left of this world." He told them and his words were like iron. They weighed down the normally jovial mood in this chamber. Then his ancient gray eyes twinkled. "In addition, I congratulate you on your ability to recover and to move on with your lives even in these troubling times." He said and there was some joke there that he was not sharing. His face and those of his entourage pretty much confirmed that. Erica glanced over at Cedric and he was smiling too. That meant that he knew what was going on. It made sense since he knew the high elf for much longer than they did. The pause drew out for a long time and then, as if he just remembered to speak again, the Grand High elf continued. "I wish only the fondest of memories for your union. May your people prosper in this new kingdom of Unity." He said holding his arms out to the side and up.

Erica stood up and stepped forward. It was an unexpected move on her part. "We thank you for your candid speech and your greetings. We thank you for making the trip here and for understanding our sacrifices." She bowed before the Grand High Elf. "Know that we do not take these things for granted." She said at the last and his hairy eyebrows rose.

"Indeed." He said with a hint of surprise in his voice.

Erica smiled warmly at the very old and wise elf before her. "You are welcome here at any time. We need not rest upon such formal situations to enjoy one another's company. Know that we honor you and your people. There is so much that we can learn from each other." She said simply.

The Grand High Elf surprised his entourage by reaching out a hand and stroking Erica's cheek. She allowed the contact without so much as a flinch. "When I came in here, I did not feel that there would be much to learn here." He said in a flat voice. Then his mood seemed to shift. "Perhaps I was mistaken on that point." He said and his ancient eyes squinted with his smile. Then he stopped, as if remembering something. "Ah, the purpose of our visit is of course to witness your union." He carried on as if there had been no pause or interruption. It was one of the perks of his position to be unpredictable and he enjoyed the anxiety that it could cause others. "We have brought you a wedding gift." He finished and the elf in the rear of the formation stepped forward. The others had been effectively hiding this individual, although it did not look like it. The difference was subtle. This male walked with that same grace that the others did, but his youthful exuberance shone brightly in contrast to the elder elves here. Erica surmised that they found his bounce a bit annoying, but none of them seemed to notice it now. The young man held out a wrapped package. Whatever it was they had wrapped it in fronds from wildflowers and the packaging was beautiful. A thin vine tied it all together in a masterful art of balance and precision. It was as if it had grown there, and not been placed there by a craftsman. The young elf held the package forward and Erica took it with a thanking nod and a slight bow. The youngling withdrew, albeit a bit awkwardly for an elf. He was not used to being in a court. He bowed once more and then resumed his position at the back of the formation where he nearly disappeared again.

Erica held up the package. "Thank you for this. Should it be opened now? Or is it customary to open it after the vows have been said?" She asked and the Grand High Elf smiled at her.

"It is your kingdom, you can whatever you wish." He said with a wink. She knew that she liked this old man, but something about him made her even more comfortable than normal.

Erica turned to look at Cedric. He had not moved from his throne and she gestured for him to come over and see. He got up and strolled over with practiced casualness. "What is it darling?" He asked and Erica jabbed an elbow into his ribs. That startled him into behaving and he held the package carefully as Erica began the unwrapping process. She didn't want to hurt any of the fronds or the vine so it took longer than normal to open the package. When they did, they were both rather shocked at the contents. Unfolded before them were two elf made cloaks. They were hooded riding cloaks with the royal seal of both houses melded into one on the back. Cedric and Erica each held up one and they looked to be perfectly sized.

Erica slung the cloak over her finery and grinned like a schoolgirl. The cloak flowed from her like a living thing. She twirled and then stopped to see who was watching her, everyone was. Cedric bailed her out though.

"Your Grace, thank you for the wonderful gifts. It is obvious that they are and will be enjoyed." He said and the whole room chuckled as Erica took a couple of steps and danced about.

She took a few more steps and then she looked up again. "Let's have a feast today." She said and Cedric rolled his eyes. "We can have all of our guests wear clothing from their homelands. Not the dress-up things, everyday clothes. It will give us even more insight into how each other lives." The other royals did not even know how to react, but Josh understood and he was impressed at his sister's insight. She had just taken a stuffy diplomatic event and turned it into a school dance. He got up and stepped over to Cedric.

"Keep your eyes open for an opportunity." He whispered and Cedric looked back confused.

"Opportunity for what?" He asked and Josh chuckled.

"To dance of course." He said and Cedric looked at him oddly. Josh continued his hints. "She wants to dance and you're the one she wants to dance with. This get-together will be your chance. Watch for it and she will respect your boldness and your assertiveness." Josh explained and Cedric nodded as understanding took him.

"I thank you for the inside information. I am surprised that her brother would tell me such things." He said his tone wary.

Josh shook his head. "Look, the only thing that is important is that she is happy. You keep her happy, and our people happy and we'll have no problems." He said with only a hint of a smile. His seriousness was controllable to such a minute degree that his face was calculated to impart the information and be intimidating at the same time. "Just do as I tell you and you're in." Josh added as an afterthought.

Cedric leaned back and smiled. "I will, trust me I will." He said and the two of them watched as Erica held the room with her dancing. She was always gifted with balance and poise, but with the cloak on, she had hit another level. She was like a cat out there and her quick and agile frame covered the ground at dizzying speed.

Josh noticed a familiar face in the back of the room and he strolled over to the wall to skirt around the assembly in the middle of the room. Some people watched him, but he was boring compared to his sister. He continued his walk as if there were no cares in the world anymore. He reached the far side of the room and he stopped and smiled at the young man he had come to see.

"Mouse! I thought that was you." He said and they both bowed to each other, a strange sight to be sure. The two would have gotten to a bit of conversation but another voice called out and broke their attention.

"It is you!" The Grand High Elf cried. All eyes turned to the aged elf and then to whom he referred. The whole room was now looking at mouse and he looked like a startled rabbit. He just wanted a place to run and hide. Of course that would not work here in court. "You are the one who warned me that we should move our people." He said and Mouse bowed more deeply this time.

Mouse seemed to take some strength from that recognition. "Your Majesty I am pleased to see that you have survived." He said humbly.

"Survived? Oh yes we did that. You told us to move just in the nick of time. We even verified your claim with Joshua here." He said and Mouse looked at Josh with wide eyes.

Josh smiled. "I told him that you had a good reason and that he had better listen." He informed the young man. "You have been very busy lately." Josh chided Mouse.

Mouse nodded solemnly. "I still didn't get to everybody on my list and those I failed to reach are all dead now." Mouse said, the weight of his actions was weighing heavily upon him.

Josh grabbed him by both shoulders and made Mouse look him in the eye. "You cannot save everybody. It is a lesson that I am still learning, but it is true. No matter how good you are, or how strong you are, or how hard you try, someone will still be lost. There are simply too many people and too many dangers out there and you are only one person, just as each of us is." He said and there was no humor at all in his voice.

Mouse swallowed. "I... I understand, but it doesn't make it any easier." He said and Josh nodded in understanding.

"No, I'm afraid that it won't. The main thing you need to remember is that you did save somebody. You did make a difference and that you have value and purpose." He said, and Mouse seemed to respond favorably to the talk.

The Grand High Elf simply nodded at each point. The young mage was doing a good enough job that he didn't feel the need to interject any of his own wisdom. "You know that he is right. We elves owe you a debt of gratitude. Focus on your successes until you can face your failures. You must go back and look at them sooner or later or they will teach you nothing. However, there is no rush to do that just now. Let the wounds heal a bit first." He offered and Mouse nodded yet again.

"Thank you sire." Mouse responded and the High Elf winked at him.

"I believe that there is a feast coming up later on today and I would like it very much if you would accompany me at least for part of the celebration." He said and Mouse nodded enthusiastically.

"I wouldn't miss that your majesty." He stammered and then he backed away as Josh chuckled.

"I know that he is a good kid. I am pleased with how he had managed to secure himself some recognition." Josh said and the High elf looked at him strangely.

"Not that I am arguing with you; but didn't you already pour accolades upon him from some earlier adventure?" He asked and Josh snorted.

"Sort of, we gave him some land and got him out of the city before any of the ruffians that were bullying him could get at him. He did help us to regain our thrones. He has a good heart and a strong will. I consider him a friend." Josh said, summing up his thoughts.

"That is a strong endorsement there, and one in which I heartily agree." The High Elf said with amusement in his tone. "I have yet to meet this wolf he speaks of, but I owe them a thank you as well." He said, a little more somber this time. "I only hope that the creature still lives so that I may get the chance to do so."

Josh locked eyes with the elf. "So do I, so do I." He said and they moved back into the festivities that were just starting to wind down a bit. Erica was moving the group to a banquet hall where the party would resume. She had diffused all protocols now and she was enjoying herself. The band was playing songs that Josh had taught them. Erica was dancing to the eighties tunes and the mood was infectious. King Cedric saw his chance and he strolled over to Erica and tapped her on the shoulder. She seemed to notice him for perhaps the first time and he held out his hand.

"May I have this dance?" He asked and Erica's curious face lit up with joy.

"Sure, if you think you can keep up." She said mockingly. The two of them started in a normal dance pose and Cedric made a quick gesture to the band. The music abruptly changed to something very quick and bold. It was a royal dancing song passed down from generation to generation. Erica had not heard it before, but the beat was easy enough to follow and Cedric was leading. He was a really good dancer she realized. The two of them were lost to the rest of the world as they twirled and swept and bowed and dipped. The dance was elaborate and precise and Cedric was amazingly well practiced. Erica was fleet of foot and very nimble and she could follow him without hesitation. It made the picture look perfect. The song finally ended and they both were panting at the end of it. The crowd around them applauded and the royal couple swept off of the floor and to the table to avoid undue embarrassment. A serving girl brought them drinks and they both sat down heavily on the overstuffed chairs that Josh had built into the grand dining hall.

"I had no idea that you could dance like that." Erica said in a joyful rush.

Cedric bowed curtly to her. "I am glad that her majesty is pleased. In truth I am amazed that you could catch on to an unfamiliar dance so quickly." He took a sip from the goblet in his hand and Erica did the same.

"Apparently there are a lot of things that we don't know about each other. It will make our lives together more entertaining as we learn and evolve." She said philosophically.

Cedric lifted his goblet in a mock toast. "Indeed." He said instead.

CHAPTER 14

T he Captain sat back in his seat as the cart made its way to the front gates of the biggest city he had ever seen. The gigantic brand new walls could only have been the work of one man, and he was honestly excited to see that man. Josh had saved his people twice, and he was ready to celebrate with him at his sister's wedding. Plus there were still unanswered questions from before. He would learn the life-saving skills that he had seen. He wanted to know if his city could be returned to its former location now that the enemy was gone. All in all, he had a lot of questions for Josh.

The gatemen were eager to move along the wedding traffic and he was easily identified and let through. He had brought only a few people with him, but they were key people. He had brought some of the troops that they had crossed the land with. These were people that knew Erica for the huntress she was and they were eager to see her again.

When the cart reached the palace, the staff ushered the newcomers in without any preamble or protocol. It was odd, but they took it in stride. They were led to a room that was getting louder as they approached. When the double doors to the banquet hall were opened, a wave of sound swept over them and the group visibly flinched from the aural assault. Then they got used to it and stepped through the threshold into the biggest party that any of them had ever seen. The

Captain was looking for Josh. The crowd was pretty dense, but he spotted the young sorcerer without too much trouble. He made his way to see the young man first. His cohorts spread out into the crowd to mingle. The spirits in this room were light and happy. It was an amazing feeling after the events of the recent past.

"So there you are." The Captain said and Josh looked up quickly.

"Captain! Good of you to come, can I get you a drink or something?" He asked, feeling the mood that the festivities were supporting.

"No no, we're fine for now. We will be needing food fairly soon, but I assume that won't present much of a problem for you." He said quirking an eyebrow. Josh made a dismissive gesture and stood up to clasp arms with his fellow sorcerer. The captain still towered over the young man, but they now looked to be closer to the same age even though Josh was much younger. "You have aged quite a bit since we last met. I hope that I have not caused that much distress in your life." He said and Josh almost lost his smile.

"No, I have had problems staying alive." He said plainly and the Captain's surprise made him laugh. "I can tell you about that later, for now we are to eat, drink, and dance as the mood strikes us." He said and then his face turned thoughtful. "Unless, that is, you need some time to freshen up from your trip. If so, just ask any of our servants here and they will escort you to anything you need. We have baths here as well if that's your fancy. I am working on the shower system and hope to have it up soon." Josh said, losing himself in his own musings.

The Captain looked at him a bit sideways. "What's a shower?" He asked.

Josh blinked and then smiled. "Oh, it's a stall you can stand in and water pours over your body to get cleaned up. It is quite refreshing, but right now, it is very labor intensive. I need to automate the process better before it becomes practical." He explained. The Captain still looked confused. Then Josh hit on the problem, imagery. "Oh, it's like washing in a waterfall." He said and this time The Captain nodded that he understood. The large fighting man scanned the crowd and he noticed Erica sitting at a side table with King Cedric. "If you'll excuse me, I need to say hello to your sister." He said in a cordial tone.

Josh waved his hand towards his sister's general direction. "Go on ahead; there are no protocols here while the dance is going on. I'm sure she'd be glad to see you." Josh said and he sat back down where his plate was still about half full. He hardly noticed the big man leaving him.

The Captain made his way to the table where Cedric and Erica were taking a breather. She noticed him as he approached and she stood up with a huge smile on her face. "There you are! I was hoping that you'd make it." She said and she threw her arms around the big man and hugged him tightly. Then she drew back and regained her composure.

The moment of discomfort at the familiarity passed and the Captain bowed. "Your majesty, I would not miss this event for the world, and we almost had to make that choice." He said with a wink. Then he turned to Cedric. "You had better take care of this one." He said almost menacingly. But in truth there was no ire in it, just a bit of joking. He knew as well as anyone did that Erica could very well take care of herself. She looked so happy that he was glad of it in any case. His demeanor turned serious and Erica noted the change right away. "We will be returning home just after the ceremony, but I will need to ask a few questions before we go. If you could schedule an audience for me and my companions I would be most grateful." He said almost formally.

Erica nodded and then added her response when he didn't move. "Of course, I would be happy to have an audience with you. We shall get back to you on exactly when, but we will take your schedule into advisement and make it as convenient for you as possible." She said like a true politician. The Captain bowed deeply and withdrew. Apparently, the dance was not to his liking, but he had made his required visit and survived. Servants led him to his quarters and he was settled in before he knew it.

Josh finished his food and found that he was not feeling so good. He had probably overeaten and it would take him a while before he felt better. His system was still rather frail and he just couldn't eat the way he used to be able to. A part of him was sad over that, but change was the nature of being and he knew that he would simply have to adjust. He excused himself from the festivities and made his way to his most comfortable place, the library. He had built an impressive library when he imagined this place. He had put a lot of thought into what books would be here and he had used a lot of magic to make it happen. Of course it wasn't like he needed to know every page of every book to make it magically appear, he only needed to know the spines of the books, the part that showed when they were aligned in their shelves. With that knowledge, he could let the universe fill in the rest for him when the spell was cast. Because of this, he had managed to put in a lot of books that he knew little more than title and author of. These were books that did not exist in this world before. He had not yet shown Erica, but he had a whole section of mystery books that he knew she would go nuts for. He made his way down the corridors a bit more slowly than usual due to his discomfort, but he made it just the same. The library was there, beckoning to him and he was surprised that it was not empty when he got there. Mom and Dad were both lounging around with their noses in a book. In fact, Mom was reading one of the Nancy Drew novels that he had made expressly for Erica. He smiled at the thought. Then he looked to see what Dad was reading. He had a large volume text, one of the oldest ever written, or at least a copy of one of the oldest ever written. It was the lore of this land. Dad seemed to be perusing it like he was searching for something. Josh strolled over casually and peered over Dad's shoulder.

"Whatcha' lookin' for?" He asked in a childish voice that would hopefully diffuse any ire from the interruption he was making.

Dad looked up and then sighed. "I am looking for the history of this land and specifically, when the devil found out about this world." He said and Josh felt it like a punch in the stomach.

"I... I never even thought about that." He admitted. "The evil creatures came from somewhere else, somewhere beyond that veil that I saw the tear in." He said aloud and Dad set the book down.

"You saw the other side didn't you?" Dad asked and Josh nodded and closed his eyes.

"Yes." Josh said and he took several deep breaths. "It was not pretty." He said at last.

Dad looked at his son with a renewed respect. "I can only imagine, and then not very well. You have seen what only a few people have ever witnessed." He said as he considered the opportunity here. "Can you tell us anything about it?" He asked directly.

Josh sat down heavily. "I… Don't know if I can. Some of it I definitely remember, and I don't like to think about it. Other things are more like a dream, or a ghost, just outside of consciousness. I think I was close to death again when I went over to the other side. At least I think I was. In any case, my trip there was short, but long enough that I will be troubled by it for a long time." He said as he considered how best to get out of this conversation.

Mom picked up on that and stepped over, placing her book open face down on the small table next to her chair. "It's alright honey, you're back now and nothing can harm you like that again." She said consolingly. Josh looked at her skeptically.

Dad dove back into the book, he wasn't sure exactly what he was looking for, but he knew that he would know it when he saw it. "There must be proof in here somewhere." He mumbled to himself.

Josh thought about what had happened on this world and he wondered how long ago it had begun. The Guardian had told him that it had been a long time coming and that had not rung any alarm bells in his brain when he said it. It was just odd that something like that had gotten by the young man's amazing attention to detail. He was concerned now though. This war had begun probably long before he was born. At least that felt right. The question was; who had started it? How did the devil find out that this world even existed? How did they discover how to breach the gap between worlds and most importantly, why did they do that? Was there a reason, would anybody left alive know what it was? He had many more questions than answers at this stage of the game and it bothered him greatly. He was into control, and order. He was heavily dependent upon ritual and organization. Part of Josh's brain would reject chaos. He was rational almost to a fault. He needed to ask someone older and wiser than he was. The Grand High Elf seemed to be the most likely prospect. He left the group in the library to find the elf at the party.

The Guardian of Balance watched from his secluded place. He could see everything from his office. The small screen on his desk showed him whatever he desired. Right now it was focusing on Josh as it had done so many times before. The conversation in the library had just turned dangerous and the young sorcerer seemed to be starting to put the pieces together. That was bad. He hit the desktop with the palm of his hand and stood up in an angry rush.

"Can't that boy ever keep to his own business?" He asked no one in particular. He looked around the cluttered office and none of his precious collectibles could help him now. He had the nasty feeling that his reign over this universe was soon about to end. He was untouchable only so long as he remained neutral. His powers were all encompassing and that had caused him to slip from time to time, but none of those infamous slips were as disastrous as this one had turned out to be. He went from angry to nervous to just plain frightened and he was not a man that you wanted to scare. He needed to do something to maintain his monopoly on the travel between realms. He needed to stop those meddling True Bloods before they could cause any irreparable damage. He started to put his kit together. He would have to go back to that stinking world sooner or later. He had to put things right again. He could feel the imbalance and he knew that he had caused it. It was a decision he had made so long ago that it hurt him now. He kept adding more and more to his list of things he needed to atone for. His soul was heavy now with the burden of guilt he had heaped onto himself.

So first, he had to silence the boy for good. Then, he would erase the young man's past and his own. Then he could start to repair things and get everything back into balance. There would be resistance though, he understood that. How could he do anything different though? He was supposed to be neutral. He was supposed to only influence things from behind the curtain. He was not supposed to act directly in the day to day events of the people he oversaw. He was the supreme authority. He was the one entitled to move freely and do his will. Why then did it feel so wrong all the time? He shook the negative energy away and set his jaw in determination. Once his meddling had been either hidden, or passed off onto the True Bloods, he could begin to rebuild. He smirked at the thought of the family being ousted for his crimes. He would not have to do too much to point all the clues to them. He was almost excited at the prospect. He had lost too much to that young know-it-all mage and his sister. He slung his pack over his shoulder and onto his back and then headed to the portal that would take him to them. He took one last look at his office before he stepped through. Somehow he got the creepy feeling that he would not be seeing that old office again. Then he was whooshed away and all he could concentrate on was moving forward.

The Grand High Elf lit his pipe as he sat in the very comfortable chair. His eyes reflected just how serene he was feeling just now. He had been asked to the library in order to answer some questions. The party he had been dragged from had been noisy and crowded, so his resistance to relocating was minimal. Mouse was by his side, for the young human seemed to have a great affection for the seasoned old elf. The chair had his attention just now. He had never felt anything like it. He looked up at Josh who was smiling down at him.

"Who made this wonderful chair?" The old one asked in utter contentment.

Josh's smile turned to a grin. "It's a Lazy Boy." He replied. The High Elf did not understand the response, but at the moment that didn't matter.

"Well this chair makes me think that humans may have more undiscovered skills than I had given them credit for." He said and then he blinked. "I'm sorry." He added in case he had offended. Of course the room full of humans was laughing now.

Josh patted the old elf's hand. "Don't worry about that, we have questions and you may be the only one alive that can answer them." He said and the mood in the library turned much more serious. "First off, when did you know about the buildup of enemy troops before this invasion?" He asked and the Grand High Elf turned suspicious.

"I was informed along with the rest of my colleagues during the mid summer meeting of the elders." He replied. Josh seemed to be doing some math in his head and then he nodded at the results.

"That matches what I had figured." He confirmed. "How long do you think the enemy had been planning this invasion?" He asked, falling more into the theoretical realm of questioning.

The Grand High Elf took a long puff on his pipe and blew the smoke out into the room. He scratched his beard in thought. "Based on the size of the army and how well they were outfitted for war. They must have been working on their plan for years." He replied at last.

Josh nodded again. "That is consistent with my thinking as well." He confirmed. Then he stepped around the room, as if putting together his next question. "Honestly, the thing that has me concerned the most is how did the devil we fought find out that this world even existed?" The question was not to anybody in particular but since the Grand High Elf had been the previous person Josh had been talking to, the default response would be expected from him.

The very old elf's eyebrows rose as he considered the question. His mannerisms suggested that he was working it over in his mind from every perspective he could imagine. When his response finally came, it was not as helpful as Josh had hoped. "I haven't considered that question before this moment. I suspect that somebody must have made contact with the dark one and then led him back here." He said, trying to be helpful. "I was thinking back in my own personal history and I cannot recall anyone making such contact with the darklings on the other side. With our love of nature, I can't imagine any Elf that would stoop to such tactics for some personal gain. There were some dark elves in our way past who could have done this, but we would have heard a lot sooner than this. They have been gone for thousands of years. You would think that the pact, if there had been one, would have severed with their demise if they had been the ones responsible for this invasion." He said, bringing that line of thinking to its conclusion. "It has to be someone else." He said triumphantly.

Josh continued to pace. "I'm not as sure as you are that they could not be the ones, but for now I will accept your explanation and move onto other possibilities." He stopped pacing and turned to his audience. "Who would benefit from the invasion we just experienced?

I mean that army was trying to kill everything and everyone here. Who would have been left to reap any benefit at all?" He asked and all he got were confused faces all around. A new voice made everyone jump.

The Sprite king, famous for his perfect timing and startling arrivals, smiled at everybody as he allowed everyone to realize that he was here. "It is obviously not someone who lives here. The only ones who could benefit from this catastrophe would be someone who lives somewhere else, and only visits here." He said and all of the startled eyes turned suspicious.

Josh balled up his fists. "Does that sound like anybody we know?" He asked and as if on cue, the Guardian of Balance appeared in the room. This would normally have surprised everyone in the room, but this time, the timing was perfect for the conversation in the room. The one who was startled was the Guardian. "Well, speak of the devil... Or rather speak *to* the devil." Josh said and the implication was bold and direct.

The Guardian dropped his backpack and looked around the room at all the hostile faces. "What?" He asked but nobody was talking to him just now. The tension in the room was nasty and he looked around for an escape. He vanished just as he had come, the only proof that he had been there at all was the backpack still lying on the floor.

Josh looked at everybody in turn. "Are there any other suspects at this time?" He asked and everybody shook their heads. Josh nodded his understanding. "Then we need to take steps. We cannot let this sort of thing happen again. We're going to need a plan." He said and there was agreement on every face in the room.

Then everyone noticed the backpack. Josh started to move but Erica was much faster and she was already in motion. She grabbed the thing by the strap and flung it out the window. It fell away towards the sea with her mighty throw and just before it hit the water it exploded!

Mom and Dad were in shock and the Sprite King was ready to bolt. The Captain was in a rage.

"How can he do this?" He screamed. "This Guardian of yours is nothing of the sort! He is trying to eliminate you from his equation.

Surely you can all see this now." He said and there were no negative responses.

Josh was furious, but his anger was controlled and shoved deep down inside where it was much more dangerous. His voice, when he spoke was low and hard as steel. "It is obvious now who we have to blame for the war." He said and again nobody argued the point. "It is also fair to assume that the Guardian has considered all of us a threat." He continued and the mood was somber. "Who has the power to even affect the Guardian's work?" He asked and he already knew his answer. He let the question hang on the air before he supplied its answer. "So it was me he wanted to kill." He concluded and the rest lowered their heads. Josh found a bit of his anger surging to the surface. He snarled as he said his next sentence. "The coward was willing to take out innocents in order to kill me." He said and his fists were turning white at the knuckles as he steamed on that. Then he seemed to calm, but it was only his outward appearance that changed. The hate was still burning underneath. "I want to know the instant that creep appears around here." He said and he looked at each of them in turn to be sure that he was understood. "Next time he will have to deal with me." He said and the steel he had before was now frosted over in his voice.

The Guardian dropped the satchel charge and fled the royals. He knew that they disliked him from the brief flash of anger he felt from all of them when he appeared. He had no time to lead the others away from Josh. He had to bail out and get clear. He teleported from the room and out to the grassy hills outside of the wall. From here he could witness the explosion when it went off in the palace. It would be a sad day for this world, but a happy one for the universe, well at least *his* universe. The rebuilding of his power could begin once this upstart has been removed. He counted off the seconds as he watched the palace window intently. Incredibly, he witness the herculean throw that sent the backpack out the window and falling impossibly far towards the ocean. It had even cleared the city wall from those towering heights. The charge timed out just before it hit the water and the explosion sent a shockwave across the water and out onto the land as well. The True Bloods were alive. What was worse was that they were also aware that he was no longer an ally. He would have to be much sneakier in the future when he dealt with them. He needed time to plan. He could return to his office, but the energy required to do so might tell the sorcerer where he was. He couldn't risk detection now, he was so close to reaching his goals. He would hide out here, outside of the accursed city and wait. It irked him to be hiding from Josh. He was the power of balance over the universe and he was afraid of one young man. It seemed laughable. However, he had to admit that it was an extraordinary young man that caused him to fear. Even so, it wouldn't be long now until that fear and its source were removed and then he would be free.

The explosion just outside of the city was cause for alarm all across the new kingdom. The average person on the streets had questions. "What caused that fire? Will it come again? Are we safe?" Of course these were all valid concerns and in the wake of the war, they were particularly heightened at this time. There were darn few humans left and those that had survived were suffering from a species wide shell shock. Fear and panic were close cousins and something had to be done to avoid utter bedlam in the streets. At the palace, the guards were getting nervous. If there was an uprising, it would be their lances at the front of the line. They did not want it to come to that. If there was anything that could avoid any further bloodshed, it would be most preferable. The chaos in the streets was for all intents and purposes being ignored by the palace. The talk in there was not of the people, but of the newly revealed enemy…

Josh was looking around, he had paced long enough where you could see wear in the carpet. He made himself stop and sit down. He had gone over things in his mind over and over and found no new avenues to pursue. He finally gave it up and announced it to the group. "I don't know how we can find him if he doesn't want to be found." He declared and the others simply nodded. For Josh this had become personal and it was now tearing at him to be powerless against his enemy.

Mom strolled over and stroked his hair. "Honey, it's all right. He will show himself eventually. His schemes seem to revolve around us for some reason. He cannot simply drop everything to stay in hiding. He will be back." She said, trying to make her son feel better.

Josh looked back at her and his eyes lit up. "Wait. I didn't feel him leave, did you?" He asked and Dad shook his head.

"How could you have felt that?" He asked and Erica looked just as confused. Mom, however, thought about her response before she gave it.

"No, now that you mention it, I didn't feel him leave." She replied and Josh seemed to be getting excited about something.

Erica was getting frustrated by this time. "What are you two talking about?" She asked, stomping her foot for their attention.

Josh started, but Mom took over the explanation. "When magic is used, it leaves a footprint behind. This small ghost of the spell can be felt by those that are sensitive to it. When the Guardian comes or goes, there is a residual trace of it. This time, neither of us felt him leave." She told them and everybody was catching up quickly.

Dad seemed to be the most closed minded about it. "But we saw him pop out of here." He complained. "He left, it's pretty cut and dried I'm afraid." He said and Mom shook her head.

"If The Guardian left this room for say, the edge of the universe, there would be a major expenditure of energy and thus a large footprint. That sort of trail is easily followed. If he went as far as the next room, or even the beach outside there, the energy spent would be substantially less and much harder to detect. Since he has left no discernable trail, he cannot have gone far." Mom turned to Josh as the whole room now understood what was going on.

Josh in turn looked at the guards posted at the doorway to this room. "Call the Guard Captain immediately. I want a thorough search of the grounds and the surrounding countryside. Mobilize anyone you need to but get it done quickly. We don't know how long the culprit will remain in the area." He said and the guard started to leave. "Hold it!" Josh shouted. "Also warn the searchers not to engage the Guardian. He is extremely dangerous and for some reason he has resorted to trying to kill us. He would not resist killing one of you either. Just report on his whereabouts, do not engage. Is that clear?" He asked in a rock solid tone of no-nonsense.

"Yes sir." The guard said and he twitched for a moment, not sure if he were properly dismissed or not. Josh felt a bit sorry for him, but his own problems were already taking much of his thinking. As an afterthought he dismissed the guard and the man bolted as if he had been restrained there, and then released. It wasn't that far from the truth, but Josh hated feeling so different from the people he served. It just made his position of authority over them even more uncomfortable.

Josh turned back to his think tank. "We should hear something soon." He surmised. "We must be ready with a plan once he is found." He said and there were nods around the room. Josh gestured for everybody to come closer and they all stood around the table that he had just conjured to make ready his plans. "Now this is what I think we should do…"

The Guard Captain had his hands full with citizens in a state of panic when the orders filtered down to him to start hunting for the Guardian of Balance in this kingdom. He shook his head at the meaning of these orders. "Someone up there doesn't like me." He said pretty much to himself. Still, orders were orders. "Alright men, let's get a skirmish line formed up. I need a full search of the city and the surrounding countryside for the Guardian of Balance." He said and there were several looks from the men. His gaze turned angry at the hesitation. "Don't just stand there, get ready to go." He ordered and the group slipped off of the current duty to reattach themselves to the search parties. In fact, they took the most unruly citizens with them to add to the number of eyes dedicated to the search. They had searched the old city before, so this was not as new as it could be. The new city was twice as large as the old one though. It would take some time to clear the whole thing. In addition, there were parties being sent out to the fields to search there as well. That meant that the troops would be scattered fairly thin. If they did encounter the Guardian, there was no sure way to ensure that he was detained, or even reported on. The man was something above a spell caster. He was the stuff of legend. Of course this was a city of legends. Josh and Erica had each secured their places in that same mythos. In fact, the city itself, being able to survive when the rest of the world had folded gave it a good chance at making history as well. The troops did the best they could. At least there were troops. The army had been newly formed and trained so they had the manpower they needed to accomplish this goal, albeit not as fast as the leaders would have liked, but surely fast enough for the purposes they were sent. At least they all hoped so.

The Guardian of Balance sat in low brush, overlooking the city across a wide field of tall grass. The grass had been trampled and bloodied before its restoration. Still, there was no sign of that now. The battle had been intense and the Guardian was just as happy that he had not had to fight in it directly. He needed to stay hidden. He had no plan. It was obvious to him that his one plan had failed and that now he was a wanted man. Normally this would not have worried him, but this city had strong leadership, magical support, and a newly formed army. His chances of evasion were slipping fast. He wanted to move away but he could see troops off in the distance, looking for someone, it had to be him. If he moved now it would give away his position. He could maybe set up an illusion to cover his own escape, but would that be detected? He did not know. Could he risk his life on the chance that it would work? So far, the answer was no. He was not desperate enough yet to try something so drastic. His worry was growing as the troops closed in, but they were not looking directly at him. They were performing a general search. They were scanning the tree line however, and he was not far enough beyond that for his personal comfort. He felt like a rabbit waiting in its hole for a pack of wolves to go by. If he could remain unnoticed long enough, he might still be able to escape without killing any of the searchers. With so few of the humans left, killing any of them could jeopardize the future drastically. In fact, it had already done so when the invasion began. He would need to repair that damage after he had cleared himself.

Much to his relief, the searchers passed by and moved on without noticing that he was there. He wasn't sure how long he had before the balance of the universe became noticeable, but he knew that it was his duty to set it right. He was one sorcerer away from going back to business as usual. The security around the royal family would be thick now. He had barely a chance at all of even seeing them again. Unless...

The answer was right in front of him. He knew that it was. The only hitch in it was that he would have to rely on the mercy of the sorcerer in question. What were the orders that were issued in his regard? If they were supposed to kill him on sight, then this plan would go terribly wrong. If they were supposed to bring him in for questioning, then he was about to succeed. He could see no other way to even get close, so he took a deep breath and then stepped out of his hiding place. He took a few steps forward and then put on his air of superiority. Chest out and shoulders back, he looked down his nose at the group that had just passed him by. "You there!" He called and they turned at once to see him, weapons drawn. "You need to take me to the city." He said boldly, as if there was not a care in the world. Inside he was shaking like a leaf. These people were so unpredictable. He hated putting himself in their care, even for brief periods like this one.

The closest man held sharp eyes on the Guardian. "Don't try to run." He said menacingly.

The Guardian smiled. "Run? Are you kidding me, take me to the city now, I grow tired of waiting for you." He said and something in his tone threw extra authority behind the request. The searchers tied his hands and then they put a lead rope on him like a leash to make sure that he couldn't run from them. Then they began the trip back into town. One of the group had brought a signal horn and he blew three short notes from it to signal that they were coming in. There was an answer horn from the city wall and he lowered the horn now that the message had been received. "You really are quite fortunate." The Guardian of Balance told them as they trudged along. "If I had not been in such a peaceable mood, you would all be dead now and I would be well on my way elsewhere." He told them to make sure that they were properly humbled around him. He got a hard shove in his lower back for his efforts. He glanced back in anger at the offending soldier. He would remember that face. That one would pay for his insolence.

The squad reached the city gates and after a brief exchange of security information, they were let through. They marched at a steady pace and groups of troops began to line the way to the palace to see the captured Guardian. The orders had been to observe and not engage, but this was something unexpected. Everyone wanted to see who had captured this man without a fight, or even a struggle. The procession continued on uninterrupted until they hit the palaces gates. There, much as the Guardian had suspected, the security was tight. There were six guards on the gates and more could be seen just in the wings. The Guardian did his best to look confident and arrogant, but even he had to admit that the palace was a frightening place when you were not invited. Joshua had known how to assemble a building. His craftsmanship was evident everywhere in this city, but especially so in the palace. The most amazing part was that he had built two of them! This was before the official unification that was about to take place. He wondered absently what they were going to do with the second palace once they combined the government into one ruling body. It seemed to be taking a long time for the guards to allow them in, and it was soon clear why. They didn't go in. The guards simply held him to the side as Josh came out of the palace. The Guardian did a few quick calculations and his hopes soared. He might be able to take out the boy all by himself.

Josh leaned in close and there was something different about him. "So, you have committed an act of treason against our government." Josh said in words of steel. Suddenly, the Guardian doubted that his plan would work. He began to fear for his life instead. "By attempting a mass murder on the royal family, you have sealed your fate within this kingdom." Josh continued unaware of the thoughts of his captive. "Is there anything you want to say before I pass judgment upon you?" He asked, his eyes were hard but his stance was actually showing signs of interest.

The ropes binding the Guardian vanished in wisps of smoke and he lunged forward to grab Josh by the collar. He expected to feel the impact with the younger man but he instead passed straight through the sorcerer. The lack of an impact made the Guardian overbalance and he stumbled forward until a guard struck him on the back of the neck. He went down face first into the cobbles and the dark tunnel sucked his will away as he passed out.

Josh turned around to see the sprawling figure on the ground. There was blood trickling from underneath The Guardian's face. "You'd better pick him up." He said to the guards and they did so roughly. This man had now tried to attack members of the royal family twice. It was clearly grounds for treason. Treason was almost always reason for death. Josh watched as the guards hauled away the offender and placed him in the dungeon. He knew that no such place could hold that particular captive, but he allowed them to go through the motions anyway. It was good for morale and he was ready to do anything that would make his citizens happier. Of course he was watching remotely. He was not actually there. He had deployed a light based doppelganger, or more precisely, a controlled spirit. The thing looked solid enough, but it was not a corporeal being. It had no physical substance; it only looked at this moment like Josh. The young sorcerer thanked the spirit for its help and dismissed it back to its home as promised.

The Captain looked on as the image faded away. "A wise precaution." He muttered behind Josh. "I'm not sure how you did it, but it was convincing enough for the Guardian." He added when Josh turned around to see him.

Josh nodded. "Yes, yes it did. I wonder what he was trying to do when he reached for me." Josh mused aloud. "He looked to be trying to grab me by the collar. Was he trying to throw me down, or to transport me somewhere else?" Josh asked. Of course nobody could have answered that question except the Guardian and Josh was not prepared to allow that particular man access to his person. Then his eyes locked back on the present and left his thoughts behind. "You know we can't hold him. If he wants out of prison, he will be out of prison." He stated flatly. "He is here for a reason and on the surface it appears to be me. That was why I went alone to test that theory and the reaction we got pretty much sealed that. He wants me dead." Josh stated and there was little chance of escaping that conclusion. All of the signs pointed that way.

Erica looked confused. "But if he wanted you dead, why didn't he just leave you that way? You were dead before and he helped you." She asked and Josh looked down unhappily.

"He helped me because he needed me to do what he could not. He needed me to get the demons back over to their side. Once they were back, he sealed the tear between worlds." Josh replied, the memory still caused him pain. He had been in hell and he would never forget that.

The Captain stepped up then. "How did he seal the tear?" He asked, trying to get a handle on things that should be unfathomable.

Josh shook his head. "I... I don't know. I was not totally cohesive then. I am only sure that he did it. It started closing before I got out." He managed to say.

Erica slammed her hand on the table in front of her. "It did?! That means that he had already tried to keep you dead!" She exclaimed. She turned from her rage to become thoughtful. "That means that he planned all along to leave you in hell." She concluded and Josh balled his fists.

Mom saw his jaw muscles tighten and she tried to soothe him, but he would have none of it. His righteous indignation flared. "He deserves to go there himself." He said and there was fire under those words. The cold steel of emotionless behavior was behind him now. "I should kill him myself." He said and it sounded dangerous.

Dad put on his best authority voice. "You know that's not the answer." He scolded and Josh looked at him with red eyes. The flash of anger was backed by magic and Dad retreated quickly.

The family seemed to be locked in emotional turmoil. The Grand High Elf just watched for quite a while, his mind turning over ideas and possible suggestions. He cleared his throat for attention. "Who has authority over the Guardian of Balance?" He asked plainly. "Unless he is a God, he has to answer to somebody." He said and Josh felt his rage subsiding just enough to consider the question. The whole situation was slowly diffusing from the masterfully played interruption.

"Yes. Who does he answer to?" Josh asked. He had no idea where to even look for information like that. But there had to be some place... "Wait!" Josh shouted and all eyes were riveted to him. "The office." He said and there were a lot of confused faces in the room.

Josh noticed it and started to explain. "The Guardian has an office outside of all of the worlds he monitors. It is a place between worlds. He has all kinds of stuff thrown about in there. There must be some kind of records, or something that will tell us who to contact about him." He said hopeful. This was the first positive turn for him since the war ended. "I must go there and look. My mind will make sense of things that look wrong. I know I can do it." He said, building up his own courage and determination.

"You will not go alone." Dad said, reinserting himself into the equation. "I will go with you in case we discover something that needs handling." He said and his tone suggested that argument would be useless on this point.

Josh turned to the rest of the crowd. "Just try to keep an eye on him. I don't want the Guardian popping into his office while I am there. He would have the home-field advantage and that could be disastrous. Dad and I will return as quickly as possible." He told them and they seemed to all agree. Josh concentrated on the image he had from his former visit to the office of the Guardian of Balance. In moments, he had the image in his mind and then he put himself and Dad right in the middle of it. He let the magic flow into the image and then "Pop" they were there, standing in the middle of the cluttered office of legends.

Dad looked around, travel like that was always disorienting, but he somehow managed not to fall over anything in this pig's sty. He made a whistle. "How are we going to find anything in here?" He asked and Josh started looking around the room closely. His image had been about ninety percent right, so a few things had changed.

"I don't think that the Guardian has had any supervisor interference for a long time, so we are looking for something that had not been disturbed in like forever." He said and Dad nodded. There was just so much stuff, that Josh could not eliminate much.

Dad started making his way through the clutter. "There've got to be files here somewhere; I'm going to look for a filing cabinet in this mess." He said and Josh nodded.

"Oh yeah, try not to disturb too much. The longer it takes him to know that we were here the better." He warned and Dad shook his head.

"This just keeps getting better and better." He said and then he gingerly stepped over a stack of books that looked like they had not moved in eons. Then he glanced back at Josh. "You'd better try the desk over there." He said and Josh nodded and started making his way over to it.

The desk, if you could call it that, was completely covered with stuff. It wasn't even stuff that you would normally find on a desk. Yes, there was a coffee cup, the normalness ended there. A birdcage sat precariously on the front corner and the place where a mat would be had baseball cards. Josh made his way around to the front of the desk and found drawer handles with flashing lights on them. There was some sort of security system in place, and by the look of it, it was high-tech. Of course the Guardian could time travel so it made sense that he had the best security that the universe could offer. But he hadn't counted on the clever mage finding his way in here. Josh stopped and closed his eyes. He began to picture the inside of the desk drawer. In a flash he had disappeared from the room and Dad started to make his way over to the desk. Inside the drawer, the miniaturized Josh turned and looked at the security latch. It had been designed to keep people out, not in, so he was able to disable it quickly. He pressed and the drawer opened just a little. Dad pulled the handle from the outside and Josh fell over as the floor beneath him shifted so fast. He looked up to see the giant Dad looking down at him.

"Well son; that was a method I wouldn't have thought of." He said and his voice was booming. Josh was already visualizing the office again and he popped back into the room and out of that cramped drawer. Dad watched him appear and shook his head. Then he started rifling through the papers in the drawer. There was nothing out of the ordinary there. It actually looked like receipts. It turns out The Guardian had bought things throughout time. Searching of the rest of the drawers revealed more of the same. Frustrated, Dad exclaimed, "This man is not a Guardian, he is a collector!" It was true that many of the articles in the office were priceless. He had paintings and first runs of just about everything. He had prototypes of things that neither of the men in the room could identify. Upon leaving the office door, they found room after room of more storage. It was all basically in the same state as the office. The hallway outside the office led down past several of these storerooms. The hallway seemed to end in a portal, quick inspection of the portal suggested that it went back home. Josh knew that going there was a mistake and he backed away from the portal.

"We need to find something useful before we run out of time." Josh said, his frustration echoing from the walls around him. "Can anybody tell us who is in charge?" He shouted at nobody in particular. He nearly jumped out of his skin when the answer came.

"Yes, I am." The voice right next to him said. Josh turned quickly to look and found nothing.

"Who said that?" Josh asked and the voice chuckled.

"Sorry, I forget that most beings can't see me. Hang on..." The voice said and Dad and Josh shrugged their shoulders at each other. Then the figure seemed to shimmer into existence before them. "I judge by your reactions that you can see me now?" The being asked.

Both men nodded, their mouths hanging open. Josh finally got his wits back under him. "Have you been here the whole time?" He asked and there was a noticeable shake of the head as the figure spoke again.

"No, I arrived shortly after you tripped an alarm in a desk drawer." The figure said. "At first I thought that you were thieves but you didn't take anything. There are so many things here that I was quite surprised." It said and Josh tried to figure out what to say next. Before he could come up with anything, the figure continued. "So tell me young wizard, why are you here?"

Josh stepped closer, but not so much as to be threatening. "The Guardian of Balance is out of control and we are trying to find out who is his boss to report it." He said in a rush.

"Out of control? I find that hard to believe." The being said and it shimmered to a reddish tint, as if trying to display emotion with colors.

Dad interjected. "It's true; he has tried to kill my son twice now." The sincerity on his face almost gave Josh a start. He sometimes forgot how his actions and those around him affected others. That was why Erica was the queen and why he was not the king. She was much more people oriented.

"What you say is not possible. The Guardian is restricted from direct action against any living being." The thing answered and Dad laughed.

"Well, he pulled me and my wife into war to save the other world and we only just barely succeeded. Many, many people were lost and the balance of the universe was no doubt upset." Dad replied and the figure actually managed to look agitated.

"What proof do you have of these allegations?" The being asked. Josh stepped forward now.

"Please look into my mind, I will show you what I know." Josh said, hoping that this was the correct approach. He visualized the tear between worlds and how the Guardian had shown it to him. He displayed the backpack attack that could have wiped out his family. He showed the final encounter when the Guardian had lunged for him and failed. When it was over Josh sighed and the being began to glitter.

"These images are troubling. The Guardian does indeed seem to be trying to murder you. He has also murdered most of your world. I have to follow protocols here, but action needs to be taken." The being said and Josh held his hope in check. Procedures sounded too much like government and that meant red tape.

"Is there any chance that you can bring the Guardian to justice?" He asked and the being twitched a bit and then settled down.

"Justice? Are you asking for revenge?" The thing asked and Josh shook his head violently.

"No, not vengeance, or even pity. No; I am more worried about him coming back with more plans and trying again to murder me or my family. None of us can afford to have that sort of thing hanging in our minds all the time." He said reasonably.

"So what do you suggest that I do in order to secure your safety?" The figure asked.

Josh thought about it for a while. What would be a good way to make sure that the Guardian did not have too much power, but still had enough to do the job he was tasked for? It was a tall order and a tough question. Josh finally got his thoughts together on it and came up with a possibility. The figure had just waited there patiently as if it had nowhere to go, ever. Perhaps he/it lived outside of time anyway.

In any case, it gave Josh all the time he needed to respond and the young man was thankful for it.

"Sir, what I suggest is that you take away the Guardian's ability to travel in time. Allow him to travel between dimensions as is required for his job, but restrict all other travel. If he cannot go back and change things in the past, then he will be much more careful about what he does in the present." Josh said and the figure changed to a golden color, perhaps it meant thinking, or processing, Josh couldn't tell either way. So Josh began to wait, just as the figure had done for him.

The delay was beginning to drag out when the figure spoke again. "I believe that your solution has merit." It said almost unwillingly. "However, the balance is sorely out of whack just now. Some time travel will be required to put things aright again." It said and Josh felt a small prick of panic edge into his mind.

"Perhaps then, could we limit the Guardian's movements through time, but allow just this one trip back to prevent the damage that he caused?" He asked. The idea seemed ludicrous. Send the one who caused serious upsetting back to fix it. He hoped that the being before him understood how problematic that would be.

"The Guardian would not restore balance if allowed to proceed with this plan." It said. "I calculate that he would use the one opportunity left to ensure that you were never born." The being said without any emotions at all. The thing sounded like a computer, cold and uncaring. Then why had it tried to portray emotions using color before?

"I agree that is the most likely thing he would do." Josh said and Dad seconded that affirmation. "So who else can rebalance the universe?" Josh asked and he was afraid that the being would select *him*. The pause this time was even longer as possibilities were thought out and rejected.

"There is nobody else with the power and skills to accomplish the deed." The being said at last and Josh felt his heart sink. "We shall discuss this with the Guardian of Balance." The being added and both humans braced themselves as the creature waved an arm and the Guardian appeared before them. He looked pretty bad from the beating he had received in the dungeon. Josh felt a pang of sympathy since he had once received the same treatment. The taskmasters were efficient at their work and he knew it all too well. He still bore the scars from that mistreatment. The being did not seem to notice anything out of the ordinary and it resumed its questioning.

"You were tasked to maintain balance in the universe and you have faltered, explain." It said and the Guardian looked up groggily.

"Wha-..." He started to ask and the being seemed to hit him with some form of energy wave. The Guardian screamed as it danced around and through him. A few agonizing seconds later it subsided and he went limp as his muscles tried to calm down.

"I repeat: You were tasked with maintaining the balance of the universe and you have faltered, explain yourself." The being asked. Josh was suddenly glad that he didn't work for this being. Dad would have agreed if he had been asked about it.

"I have not failed yet." The Guardian said defiantly. He glared at Josh. "This troublemaker has thwarted my efforts at every turn!" He spat and the being hovered in really close.

"You blame this simple sorcerer for your inability to control the balance with the vast powers that have been bestowed upon you?" It asked and the tone was emotionless, but the meaning was not. This was a key point and a lot seemed to hinge upon it.

The Guardian seemed to shy away from responding, but he knew what would happen if he held out. He swallowed hard and drove himself onward. "My efforts have been undone on more than one occasion by this young man. How am I supposed to maintain the balance with only passive means when active resistance is present?" He asked and the being seemed to process the question just like any other. The delay was stringing out and then it spoke again.

"You are the Guardian of Balance, the responsibility was yours, and yours alone. Blame cannot be transferred for the humans in question were unable to match your powers. They could not have posed a significant threat to your mandates and therefore could not be the cause for your failure." The thing said and the words were damnation. "You are to fully restore the balance that you have upset and then return here for disciplinary action." The being ordered and the Guardian looked at Josh with an evil smile and then he vanished.

A wave of fear swept through the young sorcerer as he realized what must be happening now.

"Sir, the Guardian is still going to eliminate me. I can tell that is what he has in mind." He said, beseechingly. "What can I do to protect myself from someone with so much power?" He asked and the being seemed to consider this question for even more time than he had the last one.

"You are powerful; do not underestimate your own strengths." There was a pause as if trying to decide how much information to divulge. "You are being protected at this time." The thing said and the shimmering turned golden, almost white to denote truth. "Appearances are deceiving for one such as you that cannot see all times and decisions at once." It explained when Josh looked confused. "The Guardian of Balance is being tested to see if he is corrupted or not." The thing said at last and recognition lit up Josh's face.

"So we just wait now?" Josh asked, and the thing did not respond. So, Josh and Dad each shrugged their shoulders and settled in for the wait.

The Guardian knew that this was his last chance to fix everything. How had that child managed to contact his superior? It seemed so incredibly far-fetched. He had not even spoken to the entity in eons! The state of his office was probably not helping his cause either. He had items from all over time and space. He had collected so many things that he had expanded his zone several times. In fact, his own neutral zone had actually caused a bit of imbalance when it pulled from the other worlds to fill it. He cared little for that minor problem. He was more interested in making sure that the sorcerer never existed in order to prevent the events that were transpiring even now in his office. The boy was now the biggest threat that the Guardian had ever faced. He appeared in a suburban back yard. There was a dog in the neighboring back yard, but a fence separated him from danger. The house was one he had visited only twice before. This would be the third and final time. He straightened his outfit out and healed himself from the beating he had taken. Then he strolled into the back door of the house as if he owned it. The young couple inside were caught completely unawares. He killed both of them by running them through with a fine rapier that he had materialized just as he needed it. The Grandparents of Josh and Erica were no more and they would not have children or grandchildren now. He smirked at his own brilliance.

"I should have done this long ago." He said. "It would have made all of this so much easier. The True Blood line is severed and that insignificant little world will no longer be a problem. When the evil rises up and destroys it, the balance will be slightly off, but he had a plan for that as well. He had long ago written off that troublesome world in favor of one he was creating. He wanted a world where he would be worshipped as a god. That world he would protect and nurture and teach to treat him as the deity he actually was. For being their creator was only the first phase of his plan. He would make his people strong and they would conquer other worlds, just as evil had done. He would be the ruler of everything by the time they were finished. The universe would be recreated in his image. His eyes were seeing off into the distant future and his smile was unstoppable. Then he felt a tickle in the back of his brain. He tried to ignore it, but it got stronger. Then, as if someone had grabbed him with a giant hand and pulled him across the tether of time and space itself, he was dragged back to his office. There he was deposited unceremoniously into the clutter that he had made. It was a just outcome.

The glittery being hovered so close that Josh felt like the Guardian was going to smother in the glitter. Instead, he just gawked in fear. "What had you done?" The Guardian shrieked as the being floated there motionless.

"Your powers have been stripped away. You are corrupt and have abused them. The final test was conclusive. Your predictable actions forced me to take precautions against your sabotage. The True Blood family line is secure and the world you sought to destroy will be restored to its former balance. The world you intend to create will be made, but its citizens will be free to choose whatever deity they want. That is every possible deity except you." The being corrected. "You are to be sent for punishment and your absence will make this universe better." The being declared and even the humans felt that statement was harsh. However, they were in no position to put forth any argument.

"You can't do this!" He screamed. "The universe is mine! It is my responsibility! I was the one chosen to protect it. He began to lose steam as the futility of it all started to sink in. "What is to become of me?" He asked and the entity floated there uncaring, as it always had done. "Your services are no longer required." It said instead and the Guardian started to scream as he faded out of existence. He had been erased. The being smiled at the two humans

"You have done well. It is not every day that I meet people like you, those who are willing to challenge authority and make a stand for what is right. It is good to be reminded of the troubles of mortals. We tend to forget what goes on in our worlds. I have reset yours and the balance has been restored. I shall return you home in a moment." Both men looked at each other and there was relief on their faces. "It is important that you never return to this place. It is a place outside of reality and one that should not be taken lightly. The items will be returned to the places they came from, rest assured of that. We will not meet again." The being said and Josh bowed. Dad followed suit when he realized what was going on.

"Thank you for your help and guidance." Josh said solemnly and the being shimmered a short rainbow of colors and ended up on the purest of silver.

"It is time for you to go home. You have a wedding to attend." The being said and the look of surprise on both faces startled the being into a laugh, a real laugh. "Thank you for that, I have not laughed in a very long time." Then he waved his hand and the office spun around the two humans until no details could be discerned and then they were standing dizzily on the inlaid stone floor of the grand hall. They looked down and they were both dressed in their royal finery. They looked at each other and shrugged. A young girl in a dazzling dress grabbed Dad by the arm.

"Sire, they have been waiting for you, come with me." She said and tugged on his arm. He had no choice but to follow. Josh started looking around and he knew most of the people around him. They were his people. They were their people. These were the guests to the wedding. The trumpets blasted signaling the beginning of the ceremony and Josh suddenly realized where and when they were. He put on a big grin with that realization and then he saw them. Erica was in a fine white dress with flowers stitched into the hemline and along the open sleeves. Her crown shone brightly in the perfect late morning sun and her jewels sparkled as Dad led her down the aisle. She looked picture perfect and he was glad. There was always a lot of turmoil preparing for a wedding and to have it look and feel this perfect meant that all of that hard work had paid off. He strained to see Cedric. The young man was in his royal finery as well and his crown, much larger than Erica's looked heavy and uncomfortable. He was standing ramrod straight and he had beads of sweat running down the back of his neck. Josh felt sorry for him, but only a little. He watched as the whole ceremony played out before him, everything was flawless and the mood was light and festive. It was as if the war had not ever happened. The only exception was the combined kingdom that was now being joined through marriage. Apparently some things were worth preserving. Josh wondered how much else had changed but the world would wait for this special moment to finish before it could demand his attention.

Those magical words came and the royal couple kissed as the crowd cheered. Josh was lost in the celebration. The wedding party exited and Mom made her way over to him.

"Where have you two been?" She asked. "She has one special day and you almost ruined it." She scolded and Josh simply nodded. "Do you have anything to say for yourself young man?" She asked, still a bit enraged at just how close it had been.

Josh looked at her with sincerity dripping from every pour. "I am sorry, and you have no idea just how close it came." He said and then he turned away to watch Erica and Cedric almost run down the aisle. The orderly procession began to make its way to the reception. As they walked, Josh noticed many of the people that had been lost in the war. There were leaders of cities that had been wiped out. There were trade delegations and even member of the elder races were in attendance. It was like seeing a roomful of ghosts. Josh made his way through to a table and found his name on a tag. He sat down, as did others, and soon they were being brought food and wine. His seat was close to Dad's and he spared the old man a few glances. He seemed to be just as out of place as Josh felt. At least he knew that he had someone to confide in. He would make it a point to talk later about it.

Cedric offered up his toast and there was no mention of the hardships that Josh remembered. Those things had never happened now. The army that had been assembled was now a smaller group of elite warriors that had come for a tournament sponsored by Erica. Mom was busily checking this and that detail as the gathering seemed to go off without a hitch. Josh continued to observe, feeling very much like an outsider here. With a new king and queen for the thrones, his position had been lost in the shuffle. He felt no longer needed. He was beginning to wallow in his self pity, but someone tugging on his arm brought him back.

"You got a moment?" Dad said quietly in his ear. Josh nodded and the two of them excused themselves from the get together and made their way to a side chamber that was housing the next course of the dinner. The spread looked elaborate enough.

"It seems so odd." Josh said as he looked around the room to make sure that they were alone.

Dad nodded. "You're telling me? I knew some of those people out there, and they were gone not too long ago. Of course they did not know me anymore. With the timeline changed, we have never met. Already I can feel the memories of what happened beginning to slip away." He said and there was a note of concern in his voice. "What happens if we forget entirely?" He asked.

Josh shook his head. "I remember all of it. I died out there, twice. I spent time in hell. That kind of thing is hard to forget." He lowered his head as he pulled up some images of the battles that he had fought. "I destroyed my own city in order to defeat an enemy army." He said and Dad put a hand on his shoulder.

"You fought them harder than anyone else did. You saved so many people and now they will never even know about it." Dad said and Josh sighed.

"Yeah, that's true, at least I won't have to deal with that whole hero-worship thing anymore. I did not like how the palace staff changed around me when they thought I was a god or something. I can go back to being me again." He said and his voice reflected the first real sign of hope.

Dad put on a face of caution. "I wouldn't assume that. Somebody out there must still know what happened and you are a hero, whether you want to admit it or not. This entire world was saved because of you. Sure they may not know it, but you do. It is a role that you are stuck with. Always believe in yourself, trust me it's worth it."

"What are you two doing in here?!" Erica asked, barging into the room and startling the two men. "Who gave you permission to duck out of my party?" She asked in mock concern.

Josh looked at her and his look made her stop. "It's... it's nothing." He said at last and she took that 'oh no you don't' stance.

Erica placed her hands on her hips and looked at them both with little patience. "Tell me what this is about so that I can get back to my wedding party." She demanded and both men lowered their heads. "Come on, out with it." She prompted.

Josh finally caved in. "It's just that we just saved the world and nobody will ever know about it." Josh said almost mournfully.

Erica stepped up very close and whispered her response into his ear. "We all know. Everyone remembers what happened and what you did. I placed strict orders for the festivities to go on without any undue attention. Don't let the cat out of the bag that you know and you can enjoy the rest of the day without being the center of all of that attention." She said and Josh's mouth fell open.

"Everybody knows?" He asked and Erica nodded. "Even the ones who were dead?" He asked and Erica nodded again, this time more slowly and deliberately.

"Do you have any idea how hard it is not to go all nuts over you for them? At least have the decency to enjoy their gift to you. Enjoy this day and you can go back to being yourselves tomorrow." She ordered and both responded with a "Yes Ma'am". Satisfied, Erica led them out of the room and back into the party.

Josh looked around the room again and it was somehow different. The people there were happy and celebrating. He had thought that it was just the wedding, but they were celebrating a lot more. The thought gave him a warm smile and he really did decide to enjoy the party. Whatever the new day would bring, his sister had given him a wedding gift, and he was not going to waste it. He would enjoy this day and night and deal with whatever came next. With this place, it could be anything. He grabbed a drink from a passing tray and toasted to the lucky couple. One last glance at his family enjoying themselves and he realized that they were all lucky. Everything was right in the universe again; it had been a good day.

THE END